Futuricity: Out of Time

by

Sam Smith

Published by
Llyfrau Cambria Books, Wales, United Kingdom.
*Cambria Books and Cambria Stories are imprints of
Cambria Publishing.*
Discover our other books at: www.cambriabooks.co.uk

For Stephi, who has been with me all these many ways.

CONTENTS

Part one - The Book: *Futuricity* 1

One: *Futuricity* 2

Two: *Futuricity* continued 7

Three: Ilfracombe 11

Four: Wales 17

Five: Somerset 22

Six: *Futuricity* and the state of the world 30

Seven: Julian 35

Eight: cage building 41

Nine: above Somerset 46

Ten: confirmation 49

Eleven: space [travel?] 53

Twelve: testing limits 59

Thirteen: zoom 63

Fourteen: the physical properties of light 66

Fifteen: old hands 70

Sixteen: the rings of Saturn 74

Seventeen: consolidation 77

Eighteen: linear travels 82

Nineteen: the awfulness of religions 86

Twenty: Bridgwater 91

Twenty One: the future, and only the future 94

Twenty Two: sound 97

Twenty Three: reed city 100

Twenty Four: the a b c d & e of a depressive episode 103

Twenty Five: missing 112

Twenty Six: Ilfracombe 117

Twenty Seven: another's cage 121

Twenty Eight: Exmoor 129

Twenty Nine: survival? 135

Thirty: more settlements 140

Thirty One: manic 149

Thirty Two: only connect 152

Thirty Three: The New Neroche 157

Thirty Four: a proposition 161

Thirty Five: an erection 165

Thirty Six: in residence 170

Thirty Seven: Galloway 173

Part Two: Out of Time 179

Testimony 180

Part Three: The Enquiry 255

Session One: Part One 256

Session One: Part Two 261

Session Two 265

Session Three 276

Session Four 283

Session Five 292

Session Six 301

Part Four: Confession 307

Part Five: Analysis 322

Inquisitor: If I may suggest, Senior One, that you skip the first 5 chapters of The Book. They are of little concern to The Enquiry, give but background to the four main characters initially involved. Can be of passing interest only. Mention is made of the original Faraday Cage in Chapter Three, but again solely as background. Chapter Six onwards is what leads directly to our Enquiry.

Senior One: Appreciate your advice, but I'm already on Chapter Three. And there are clues.

Inquisitor: Really? Such as?

Senior One: Attitudes, mindsets maybe, more than clues as such. These four were on the island of Britain?

Inquisitor: Yes.

Senior One: [after a pause] Once our Enquiry into his disappearance begins in earnest, we will work on the assumption that not everything was/is what it seems/seemed. We therefore need to know everything.

Part one - The Book: *Futuricity*

One: *Futuricity*

Futuricity, the name of our website, is where for the past twenty plus years we have been assessing works of science fiction. Any member – almost fifty of us active at one point – can put up a 'discussion paper.'

'Paper' can make us sound like scientists, academics, intellectuals, even more like poseurs. Nevertheless 'papers' is what they still get to be called; and in the online discussions that follow the posting of new papers we continue to refer to them as 'papers.'

Although we are all enamoured of SF/Sci-fi we do try to keep our discussions of the merits/aspects of this or that author/sub-genre down to earth. Which, given *Futuricity*'s *causa causans* – chucking in a Latin or otherwise foreign phrase or two can certainly add to the 'paper' pretentiousness – has by no means been easy.

Before it was called *Futuricity* one of the many titles Steve and I considered was *The Future Remembered,* its credo 'Remembering the Once Future.' When historian Bart became a regular, he suggested changing it to *Future History.* Having by then though settled on *Futuricity* it was my idea, when 'Fake News' as a misleading concept came along, to have under *Futuricity* by way of explanation, the epigraph, 'Is Science Fiction the only route we now have to the truth?' Which drew the comment, 'Aren't all SF authors perpetrators of fraud?' Discuss.

Steve and I originally met on another social media SF and fantasy forum. Where we, at various times, both voiced our despair at contemporary SFers ignorance of century-old SF. We had both shaken our metaphorical heads at their enthusiasms for 'new' concepts, many of which had been articulated better way back when.

One book, for instance, that I still keep virtually ramming

into peoples' faces, is John Brunner's *Stand on Zanzibar.*

We are now living upon the overpopulated world that John Brunner described. Yet *Stand on Zanzibar* nowadays hardly ever gets referenced, let alone read. What John Brunner describes – for anyone who doesn't know – is a world so overcrowded that it drives some individuals berserk, where they attack whoever is at hand. Senseless killings. Bombs in public places, school shootings, knife and machete attacks, cars used as lethal weapons... All so familiar to our news feeds today and written by a Somerset author in the early 1950s. Possibly before.

Consequently, one of my early 'discussion papers' on *Futuricity* extolled *Stand on Zanzibar.* I say 'discussion paper' but *Stand on Zanzibar*'s central hypothesis having become self-evident my 'paper' didn't provoke much in the way of discussion. Had been good though to get it off my chest.

What Steve and I had wanted for *Futuricity* was a discussion, an exploration of SF's multitudinous futures, the airing of a myriad alternatives. Neither of us was particularly keen on SF tales that slipped over into Lovecraftian-type horror, or with battle-heavy SF, where aliens were always the counter-cultural enemy.

Unfortunately, we never did get the debates *per se* that we were after. Or only in the sense that some 'papers' started a thread of people putting up their own take on the same book. Or we got someone gleefully pointing out an anachronism. As there inevitably is in any book of the future, especially those written a while back, including even the more recent internalised high-tech dreamstate takes on the future. But where, peradventure, there are still cigarettes and newsprint when, within our time, most have already become largely defunct.

Wasn't long before we began to see that many *Futuricity* subscribers only joined in order to deliver up their response to one work, or to publicise a favourite author who hadn't yet got a *Futuricity* mention. They might go on to put up 'papers' on two or three more books/authors; but what we came to realise was that if that was all they did and they didn't interact with any other contributors then they wouldn't be long for *Futuricity*.

Vortex man came, said all that he wanted to say in three highly technical papers, actual science mixed with speculation upon far out speculation, and he disappeared never to be heard from again. While we got only the one 'paper' from a woman confused by Bode's Law. She was obsessed, she said, with the idea that there is a planet missing between Mars and Jupiter, and which hasn't, and certainly not to her satisfaction, been explained.

We also soon found that K-Dickers, and other single author fans, were only interested in, and fiercely defensive of, that one author. When what we were after, almost regardless of the author, were ideas for their own sake. Not quotations – with exclamation marks! – to be shouted at fellow shouters. Not zealots who chose to misunderstand what had been said just so their author/cause could get a mention, and they could start into their spiel, finger-stabbing [virtually] outrage and condemnation of all us non-zealots.

After a spate of such shoutings, I considered adding another epigraph: 'No SF book is a bible.' L Ron Hubbard's aside of course. Scientology anyone?

We wanted *Futuricity* to be educational in the widest sense, an online tool for the gaining of knowledge, new knowledge that might prise open yet more knowledge. Not a cosmetic or colourful quotation coat for a 'paper' to be wrapped in, to be resentfully admired. While as webmaster I was determined not to be proscriptive: I even let post those authors of supposed flow-of-machine-consciousness, if incomprehensible.

Noticeably what no-one did, not us four regulars nor any of the visitors, was attempt to critique or otherwise promote film versions of SF. Probably because us readers of SF have little in common with fans of SF film and TV franchises, which are generally space/time-shift drama rather than explorations of concepts.

Such SF adventure films often include, if not a cute and cuddly alien animal then a simple robot or alien, both with a charming and insatiable curiosity. The robots/cyborgs behaving with no mention of the quandaries caused by Artificial Intelligence, to wit Isaac Asimov's four laws of robotics. Those four laws only getting a cinematic airing in the film version of his *I Robot.*

Personally, I dislike, despair of, SF movies that don't see beyond present technologies, behavioural tropes, where every assumption of their imagined future is taken from today's cultures.

There are exceptions of course. I confess to a soft spot for an early *Star Trek*'s discovery of a silicon intelligence. A seductive concept, and Spock's delight in ascertaining a slow rock's vitality did have an impact on me. *Futuricity*'s own mission [statement] is to find futures before they are lost to us. Not said unboldly. To find remembered futures and transport ourselves to one. [That comes later.]

Another film exception is Arthur C. Clarke's long ago *2001.* Despite my being in awe of the great majority of Arthur's written work, this film adaptation is I believe an improvement on the book.

Few other film versions though can be called an improvement. In fact, any SF film that has actors holding handguns or their equivalent has usually missed the point of SF. I can't for instance think of any *Dune* film version that has come anywhere near close to capturing Frank Herbert's preoccupation with the formation and exploitation and corruption of religions.

Film fans are usually more conversant with the arcana behind the film, or series, are more interested in who the actors, who the directors. Generally, it is neither the science nor the fiction that appeals to those fans, could just as easily be a well-crafted Western or a gangster movie.

So, for the twenty odd years that *Futuricity* has been running, SF fans have discovered us, have left their tuppence worth, and have shortly thereafter abandoned our multiverse. Leaving a core, a stalwart four of us. Myself here in Somerset, Julian in North Devon, Bart in South Wales and Steve in Cumbria.

So far as each of our four lives go we are all where we have ended up. And while we may have settled into lives where we are now, we are none of us settled men.

As part of my day job, I have met many men who, having always lived in the one place, are unable to believe that they could exist as themselves in another environment, so much are they a part of where they are. Not us four.

We four know that we are not fixed, that we live within an ever-changing climate upon an unstable planet, with people disappearing, moving on, taking up lives elsewhere. We four know that we ourselves could as easily have had other lives, have been other people.

That said, we four at the beginning of this tale, we also considered ourselves for the moment domestically stuck and could see no further ahead than the sharing of our enthusiasms and ideas.

No way did we then assume – was it only a year or so back? – that we four too would become capable of space travel. Yet here we four Futurists go, looking forward, while recalling older futures.

Two: *Futuricity* continued

(Cumbria & Somerset)

Pre-*Futuricity* Steve Packworth and I – Steve in Workington, myself in rural Somerset – had found ourselves more than the once, supporting one another on various SF sites or social media threads. Especially when, as said before, it came to new SFers believing that only SciFi films or franchises were all that rated an SF mention.

For Steve it was *Dune*. Pre-*Futuricity* Steve became almost possessively incensed with any film's concentration on the giant worms of *Dune*, then on the battles; rather than on author Frank Herbert's invention of myths, his analyses of religion; plus all the many concepts that the film versions failed to explore – tank births, Bene Gesserit use of 'voice', navigation by spice exploitation, and the political machinations beyond the battling fremen and the thuggish Harkonnens.

This huge, many volumed work of imagination and speculation, father and son co-authored, could no way be successfully reduced – Steve resolutely maintained – to a few formulaic tropes.

Nor was it solely the filmic trivialisation of *Dune* that had us voicing our outrage. Science fiction had existed long before TV's *Quatermas* and H G Wells' radio reading of *War of the Worlds*. Nor were Wells' time travels backwards and forwards only about meeting up with strange and frightening creatures. Read his *Kipps,* I told an argumentative but snobbish ignoramus on a social media thread and learn how it had been in Wells' time to be poor, socially awkward, and what a struggle it had been to better oneself.

Widely read as both Steve and I were, what gave us most annoyance was the film buffs' right to call themselves SF fans.

Gratingly so when they believed their latest SF to be the newest of the new; and they had never heard of Jules Verne's *Voyage to the Centre of the Earth*, written in the 1800s. Let alone Cyrano de Bergerac's 16th century *Voyage to the Moon*.

Let me be clear, lest I unnecessarily cause offence: neither Steve nor I were out-and-out opposed to TV and film versions. Both Steve and I could unselfconsciously come out with TV and film catchphrases. 'May the Force be with you.' 'Live long and prosper.' What we wanted was to tell film fans, and not in a condescending way, that there was more, so much more.

On any thread that descended into filmdom 'Read' came to be our recognisable response, our instruction. And as readily, wearily mocked: 'Yup. I know. Go to the book.'

When I came to realise that response was what Steve and I were regularly receiving I privately messaged him and suggested that he and I set up a website to promote SF books and authors both old and new. Steve enthusiastically agreed. Our initial working title was to be, from our joint emphases on the old, *Remembering the Future.* The website was to be where we would encourage those already inclined towards SF to read the hundreds and thousands of novels that explored the many alternative futures and pasts.

For the website software I was wholly dependent on Steve. My own contribution to the new site was a piece aimed at *Blade Runner* enthusiasts, directing them to the many other Philip K Dick short stories. My own K-Dick favourite, beyond *Electric Sheep*, is his offhand reference – and Dick comes up with many such incidental characters – to [again!] Gannymede Slime.

My second SF evangelical effort was intended to take film fans beyond A C Clarke's *2001.* (As with John Brunner's *Zanzibar* I'm always happy to promote fellow Somerset authors.) And of all ACC's books the one that I wanted film fans to pick up was his *Childhood's End.* Steve too loved that book's ending, with everything preceding stood on its head.

ACC is just so good on otherness, as in his *Rendezvous With Rama* trilogy. And of course, I always urge new readers to his non-fiction *Profiles of the Future.* So many of those futures still waiting to come into being.

Steve's first contribution to the pre-*Futuricity* website, after the software and web design, was a strange one. One where I feared he may have set out to deliberately cause offence.

Later on, I realised that it had been more about his ex-wife and her preoccupation with image. I know this as I have since asked Steve how his marriage had fallen apart. This Q&A coming about after his wondering about my own many failed relationships. I had therefore felt it OK to ask. Steve had said that she hadn't liked being called Mrs Packworth. Had to be more than that, I had said.

"No. Image was everything to her. All life was a mirror to her. How she might look at that moment, in that place. If she was being flirty, she'd even pretend not to be a mother. Of three!"

Steve's first pre-*Futuricity* paper therefore – provoked by this image-consciousness – was critical of, indeed sought to laugh at, comi-cons.

Now comi-cons may have started out as a celebration, a chance to promote and sell SF comics; but they have become, since the film franchises, a chance for – sometimes entire families – to dress up as their favourite film characters.

Nubile young ladies parade around the few stalls in second-skin lycra. Those women who don't have comic book cleavages or peach-pert buttocks, but who still like dressing up, they come as ghost-busters. Men without muscles slip into padded vests and don the latest Marvel rig; or, channelling their inner psyche, they sport some grotesque plastic form. Small children are recruited into peculiar alien suits. Then of course there are the store-bought Wookies, Storm Troopers, Spocks; and every other film creation. All parading self-consciously past one another.

On comi-con stalls will be DVDs, toys and posters, a few comics; but with not a solid book in sight. And they have the gall, Steve said, to claim this as a Science Fiction event.

When this was uploaded onto pre-*Futuricity* I readied myself, as webmaster, to deal with outrage. Instead, it proved our biggest recruiter. Obviously attracting those who do not enjoy dressing up.

Futuricity was go.

Three: Ilfracombe

In any life there are many an if: if that someone had not been brown, white, in front, behind... There are as many ifs in this tale. For instance, and foremost, if it hadn't been for Julian Featherstone, and if Julian hadn't lived in Ilfracombe, this tale would not be being told.

Within himself Julian is a man of as many ifs, coincidences and contradictions.

An unashamed techie, Julian refers to himself as a nerd, a geek, self-wired, and happily confesses to being a fan of, of all things, pulp science fiction, the penny dreadfuls of our once brave new world. [Apologies to Aldous Huxley.]

Julian made his entry into *Futuricity* with a consideration of pulp SF, how it has so often – even if as an inadvertent plot device – accurately predicted aspects of this world.

Killer Crabs by Guy N Smith I recall as one of his all-time favourites, though as much for its cover as its content. When I said that nothing within *Killer Crabs* had so far come to pass, his unarguable response had been, 'Not yet.'

Further 'papers' on aspects of pulp SF followed. One I recall, probably because so garishly illustrated, was on how some pulp SF had been saved by their cover art, while others were let down by an unimaginative visual trope, usually – and regardless of the story – a full-breasted semi-naked woman in warrior costume.

Still more promotion of pulp SF on *Futuricity* gave examples of how some pulp authors could write well, although they then had plots and characteristics wholly preposterous. Albeit with some neat notions. EC Trubb for instance.

No pulp SF writer could nowadays however be anywhere near as successful as EC Trubb; and I say this from the heart, could expect anywhere near the following that those old SF writers got, often verging on cult status. This is primarily because way too much is getting published these days and with so much choice it is hard for any pulp author to get any kind of following let alone a cult following.

Julian made no claims of literary excellence for pulp SF, readily conceded that most had heroes who were unnecessarily macho and ladies who were seductively luscious, and plots – with their plethora of non-sequitors – near chaotic. There would also often be an encounter with a savage tribe and some strange beasts; a bit like those archaeological, treasure hunt films.

Preposterous as maybe, Julian nonetheless lamented pulp SF's passing. Which passing had been brought about initially by repeal of the Net Book Agreement, and completely killed off by the arrival of online Print On Demand and self-publishing.

Old time pulp though Julian still defended, one of his defences being, 'Why not two or more moons? Or whatever natural unnatural phenomena? We accept sky discharges of static electricity. Having ice balls rain down on us. Occluding mists. Rainbows for goodness sake. And that's before we get to Austro or Aurora Borealis.'

What is also untypical for this self-acknowledged techie, besides his having been happily married to glamorous Glynis for years, is his sense of humour. And it is not only defensive self-deprecation, he is quick to find the ridiculous in any and everything.

Before I go any further in describing Julian though I'd best point out that if this was Julian himself in conversation, he would very soon let it be known that he did not want, no matter how close a friend, his name shortened to Jules.

"I am not a unit of electrical energy. My name is Julian."

For some reason this insistence on his full name makes him, in my mind, sound tall. Julian isn't. Julian is a round man. Wife Glynis fractionally taller. In olden times Glynis would have been described as tightly corseted. These days it is more that she is upright and athletic, well-groomed in even her hiking boots. Although for business she becomes noticeably taller in sharp high heels.

Of much more importance to this reiteration of ifs is where Julian happens to live.

If Julian had not inherited that tall block of Ilfracombe flats, flats which had begun life as a posh seaside hotel, then this tale entire would not be being told.

I should have said cliffside hotel. Julian thus has an invested interest in global warming, its effects of coastal erosion; can quote if provoked whole passages from JE Lovelock's *Gaia* and JG Ballard's *The Drowned World.*

Of this tall block of flats Julian and Glynis have the top floor flat. Of this flat estate agent Glynis, who also makes quilts, has a spare bedroom given over to their production. As an estate agent Glynis would often drape one of her quilts over a bed in a top-end property, and had by this ruse acquired a couple of on-the-side sales.

For his part Julian has the entire large attic. Of this whole floor sections are given over to the residue of his various enterprises. The greater area though is given to what, when busy he calls his workroom, when excited and pleased with an outcome he calls his laboratory.

Not only is Julian's Glynis unexpectedly attractive, she is also sharp-tongued. She said of Julian – during a living room zoom we four had and she was popping in and out – at some point in our chatter one of us had said we all had to admit to having different bees in our bonnets – Glynis said, "Should be so lucky. Got a single bat in my belfry."

Exit left cackling.

Although still in his early thirties Julian has already had several enterprises. One of which was of course his trading in pulp SF and SF figurines, along with his buying and selling of general antiques. With the latest recession and his trading having trickled to a halt, with the patent on his two inventions outdated, his main source of income at the beginning of this tale, other than rents from the flats below, came from repairing iPhones and cleaning various other electronic devices back to factory settings for a Barnstaple pawnbroker.

But let us go back to the attic as laboratory.

The longest lasting of Julian's experiments – going way back to a childhood crystal set – was his creation of a unique receiver. He threaded an aerial up inside the old chimney stack. The flats were listed – 'a fine example of Victorian seaside architecture' – and although the stack had not been in use as a chimney for at least a century, the stack was noted as 'a fine example of its type.' Even so a chrome aerial now discreetly protrudes, ever so slightly, above one of its glazed terracotta pots, also fine examples of their type.

That one tall aerial alone would have made for good radio reception – for ordinary radios. For ordinary radios, Julian told us, being shut off by hills inland the strongest signal came from a Welsh-language transmitter the other side of the Bristol Channel. Not that Julian has been keen to learn Welsh. Any Welsh he has picked up has come from his many calls with Bart. Which Julian claims aren't really conversations but steam-punk Bart picking antique-dealing Julian's knowledge of Victorian arcana.

But back to the aerial.

The chrome chimney aerial was augmented by what Julian claimed to be the world's longest carbon rod. It ran the length of the attic, from one apex end to the other. Using just a crystal set – Julian confided that it was both his start-of-the-working-day ritual and what he did prior to leaving the laboratory – he would slide the contact along the carbon rod picking up the world's transmissions.

Has to go almost without saying here that what Julian really wanted was to pick up an out-of-this-world transmission.

What Julian reported back to *Futuricity* was, 'Hugo

14

Gernsbach would have been so impressed with what I have done in this attic. Here I am listening for aliens beside a heap of classic pulp SF.' [For those who might not know, Hugo Gernsbach was both an inventor and publisher/editor of the very first science fiction magazine.]

In that same 'paper', Julian referred to his attic set-up as The New Machiavellian Intervention. Which title may have been what led to him and *Futuricity*, much to our amusement, being investigated by one of the Secret Services. Could have been Special Branch, MI5 or 6; we never did find out.

The reason for Julian being under suspicion was because, historically, the Russians have always been way ahead of Western powers when it comes to radio astronomy. Propaganda of the Western powers claims that this is because Soviet Russia, as it was then, initially opted for radio astronomy because it suited their 'autocratic systems of governance.'

Politics large and small revelling in its usual name-calling mess.

Futuricity was found not be a fifth column.

But back to Julian's daily listening ritual. On those days when he thought he may have picked up something extraterrestrial from a frequency unrecognised he connected the crystal set to the electrics and pumped up the volume.

Julian said that those faint signals always seemed to come whenever there was a storm battering the roof tiles. Although he had inserted solid foam insulation panels between the attic rafters - having removed the silver foil from the panels - still the clifftop gales, even with the headphones on, would drown out the fainter bleeps and whispers.

With little confidence that Jodrell Bank, or any of Russia's or America's giant dishes, would disclose their having received alien transmissions, Julian set about wiring the attic floor and rafters, making of it an internal dish. Only to discover, cursing his lack of foresight, that what he had created was a Faraday

Cage, wherein even his workaday transistor radio failed to function, couldn't even pick up the Welsh language station.

Concerned that all the new wiring might also inhibit his long carbon listening for aliens, Julian dismantled the all-round wiring and, but of course, knocked out a 'paper' for *Futuricity* on the experiment/misadventure.

Four: Wales

Bart, in South Wales, is our historian. Not yet the historian of *Futuricity* (that lot would seem to have fallen to me). Bart's is more a bent for history in general. Not completely general: he has researched and published a booklet on the pre-mining history of his one Welsh valley. His aim, he said, had been to counter what he called the tendency to myth-creation of other Welsh historians.

'Have they truly been plumbing the past? Or have they too been seeking to create, often out of hints and accidentally found artefacts, myths?'

Although he is along with us enamoured of the future-fantastic, Bart nonetheless has fierce strictures when it comes to actual history; castigating those who go looking into medieval history (legend) only to be able to tell, via SF, of ghosts, strange spirits, hauntings...

'History of a land,' he wrote, 'is the record of migrations over it. There may have well been battles, wars even, but what matters is the record, the pressure of the migrations underlying those conflicts. Romans, Vikings, Normans, Saxons, Huguenots... There began the cultural evolutions...'

Has to be said however – and this from a third person's point of view – that Bart's interest in the past is also what he himself can take from it. A fan of steam punk all of Victorian history – as with Julian's flats and antiquities – is grist to Bart's mill.

I once questioned Bart's insistence on his being described as an 'amateur historian.' 'A professional historian gets paid,' he responded. 'Amateurs not. Pay me and I'll call myself professional.'

'By the time history happens I'm going to be dead.' John Brunner

After me, Bart is the next oldest of us four, although at times one might think of him as the youngest. This I believe is down to his several years younger, and totally tattooed, live-in girlfriend, Rhean. Even Rhean's face, to beyond her scalp hairline, is geometrically tattooed.

Julian had first physically met up with Bart at a Porthcawl comi-con, where Rhean had joined the costume parade barely covered in latex. Bart had told Julian that he knew of no area of her skin that hadn't been tattooed.

While the twenty-year difference in their ages might be remarkable, given the current fashion, Rhean's tattoos were not. Both Bart and Rhean were, as if this might explain much, occasional musicians, and had got together after they had appeared a few times at the same venues. Which explains little. Probably because Bart is so difficult to typecast, so different to me. Apparently, donning his musician's cap, literally, on stage he also wears a jacket with tassels, and switches between saxophone and guitar.

But back to *Futuricity*.

Most of Bart's contributions to *Futuricity* have pursued two themes, steam punk and exploring such as Von Daniken's theories of alien visits to planet Earth. This has had him extensively investigate Stonehenge, its Welsh connection (the Preseli stones); other Welsh barrows and stone circles; and of course pyramids, Mayan temples, Nasca lines... and all the associated religions and cultures. He and Steve particularly get off on these speculations.

"Here I am in Wales," Bart said once in a zoom, "investigating the origins of hard objects, and there's Steve up there in Cumbria wondering at the shamanistic influence of magic mushrooms."

Which handily demonstrates *Futuricity's* many pairings.

Because although I may have started *Futuricity,* I am by no means its focal point. Steve and Julian regularly confer on various technologies. Bart and photographer Steve are both nature-loving conservationists. As am I. And, in their criss-crossing over and around the Bristol Channel, Bart's and Julian's entire families seem to have become solid friends.

In his contributions to *Futuricity* Bart has, I believe, the best authorial handle, signing off his 'papers' as Bartholomew Montgomery. Nor does he seem to mind our shortening it to Bart.

Talking of Bart and names brings me to his son. When said son was London-living he had been a comedy rapper, with the tag Lou Quickly.

Lou had been Bart's only son. He had died a couple of years prior to our meeting. The inquest came up with a 'narrative verdict,' cause of his sudden death possibly an underlying genetic heart condition, exacerbated possibly by use of Class A drugs, with a rare form of cancer also implicated.

Father Bart and Lou's emotionally unstable mother had already been living apart. Long before her son's death she had returned to her valley parents. Bart had remained in the family home, had more or less single-handedly brought up his son. Lou, even after moving to London, had continued to use the house as his base.

Bart had grieved, had looked for someone, something to blame. Lou's mother had come even more undone.

In the awkwardness surrounding even belated mention of death, I yet felt duty-bound to ask Bart about his son. Not that I was alone: we all of us sympathised with Bart - *'...a strong desire to share the burden of another's pain.'* Cixin Liu: *The Three Body Problem.*

"How did Lou become a rapper?" I had assumed Lou had followed his musician father onto the stage.

"No real idea," Bart said. "He never did any of it down here. But in London he became really popular. Still can't make

19

out how or why. He talked so fast in a strong valley accent. How Londoners understood a word of it I'll never know."

But back to *Futuricity.*

The SF authors Bart mostly promoted, aside from steam punk, were Chiana Melville and JG Ballard. Beyond that he goes for time travel concepts, calls it 'Forward History.' As with all four of us though nothing is that clear-cut.

'Past and future', Bart defended his mix of the pair on a thread, 'are said one moment to be irrelevant to the present. The next necessary to an understanding of the human condition. Who of us can live without a past or a future? Science fiction is forward history.'

'I just don't understand where the past goes when it goes.'
Phillip K Dick

Bart has a liking for historical ironies, rubs his hands in glee over any paradox, exults over quantum leaps and has a penchant for alternative histories and bizarre pairings.

"Take apples," he said once. "A single apple fell – bonk! – on comic Antiphane's head. It killed him. Another apple, much later, fell – bonk! – on Newton's head. From which apple event Newton eventually deduced gravity. Think Antiphanes would've found that funny?"

One 'paper' of Bart's was on Jules Verne's *Voyage* series. Bart maintained that Jules Verne's use of 'voyage' was deliberate, redolent as it then was of both adventure and the exotic. In Verne's recent history there had been celebrated travellers such as Magellan, Columbus, even Marco Polo and Raleigh; all of whom had returned to Europe with tales of the fantastic.

In Verne's original French, which Bart claimed to prefer, *Voyage to...*had been used as titles rather than the English language versions of *Journey to...*'Journey,' Bart had written, 'sounded like Jules Verne had bought a ticket for a regular bus route rather than having taken a step into the great and exciting unknown.'

At the time of Bart's writing those words we four had yet to take our own steps into that great and exciting unknown.

Five: Somerset

As I will be divulging details of the personal lives of *Futuricity*'s other three stalwarts, I feel it only fair to disclose some of mine. Although, childless as I am, little there is to tell.

My name is Benjamin Barraclough. Langport, Somerset is where I was born. Somerset is where I continue to live. At that time, to be precise, on one of Somerset's wooded hillsides. To be even more precise, in a caravan.

I did not choose to spend my last years on planet Earth in a caravan. This caravan was where, in my early seventies, my life's pressed-upon-me decisions had dumped me.

This was where, a retirement project, I was supposed to be building my own eco-house, while keeping a jokey journalistic record of the process, its setbacks and successes. All came to a halt soon after the laying of the concrete raft and the installation of the septic tank, the onset of Brexit, the beginning of the pandemic, recessions and distant wars, et al.

The rectangular caravan was already there – water, mains electric and telephone connected – for me to live in while the house was being built. And who knows? With luck, the luck that had to date deserted me, that much-imagined house – oriel window with a view out over the Deane – might indeed get built.

In the meantime, my money having run out, or rather the price of materials having overtaken my budget and local newspapers having gone bust, so not even an irregular income, there I stayed in the caravan. Which was, I used to console myself, ten hundred times better than being shop-doorway homeless.

The caravan was not the only place where I have lived in Somerset.

I began as a homeowner down on the Chedzoy Levels,

stayed thereabouts a good many years. Before moving to Burnham, then around the coast to Arthur C Clarke's birthplace, Minehead; then disastrously – during a surge in the housing market – to an ex-council house beside the River Tone. Which was underneath some electric pylons whose buzzing interfered with my thinking, and which is what desperately led me in my dotage to want to build a house of my original own on a plot up here.

In this dotage I'm still not sure what to give as my life's driving force. Whether it has been my having a need for solitude in which to write; or has it been my desire for solitude and my giving writing as a socially acceptable alibi?

My several partners came to suspect that alibi and, feeling abandoned, unwanted, they left. With few regrets on my part. Each time I re-embraced my solitude.

I am self-evidently not good at relationships. I can analyse them, tell you afterwards what went wrong – misplaced expectations mostly. What I have been unable to do is manage those expectations and live within any of those relationships.

My writing was more than a job. But a day-job it was, paid me a wage. And as I was the wage-earner with a mortgage years before Lilith moved in with me, the house on the Levels remained mine when she eventually moved out.

While partnered with Lilith we had acquired a social group that, without her, I no longer felt a part of. (One of 21st century life rules has it that the more people there are around you the more isolated you will feel.) So I sold up there and moved across to Burnham, which was closer commuting-wise to my then job in Weston-super-Mare.

That set the pattern for all my future moves. Partner left, I sold up; with each move leaving me, peradventure, with a smaller mortgage.

When each of my live-in women left, they made a scene. Felt it behoved them, I supposed, to dramatically mark the breach. Within the scene I would be accused of many things, but predominantly of neglect, social and emotional.

I knew myself each time not to have been the only one with character faults. Yet mine were the only ones that, each time, got a snarled mention. Lilith even maintained, long after our separation, that my neglect of her had verged on domestic abuse.

Lynne told me that I'd been absent even when I'd been physically beside her. Carole named me 'Distracted.' At a lunch with her friends, near our end, I got up to go to the lavatory. Carole said, "There goes Distracted. Not a word of apology. Not even an Excuse Me." The side twist to her mouth said that she had planned saying something like that in front of her sympathetic friends.

'Some people never observe anything. Life just happens to them. They get by on little more than dumb persistence.' Frank Herbert

Scene behind me, another day or two after the latest had packed up and gone, I would unencumbered come again happily to the page. Even greeted by a blank page I'd be confident that in my brief absence my subconscious would have been simmering away, and on this new day the page would tell me what. And somehow most times it did.

Alone with the page I would be in awe once again of the power of language. (Language is where, should it have passed you by, some creatures exist only as their names – angel, unicorn, phoenix.) And I would delight again in writing for its own sake, relishing those productive periods when writing has been my one and only confidante.

Such days however have to be weighed against those many others when, pen in hand, fingers floating over the keyboard, when writing has been – but to me still retained an attractive aspect – possessed of an aura of mindless ritual. So here I am again: why do I bother?

'Sometimes you don't know what you think until you try to explain it.' Brian M Stableford

In my newspaper columnist day jobs, I specialised in self-mockery, or rather in self-pity with an undertone of wry self-approval. Or, looked at generously, a simple monitoring of mine own responses to life's stimuli.

So self-negating was I that in one article I quoted the one review of my one poetry collection - '...far less than the sum of its parts.'

Nowadays I console my poet-self that, dismal as that review may have been, at the very least throughout my poetry 'career' I placed no reliance on ornate fonts.

'...lyric poetry was left to untalented screwballs who had to shriek for attention and compete by eccentricity.' Pohl/Kornbluth – The Space Merchants

I think it was from that ego-pricking review onwards that I stopped taking my own authorship seriously, came to see myself as no longer in competition with the likes of Clarke and Brummer, and most certainly not with that pair of Somerset literary grandees, Coleridge and Wordsworth. From thence onwards I reconciled myself to being but another second-hand chronicler of the absurd; and as a journalist – not that differently – reporting on the sillinesses and hypocrisies of Somerset folk, and of politicians both local and national.

'He had never seduced his clerkly soul with the thought that he was either born great or would under any circumstances achieve greatness.' Isaac Asimov

For clarity I have to state that, although I might relish solitude, here I have not been that solitary. Two cats, a tortoiseshell and a tabby, within a year of each other have found me. Not that I let them and their fleas indoors. Both live under the caravan, and from there have been company enough. Idle moments they might sit on the steps with me, sheltered by the canopy I had built over the caravan's front door, the three of us looking out over the concrete platform, foundations of a house never to be built, two blue pipe ends sticking out of the grey concrete, their opposing arches making different shadows.

Those two cats undid my hermit status. As did/do my three *Futuricity* compadres. I also maintained a rivalrous and distant friendship with many other writers. In whom I readily recognised aspects of my solitary self, even in those at the time with their partners. All of us content with our own company. The cats likewise. No fealty with cats. Much as they might have enjoyed my food and occasional petting, both went their own way, followed their own woodland tracks and trails.

The outstanding consequence of all my failed relationships, each subsequent house move decreasing my mortgage, was that I inadvertently made enough, come my late sixties, to buy this woodland plot and with retirement savings enough to self-build my dream house. As already said the house remained a dream. Instead, there I was in a tin shelter getting woken mornings by twigs and acorns falling on the roof.

No real rancour at fate though. I had grown accustomed to life's struggles and disappointments. My one struggle with the caravan was pushing bike and trailer full of supplies back up from Wellington, seeming even back then to have to pause more and more often to catch my breath.

In many ways that caravan has left me better off. Compared to a house a stationary caravan requires little in the way of upkeep, beyond maybe an annual touch of oil on door and window hinges. Having also been gainfully employed most of my adult life my state pension alone has covered my day-to-day needs. No longer do I have to prep for interviews, hustle for freelance work.

I have been free to write what entertained me. Least ways I

26

was before I began this book.

Back in those days however I couldn't help but feel that the absurd, the more ridiculous end of SF, had to be a more accurate representation of our lives than anything supposedly grittily authentic. In which case I will have to retrospectively count myself a late-coming associate of the K-Dickers.

All of this is how I see myself. Is probably not how others saw/see me.

As an SF writer in Somerset, I believed that my efforts would inevitably get compared to those two Somerset heavyweights, Brummer and Clarke. I believed, back before *Futuricity*, that one had to either deny their influence or to live with it. Living with it was what foolishly decided me to buy the beside-the-Tone house: it was only a couple of cycling miles from Arthur's last known Somerset address. Although by that time Arthur had long before taken up residence in Sri Lanka. His brother Fred had been the last to live in Dene Court, from where he had put out occasional paper issues of his *Rocket* magazine. (I learned later that Arthur had never lived there at all, but had been brought up in a farm at Ash Priors.)

My buying that Tone house had been a silly idea all round. Took me several frustrating years to get someone to take that unwholesome dwelling off my hands.

Burdened by those reputations, come *Futuricity*, and being another Somerset author, I yet believed it behove me to champion both John Brummer as well as Arthur C Clarke. Blogging a homage to Brummer's *Stand on Zanzibar* I set my short story in an overcrowded, jampacked but still very polite England, and I titled it, *Excuse Me, Sorry.*

Self-evidently I have never relied for income on my SF output. Didn't take much hindsight to see that my own SF suffered from the same air of facetiousness, as if reluctant to take itself seriously, as so much other amateurish SF. But I did, as Ben Barraclough, sell more than a few formulaic crime tales. Likewise, I have also been able to pen a magazine/periodical/newspaper piece to order, lately knocking out an occasional piece for the online Gazette.

Doesn't mean that I was in the least self-satisfied. I was much given in my early seventies to glancing back – to opportunities missed, messed up, to live-in women misread. Each introspection leaving me surprised just how quickly the future had come – things once SF now all around, turbines, solar-fields and handheld phones – and simultaneously dismayed at how much had remained the same – use of pesticides, car-thrown litter and corrupt politicians.

There in that caravan, in Somerset, I felt stuck.

Oddly, in that then looking back, I believed that my SF efforts were way more important than any of my other scribblings. And I must have thought so at the time of writing. Much as Iain M Banks added or removed the M for books he considered less or more important, those SF books of mine were the only ones to which I affixed my full name, Benjamin Barraclough. (Can't recall offhand whether Banks' *The Wasp Factory* was authored with an M or without.)

Even when offering arty poems for publication I did so as Ben. Not that I have written much poetry, arty or otherwise, while in this caravan. I had been on my lonesome here for too long; and poets need new people, new places, fresh input. Why do you think they travel so much? The trees, roads, seasons here quote themselves back at me.

Stuck and directionless: as founder and web-master of *Futuricity* I believed that I was the one getting the most out of it, used *Futuricity* to test out possible plots. Mostly I asked what more was needed to make a plot credible. Or as credible as my readers' imaginations would allow that plot to be.

As I wrote 'stuck and directionless' a small voice in the back of my head was wondering what our space travels might soon have me say. How they might have me say it.

Remains to be seen. For the moment I will go on fulfilling

28

my self-assigned role of privately – for now – documenting what we have so far achieved. While keeping *Futuricity* as cover.

Six: *Futuricity* and the state of the world

We noticed only later that Julian had contributed little if anything to *Futuricity* for six months or more. Within those six months Julian's absence hadn't been that remarkable: we all four of us, when we had nothing pressing to be said, myself included, often took a break.

It was my posting about Apollo that got us four off on this particular track.

Being called *Futuricity* didn't mean that we couldn't post about the past, especially when we believed something old relevant to our future.

'Concept of conservation, of valuing all life,' I wrote, 'is by no means new. Take the ancient beliefs surrounding Apollo. The griffin, the cock, the grasshopper, the wolf, the crow, the swan, the hawk, the olive, the laurel, the palm tree... All were considered sacred to Apollo. Albeit that Apollo's championing of all life was even then brought into question – by critics of Apollo worship. They pointed out that wolves and hawks were seen as suitable sacrifices to Apollo. Defenders of Apollo responded by saying that as a god Apollo also represented shepherds. Wolves and lamb-taking hawks were the natural enemies of the flocks over which Apollo, as god, presided...'

And I went on to bring up the interconnectedness of all global life.

'This has an awful contemporary ring to it,' Steve started the thread critical of the obvious inconsistencies within Apollo worship. 'Even then always an opt-out. Bit like those who still come up with reasons to continue using fossil fuels and nuclear.'

A peculiarity of online threads, keyboard campaigners all, is that they aren't strictly consequential, bear little resemblance to a same-time same-place face-to-face conversation, a conversation that can be led as much by gesture and grimace as the words used. And in any online thread not all the contributions from all the correspondents arrive at once. A participant can well be responding to something said, thought about, several days before.

Bart for instance, and in apparent response to Steve, came up with this, 'We stand each in our country on our invisible planet.'

'Not invisible,' Steve came back. 'You poet you. We all know that we're on a small planet. Small, but one large enough for us to be able to appreciate how life, in its seasonal migrations, moves over the surface of the planet. The assumption, the near blessing of ignorance, of small-mindedness, is of no help at all.'

'That's you told Bart.' My attempt to lighten the thread. 'You poet you.'

Any discussion of Earth's probable demise is depressing. And with just us *Futuricity* four, fruitless. Unlikely that we four alone can change anything.

Steve though is *Futuricity*'s premier nature writer. Steve it is who excitedly puts up photos of red squirrels, geese in fight, says how pleased and proud he is to have captured the green sheen of a plover's plumage, its crest erect. And on this thread, he inevitably laments that, as with so many other species no longer at ease in their ecological niche, the lapwing too is in danger of extinction. If not from seasonal misalignment of food staple, then from disease enabled by global warming.

'Nothing new,' I told Steve. 'In 1938 Edgar Rice Burroughs had this in his *Carson of Venus*: 'Earth, where overpopulation and increased means of transport have greatly spread and increased the number of bacteria."

The one book nature-loving Steve promotes above all others is Ursula K. Le Guin's *The Word for World is Forest.*

Talking of trees, Bart in South Wales was happy to tell us

31

how exciting it was, after the depredations of the coal mines, to see how year on year even the spoil tips were being colonised. First by lichens and mosses, low-lying plants, then a willow or an odd spruce seedling taking root. And on top of that natural regeneration, Bart was pleased to tell us, the Welsh government had a tree-planting programme – for every child born in Wales a tree had to be planted somewhere in Wales.

A result of that programme, Bart told us, was that his valley sides were becoming forested. Oak, beech, birch and even sweet chestnuts were taking over from the bracken. Self-seeded sycamores and maples too were spreading. Countering this optimism daylight gaps were appearing in the new canopy, where diseased ash and larch were dying back.

That same two-steps-forward-one-back holds sway too here in Somerset. The Levels have for decades now been returned to their natural state, flooded in winter and farmed in summer, that being how Somerset came by its name. That programme of reversal has seen cranes come to regularly nest, bitterns return to the reed beds, and in the narrow tines [drainage ditches] white egrets small and large competing with our indigenous grey herons.

Set against that Somerset positive is the amount of building that has gone on along the M5 corridor. Since the motorway's coming Bridgwater, Taunton and Wellington have quintupled in size, and not with anything of architectural merit – housing estates of kit-built houses, some on flood plains, along with huge retail estates and the seemingly endlessly grey roofs of industrial estates.

Fortunately, low-lying Somerset is cut about by hills. The Mendips, Quantocks, Blackdowns, Brendons and Poldens. But, and as with Wales, on their wooded hillsides the ash are diseased and dying back.

'And what with agricultural herbicides and pesticides,' I complained to my three friends, 'towns here have become wildlife reservoirs, the farmed fields a too-green wasteland.'

Regards global warming what we on *Futuricity* most lamented was that all the many futures imagined by SF writers will be lost in a humanless future. At the same time, we drew a perverse solace from those SF writers who had so predicted. Steve, his house not that far from the prone-to-flooding River Derwent, often cited as handbook J G Ballard's *The Drowned World.* Such drowning would see the Levels under water the year round. Possibly even the Deane.

Looking to a positive future, to what might await a surviving humankind, exemplified how different are us four lovers of SF. For instance, when we as humans go beyond *homo sapiens* Julian thinks the metamorphosis will be by machine, Steve by – his own definition – mind-flight, and Bart by something he calls time-melding. My own guess, and it is not necessarily a good thing, is that the transition from human will come about, not by state eugenics, but – given the choices already on offer by IVF and gene manipulation – by privately-funded selective breeding.

Often, I have consoled myself, during my less than successful literary career, that although my work might not have been widely read during my own lifetime there could come future times when my books might find a devoted readership. Increasingly however that posterity – in which my efforts might find a readership – is becoming only a possibility.

In the valleys, Bart told us, year on year landslips are becoming more frequent. 'Climate change means all year-round weather extremes. Even here in Wales. I've actually found myself lamenting those long-gone wet Welsh summers, those gentle drizzles drifting up the valley. Droughts are now followed by torrential downpours, which increase the likelihood of yet more landslides. And this is not just the UK. Look what's happening in Africa. The landmass entire is baking.'

'Human life on this planet is nearing its end,' Steve put in. 'It may continue to exist in small pockets, but the human species will be unlikely to dominate again.'

Bart told us of the Welsh poet Dannie Abse describing humanity's absence from early history as *The Great Silence*. In his *Wanderers of Time* John Wyndham said that mankind, like the dinosaurs, just 'ceased to be.' And he wrote that in 1933.

'We're returning to silence,' Steve wrote.

Followed by Bart asking, 'Think we should put up a sign – for visiting aliens post-Climate Change? Have the sign say, 'It was our fault that so little's left. Sorry."

We on *Futuricity* however claim to be not of those minded to revel in post-apocalyptic futures.

Steve: 'Those SF folk who desire a clean post-Armageddon slate fail to comprehend the intricate continuity of life here, the many smallnesses of it, but smallnesses which can nevertheless produce gigantic structures. I sometimes look up in awe at what civilised humanity has built, and with despair at what uncivilised humanity has destroyed.'

'I'm no Johnny-cum-lately nationalist,' Bart almost spoke my mind. Then didn't. 'Don't think I've ever joined in the singing of *Land of my Fathers*. I was more concerned about keeping a home for my sons. My son.'

It was just as well at this point, before we three sank into the pit of despair, the slough of despond, that Julian came to our rescue with news of his space adventure.

Seven: Julian

It was only when I got a private message from Julian, saying that he was setting up a zoom meeting, that I realised I hadn't heard from him for at least six months. Maybe more.

Nothing unusual in that. We were all busy with our own projects. I'd get a notification if someone posted or passed comment on *Futuricity*. Otherwise, and unless I had something of my own to post, I didn't look at the site.

What was unusual for this zoom was Julian insisting that it was to be just us four.

I told Julian that the proposed evening, two days later, was fine by me, asked what it was about. Julian said that all would be revealed on the night.

Which left me wondering if it concerned *Futuricity*. But I didn't see how. Someone doing their PhD had been the last to post. They had been looking at the use of plants as characters in SF. Their own starting example had been John Wyndham's *Triffids*. A K-Dicker had almost immediately popped up with Ganymede Slime. My own two offerings had been Brian Stableford's intelligent fungus and Herbert's sentient kelp in *Lazarus*. Of course, Le Guin's forest and Tolkien's walking trees had had to get a thread mention. Best of all though was the aragami, the plant monsters of *Blue Seed*. [I had to look that one up.]

Beyond that, and my much earlier Apollo posting, I hadn't paid much recent attention to *Futuricity*.

The pre-zoom on the evening followed the usual pattern, hellos and asking after family – Bart's partner, Steve's daughters – weary mention of the latest political news; and as usual our joint despairing of this island of thickos off the north coast of France.

Julian, arriving, called us to order, each in our screen

35

quadrant.

"I've been to the moon," Julian said.

We three looked to each other's square for a reaction. Julian's chubby cheeks beamed out at us.

"This is a closed zoom." He adopted a serious face: "What I have to say must go no further. No further than us four. I must be certain of that."

If our three faces were each in their own way a little sideways sceptical, we nevertheless all gave nods or sounds of agreement.

"You recall that I once accidentally turned my loft laboratory into a Faraday cage?"

He waited for each of us to acknowledge: "Well I was working on some new stuff. I mentioned parts of it to Steve. That gaming app?" Steve nodded. "And I know, I accept that every idea has its time. That concurrence of coincidence. If I hadn't been working on that gaming app someone else would have been. Its time had come. And I got beaten to it. Fair enough.

"Except that, over these last four years, this has seemed to happen time and again. And all too often they have been patents way too much like mine to be a coincidence. Got me into a right state. How was I being hacked? I stripped down a laptop to its factory settings, put my own basic programs in. Worked only through that laptop on the next project. And still someone beat me to it."

Julian waited a moment, seemed to be communing with himself. A going back over what he had already told us? Or working out what next he wanted to say?

We three in our previous meetings/conversations with Julian were used to his mental wanderings off. This time though this gathering of his thoughts had me wondering if we three were about to be accused.

"I know this sounds like paranoia," he picked up his tale. "I even suspected you three. Maybe passing on info. Don't ask me how you were supposed to be doing that. Pure paranoia. Glynis definitely thought so, even suggested medication."

'Thought joined on to thought like things that whisper warmly in the shadows.' H G Wells

If all relationships are a power struggle, as Adler would have us believe, then one would presume that in their marriage Glynis, being the inferior partner in that she came property-less to the partnership, would be the more circumspect in her offering advice to Julian. From my week-long stay with them however I can vouch that the opposite holds sway. Buxom she may be, but sharp as a green apple is Glynis.

"I naturally considered," Julian went on, "removing the wireless from the stripped back laptop. But my whole laboratory set up is wireless – printers, scanner, everything. Frustration upon frustration. But you know how," he brightened, "sometimes you look back at something you tried; and, in looking back, you realise that what you tried, or did, was more interesting than what you at the time supposed?

"So it was that I recalled my accidental, my unintentional Faraday Cage. Result? I set about deliberately building a cage. Copper mesh mostly, and in just the one end of the lab.

"I don't know, yet, if it has stopped me getting hacked. What I do know is that I was sitting in that cage, playing around with an oscilloscope, a gaming switch and a length of carbon fibre. Some of the carbon fibre touched the copper mesh, and I found myself in space.

"Eighty-seven miles up, just hanging there. The Bristol Channel way down below me. I could've waved to you Bart."

Bart may have politely smiled acknowledgement. I seem to remember though that not one of us, in our three corners of the screen, overtly reacted.

"Of course, I thought I was hallucinating," Julian smiled. "Or in a dream state. Had maybe nodded off while in the cage.

Wouldn't be the first time I've woken up staring at a screen. But it was no screen I was looking at. There I was, the copper mesh of the cage all around me, and beyond the cage the black of space. I could breathe. In airless space. So was I really there? I saw some carbon fibre touching the mesh and lifted it away. And I was back in my corner of the loft.

"That took more than a few minutes to process. I am, however, I regard myself as, a scientist. And as a scientist I know that experiments have to be replicable. So, keeping all else the same, I touched the fibres to the mesh. And again, there I was eighty-seven miles above the Bristol Channel, sitting on my chair in the cage, laptop on my knees."

"It's a projection," Steve decided.

"More, much more than that," Julian grinned at him. "I began by telling you that I've been to the moon. Not that I went that afternoon. To which I have to add – about that afternoon. When I went up that first time it was just after sunset in Ilfracombe." Julian would have known this by the two porthole-like windows at either end of his laboratory. "Up there though the sun had still been above the horizon. I'd had to turn my eyes away from it. Still a projection possibly. But a projection of a new kind. What I do know is that I was most definitely up there."

"The moon?" Bart's dark eyebrows were raised.

"That took weeks. I didn't know which of the objects that I'd had with me in the cage had caused my being up there. I took out the gaming switch, touched fibres to the mesh. Stayed where I was. I unhitched the oscilloscope – it was outside the cage – found a jack to connect the gaming switch to laptop and fibre. I pressed 'return' and straight away I was up there again, same place above the Bristol Channel.

"Although that day I'd had to wait for the cloud cover to break before I could see the ground shapes."

Julian wandered off into his own thoughts again. We three waited, knew that there was more, credible or not, to come.

"What I had to work out," Julian said, "supposing that the hardware was set, was what the laptop software was telling it to do. The program I'd been working with had all been about moving blocks of data. So, was it the program itself or one of the data blocks that decided where I went? I isolated all the data, touched fibre to mesh. Stayed where I was. Ran program with data, touched fibre to mesh; and there I was again looking down on the Bristol Channel. Something in the blocks of data it was that decided where cage and I were being sent.

"That took much longer to work out. And it's this Steve that I want to work on with you. How program and data combine. For now, I've got it down to the one block. Its operative numbers begin with 01. Which I have taken to be my starting point, the loft. Won't work without the 01. Getting that far was comparatively easy; it has been what in the other 260 characters of that block that has taken some working out. But that's where I found the sequence corresponding to the eighty-seven miles. Was how I came to know that it was precisely eighty-seven miles. It was accepting that section of the data that got me to the moon."

"This is true then?" Bart it was who broke the growing silence.

"Absolutely." Julian smiled around at us three. "I've been to the moon. You three are going as well. I need validation. I've stripped down three more laptops and I'm sending one to each of you by courier tomorrow. All the laptop has on it is this one program. With it will be a gaming switch and a coil of carbon fibre. I expect you to supply your own copper mesh. Shouldn't be that expensive."

"How expensive?" Bart asked.

"If you need help getting it," Julian continued, "or cash to buy it, let me know. After all you three are now my tax-deductible research assistants. When you've got your cages set up, let me know and I'll send you the data block. See you on the moon."

What else, believing it or not, could we four futurists do but look to one another and chuckle.

Eight: cage building

'Every time we act, we commit ourselves to the future.' Colin Wilson

I was first off the mark. Not that I was that quick.

Grey laptop, gaming switch, connecting cable and a coil of carbon fibre – all in the one box – arrived by courier, instructions from Julian within as to where online I would be able to purchase the copper mesh. Good fellowship and charity apparently had their limits.

Although my rectangular caravan is long and has, allegedly, three bedrooms, in only two of those bedrooms does a double bed fit that allows a theoretically slim couple space enough to squeeze out each their side of the bed. On the outer side a bare bum has to squeak past a cold windowpane. Only one of my rooms is therefore given over to a double bed. (Even at my advanced age I live in hope.) The other double is my office, the smaller my wardrobe and general junk room.

There is consequently nowhere in the caravan for a non-Faraday Cage. Plus, the suspicion that the caravan, given its metal sides and metal roof, would stop the cage working. Radio reception inside is certainly poor to hopeless. Following Julian's advice, I had earlier rigged an aerial further up the hillside among the trees; and that was just for my old transistor radio. TV and PC all came courtesy of landline and router.

The groundwork builders had left behind a blue and green portaloo. The portaloo company had gone bust in the same slump that had brought a halt to my building efforts. No-one came to collect the chemical-stinking portaloo. The caravan has its own lavatory temporarily[?] connected to the sewage mains.

After a year of the faded blue and green portaloo sitting

away to the side I considered it mine, renamed it the Turdis. And I have ever since kept my gardening tools in there, along with the tools that I used to build the door canopy and the bike lean-to at the back of the caravan.

At first, I considered emptying the tools out of the Turdis and making the non-Faraday Cage within. Except, although the Turdis appears to be principally of fibre glass and plastic, I suspect – so sturdy is it – that its skeleton might well be metal, which again might interfere with the functioning of the cage. And sceptical as I instructed my reporter self to be, I still wanted Julian's cage to be given every chance.

Telling myself that I could always find alternative uses (the desire to appear sensible is strong in Somerset male humans) and making sure that I exceeded the cage dimension that Julian had given me, I ordered online a wooden shed. It came flat-packed two days later.

Still days ahead of my two *Futuricity* confrères.

You might think that with all these consideration, preparations of mine, that Steve and Bart would have been way ahead of me. But Bart in his hillside terrace had his office way up the top of his steep garden. That shed/office was block-built, insulated and fully electric. There Bart did his historical research, kept his library; and there was nowhere else in his terraced garden for a shed even as small as mine.

What Bart did have in his house was his late son's bedroom. Rhean had been striving to de-shrine that bedroom for some time. She suggested that Bart put his cage in there. When Bart equivocated, she assured him that the cage would be temporary and that everything that needed to be moved – the electric train track and airship mobiles – could be returned to their original positions.

Fortunately, there were no lingering family resentments to negotiate: Rhean and her stepson, being of a similar age, had got on really well, had both been steam train enthusiasts, had gone on trips together. Tattooed Rhean also got on well with

Julian and Glynis, she and Bart having been across on the *SS Balmoral* and paddle steamer *Waverley* to visit a few times. And all of them, stepson Lou and girlfriend included, had gone together on an East Coast excursion as far north as the track took them. [See *Futuricity* archive for photos and comments.]

Finally convinced that the cage could be, would be, easily collapsed, Bart began to work out ways of building it in his late son's bedroom.

Steve had been faced with similar spatial impediments and family considerations.

Steve's Workington ex-council house had rooms, like my caravan's, not excessively big. More to the point he had three grown daughters regularly returning to the family home. When the box containing the cage makings came one daughter and granddaughter – a partnership break-up – had been living with him for some time. Steve consequently had no regular available space within the house.

Like Bart Steve too had a shed/office, further stroke, studio; but his was at the end of his long and flat garden. Both gardens, front and back, had been given over to vegetables – Steve is keen on self-sufficiency – so no room there for an extra shed, for even one as small as mine.

Steve's end-of-garden shed was sturdily wooden, also insulated and fully electrical. This sometimes photography studio also served as his workspace – for software repairs and PC and laptop upgrades. Steve also promoted and sold his own software, and he kept his bike there. Which shed occupations and activities again left him with little space for a non-Faraday cage.

However, what Steve's ex-council house did have, running part way alongside the back concrete path, was an old block-built wash-house and outside lavatory. The old washhouse, painted white inside and out, had become a utility room long before Steve had bought the house. While the outside lavatory, as with previous owners, had become a dumping room – for old paint tins, compost bags, plastic pots and garden tools.

Steve found a plastic chest on a local free-to-collect website, got it home in the back of his car and squeezed it off the path at the back of the lavatory, where the old tin coal bunker had been. He transferred the outside lavatory's contents to the chest, and he converted the lavatory to his cage, putting a padlock on the outside of the door to stop his daughter and granddaughter in desperation using it for its original purpose.

All of which took place long after my cage-making.

I had no such familial difficulties to negotiate, to slow me down. Steve and Bart's scepticism too had had them in no great hurry. Whereas, with nothing else pressing, it took me but one day to flatten a piece of ground up behind the caravan, and another day to screw the shed's eight pieces together. The two extra pieces were on either side of the door. No window.

Took me another day to lay the copper mesh around the insides, over the floor and pin it under the roof. I nailed another sheet to the back of the door. Left me with mesh to spare. I rolled that up and stored it in the portaloo.

That done I messaged Julian to tell him that I was ready for the data block. For once Julian replied almost immediately, said that it was on its way and to check my emails.

The data block came attached to an explanatory note saying that it had been extended to include other 'contingencies', and telling me to transfer it to the stripped-back laptop via a USB flash drive. Julian also attached the operating sequence for such a *Window*less basic task.

That done, and by this time excited, I ran an extension lead out through the caravan side window, took the swivel chair from my office, gathered up the laptop, gaming switch and carbon fibre.

With the shed door ajar to give me light – from the caravan's back windows – I first set up the laptop. Pulling the door shut, and with illumination enough from the laptop screen, I then made sure that the copper mesh was joined; and

44

connecting the gaming switch I touched the fibre to the mesh.

Feeling a little foolish, reassuring myself that the shed could always be used for something else – caravans notoriously have little storage space – I checked again best I could that the mesh on the back of the closed door was making contact on all sides, and I pressed Return.

I was in the black of space, star glimmer all around, planet Earth questioningly dark below me.

Nine: above Somerset

I could still see the copper mesh enclosing me and beyond that, free of Earth's occluding atmosphere, stars of so many sizes; groupings seen before only through the clearest and cleanest of telescopes.

And I could breathe. I took deep chest-expanding breaths. Yes, I was in airless space and I could breathe.

How high was I? Beyond Earth's atmosphere. I guessed about 80 miles up. A hundred?

Up? Out?

Panic-knowledge came at me. I don't even remember reading about the Karman Line but knew that I must be way above it. How far above?

I was in space where horizons curved. Leastwise the dark one that I could make out curved.

Looking past my feet I could see Somerset's dark mass, I assumed peppered with Wellington streetlights, and over to the east Taunton's sprawl. Further out, maybe, villages with one or two lights. Maybe.

Not knowing what else to do, sitting there in the black of space, I felt the breathlessness of real panic coming on and, very deliberately following Julian's instructions, I simultaneously pressed 'Control' and D.

I was back in the shed looking at what I could see of its wooden walls by the grey-blue light of the laptop screen.

My heart was beating so fast that it had my fingers all a-tremble. I had difficulty unhitching the copper mesh before I could open the shed door.

With no satisfactory explanation for what just happened to me I walked in small frantic circles between the shed door and the back of the caravan. I told myself on each circuit that I knew what Julian had said, but... Yes, but...

Although I had chosen to believe, to indulge Julian, I now found it hard to credit my own experience. Had I really been in space? Among the stars? If so, how?

How?

Tired of staring into the shed as if it would tell me, I took myself into the caravan and switched on the kettle.

"A refreshing cuppa." For this newbie astronaut.

The cuppa took me no further.

*

When not asleep that night I moved between the exhilarating acceptance of my having been in space – Out There Up There – and my doubting how. How? Just how? Had it been real? Or was it something Julian had concocted that triggered mental projections? Had I seen what I had expected to see? Auto-suggestion based on a planetarium set of stars, satellite views of Earth? And if I had been truly there, in airless space, how had I been breathing?

I'm presuming that I eventually slept. Must have, because at day's first grey light I awoke.

After a gobbled down breakfast, I hurried out to the shed with the laptop. I had left the extension and office chair in there. Seated, laptop and gaming switch connected, carbon fibre touching the mesh, program set, I pressed Return and was blinded by the sun.

Ducking my head I shuffled the seat around to put the sun at my back.

I was again breathing fast and my heart was hammering, but I was definitely in the black of space again, my feet up above the green broccoli tops of my woods, but so far up that my caravan roof was not visible, even when I squinted. Although was that? Part shaded, the white of my concrete platform?

47

There was Wellington's uneven drift of speckled rooftops, the playing fields of the private school, the big off-white roofs of the Chelston industrial estate, grey motorway skirting the hills beyond. There was Milverton, Wiveliscombe; and I realised that I could feel no warmth from the sun.

How was this possible? The light spectrum was open to me, but not all the rest of the spectrum. Actual astronauts absorbed radiation even within their spacecrafts. Just being in space, outside of Earth's protective atmosphere, they became subject to gamma radiation. Yet there I was, breathing while in the vacuum of space, and not feeling even the warmth of the sun. This didn't make any sense. No sense at all.

And yet...

Yet there I was in real time, creamy grey clouds obscuring parts of the Brendon Hills; and was that..? Yes, I could just make out the grey rectangle of a lorry moving along the motorway.

At that my brain couldn't take any more. My breathing had accelerated to the point where I was panting. I hit Control D, was back in the shed, the woodland's green light peeping through cracks, splits and knotholes in the shed's thin walls; and I was facing away from the door.

Ten: confirmation

'Knowing the results of an experience is not the same as understanding the experience itself.' Aldous Huxley

I called Julian.

"How is this possible?"

"Sorry?"

"I've done it. Been out there. Up there. How is this possible?"

"Right. Sorry. Still in bed. Glynis just brought my first coffee." A pause as, I guessed, he reached for the aforesaid coffee. "You've been out?"

"I think I have. Or imagine I have. Twice. Went up last night. Again, this morning. Is it real? Was I really there? Not some clever auto-suggestion? Believe it and be there?"

"So cynical?"

"I have spent a large part of my life, Julian, creating works of the imagination. Credible works of the imagination I might say. But works nonetheless that have to appear credible, acceptably credible. How's it done?"

"Physics of it," Julian carefully said, "are beyond me. I had all the same doubts as you. Even while doing it. This can't be true."

"Yet it is. I was there. I believed I was there."

"Which is... I have given this so much thought." Julian took a loud inhalation, sighed it out. "Possibly we don't yet have the terminology for such an experience. An experience neither virtual nor actual. Although your collaboration does go some way to making it actual. Shareable. Which is precisely why I passed on the details to you three. Because there is no way, based on only my own experience, I could patent this."

I heard him move about his bed, take a glug of coffee.

"Could still be some kind of mass hysteria," I said. "Groupthink?"

"How groupthink? When it is, so far, just you and I. Not that you're wrong to question it. My own first doubt was that if I was physically, corporeally up there, then I had to be in geostationary orbit. So I went up, stayed up for several hours. I turned with the planet, watched the sun travel overhead. A weather system started to come in from the west. When it obscured Lundy I went back to the lab, waited for the rain. It came."

I was neither convinced nor reassured: "Proves nothing."

"Which is why I went to the moon. That strange dust bowl wasn't what I had expected. No erosion. Not as here on Earth. That's what struck me. Everything jagged. I hadn't consciously foreseen that. Or was it something that I'd subconsciously stored away? Like in dreams you can sometimes be surprised by what you know?"

"Can't say that's happened to me of late," I said for something to say.

But his thoughts, although not identical, were along similar lines to my own. Mine had been on percipience, that mental state where you know with near certainty what is about to happen. Those times for instance when playing darts you know, even before the dart has left your hand, that its point will embed itself in the treble. Not that it has happened that often to me. Twice maybe. Or it is like selling a house. You sometimes know that the transaction is done almost before it has started. In a state of prescience, I can feel it. And even more so with a multi-stranded event. Comes a moment when I know that it is touchable, all strands about to coalesce.

"How precisely does it work?" I asked Julian.

"Dunno," he grunted. "But work it does."

"Can't see how you're going to prove this. How did you find out how to get to the moon?"

50

I heard Julian call out a distant 'Bye!' to Glynis, then he said, "Take a look at the laptop software. The zero one [01] is where you are. After that it gets complicated. First instruction sends you to the gaming switch, which comes back to the laptop, then back to the switch; and whatever the two of them wants it goes to the data block. It was Steve pointed out that the data block is not inert. Which I'd already guessed, but not how the switch was activating it, making it in effect part of the code."

"Surely a data block is just that, a data block?"

"Precisely. It was only once Steve had showed me what was doing what... It was from then on that I proceeded in leaps and bounds.

"Steve hasn't even got his cage built yet."

"This was all hypothetical then as far as Steve knew. He assumed, given the gaming switch, the problem was with a video game. I just sent him the numbers he asked for. Which was how high I'd got in miles and in kilometres. He worked out what in the data block was being used."

"Which is?"

In his pause I sensed Julian, even propped up in bed, raising his plump hand for quiet.

Finally he continued, "Which is, for instance, to get to the moon I first went looking for a string of numbers in the data that corresponded to the height, distance – call it what you will – that I'd so far been up. If you look in yours it'll be exactly the same distance you went up. Actually, in your data block I've enclosed the measurement in sharp brackets. The moon distance I put it within those self-same brackets. But to get to the moon I also had to specify the angle, couldn't wait for the moon to be directly line-of-sight above me. So, I had another look at the gaming switch software. Which is basically the video gun sight.

"I tried using that, but not to get to the moon. Not yet. I used the same distance as I sent you. I ended up almost

51

midstream between Cardiff and Hinkley.

"Working backwards from that elevation I found the angle required for me to have done that in the data block. Enclosing those numbers in brackets, I then exchanged the numerals necessary for the moon."

I must have audibly sighed or shifted.

"I know," Julian said. "Still doesn't prove that you or I were in space, or that I was on the moon. Could still be what I expected to see there. That said, there's all this hard and fast physics involved. There was a definite time lapse between my leaving here and my arriving," I heard Julian put 'arriving' within quotation marks, "on the moon. 1.3 seconds to be precise. And took even longer when I went further out. Which I believe means that we can only travel," again the quotation marks but this time around 'travel,' "at the speed of light."

Silence.

"Except," I felt compelled to say, "wherever you were, you weren't really there. Hard and fast physics?"

"Which is why I am holding fire on further experimentation. Until Steve and Bart have finished their cages. See how they both get on, then see what our hive mind can come up with by way of practical, repeatable demonstrations."

Eleven: space [travel?]

'My mind was like a rat in a maze, being both rat and maze.'
Brian Aldiss

I wanted more than inventor Julian's attempts at explaining what he thought had taken him and I up there. I called Bart and Steve to see how their cages were progressing.

Neither of their cages were anywhere near complete.

The hold up so far as Bart was concerned was his continuing reluctance to make use of Lou's bedroom. And I could understand that reluctance, especially when he was still battling to discover the actual cause of his son's death. Since the inquest Bart had subsequently discovered that others his son's age, and who had performed at some of the same London venues, had fallen foul of a similar type of cancer.

As he had tried to get his MP or anyone official to admit to the connection, let alone the cause, Bart's frustration had built. Even the other two relatives, granting it was a coincidence, hadn't been convinced there was a direct connection. Which had only served to make Bart dig deeper.

Bart had even had a BBC crew around filming his son's room as part of their 'investigation.' Nothing came of it.

But with nowhere else within or without the house for the cage Rhean it was who was pressing hard for, finally, an alternative use for the room.

"Time was long overdue for the grieving process to be brought to an end," she later told Julian and Glynis.

*

Steve's cage-building tardiness up in Cumbria was due more to everyday nuisances – his having to earn a living, and one of his daughters plus her child having come back to live.

One or other of Steve's daughters were always coming back to live or were in other ways in need of his help, his time. In fact, I knew more of Steve's three daughters than I did of his missing wife. Knew only that she was somewhere abroad with a new man.

The outside lavatory, the new Turdis-to-be, that was to become Steve's cage was not an easy conversion. Getting the copper mesh to fit over the lavatory pan proved the most challenging part; after that was running an extension through the wall from the utility room, and then keeping his infant granddaughter at bay, or amused.

*

If memory serves, I think that's where Steve and Bart were. So easy though to get out of sequence recalling all that has happened and was happening so quickly.

While waiting for their corroboration I investigated the screen pages of code on the stripped back laptop, worked out what was fed to the gaming switch, and then what the gaming switch wanted of the data block.

At that point I was suspicious of the data block: it seemed to me then too convenient for an 'accidental' discovery, too neat. What was Julian not telling me?

It took Steve later to explain to me that the data block could have contained any lump of numbers. Steve convinced me that it was the program, along with the gaming switch, that went looking for instruction and interpreted lengths of data as the measurements needed for what it was being asked to do, and then doing it at speed.

Julian had told me that one set of data numbers was the height I had been going above my 01 base. Having increased that set of numbers, now within sharp brackets, I took laptop and lead out to the shed and almost up to the moon.

Closer to the moon that is, sitting there within the black of space, Earth a dark oblate spheroid way below, off to my right the surface of the moon, its dry seas and mountains clearer than ever before seen – seen by me that is – even through a strong telescope.

My straight up angle and distance that time were wrong for a moon 'landing.' But, working backwards through the data block, it did show me which set of numerals probably directed the angle I would have to use.

First though I wanted to see what would happen within Earth's breathable atmosphere. So, I brought the angle to almost my horizontal, and pressed Return. Nothing happened.

With that angle nothing happened for several small plus and minus changes I made. But if I reverted to the straight up I still, at different times of day and night, went out into space.

I could make no sense of it. My mind a blur of numbers I got back in touch with Julian, told him what I had tried.

"Has to be line of sight. No obstructions. You're in an awkward place behind your caravan and surrounded by trees."

"The shed is actually up and behind the caravan. Can see out over the caravan roof."

"Then that's the direction to go in. Identify the blocks of data the program finds – for what you do – then adapt them to your future needs. I'll send you over my new data block with the elevation and direction sections et cetera all picked out. I'm stymied by the hills to the south of me. But I've been north over Bart's place in Wales. Never saw him. I was still plane height. It's all trial-and-error Ben. This is just the beginning."

Once the new data block arrived, I replaced Julian's direction and distance, added elevation. 3D thinking now. And straight away there I was a little above and before Barrow Mump out on the Levels. I was low enough to see a white egret on the edge of a rine, a couple of plump swans leaving dark trails through green weed. And a man and a woman climbing the Mump's dried grass to the grey ruins of the church.

The man and the woman, pausing to catch their breath, looked out over the Levels; then looked up, seemingly at one point straight at me in my cage. Neither reacted as if having seen me sitting on my swivel chair in the sky. Which begged the question yet again: how was I there and not there? And if I was truly there, could see them, how was I not being seen?

I couldn't get hold of any of the other three for a day or so. So I continued playing around with direction, elevation, distance; and I found myself over the east coast, twist of the River Thames below. I went further and, given the curvature of the planet, higher, found myself almost in space looking down on the Baltic Sea.

Leaving the shed I went indoors to find missed calls from Steve.

"Been up," Steve said. "Thought it best to wait till the girls," daughter and granddaughter, "weren't around. And there I was in my outside lav looking down on planet Earth. Still can't believe it's real. Is it real?"

I told Steve about my hanging above Barrow Mump and the couple on the Mump not acting as if they'd seen me.

"Pretty sure I had the same," Steve said. "Julian had warned me about line-of-sight when I told him I wanted to go to Mars. Not risen yet. So, I went out over the Solway to Balcarry Bay."

I wasn't surprised that software analyst Steve had mastered the code so much quicker than I. Debugging codes was part and parcel of his day job. And which had probably led to his attraction to other codes. Don't ask Steve about the Petroglyphs of Judaculla unless you have at the very least a good hour to spare.

"How did you get there so precisely? Mine's been all hit and miss."

"You have to work out the co-ordinates. Not the OS map co-ordinates. Although you'll need the map – for line-of-sight

56

distance. The distance from you, your zero base. You are your own zero latitude, zero median. Then plot a graph, work out the new co-ordinates. Your own East/West, North/South quadrants. Hit Return, and there you are. Will be. I'll show you where the co-ordinates go in the data block."

"Thanks." I'd been wondering where next to go. "Balcarry Bay?"

"You won't get there line of sight. Balcarry is over in Galloway. The most perfectly visual bay. Long sweep of it. A few cottages out towards one point. Car park beyond the woods the other. Nothing in between but this sublime arc. I love everything about Balcarry Bay, daydream about living in one the cottages. More shacks than cottages. I even love saying it, Balcarry Bay. As singularly poetic as Greylag Goose. Balcarry Bay. Greylag Goose. Balcarry Bay..."

I could hear him smiling.

"I even envy the alliteration in yours. Mister Benjamin Barraclough. What a lovely bloke Benjamin Barraclough."

And there I'd been envying Bart his moniker, none of us ever satisfied.

Before I could ask my next question Steve excitedly continued, "I took a few shots." Steve had contributed wildlife photographs to *Futuricity*, many taken on Cumbria's coastal plain, agricultural land mostly, some reclaimed from mining; all as part of his one-man campaign to show the perils of global warming, what we could lose.

"Thing is, these didn't come out well. Mesh of the cage blurred in the foreground. While I was trying to get past that, holding the lens against the mesh, a group of walkers came around the western end of the bay. And not one of them down there, as they made their way towards the cottages – shacks then – paid me the least attention. So I ask again; we breathe in space, are invisible here. How does this work?"

"No idea. Not that makes any sense."

"What's Bart say?"

"Don't think he's been up yet."

"What about Julian?"

"Couldn't get hold of him earlier."

"Well, I'm off to the moon shortly. Join me?"

Twelve: testing limits

"OK. OK." Bart at last answered. "I'm doing it. Cage keeps collapsing though. Rhean had the bright idea of using a set of plastic rods from a tent. Dimensions though aren't right for the cage. Have had to adapt. Good 'ol musicians' gaffer tape coming into play. Almost solid now."

"Steve and I are off to the moon in half'n hour. Care to join us? I'll send along our data block."

"I keep telling Rhean that I'm not sure about this at all. All I get back from her is 'boldly go.'"

"Takes some adjusting," I said. "But I'm getting there. Be interested in your take. Your being, like me, non-scientific."

"OK. OK. I'll let you know. I'm going to try space first. The initial settings?"

"Of course."

In a time when there's an app for everything you can find out the exact distance the moon is from your point on Earth; and the closer the moon the stronger will be the tides near you. Stronger still when the moon is aligned with the sun.

Such astrological considerations however were put to one side: for this moon trip all that I required was direction and distance.

Steve and I had decided to meet up in the large crater *Bullialdus*. I was there an expectant second after pressing Return. Smiling I looked all around the crater's sides, leaned to left and right to see either side of the little mountain in the middle of the crater. Only to decide that, within all of its 38 miles, there was no sign of Steve or Bart. Bart I hadn't truly expected.

My sagging onto my chair told me of my disappointment. I had fantasised on us four futurists holding discussions on the moon.

I pressed Control D and returned to my shed walls.

Was no point calling Steve or Bart from my Faraday cage. Unhitching the shed door, I took myself around to the caravan's front steps. Second step down was usually guaranteed a signal.

Mid-afternoon there was a faint half-moon high above me.

"Where were you?" I asked Steve. He finally answered.

"*Bullialdus* ten minutes ago."

"Me too. Which must mean that we're invisible to one another while up."

"Seems so. Sun was scary bright though."

"Which has given me an idea. I looked to see if I cast a shadow. Didn't. Didn't disturb the surface dust either. Got me to wondering if I took my little laser pen with me I could establish in some other way that I was actually there."

"My photos still look photo-shopped." Steve had his own light preoccupations. "I got those sharp crevices around the edge of the crater, but every black crack and crag are all beyond mesh blur. I'm going to have to make apertures in the mesh on all four sides of the cage. Poke my lens through. Against the door and walls that is. Just gotta hope that the holes I make don't damage the cage."

"I'm going to try with the laser pen."

Twenty minutes later I was back on the front steps and on the phone to Steve.

"Here's interesting. The pen worked. That little green dot travelled over the crater's sides. So, I was there and interacting with my surroundings. Had me tempted to point the laser back at Earth. Need someone here though to be watching for it."

Steve gave a prefatory laugh: "My own discovery was more, literally, down to Earth. While I was pressing my camera against solid walls and door, and keeping an eye out for your green dot, my daughter came banging on the lavatory door asking if I was alright." Another laugh: "Was so weird being busy up on *Bullialdus* and having to shout, 'I'll be out in a minute.'I've already put a padlock on the outside of the door so they can't get in and mess up the mesh when I'm not around."

All new information is almost unthinkingly checked against one's own experience. Steve telling me of having to shout to his daughter had me realise that while I'd been out over Barrow Mump, and even when eighty plus miles up in the black of space, I'd been hearing shed noises; the creak of my office chair, wind rustling through leaves, fluting call of a blackbird. All so familiar that I hadn't paid them any attention.

Bart was next to call: "My calculations are going to need some finessing. I ended up on the Bay of Rainbows"

"On the moon?" I asked to be sure, Balcarry Bay still on my mind.

"*Mare Imbrium*. Nowhere near you and Steve. Something else this, innit? How the hell does it work? Makes no sense. No sense at all. We can breathe in space."

"And we can see, but not be seen."

"In what band of radiation does that work?"

"Two-way mirrors?"

"Maybe. But how?

'But how?' was to become our refrain over the next few days as we four attempted to reconcile experience with known physics.

"Don't suppose we've been neuromanced?" I asked Steve later.

"How could we, each time, without knowingly ingesting something?"

"Odourless gas?"

"From where? In a cage with holes?"

We had none of William Gibson's dermatrodes affixed nor his neuromancing 'lines of light ranged in the non-space of the mind.' We were each in our own cage and once there we each prosaically pressed Return and we were somewhere else.

To Bart's 'How?' that day I told him to ask Julian.

"Can't get hold of him," Bart said.

"How about I arrange a zoom? All four of us. And we try to make better sense of this?"

"You're on."

In the meantime, I think we all went a bit space mad.

Thirteen: zoom

The hellos over.

Bart: I can only go straight up from my valley. Have got to know the moon quite well. Still no idea how this works though. Two hundred and thirty odd thousand miles from Earth, and there in seconds. Who knew?

Me: I tried Venus. Edgar Rice and all that. Got through the first gas layers. Wouldn't let me into the denser though. Never got anywhere near the surface.

Julian: How long did that take?

Me: Minutes. Between each try.

Steve: I plotted in Ross 128. [At the time of writing Ross 128 is our closest habitable planet.] See if we do have any galactic neighbours.

Julian: You didn't get there?

Steve: No.

Julian: Because Ross 128 is eleven light years away. While we travel, if travel is the right word, at the speed of light. Given that... I suppose that if you were to set the program running and left it on... [he pauses again, gives up on the calculation] ...then after more than eleven years you'd get there.

Me: This light business... [I told them again about the laser pen, and that Steve had said that his camera flash had lit up the inside of a moon chasm.] Us being there and not being there...

Julian: Granted, sense it does not make.

Steve: Is this real? Have we really gone to the moon? And if we have, why hasn't anyone else found out how to do it?

Julian: This is precisely what I wanted you three to help me find out.

Steve: What if the cage thinks it's a part of a game?

Julian: How would that work?

Steve: A tailored hallucination? Matrix-like?

Julian: Our cerebral cortexes aren't plugged in. And there's nothing in the software, of either the laptop or the gaming switch, would even suggest that.

Steve: Taken all together? The combination?

Julian: [Pause.] No, still don't see how.

A lull, four faces apparently lost in thought.

Steve: I wanted to see if I could get under water. Did a minus calculation. Which got me to the surface. Sitting there in the middle of the Solway. A calm day. Next time I tried it was windy. But precisely the same minus elevation. The second that a wave 'touched' the cage the connection broke and I was back in the lav.

Julian: Like all of you I wanted to know where I actually was while in space. Where me, corporeal me was, when to all intents and purposes I was looking around the *Sea of Tranquillity*. So, I set a camera on me in the cage while I went to the moon. Times of the film and my going up were the same. While I was on the moon, there I was in the cage looking around at whatever it was taking my attention on the moon.

Bart: Rhean wanted a go. As she was the one pressured me into building the cage, was hard to refuse. I set the data block for nearest space. Got her sitting in the cage, closed the mesh... Know what she said? Apologies everyone. "Beam me up Scotty." [Laughter.] What was weird was my standing there in our spare room watching her inside our makeshift cage. I could see her looking around. She even said Wow. But to know that she was in two places at once. That was, that is, so weird.

Julian: No escaping that.

Another thoughtful lull. In which – couldn't help myself – I held in my unwholesome mind's eye the image of a totally tattooed Rhean squeezed into one of her minimal comi-con Lycra outfits and suspended in a wonky copper cage within the black of space. Perfect lurid pulp cover for Julian.

Julian: Hate to bring this up, but I take it you impressed on Rhean the need for secrecy?

Bart: Threatened to remove her tattoos one by one if she told a living soul. But tell you what is weirder – weirder than our being there and not being there. Because, and I don't know if this was a coincidence, but I must have slightly – only slightly – mismeasured my distance. On my arrival – finally! – I displaced some dust of *Mare Imbrium.* I watched the white dust rise and settle again. Or did I really see it? Or was I seeing what I expected to see? Dunno. I went back to see if the cage had left an impression. There was none.

A semi-lull. I tried to recall if the gases on Venus had swirled and eddied around me. Couldn't decide if I'd been even a part of the swirling and eddying. At the time I had been mostly relieved to be still breathing the shed's woody smell.

Julian: I think we should all go beyond the moon. Did consider Mercury. Sunlight there is too dazzling though. And Mercury's too hostile an environment. What I'd like is for all four of us to do impact experiments on Mars. Should be in line of sight in a couple of weeks.

Fourteen: the physical properties of light

On a call Steve said – we usually speak at least once a week – that he envied us three our swivel chairs: "More than surreal my sitting on a lavatory in space, and then having to twist around to snap things – always behind me – that I want to take."

Even with our moveable chair seats we three were as handicapped. We had laptops balanced on our knees limiting our movements; and their cable connections to the gaming switch, the switch's grip on the flimsy carbon fibre, the fibre attached – stuffed into – the copper mesh.

Steve was nevertheless happy to believe that he had mastered the taking of photos in space by leaving at home his big cameras and taking only his mobile. By contorting his torso and squeezing open the cage mesh in front of the phone's lens he could take photos with no foreground blurring.

The properties of light however continued to bother Steve: "What I still don't get is how I can photograph what's there while not being physically there. Or rather, and at best, being simultaneously in the two places. And, as well discovered on the moon, not casting a shadow."

"Could it be we're on the astral plane?"

I was ignored.

Steve does tend to go on, not so much like a dog with a bone, more a cat with its prey, tossing it up and pawing it aside. Which analogy would annoy him.

My fellow founding member of *Futuricity* dislikes unthinking animal analogies. So much so that he had me believing that he disliked the entire animal world. I actually held back from telling him about my two under-the-caravan cats. Until that is I fully grasped his love of photographs, was told of his cycling miles to snap a particular bird or, more likely, a scene. Or, this last time, a perfectly posed red squirrel.

Steve is really proud – uses it as a screensaver – of a snow-topped Skiddaw beyond the coastal plains' green fields. *Cumbria's floating Kilimanjaro* he calls that view of Skiddaw.

"What it is I find so frustrating," Steve attempted to explain to me once, "in this drawing of comparisons with the natural world, is the making of animal behaviour analogous with the human, and then the one getting anthropomorphically reflected back into the other and skewing our understanding of both."

Photographer Steve also gets the occasional commission, did one on a Barrow dancing troupe specialising in period jitterbug. He titled the dance hall exhibition *Still Jives.*

What Julian and Bart early discovered, and Steve shut in his dark lavatory only later came to realise, was that the photos we took in space were, like old-fashioned double-exposure prints, of both stars and of each our place on Earth. So the very first photos that Julian took were of the long inside of his well-lit laboratory with stars or moonscape superimposed. Likewise, Bart had the wall posters of his son's bedroom pierced by stars.

Being belatedly told of this, and on closer examination, Steve and I too discovered that our own space photos were similarly superimposed on our darker Earthly surroundings. Took Steve longer than I to concede, seeing is believing, as he kept the light off in his back path lavatory so that his daughter and granddaughter wouldn't realise that he was in there. And leaning forward to take photos in space he shut the lid on his laptop to stop it toppling off his lap. The sole, and faint source of light in his lav had therefore been his mobile screen showing him the shot in space that he was about to take.

My own absolute confirmation came about when I became puzzled by a sun I couldn't recall having seen up there. Turned out to be a knot hole in my shed wall.

Even with that solved, the properties of our space-travel

light continued to perplex scientist/software engineer Steve: "How can we see, but not be seen? Makes no sense, whichever way I look at it. Our eyes receive light waves and photons. The mind makes sense of those patterns. Yet the head which holds the mind, the eyes; the body which supports the head, casts no shadow. It is simply not logical. Makes no kind of natural sense."

This despite a paper he wrote on the blind pineal gland's eye-like structure, its lens, retina and potentially optic nerve. He then expanded that consideration to fantastically discuss ways we might become capable of re-animating the gland, the uses an optical pineal gland could be put to...

Frustrating for Steve that his perspective appears to be first and foremost visual. On one zoom he entertained us with impressions of his then teenage daughters' lexicon of facial expressions, from anxious doubt to mock despair.

He is mostly visual in his descriptive writing too. Telling of an early morning up in the fells: 'White-grey mist creeping through green trees, drops clinging to every grass-head and pine needle, boughs en masse silvered, a raven calling above the treetops. Views from the rocky crags down through broken clouds to the hyper-green valley bottoms.'

In my *Futuricity* championing of Asimov and Clarke, scientists both, I'd oft repeat their assertion that in science fiction a difference always has to be made between fantastic and futuristic science. What I have never been sure of is where software engineer Steve, with his fascination for religiosity, sits with that assertion. What I do know is that he was the one of us most unable to accept what his senses seemed to be telling him. As he said, seemingly as complaint, "We are there, but don't exist there."

That wasn't Steve's, or our, only frustration. Line of sight was confining our travels over planet Earth. Setting random co-ordinates found us in some odd places at unwanted heights.

"But not within hollow spaces underground. Definite

limits," Steve said, "to our supposed travels."

Line of sight also meant that, even those of us able to travel in any lateral direction, we were still confined to the one hemisphere. And to our up-above space. With Mars close to rising.

Fifteen: old hands

Got so we were very soon old hands at space travel. Leastwise I got to feel like an old hand. Could have been my age: space travel was certainly tiring. I restricted my going around to the shed to every other day. The day between I needed to process all from the day before and to decide – possibly – what and where next.

My keeping-up calls with the others, especially Steve, had me wanting to replicate some of what they'd done. Not that I wanted to go to Balcarry Bay, but I did want to see if the cage could take me underwater.

Although I had found the gases on Venus claustrophobic, and I had no wish to repeat my visit; and although I had known that I had been safe in my shed, with oxygen aplenty coming in through the cracks and the knotholes, still having those gases eddying about me had felt suffocating.

But if I could enter those gases unharmed then surely I could go underwater, investigate marine life? Planet Earth's own alternative universe.

Steve's attempts to go under the silted Solway hadn't convinced me. I couldn't work out though how to lower my elevation to a watery level, was finding it difficult even to get down to wet ground on the Levels.

I called Julian, asked him to try dipping under the Bristol Channel.

"Can't be done," he assured me. "I've tried. Water really is like a solid surface."

Which set me to wondering if it might be possible to go into empty spaces underground. I very carefully set a course for Cheddar Caves, pressed Return.

I remained in the shed at the back of the caravan.

I decreased the distance slightly in the data block, pressed

Return. I was on this side of the Mendip hills sitting above a partially filled car park.

No-one, couple or family group getting out of their car and walking through the car park, acted as if they had seen me sitting above their gleaming car roofs. There and not there. Which had me wondering if what we were doing was akin – electronically induced? – to what the shamans did. Only we were doing it without the spirit animals to lead us onto our astral planes.

Or whatever.

Shamanistic had to be an off-kilter comparison: our trips were too immediate, too technicolor real. Dab a thumb on Return and we were there.

With his interest in religion's altered states, I thought to try my shaman theory on Steve. Couldn't get hold of him.

Why was I bothering with what the cage couldn't do on planet Earth? "Go back to space," I told myself, and I set course for Mars.

Didn't happen of a moment. Getting the course right took me several days, each misfire leading to my hanging among stars (my back quickly to the sun) with Earth the tiniest of dots below me, the big red wall of Mars somewhere to my left or to my right.

All of my space travels were hit and miss. Brought to mind my 1960's attempts at technical SF, the writing all so pedestrian and clunky. Being fair to my much younger self I had even then been correct in fictional concept if not in actual terminology. For instance, I had believed there would come a time when electricity could be converted from any atom. What I should have been saying, instead of electricity, was that energy could one day be so converted.

Puzzling over the packed mass of the data block, learning as much as this old brain was capable of retaining, finally I landed on the Martian surface, noticing that as I did that I displaced some red dust. Leastwise the fine dust rose up and settled again. A coincidental Martian gust? Or a consequence of my arrival?

Two nights later, having unpinned the copper mesh from the shed door and with the wooden door ajar, mesh cage intact, I returned to Mars with a bamboo cane long enough to reach down beyond the cage.

This time no dust rose on my arrival. Nevertheless, I poked the slim cane down through the copper mesh and drew a circle in the red dust. When I pulled the cane back up into the cage the circle stayed.

Were we four then active projections? Could we four – me in my shed cage, Steve in his lavatory cage, Bart in his spare bedroom wonky cage, Julian in his end of the laboratory cage – interact with the environments we projected ourselves into?

I was just so excited, sitting there in my cage on Mars, I decided to leave a message, and I wrote as distinctly as I could in the deep dust, 'Arthur C Clarke wasn't here.'

While with patient difficulty doing the writing I had wondered what a delivery driver – when I wasn't home, they left parcels around the back of the caravan – would make of the cane sticking out of the shed and twiddling about.

I smiled down at my handiwork. I had at last gone one better than Arthur. He had only written *The Sands of Mars*. I, Benjamin Barraclough, had written in the very dust of Mars.

Back on Earth I scrambled out of the shed, but couldn't get hold of Steve or Julian, so asked Bart to go to Mars, check out what I had written. I gave him my Martian co-ordinates.

Then I waited. And waited.

I had so much trouble containing myself. Was tempted to go back to Mars myself and check on my dust-writing. But would my arrival there this time raise the dust? And would that dust obliterate my message? And what if my being there interfered with Bart's arrival?

Instead, and as diversion, I considered going back to Venus and leaving another message there. But to write on what? On the swirling gases? 'Edgar Rice may well have been here. Carson definitely wasn't.'

I loved E R Burroughs' SF, his invention of upside-down cultures, the women warriors, men become apes.

Bart finally called, said that it had taken him several attempts to get to the exact same spot. Had been so much to take into account, he said, the rotation of the earth, rotation of Mars, both their orbits around the sun, Bart's own starting point, time of day... But, with an air of self-congratulation, he told me that he had done it.

"Couldn't decipher all your writing. But got part of, was it 'Arthur'? And 'wasn't here'?"

"Know what this means?" I asked him. "If we reach beyond our cages, we can have some influence on where we are in space. Maybe here too."

Our relationship in space with light, or rather our non-relationship, had been a puzzle to us all. Direct sunlight blinded us, yet on the moon and Mars we in our cages had felt no heat, had cast no shadow. How was that possible? There and not there? Yet I had now left a message on Mars.

"Bit like that old joke," Bart said. "Told about two stupid Englishmen." He continued in a posh BBC/Etonian voice, "If I get there first, old chap, I'll write on the wall. And if you get there first, old man, you rub it out. No offence."

"None taken. We'd best let Julian know. Steve too."

Sixteen: the rings of Saturn

Our navigation skills having exponentially increased we agreed to meet up on Saturn's rings.

I say 'our' skills. The improvements, each and every tweak, had come from Julian and Steve. One or other told Bart and I what and where to add into the data block.

"We've gone beyond line of sight," Julian confidently assured me, "are leaving behind simple Cartesian co-ordinates. Steve and I have brought our methodology up to space age date."

So it was that, at the appointed hour, we four each made our own way to each our cage, sat ourselves down, made sure that the mesh door was closed, and again checking the time, we pressed Return and found ourselves on, or in my case below, Saturn's rings.

Although prior to entering our cages we had all said, "See you there," we knew of course that we wouldn't be able to see each other, nor communicate while we were there – how so from inside a Faraday cage?

At the same time, with those threaded cream and caramel rings above me, the orangey glow of Saturn beside me, it was comforting to know that my three friends nearby – all four of us there breathing the atmosphere of each our own room, lavatory, shed – were in close-up witness to the same thing.

And what a thing.

Saturn itself, the gaseous bands of hydrogen and helium held to its surface and underpainted by an orangey glow that also somehow ranged from blue to white, was a wondrous world to behold.

So wondrous was it that I came over all *Vanity Fair* and found myself bellowing out, "If Freddy Hoyle could see me now, that old hack of mine..." And laughing like a drain because of course that old SF pragmatist wouldn't have been able to see me. If however there happened to be a delivery man or walker near the caravan they might wonder at this strange croaking coming from the shed, which image had me cackling all the more as I turned on my chair just below the rings of Saturn.

"Saturn's rings!" I shouted out my joy. Each and every one of those rings an effect of Saturn's 83 moons. The moonlets and dust making up the rings were held there by Saturn's gravity but influenced also by the mass of moonlets within the rings and by the larger of Saturn's moons beyond. I could see Enceladus quite close, had been hoping to see Titan emerging from behind the rings.

My wide-eyed attention though was and was for breath-held moments fixed on the rings; a couple of rings especially that competing gravities had woven in and around one another. I don't think there is anything within our solar system to match that phenomenon. And there I was, and wasn't, those flattened discs my temporary ceiling, wondering what it was of them that my three friends were seeing.

And then...

And then Titan rose; and there was a moon with an atmosphere akin to that of Earth's. Not a breathable atmosphere unfortunately, mostly nitrogen. So not habitable. But there was little ol' me, Benjamin Barraclough, gazing enraptured upon it. Albeit Titan's colour is that of every new house's magnolia paint. Even so, what a wondrous wondrous privilege.

Julian had lately become concerned over our staying in space for hours at a time, had grown less confident that our space alter egos were not after all protected from gamma radiation, even though the personal radiation meters he had sent us, and which we obediently wore pinned to our chests, hadn't shown increased measurement.

Julian had subsequently got hold of an RIID, a Radiation

Isotope Identification Device, and had applied it to his cage. It showed that the copper mesh had absorbed gamma radiation. Unsure of the effects on his own soft tissue from this radioactive cage in the corner of his lab – his own personal radiation meter still showing nothing above normal – he had told us to limit our trips into space to an hour only, or until such time that he could be sure our cages were safe.

I had set my mobile's alarm. When it sounded in my shirt pocket, I dutifully bid farewell to creamy Titan and Saturn's glorious rings and returned to my mid-afternoon shed, letting out one long contented sigh.

*

An hour later, as agreed, we all four met up on zoom. Four very excited individuals.

"Did you see..?" and "Did you get a look at..?" and "Wow! Wasn't that something?" And Steve saying to anyone who'd stop talking long enough to listen, "The shots I've got. Better than Voyager. I'm telling you..." And from me, time and again, "I saw Titan. Titan!"

"This time..." Julian began.

"Whadya mean? This time?" from Steve.

"I checked out Saturn before. Make sure it could work for all of us. Anyway, this time I went up over the pole so I could look down on the rings. Stupendous whichever way."

No whisper of disagreement there.

Seventeen: consolidation

The exteriors of all space vessels become irradiated. The cage at the end of Julian's attic-laboratory had become irradiated. If his cage was picking up cosmic radiation did that mean our cages were too? Were we?

None of our clip-on meters showed anything other than ambient radiation.

The cage irradiation added to the contradictory nature of our space travels, their illogicality – not seen, but can see; sun-blinded, but cast no shadow. Those uncertainties had us readily bowing to Julian's decision that we best limit our extra-planetary activities. He suggested that if we were to do any cage-travelling then best keep them to within Earth's protective atmosphere.

"Unless" Julian said, "we need to go up for a specific purpose."

His own specific purpose was to follow up on my telling him of my green laser spot travelling over the moon rocks and cliffs. Julian went back up to the moon but with a more powerful laser.

Julian the inventor/entrepreneur has to have a purpose beyond Wow! That such a thing can be done. His moon trip hoped to find that this, his latest and accidental invention, had commercial prospects.

He arranged for Bart to set up a telescope atop the hill above his terrace, and there to see if Julian's green laser was visible from Earth. At that trajectory Bart was the closest of us three to Julian in Ilfracombe. Plus, Wales has a dark sky policy, their streetlights all directed down.

What Bart's Welsh valley didn't have for several frustrating days prior to the full moon was cloud-free skies. Just after full moon however Bart carried the big scope up the hill, got it aligned, and for the whole of the appointed hour he concentrated on the Copernicus crater. (We futurists are nothing if not romantics.)

Julian and Steve had already tried calling one another from space, while physically still in their lab and outside lavatory respectively. The Faraday cages did as they should however and had stopped their calls. So, when it had come to the moon experiment the times had had to be agreed beforehand. If the maths were right the spread of the laser, magnified by the scope atop that Welsh hill, should have been visible. But although Bart looked and looked, although he thought that once he may have detected a speck of green, he blinked once and it had gone.

As with all true innovators, who usually begin by being disbelieved and derided, be they the man with the metal nose who mapped comets or he who first charted blood's flow, in his need to find ways to, not only prove what his invention could do but show how it worked, I sensed Julian withdrawing, guessed he was hunkering down for a long think.

"I'll register the patent," he told us. "When, and only when, I've proved its worth. For the moment, all of you, hang onto the prototype. No sharing outside the group." Which I assumed now included space-travelled Rhean.

While Julian and Bart had been playing with lasers and scopes Steve and I had found ourselves frustrated by the hemisphere limits of our earthly cage travels. We had a joint moan and Steve said that he would see what he could do.

In retrospect this largely post-space pause was almost as if us four were reluctant to take the next step. The more likely reality was that we simply hadn't known what next to do. All four of us had no doubt that this was each our great adventure. Nothing preceded matched it. I, like Steve, have never felt that I belonged to this world, this era: where though were our mesh cages to take us?

There have been times when Steve has seemed to contain

all the contradictions of contemporary humanity. First and foremost quirk of this single parent father of three – all three daughters being fiercely defensive of his quirks – is his being near besotted with alternative religions: a software engineer puzzling over the soft anthropological science of myth and legend? Add to that this techie being as fascinated as much by the natural world as he is by machines. No stereotypes for Steve.

When he got back in touch with me, he had already stripped down the block of data to those functioning parts that had sent us into space, direction and distance; and he had started putting back, section by section, other parts. He discovered them to be elevation and co-ordinates. It was the latter that had him work out that if, after the first set of direction/elevation/distance/co-ordinates, he added the direction/elevation etc to another, then – and certainly within Earth's atmosphere – the second acted as a new starting point.

"Basically, what I've done is found a way to bounce the signal. A bit like working out a SatNav route that takes in various points along the way. I call them notional beacons."

Steve sent me the example he had used, that had taken him from low-lying Workington to the top of Sca Fell Pike.

"Take a look at the data block where it repeats distance and co-ordinates. I've highlighted them."

The repeated number string was divided by a double slash and highlighted on my screen in a yellowy orange.

"The second string is direction and distance from the church tower to Sca Fell. What you'll have to do is find a high spot in your own line of sight and go from there. Direction, elevation, distance: no reason we can't make leap after leap. Next time I went from Sca Fell Pike down to Morecambe. Negative elevation. And on Control D disconnect I came straight back here each time."

I decided to use direction, elevation and distance to the first point, Willets Tower; then work out a way up to Dunkery

Beacon (would be some satisfaction in my being the first of us to use an actual beacon), and finally out over Ilfracombe.

The code painstakingly calculated, entered, I closed the shed door and pressed Return. I was closer to Lundy Island than to Ilfracombe, in that I was way above both. But it had worked.

"World's our oyster," I happily reported back to Steve.

"Just wish I was confident what made it work," Steve said. "When I told Julian how we had extended our range he was all for patenting the set up there and then, and marketing it as spyware. I talked him down, said it was too early. Reminded him of our cages absorbing radiation. Says he'll consult us before selling his invention to possible governments." Steve doesn't like governments.

Bart, limited by the hills all around his valley, was delighted by Steve's innovation: 'Means I can now get to Africa. Home to us all. All who recognise our ancestry.'

He concedes that such a trip would take some line-of-sight working out.

Julian alarmed us in a copied-in email saying that he had been to the sun. He had wanted to see what effect the nuclear heat of the sun would have on the cage. Said he couldn't get that close: 'Closer than Mercury. But I was still not hot. Light though was intolerable.'

Which got us three anxious about the desperation that had driven Julian to attempt such a trip; and all four of us again wondering about the precise properties of our space travels. By going near the sun, the contamination count on Julian's cage had of course shot up. Giving him concerns over any effects this irradiation might have on everything else in his lab.

So, what next was to be done?

When there is a hiccup in any onwardgoingness always best to go back, if briefly, to basics. *Futuricity* basics is where we usually, when presented with a new book/author, we compared the book's plot/style to previous SF scenarios, and we assessed the new/latecomer's credibility/probability.

For what was happening to us and our cages we each went back to our individual SF libraries, looked at the many What-ifs of the human imagination; and we found nothing directly comparable to what we were doing.

Eighteen: linear travels

I was the least ambitious of us four when it came to using 'beacons'/staging posts, call them what you will. My second bouncing from line of sight, point to point, was from Barrow Mump to Glastonbury Tor to a trig point on Salisbury Plain, before dropping down to sit above Stonehenge.

I name all those points, but didn't experience any of the intervening places before Stonehenge. One moment I was in my shed and the next sitting on my office chair within my mesh cage looking down on people wandering around the roped-off standing stones.

I suppose drone spies must come by a similar at-a-remove neutrality regards what they are looking at. They though are physically miles away from what they are watching on their screens, added to which someone below might glance up to their drone and become aware that they are being watched. While none of the people below the mesh bottom of my cage, possibly discussing ley lines that possibly connect standing stones, had no idea that me, my chair and laptop were up above.

Invisibility is a fantasy that has long held voyeuristic appeal. To spy on suspected lovers, play pranks on friends, discombobulate enemies. The reality of our invisibility though, maybe due to the impersonal height we godlike sat at, made us all uncomfortable.

My next chain of beacons got me to sit above the Thames, its silver curves chopped into sections by all the dark bridges. Sitting there though didn't confer on me the least sense of superiority. I was too aware of planes above, helicopters below, and wondering what would become of me should one or other come straight at me.

Julian used Lundy's old lighthouse as his first beacon and explored Ireland. Reported back that he was trying to figure a way of getting across the Atlantic. His aim, in the belief that someone in Silicon Valley might be interested in his space-cage, was to then get right across America. He failed to say how, being invisible, he would communicate with them once there.

Bart made it as instantaneously from Wales to Africa. To the Atlas Mountains his first time. Then to somewhere over the Sahara.

Bart said that he had to take at least a day between each trip to work out all the jump points. He also needed time to recover. So disconcerting was it, he said, being in two so very different environments at once. The green lushness of his valley, if he stepped out his front door and it not actually raining, would still have him encounter a tangible moistness in the air. While over there he was up above the baked rocks and dust of mountains or hanging over the seemingly endless sweep of ungrassed dunes.

No sooner recovered however than Bart was looking for beacons to carry him to the tropical rainforests off the Gulf of Guinea. There and back in moments. Which is what, with these global surface excursions, bothered us more than when we had been in space. Say we got physically stranded where we were? How, for instance, Would Bart get home from the Congo?

We knew that wherever we were we weren't there. Sounds remained always at base, the leaf rustle above my shed, coo-coo of a wood pigeon. But say we got a power cut, that we weren't able to do a Control D?

Bart it was who found out. Via, of all things predictable, a toaster shorting out the electrics in his house.

He had got up especially early, had been mid-journey. When he had 'left' Rhean had still been in her dressing gown, about to make breakfast. Bart arrived, he thought, at Mount Kenya prior to Kilimanjaro, and for the briefest of moments registered where he was. Before being wide-eyed back in his son's bedroom with Rhean calling up the stairs, "Fuse tripped. Sorry.

Hot cross bun."

This incident offered some reassurance to us cage travellers. Certainly, it encouraged Steve.

An older cousin of Steve's, unable to find work locally, had reluctantly joined the army. Having been in the army a couple of years he had disapproved of Steve joining a demonstration against the invasion of Iraq. Soon after the invasion his cousin had been killed.

That unnecessary loss of life had so angered Steve; and the more that Steve had subsequently learned of the lies told about Iraq's non-existent weapons of mass destruction, of the political deals done, with every fresh disclosure/denial the angrier had Steve become.

Came as no surprise therefore that Steve's first major excursion was to Basrah, the second to somewhere near Baghdad.

"The waste," he reported back. "All that unnecessary damage. Gas and god knows what else being flared off. You know they used to say that no-one could be certain who'd win World War Three, but that the wars after that would most definitely be waged with sticks and stones? Over there you can almost see that reversion taking place."

Steve of course didn't stop his rant there, as usual went on to lament the huge loss of life throughout the region, to blame the inept politicians and ambitious religious leaders, especially the didactic heads of different sects. "So much of any religion is pure whimsy, from Adam and Eve onwards. And there they still go slaughtering one another over it. Buildings smashed to pieces..."

By which time I had long stopped listening, knew all that he was going to say, knew too that there was little that any of us could do to bring about actual change.

What I did do was envy my three compadres their desire to see places new. New that is on the surface of planet Earth. When what I really wanted to do was to go back to space. The meter I had acquired however had showed my cage and shed to be mildly radioactive, above ambient radiation that is. Turdis and caravan not so.

Nineteen: the awfulness of religions
and the possible nature of time

Steve described his keeping on going back to Iraq as 'an awful fascination.'

'There is no need for killing as a tool of government. Ever.'
Harry Harrison

"To see a country in the process of steady destruction, every single step forward followed by two sectarian steps backwards. Can't remember who said it, but they were right: 'Every reform movement within a religion degenerates into a sect.' And every new sect is fiercely attacked by the old school religion. Which then has the new as fiercely defending itself. No hope for Iraq while there's so many religions there."

'Rules for war – a conceit worthy only of children or imbeciles.' John Wyndham

Steve had a need to talk. His daughters, while kind to him and tolerant of his oddities, knew nothing of his cage travels, his preoccupations; and they were often busy or elsewhere. While I, being retired, was always pretty much available to lend an ear.

"Like with Ireland," Steve said, "Always some group objecting to something or other. Their objections alone sound threatening. And fear makes any group gather more closely together. Being afraid they are then instantly hostile to other groups.

"Seeing no future for Iraq I went back to the Sumerian valley, that cradle of civilisation. I looked too at ziggurats, searched out the soggy confluence of the Tigris and Euphrates..."

He sighed: "All so frustrating. So I went across to Iran. Don't know how I got there, but I was sat on my lavatory pan above row upon row of date palms. Rows weren't straight, had slight curves where they followed the lay of the land. And there was something so reassuring about their calm orderliness. Maybe it was only having to consider a vanishing point perspective..."

The peculiar wiring of Steve's brain had that vanishing point perspective somehow sending him to look again at the laptop's program. Ensuring that no matter what alterations he made to the program or the data block, Control D would always bring him back, he set about some radical tinkering.

'To see a candle's light, one must take it into a dark place.'
Ursula K Le Guin

This is my understanding of the process.

First Steve set about cutting away all material so far not used in the data block. Several days of experiments with the modified data followed.

"But resulted in nothing that different. Nothing that better or worse. I went back to retrospectively working out where the data this last time had sent me. Distance has been, as we all know by now, the easiest to find, to work out. Next came exact co-ordinates. Quite a complex string that, but once found... After that elevation..."

Julian was unreachable again, was why Steve was using me as his sounding board. All that I had to do was to make appropriate responses.

"Then I realised what it was my pointless tinkering had been looking for. What has all this time been missing. Time! A chronometer. No clock in Julian's stripped-back laptop. And yet most programs, if not all others, make use of a chronometer, if only as a ready-made random number generator. Or even if, paradoxically, requiring a constant. Such is time's contradictions."

Steve paused. I guessed to gather his thoughts, his words.

'You don't get to new places by following established tracks.'
Carlo Rovelli

"To start with," Steve said, "having added both calendar and clock, I only played about with the clock frequency, trying to see why Julian might have removed it. Other than his liking to keep things simple. Having the clock made no difference. I could still pop across to Basrah and Baghdad. Usual time-of-day difference. Except that, although I was using the same beacon points, it felt to be taking just that little bit longer. I wondered if the program, or the gaming switch, was now looking for something they couldn't find.

"I changed the data block to take me to places near and far. Even for the near though there was now an identifiable pause. Obviously having the clock was having some effect. So what I did was to add that moment's clock data to the data block. I hit Return, and nothing happened. I stayed shut in my lav.

"Brought to mind those times when we had tried to go underground, or under the sea. The same stubborn refusal to work. I removed the clock data, hit Return, went across to Balcarry. I put the clock data back in, but a couple of decades ahead. Lo and behold I was above Balcarry again. Then I thought I'd try the same with Basrah.

"No pause sensed this time. And remember I'm making all these amendments, laptop slipping off my lap, in my outside lav, my mind half inside the laptop and half looking around the place it's taken me. Which is when I noticed a minaret was missing. And two other big buildings gone.

"I tell you Ben that frightened me. So much so that I left the lav and went along to my studio to do some serious thinking. A note there though told me that I had to pick up my granddaughter. And she is... She is an absolute priority. Suffice to say I breathe in happiness every time I see her."

I tried to recall any of my rarely seen grandparents breathing in happiness when they had seen me. So stiff had been their encounters with my parents though that I doubt the small weird boy that had been me had barely registered.

I re-listened to what Steve had said before mention of his granddaughter: "You're telling me that you went forward in time? That you time-travelled?"

"I took it as a given that I must have travelled into the future. How far into the future though? That's what I needed to find out. Had to be something external, something uninvolved with the cage. Something I can measure against the here-and-now.

"Following from your idea of building your own house. Feasibility study, nothing more. Not at the moment any road. I've been looking at local planning permissions. And there's been an ongoing dispute up near Lamplugh. Locals objecting to a house extension coupled with a holiday home in the grounds. To cut a long story short, permission has recently been granted.

"First off, I paid a visit – on our astral plane – in the present. The house doesn't have an extension, doesn't look lived in, and the garden is scrub. A few bushes. Grass and thistles.

"Coming back to the lav, I set the code ten years hence. There is now... No, not now. In ten years time, there is a glass and concrete extension with a sloping lead roof. And in the very tidy grounds is a small cottage. Airbnb place I should think. Has its own parking space. All tidy. We can go into the future."

"You sure?"

"Pretty much. To make absolutely sure I'm cycling up there tomorrow."

Steve and I are both keen cyclists. He had invited me up there once for a cycling holiday, but getting my bike onto those trains that allowed bikes had proved problematic. I hadn't gone.

"Forecast is good," Steve said. "And it's a more or less easy ride. Once up past Lamplugh I usually go along a flattish top bit, then drop down beside Loweswater. Just before Crummock I grab a left. Margaret Forster used to live there. Know her? Great writer, don't know if she produced any Sci-fi. Then I do a circuit back through Greysouthen and Bridgefoot.

"Principal purpose though is to check out if the grounds around the house are still scrub. If there is no cottage, no extension... And that being the case when I get back home, I'll send along instructions to you three on how to add the clock, and where to place the time you want to go to in the data block. Easiest way is to use the day's date and just change the year."

*

Most of our conversation had taken place with me wandering about the concrete platform, phone flattened to my ear.

The call over I had come into the caravan, had part lain myself down at the living room window end looking out over the still bare treetops, thoughts circling with a lone buzzard.

"Cyclists, space and time travellers," I heard myself say. "Wow."

Twenty: Bridgwater

I know Somerset, have lived and worked all over the county. Not so much North Somerset where it edges towards Bristol and Bath, but certainly to the west of Cheddar and the Mendips; and where my Somerset towns seem to fall naturally into pairs, Yeovil and Crewkerne, Taunton and Wellington. So too the old mining towns of Midsomer Norton and Radstock.

I have reported on agricultural fairs, pop concerts, air shows, dozed in Somerset courtrooms and council chambers, have taken details from organisers of fêtes and festivals, written up stories on fines, fires and floods, thefts of agricultural livestock and equipment; even followed up a UFO sighting once.

Armed with the clock-modified laptop, memorising Steve's instructions – "For the purpose of this navigation we each begin at Ground Zero, Time Zero" – I took my cynical, seen-it-all reporter's mindset around to the shed. I set the date 300 hundred years ahead and pressed Return.

My cage and I were in full sunlight above the submerged roofs of Bridgwater.

In rural Somerset Bridgwater has always been one of a kind, more an industrial than a market town. Burgh of Sir Walter was how its name originated, gift of a conquering monarch and nothing to do with a bridge or with water. Although bridges over the River Parrett there have been, are, were.

Now, or in this confusion of tenses, 300 years hence, there is/was/to be a distinct absence of bridges. A surfeit of water however.

Some grey and red roofs were still visible below me, the tide slipping and sliding over a nearby slope of once-red tiles. A jagged black hole in one of the other roofs. No sign at all of

Chilton Trinity.

Looking back over the Levels the silvered water stopped at one of the yellow green Polden Hills. Nothing broke the surface 'twixt.

Was this winter? I'd left in May. A straightforward 300 years ahead it would be early summer here too. I could make out trees on the Quantocks in full leaf.

Nothing though of the Levels to be seen. Not a drooping willow or a stubborn alder. The roads and turnings that I knew/know, all were underwater. Gone my favourite broken railings lay-by where I used to go out of my way to park up, take a speculative stroll along a tine one way or the other.

I looked back to what would have been the mouth of the River Parrett, could see only the broad inlet of the Bristol Channel. No obvious sign of Cardiff this day, this elevation.

A white haze lay along the sea's surface, light blue lumps of the distant Welsh hills and mountains beyond.

I returned my gaze to the submerged roofs. The smallest of wavelets slipped and slithered, slipped and slithered.

Once the Bridgwater levee had been breached that would have been the end of Bridgie.

Away to the left, the land rising to the long lump of the Quantock Hills, was a single house above the flood, a grey flat-bottomed boat pulled up beside it.

Wondering what the house's inhabitants did to survive here I looked for fishing gear in and around the grey boat. None, which had me realise that with a flood this high there'd be no fish. No edible fish. With a flood this high Hinkley Point would also be underwater and this sea radioactive, with who knew what effect on the fish?

I looked despondently back over what had been the Levels. Tried to think what all the marsh fowl – the bitterns, cranes, herons, egrets, water rails – will/would have done. Moved/adapted to higher ground? Or will they have sought out other marshes? Will there be other marshes?

I lingered over Bridgie an hour or more, the hypnotic power of moving water, watched the tide come to cover more of the roofs, colonies of barnacles and limpets glimpsed in corners and crevices, green and brown weeds wafting with the tides slow increase.

Still I lingered on. To keep myself from going to see how county town Taunton had fared.

Twenty One: the future, and only the future

The only one of us four never to call himself a futurist Bart was unhappy. His unhappiness unlike mine was not with what was happening in the future, more that, no matter how he reset the laptop's clock or played around with the data block, even applying various square roots, it wouldn't let him visit the past. He tried to get Steve – bemused by these many mathematical suggestions – to come up with a formula. Nothing worked.

"A time-travelling historian denied the past. Such a disappointment to have only the future." That last said with heavy, self-mocking irony.

It wasn't only interest in things historical that had had Bart wanting to go back in time: I doubt I was the only one suspecting that Bart had nursed a dream of having been able to go back to save his son. In all our dealings with Bart investigations into possible contributing factors to Lou's cancer had rumbled on in the background. Only for Bart to find now that if he set the years back five or a hundred, as with solid rock or the sea's surface, he and the cage stayed in Lou's bedroom.

That left Bart with zilch chance of showing that his son's death had not been due to a cocaine overdose but to a preventable and therefore curable cancer. If not saved son and father would then at least have both been rendered blameless.

With the past entire closed to him the future was of little consolation: "Archaeologists build whole empires on the evidence of a single ceramic shard. Imagine if these cages made it possible for us to go back and check out those empires of the mind? To not only see if the archaeologists got it right, but for us to see the whole, in action. See it alive and busy."

Denied the living past Bart did, with Rhean's

encouragement, go truculently into the future, staying at first, geographically, mostly in Wales. Five years, a hundred years ahead, he sat just above his own house, could see new neighbours, fewer cars. Three hundred years hence the valley terraces were, with a few more gaps, more or less otherwise unchanged. The sea though had encroached over parts of the motorway and completely over the steelworks.

From these disconsolate trips into his valley's future, he reported back that valley topography looked pretty much as it would have been before the coal mines. Except that a few of the landslips had become longer, wider, deeper into the hillsides.

He and Rhean went further into the future – they took turns – and the further they went more of the valley houses became abandoned, their own included. Those that remained seemed to have either extended their gardens up the hillside and/or spread sideways into their old neighbours' gardens.

"Everywhere everywhen is now. Always now," he dismissively told Steve when Steve had suggested that he try looking elsewhere.

"Future history," Bart harked back to our old terminology, and rehashed it for what the future had shown him, "is as educational as past history. Both educate, at public and personal levels. Histories, past and future, hand us lessons in humility, how powerless are our vanities when it comes to posterity." Bart even sent me a piece for *Futuricity*, 'The past lost to us, the future ruined.'

As his piece implicated the cages I didn't post it.

Where Bart and I differed in our reactions to the future was that, while I couldn't cope with what was to become of Somerset, and I wanted to see no more, anywhere; Bart, with Rhean's encouragement, worked out beacon routes to take them to future Africa. In very short order the pair of them became taken with the centuries ahead growing of Africa's green latitudes, excitedly reporting back on the different trees being planted.

Bart declared himself, '...greedy for life again. I so needed to come out from under the dead.'

Had they been his own words, I wondered, or Rhean's. Whoever's, on and on he and Rhean went about the benefits of this kind of tree and which trees in which area were proving the most successful.

Trees in SF, Ursula K Le Guin aside, are usually allied in some way with aliens. For Bart and Rhean though they came to represent the innocent re-greening of the planet.

Twenty Two: sound

"Here's new," Julian reported back. "But only works future-wise."

He had arranged this zoom. My suspicion beforehand had been that he had picked up on our flagging interest, if not our despondency. This zoom he was to do most of the talking.

"I became interested in Ireland. Easiest for me to reach. Use Lundy's old lighthouse as my first beacon and go on from there. Though, that said, Ireland isn't the easiest of places to view from above. Indisputably green. If you can see down through the clouds.

"It was its future though that is of interest to me. Three hundred years hence one could hardly credit its troubled past. That's what had me curious. Lay of the land not as dramatically changed as this side of the Irish Sea."

Julian paused here, eyes down, hand going over his chubby chin's dark stubble. We waited for him to gather his thoughts.

"No," he said to himself more than to us. "With so much to learn it's so very easy to get sidetracked. The important thing I found, those three hundred years hence, was when I got myself low enough to get a good look at what I thought were new construction techniques. They weren't. New that is. Prefab kit building. Look to be what could be ordered on their future equivalent of Amazon. Except with the kit the workmen came in the same lorry.

"Sorry. Sidetracked again.

"There was a lot of shouting from these men. Irish brogue to the fore. And that's when the realisation came to me – in the future I can hear what is happening."

Had me re-listening to my hanging above flooded Bridgwater. Had I imagined it? Had I heard the water sluicing and slopping under the roof eaves?

97

"I checked," Julian said. "Ireland again in the present. Left my radio on back in the lab. And that is all that I could hear sitting over present-day busy Limerick. With time added to the mix I took myself to future Limerick. And in future Limerick I couldn't hear the lab radio, but I did pick up on traffic noises and the fierce whoosh of a hailstorm bouncing off Limerick roofs."

No-one spoke, the three of us I suspect re-examining our own ventures into the future.

"This adds puzzle to puzzle," Steve said. "But you're right. So many assumptions that screen-watching has had us make." He indicated us four on the screen. "Of course, I realise now, I was hearing sounds in future Iraq."

"More like complication atop complication," Bart complained. "Not as if I didn't have trouble enough already working out where and when I get to."

A long-ago instruction to my reporter self, had been to never be afraid to state the obvious. Plus its precursor, never be afraid to ask the obvious.

"If you could hear the builders," I asked Julian, "could they hear you?"

"Not too sure," Julian blessed me with a half-smile. "I did shout. Just the once. When they were unloading the lorry and calling to one another. One of them looked around. Couldn't see me of course. So... I didn't see the point of continuing."

'...didn't see the point of continuing': that struck a chord with me. What would be the point of us, seen or unseen, talking with anyone in the future? What was the point of us going into the future? What if we were to tell them of now? How would that be of benefit to them? Who can know what of our present, or of the past, what the future will find even noteworthy? And who will it be in that future decides what it is that is noteworthy? What journalist, what scholar looking for a thesis, what political bombast?

As for us four... No matter what we might learn on our

visits to the future, just us four weren't going to be able to affect our own present nor their future. So what, dear reader, was the point?

*

In the follow-up zoom, all now sound aware, Bart was the first to speak, "I'd have thought, what with the coastline disappearing, and with the land sliding towards the sea, more people would have moved inland. Seems though that our valley is set to return to something like its partially populated, pre-mining state. A few hangers-on trying to scratch a living."

"My suspicion," Steve said, "is that populations in general have been decimated."

"More than likely," Bart agreed. "And all too depressing. A few hundred years hence I listened to the eerie silence of this valley. No traffic. No whoosh-whoosh of the turbines. No industry. No-one calling out to neighbours, wife or child. No sign of lights at night. Darkness complete. Other than grey starshine. No sign of electricity, solar panels or turbines. Brought to mind an RS Thomas poem, the one where he talks about the grass creeping towards 'this last outpost of a time past.' With such a future one has to ask, what's the point?"

My mind-set echoed.

Twenty Three: reed city

Julian and Steve seemed less dumbstruck by the future than Bart and I. For instance, Steve's fixation on the Tigris and Euphrates had been taking him into Future Mesopotamia.

All this because of the one and only political demo that young father Steve had attended had been against Blair's proposed invasion of Iraq. He and the million others who had marched had been ignored. The lies that had been told to justify the destructive invasion still angered Steve.

Now, presented with the opportunity, Steve first went decades ahead to see if the gas was still flaring. 'Been flattened,' he reported back. 'Whole area dark and desolate. Unpopulated. Toxic I should think.'

Totalitarian dictatorships can't tolerate difference, even if the different are in all other respects prepared to follow diktats. Where before Steve had lamented dictator Saddam Hussein's draining of the marshland – marshland that had supported the unique and centuries old reed city – now he was pleased to see that, in his visits to the future, the post-war neglect of the drainage was resulting in, especially wet winters, a gradual return of the reeds and lagoons.

'After all the desperate cruelties, the random bombings, the casual street executions, enough folk must have drifted back towards the quiet marshes. So that gradually, within the sanctuary of the lagoons, and with cultural memory at work maybe, raft by reed-raft, boat by reed-boat, house by house reed townships got rebuilt.'

One might have supposed that of us four, given that huge area of marshland and given my upset over the future flooding of the Levels, that I would have been the one drawn to the marshland's renewal. The Levels though had fallen foul of the sea's encroachment. Those marshlands were freshwater and deep inland. Not comparable.

Where I was in despair over what was to become of The Levels, Steve was full of excitement over the marshland's expansion. Year upon future year, especially future winters with the excess rain and with snowmelt from the Zagros and Taurus mountains, the marshland became more and more established.

Steve kept going back [forward] century after century. Only the climate extremes worried him. Some summers the rivers fell to such low levels that he feared the marshes would again dry out. Only to be relieved by the onset of the autumn rains.

Making this his pet project Steve took great satisfaction of finding evidence of the relearning of the marsh way of life. That building of reed rafts to begin with, old skills remembered, recalled, re-learnt; that resulted in reed boats being rewoven, remade. Shelters had been first, shelters became houses and, a century or more on from the drainage, a reed township was again afloat. With a few more dry summers survived Steve took great delight in reporting that one township had become two and the reed city was back.

Whether its pre-drainage customs and way of life were also restored would be left, he said, open to debate.

Although I was pleased for Steve, the pleasure he took from this side project, all that I could see of Somerset's future was seawater lapping up against the Polden Hills.

For his own Cumbrian coast, the future that Steve had seen was for it to become near islands, and them with mostly abandoned houses. His own house, all of the estate, was underwater. A few of the island houses, he said, were remarkably intact, but with few people to be seen. Steve believed because the sea there too would be contaminated – nuclear waste having been bulk-stored a few miles down the coast from Workington.

All that wet devastation Steve seemed to accept as Cumbria's due: 'Can't say they weren't warned.'

On Steve's next century visit to Iraq the marshland had

101

visibly increased, while the dryland population seemed to have dwindled. Bart had also noted – in his own ahead time – fewer collections of people among Africa's green latitudes. Steve and Bart both assumed pandemics. One consequence of this depopulation was that upstream of the Tigris and Euphrates less water was being taken for irrigation, more was arriving in the marshes.

My Somerset levels during all those same years remained underwater. So it is that I have to confess to a touch of schadenfreude when Steve reported – from centuries into the future – of a flood of such scope that pretty much the entire reed city went floating down the Shatt-al-Arab.

Steve followed, watched households he had come to know desperately clinging on to their floating neighbours. As the big river carried them ever downward, eddies offering them no sanctuary, the lands on either side jealously guarded, lines of date palms disappearing underwater and rendering landfall difficult if not near impossible.

Those lines of date palms – Steve said – curving inland. And while he rejoiced in the curves, he watched the reed people turning in their eddies and knew that they wouldn't see the same curve twice. "Don't know why," Steve said later, "but that, their desperate circumstances aside, really saddened me."

Ropes of woven reed not anyway that sturdy came apart so that, by the time the flotilla reached flooded Khorramshar, the various ironworks that stuck above the waterline tore into the few reed houses still afloat. Their upended occupants struggled to reach ever distant shores.

Although Steve had hoped that the creation of a new swamp at Khorramshar would have possibly enabled the reed people to start afresh, the marsh was not of the same extent. A century further on nothing was left among the iron and weed-clad ruins to say that the new reed city had ended there.

So did Steve briefly share in my sadness over this fast forward future.

Twenty Four: the a b c d & e of a depressive episode

'He had always accepted his own madness. His big task – always – had been to keep other people from finding out how unstable he was.' A E Von Vogt

a)

I can see that it might be difficult for anyone who has never been around depression, the clinical state, to accept how that one trip to submerged Bridgwater could have sunk me so low. It did though. And as usual I even had difficulty breathing. Or rather of reminding myself to breathe.

It's not like the future was a surprise. We all knew something like it was going to happen. Had received plenty of warnings. But to actually see the roofs with the tide lapping over them... There is no other way of saying it, I had been shocked to my core. Only three hundred years or so and it had happened, sea levels had risen...

I had had no need to go further forward, or to take a look at Langport. Langport has always – in memory – been wet underfoot. Three hundred years hence it too will be underwater with all my boyhood back-alley familiarity washed away. I felt myself undone, illogical as this may seem, by all those centuries beyond.

As you may have surmised this was not to be the first time that I have sunk into a funk, have wallowed in depression. Previously I have been helped out of my pit of existential despair with medication. This time I couldn't see the point of even making that journey. To what future end?

It is in the nature of depression that everything serves to drag one down. The first daffodils, a garden swathe of golden crocii... Pretty yes, but what was the point? Who would be here to appreciate them in a few hundred years?

We are all made of our time and of what our time makes of our futures. And suddenly I was futureless. For all my own travels into space, and into the future, there'd be not even a trail of ions to mark my passage through space and time. I counted for nothing, was nothing.

I have lived my life through books, and of books mostly science fiction. All of science fiction needs a future to happen in. At the very least a continuation, not a wet stop.

To me civilisation is science and arts, arts and science. And arts and science won't be finding a place in the simple, self-sustaining villages that Julian has been so enthusiastically telling us of in future Ireland.

Can't see much of a future for the likes of me in a village. I have reported on too many neighbourhood spats that got out of hand, have come away thinking how small, how narrow village thought. There had to be, there has to be more. I have found that more in museums and galleries, in science documentaries, in science fiction's futures.

Even so I do like human beings, their many guises. As a reporter their doings have been my bread and butter. Not politicians. Politicians of all stamps, especially the controlling kind, I hold in unprintable contempt. Their global doings will be what will lead to Bridgwater being underwater. Not that I have ever been fond of industrial Bridgwater. Because it won't be only Bridgwater underwater. All of the world's major cities are low-lying. Therein the galleries and museums, the universities and much of industry. All, like Bridgwater, will be drowned. Where then civilisation? Not, I believed, in small, self-contained rural communities.

It wasn't only Julian's Irish communities, they had all been telling me of their time-forward adventures. Out of habit I suppose. Because, before being sworn to secrecy, I would have been the one posting, or suggesting they post their tales on

Futuricity.

When we had talked of apocalyptic futures before, of post-nuclear winters, post-pestilence, we had all considered going – literally – underground. Had cast about for where best to go, what hillside to begin tunnelling into. Bart, like Steve, had opted for adapting the old mines local to them. Not though a coal mine for Steve: Cumbrian coal mines had gone out under the Irish Sea, had needed pumping. Steve had had his eye on those old mineral mines in the sides of the fells. While Julian and I had favoured making use of old Ministry of Defence WW3 bunkers.

All now childish fancies. Nothing of us will be preserved. And even should we have survived those hypothetical cataclysmic futures, to what would we have realistically emerged? From our new cave age? To more seawater and isolated rural villages?

I kept seeing that unused boat by the Bridgwater flood.

I repeat: my response to that future-distant flood might seem excessive, I was however undone.

'The mind's delight in truth at all costs, even if that truth is destructive.' Colin Wilson

b)

We four had all been fascinated by futures beyond expectation; in new sciences, new technologies, in new ways of this world, of how the cosmos to come might be organised. And here we were, those futures lost, because, as expected, human beings were about to mess up their one world and lose everything that mattered.

The living past having been denied him Bart appeared to be overcoming his disappointment. His every utterance of late seemed to be trying to convince himself, and us, that we had found ourselves in a unique position, historically, in that we were able to study both the making past along with the results of the making present.

Of us four I alone seemed the one determined to take no comfort from the future. Nor any from the past. Like Bart I would have loved to go back, in my case to that marvellous moment in the early sixties when humankind began to make their own stars.

Denied the past Bart talked up the future: "Radiation aside, at the speed of light the solar system has always been our realistic limit. So, as we are now doing, what we do is we explore planet Earth."

Bart refused to share in my desolation. I had early called on him, thinking he would have been of like mind. But "Bugger it," he said, "I'm off to future Africa."

Call cut.

Thus, it was Bart who brought home to me my timidity, showed me that I was the least adventurous of us four. When I had always assumed that Bart, in his thinking the most conservative of us, would be least likely to follow a fancy. I had overlooked his also being a musician, his having been to gigs all over Europe. Travel was nothing to him.

It was me, Somerset me, born and bred, who was the most timid.

Risking all Bart went so far ahead, reported back that Tarkovsky's spiders hadn't taken over. Nor so far as he could tell from that underpopulated world, had anything else. Foliage excepted.

To me these now known futures – the desolation of Mesopotamia, the reed city lost – felt like a betrayal of all SF. No space travel, no intergalactic colonies. Even the much harped-on catastrophes I now saw as part of that betrayal. In that all warnings had been ignored.

And we had been warned so many times.

All those possible futures lost to us. All chances of those futures lost to us. All that cleverness gone to waste.

'Sanity's a handicap and a liability if you're living in a mad world.' Anthony Burgess

c)

Have to admit that by this time I was in a real funk. No future. No point.

I did try to lose myself in some writing. Came up with a title, 'Do I Still Belong To The Human Race?' and got no further. What more to say? Welcome to the end? Give up, human beings are just not capable of seeing futures?

The prospect, the anticipation, being able to imagine so many alternative futures had mattered so much to me, far more than the nearby realisable futures. The distant, the far off, I could live in them in my mind. But not while Bridgwater's roofs were being washed by the tide.

Religion offered, as usual, no consolation. Where in that wet desolation was God? Where infinity? My faith, my belief had been in the unknown, in the unknowable future.

For some reason that watery image kept bringing to mind my own short story, *8391AD*. That apocalyptic tale had ended by saying, 'We knew at last that man was alone in the universe. No-one else but us. While some of us felt elated at being part of such an elite many more were disappointed. We, our sorry species, was all that there was? Hope left our lives. With only human beings, more human beings, there was going to be nothing new, only variations on times past.'

Fred Hoyle said that the universe did not have a beginning and it will not have an end. Meanwhile there I was, somewhere in the nowhere middle again, lost to my small purpose on this small planet.

I did try, really tried, to join in Bart's deliberate excitement, to talk myself into optimism. Didn't get very far. His every other word was an exasperation. Steve wasn't much better. He would chatter on so about his daughters and grandchildren, jobs and schools respectively, as if the future we had seen wasn't going to happen.

I have no children. Count myself lucky.

Sometimes.

'Of course it is exhausting, having to reason all the time in a universe which wasn't meant to be reasonable.' Kurt Vonnegut

d)

During these lows I often began by envying my three friends the fall-back solidity of their partnerships, Julian his Glynis, Bart his Rhean, and Steve the devotion of his daughters. I have no-one. I didn't even have the solace of once-doting parents.

An only and sat-about bookish child I had been at best a bothersome nuisance to my busy mother and father. And when I became set – 'recklessly set' – on becoming a reporter they told me that I had thrown my Millfield education in their faces. I had, with no conscious effort on my part, won a scholarship.

Then, when I had let 'that slut Lillith' move in with me, they had, and with near indecent haste, 'completely washed their hands' of me.

A year or more later, out of touch, I had learnt that soon after the washing-of-hands they had sold up both house and businesses and they had – and this was way before Brexit – moved to Sicily-by-the-sea. They haven't written.

As to my adult relationships... You probably may have already surmised from my many subsequent house moves that each of those moves marked the end of another of my cohabitations. House, place and relationship belonged together. Thus can my many moves in and around Somerset tell their own tale – of a man prone to bouts of depression with each new move having been intended to be the cure.

Those like cruel Carole, with only a passing knowledge of depression, assumed that because I landed in the pits of despair then I must also be bipolar and at other times would, apparently, reach delightful manic heights. In my case unfortunately not, that is if mania is to be enjoyed. I am either on the level or I go ever further down the Eeyore road. Carole declared herself disappointed and me 'no fun at all.'

As you may also have surmised, I am not very good at relationships. While within them I have generally done what I believed was expected of me. Until I got something wrong. My having once miscalculated then the relationship, every time, went rapidly from uncomfortable to unlivable. Leaving me as onlooker at the centre of my own disaster.

I have been shouted at a lot by my partners. And way before they were on the road to becoming ex. Probably because I am naturally given to interiority, to dwelling in the mind, and according to my female world I had to be shouted out of it.

At the same time, I came to resent any assumptions made of me. I obstinately would not be fitted into any of their stereotypes. Just what was this much-vaunted 'family' to which I was supposed to make myself belong? So far as I could see 'family' was but another accidental grouping. Friends, jobs, places I happened to live, too-friendly neighbours... Move on.

I am aware of the contradictions in myself. And aware that I resent not only those assumptions made of me, but any of the [then] unknowable future.

I have been completely fazed by people who seem to know why they are doing what they are doing while they are doing it. I often have no idea why I acted as I did until a mental door opens years later. Much of my time here alone in the caravan has been given over to introspection.

That realisation was prompted in part by my reading of JG Ballard's autobiography. I too am more at ease with those who, like me, are haunted by a not understood past. Even though that haunting can have us behaving erratically.

I have looked at other people's partnerships and tried to figure out how they worked. Motives I ascribed to them have often appeared later to have not been the case. I was so much happier in my role as reporter – find the stereotype and apply it. Everything yesterday's news.

e)

To Steve his children and grandchildren are each individuals in their own right. To me they are cyphers, mere adjuncts to Steve. Nor is that I have secretly wanted to be a father. I see my sperm's failure as a lucky escape: I wouldn't have known how.

All those failed personal relationships haven't been my only route to despair. Years of trying to get work published has had me as both fish and angler. I'd go fishing for a publisher, for an agent; and when I got a nibble, I then became the fish being slowly reeled in, the angler looking to see if I was worth landing. Or it'd be me as the angler nervously reeling in the publisher. Only for one or other of us to slip the hook, cut the line.

Using the same bait, I'd cast out again.

And now? The future known? The consequence of all that repeated effort? For futurist writers like me we are looking at the end of posterity.

To despairing me Steve did sympathetically concede future's loss: "We were to have all those Arthur C Clarke hospitals on the moon. My grandson Theo – you know he was born with a dodgy heart? – he was to have had his ultimate heart operation up there."

Steve though was far from idealising his own young. "Strange," he said in one of our weekly catch-ups, "how the young – those between ten and twenty say – couldn't care less about the future. The planet's future that is. This age group it is, plus the ageless stupid, who are responsible around here for most of the litter and vandalism."

Readers of SF like Steve and I, living through our own dystopias, have tended to avoid fictional dystopias such as

Bradbury's *Fahrenheit 451*. Knowing now the slow catastrophe that is our future maybe we should have read more, have paid more attention.

Bridgwater's underwater roofs had shown me that there was now no future for SciFi to happen in. This was the end of civilisation. Not that I have ever seen Bridgie as the acme of civilisation. Far from it. But if low-lying Bridgie was gone then so too would be most of the world's cities, along with their art galleries, museums and national libraries.

Actual science and the many predicted futures had been ignored. If my up and down life had had any purpose at all, now it demonstrably had none.

"Flash I love you. We have only fourteen hours to save the Earth." Dale Arden: the Flash Gordon film.

Twenty Five: missing

I got a call seven in the morning from Glynis. She told me that Julian was missing.

"How do you mean, missing?" So far as I was concerned Julian was very often missing, unreachable.

"Not here, not there. Not anywhere I can think of. Missing."

I established – Glynis somewhat impatiently answering my every question – that Julian had last been seen going up to his attic laboratory two days ago. None of their neighbours in the flats below had been aware of him leaving the building – he makes a show of firmly closing the outside door if left open – nor had he been to any of the local shops.

"His house and car keys are still here. Outside coats too. And all his shoes. His mobile – I think it's his – is on the bench in the lab. Lights in the attic were all still on."

Julian is punctilious about energy-saving, forever castigating me for failing to recycle torch batteries.

I asked if she had phoned the police: more than 24 hours had passed so they would have to register him as officially missing.

"I will, but not yet. Julian wouldn't forgive me for letting them poke about his attic. You know how paranoid he can get."

"Hospitals?"

"No. I'm convinced he has disappeared from here in the flat."

"This why you are calling me?"

"I know he has had you lot going into space, and I think," a sigh, reluctant to put into words something so outrageous, "he's lost somewhere up there. I've looked all around the attic. Not a clue. Not that I can see. If he is in space, I've simply no idea how, or where, to start looking."

"Can't Steve or Bart help?"

A nature of depression is that one doesn't greet an unanticipated change in one's circumstances with relief, thinking that the change might lead somehow to one's salvation. No, one thinks despairingly, What now? Now what?

Would be easier for Bart and Rhean to get to Ilfracombe than me. Bart told me they usually drive to Penarth and get a boat across. Or was that summer weekends only?

"Steve's got a hospital visit with one of his grandchildren," Glynis said. "Bart and Rhean are up country on a week-long music gig. You're all I've got."

"Take me forever to get to you."

A trek to Ilfracombe didn't appeal at all. I'd have to cycle into Wellington, get a bus to Taunton, train to Exeter, another to Barnstaple, then a bus to Ilfracombe. The last time, the only time I'd gone, had taken me a whole day getting to them. When it came to my going home, and Julian saw me working out times and connections, he felt so sorry for me that he drove me to Tiverton Parkway and I had caught the train the one stop to Taunton from there. Julian had offered to drive me all the way home, but I had already been embarrassed enough. The amount of extra petrol consumed had rather defeated my attempts to cut back on carbon.

Glynis must have heard me sigh or been doing her own calculations: "I'll come and get you. Should be there before lunch. Be ready to leave the minute I get there."

"Wouldn't Steve be better at this? Knows more."

"Said he'd make himself available on the phone. I need your help Ben. Please."

"OK," said reluctantly.

"Be ready."

*

As part of my post-retirement ambition to be self-sustaining in my to-be-self-built house, just as soon as I had the caravan as a 'temporary' home I had given up my petrol car. I had not anyway been what one might call a proficient driver. Always a minor knock or bump, which had left me with prohibitive insurance.

I had thought that my poor driving might have been because I have never seemed able to co-ordinate my limbs. And my caring mother and father had enthusiastically packed me off to sports-centred Millfield, where I had been near guaranteed to become an object of curiosity – But why can't you? - and/or the object of occasional peer-driven derision.

Even with automatic cars I never seemed able to park without scraping the side of the car next to me, or knocking over a bollard, or driving into a wall; and with near always someone watching who was not only willing but keen to report me.

The unbuilt house was to have been my eco-home, south-facing windows, brick floors to absorb the day's heat; an all-round self-sustaining existence. No car. No great sacrifice. I liked cycling, so it was no real hardship, kept me healthy. The trailer-towed shopping trips down to Wellington, or even – feeling in need of exercise, or simply desirous of a change – working out less-used routes uphill and down, I would cycle over to Hemyock or up into the Brendons.

Waiting for Glynis I packed a change of clothes, found my toilet bag, decided I needed a shower and to deodorise if I was to be sitting in a closed car alongside the always precisely-attired Glynis.

That done, and not knowing what to do with the rest of a reasonably new loaf, I made some cheese and chutney sarnies for our trip. Given the urgency in her tone I doubted that Glynis would stop or would want to pull in somewhere for lunch. I did consider making a flask of coffee, but she and Julian were of a generation particular about their coffee. And my ordinary tea brand was out of the question: they favoured scented herbal teas.

With nothing else to do I sat myself down on the front steps, where the two cats – unseen until that moment – found me. Glynis too.

"Need a pee." She bounded past me, scattering cats, found the lavatory the second door she opened.

I gathered up my stuff, including my office laptop in case... In case of what I had no idea... and I stood by the caravan steps, key in hand, waiting for Glynis to emerge.

"Don't know what you lot have been up to," she said as she came out of the caravan. "Not a hint to where he might be."

She was wearing what looked like sports shoes, not trainers. The rest of her garb, skirt, blouse, said she had been dressed for her estate agent work.

"Or when," I said, caravan door locked.

Glynis made a disgruntled noise to that, headed across the concrete to her green car. A petrol/electric hybrid, her eco-compromise, Julian her eco-conscience.

She drove off before I was buckled in and was speeding around bends that as a cyclist, I deemed blind.

"Where now?" she demanded at the first junction.

"For the motorway? Right."

Even with my seatbelt buckled I clutched the sides of my seat as she got onto the wider road but still with no white line down its middle; and then we were around the roundabout and onto the motorway. Although Glynis accelerated away, in the sense that I slumped back, I heard myself breathe a little easier.

"Got some sarnies for us," I told her. "'Case you hadn't eaten." My bag and laptop were at my feet.

"Thanks," she flashed a smile at me, took a deep breath. "Time, Steve told me." She must have talked with him on her way to me: the car came with hands-free. "What the fuck?"

So did the journey begin, no sooner on the motorway than off at Tiverton Parkway and onto sometimes dual carriageway, sometimes two-way traffic, taking us towards Barnstaple, before we would have to turn off to Ilfracombe.

While we ate the sandwiches, I tried to tell Glynis where and why we had all been going in our cages – Bart to future Africa, Steve to Iraq, Julian to Ireland.

"Think it was somewhere else." She threw a frown my way. "He stopped using his silly Oirish accent. Was somewhere else. What's the daft sod done?"

Glynis said that last bit several times, including that there had been storms in the two nights now that he had been gone. "What if he's not able to get back?"

After that Glynis talked more to herself than to me. I didn't understand all that she said, but then I have never, even at my best, been at ease in the quick company of Julian and Glynis. They are so much younger than me, think differently, use expressions unknown to me. And in my current state, just this side of medication, I'd like to claim that my taciturnity was due to my doing more thinking than talking. Truth is, I heard her words going past me and they seemed to have no connection to me.

I'm not anyway good with people in close proximity. As a reporter I had simply asked questions, noted what the person had to say, took their name, other particulars. A role I knew. In that car though, even when she wasn't talking, I could hear her breathing.

"No point getting the two of us killed," I dared say after she had completed a silly overtake, an oncoming lorry having blared its horn and flashed all its lights, including those on the top of its cab.

She nodded without looking at me. "You're right. It's just... Time," she said, "Fucking time."

Twenty Six: Ilfracombe

Glynis drove us in through what she called 'the back way' to Ilfracombe. Branches arched over country roads; the year's first leaves a dimpled green. We went through a deep wooded valley, passed a quarry, and rose up and up, to skirt the long edge of barren Exmoor.

Eventually, several junctions having had me confused, signposts pointing in directions other than Ilfracombe, we began the long drop down to the town, the sea glinting blue between the green hills. We passed an out-of-town supermarket, a holiday camp, a school; and we dropped on down through a housing estate into the old town. I recognised the turning near the church that would take us to the single tower of Julian's flats.

Glynis pulled into what was apparently her parking space, beside Julian's dusty Volvo estate. She began unbuckling her seatbelt with the same movement that she pulled up the handbrake.

"I'll go ahead," she said opening the car door, "put the kettle on." And with that she told me my age and the many slow steps I'd have to climb.

When I was their guest the last time here, with the pair of them busy in the days I had taken myself up onto the clifftops that they called the Torrs. At the end of that summer, it had been entrancing for this landlocked Somerset dweller: the rhythms of the blue-grey sea far below, a few sheep or cows roaming the glass sloping down to the cliff edges, glimpse of a peregrine, a family of gruff ravens.

Most days I had looked west, past the thick black chimneys of Bull Point and on out to the dark wedge of Lundy island, the Atlantic Ocean beyond. One day I had watched a tall ship appear mast first above the horizon, followed by the rest of it as it had slowly closed on Lundy, making me aware then that the ship and I were both on the outside of a sphere. Had been my only actual sensation of being on a planet prior to my going into space.

As I trod on up the tower's flight after flight, I told myself, the closed-mouth sourness of my depression itching for clean cliff air, that I doubted I'd have time this visit to get up to the Torrs. Nor did I make any attempt to hurry after Glynis. Although I ordinarily count myself fit from my cycling my male vanity was wise enough to know not to compete with a gym-going/pilates/yoga muscular thirty something.

My last time here Glynis had told me that she had two regular runs, one out over the Torrs and along the coastal path to Morte Point, and back along the inland cycle track. The second, apparently the least favoured – wind direction had something to do with the choice – was from Ilfracombe to Combe Martin and back across the hills.

Their door on the top landing was open. Glynis was not in any of the rooms, all the flat doors ajar. I guessed that she'd gone straight up to the attic. A basic timber stair led up, had hanging from its square bannister a cut out wooden hand with 'office' painted on it.

Julian wasn't there.

Glynis was, stood at the long work bench and moving papers around. The carbon rod was on the other side of the attic.

"Anything changed?" I asked her. She shook her head still looking down at the papers. My guess was that she had looked through them before, was scanning through again in light of what Steve and I had told her.

I walked past her to the end of the laboratory. Julian's cage was smaller and lower than mine, squeezed in under the sloping ceiling. Its mesh door, bending under its own flimsy weight, was open.

"You open it?" I asked Glynis.

Still looking at the papers she shook her head.

Five hooks were tied to the copper mesh that Julian must use to close the door. All would have to be hooked onto the mesh from within the cage and, to leave, be undone from within the cage.

With all of our lamenting the future state of our planet, our wondering what best next to do, my first thought was – treacherous in the concerned company of Glynis – had Julian escaped into the future?

"Pretty certain the cage was like that when I first came up looking for him," she said as she came towards me. "I did shut the laptop. Save the battery."

The grey laptop, twin of the one in my shed-cage, was on the low stool that Julian must use when space/time bound. The laptop, gaming switch and carbon fibre were all connected.

I had always imagined Julian sitting upright on an office chair similar to mine, not almost squatting down.

"Two things," I said, "I hadn't realised his cage was so small. And I'm surprised he didn't keep his laptop on charge. I think we'd best hook it up and leave it open. If he is stuck somewhere, wherever that might be, the laptop will be his one way of getting back to us. Got an extension?"

"Should be loads up here." She went marching back along the workbench bending to look in cabinets and pulling out boxes. "Won't an extension lead interfere with the cage's workings?"

"I use one," I reassured her, "every time I go up. So does Steve. Bart too." I was about to tell her what happened to Bart when Rhean's toaster had tripped their electrics, how it had brought him straight home. But that had been before we had started time travelling, before we had started hearing sounds there. And there had been storms here...

I checked that the gaming switch and carbon fibre were both securely attached.

"Got one." She began unwrapping the cable.

"Will it reach?"

119

"He's got sockets all along the bench." She found one, plugged in the extension. I found nearby what looked like the charger for the laptop, leastwise it looked enough like the one for mine, and I connected that.

The laptop was down to two percent charge.

I wondered what to do about the cage door. Assuming that Julian had indeed travelled somewhere and, whatever his reason, had got out of his cage, then to get back home he would need to get back into the cage, and if the door was closed it would be near impossible for him to unhook it from outside the cage.

"Best we leave the laptop to get fully charged," I told Glynis. "Then I'll try to find out where it took him."

"Will it be safe?"

"I'm going to leave it connected."

"You sure?"

"Process of elimination. If he's not the other end of this he'll have to be somewhere else. Time then to call the police. Let's leave this to charge. I need the loo."

"I'll sort you out a room. Then I'll rustle us some grub."

Twenty Seven: another's cage

When Glynis began clearing away the dishes, I took my dull head up the wooden stairs to the laboratory. To wander the length of the work bench wondering what magic Glynis thought me capable of, just what I could do...

One section of the bench held the ordered chaos of most writers' offices. In a wicker basket – I guessed a one-time fruit basket – paper scraps, some torn from notebooks, the bottom half of a page... On one was written, 'Ilfracombe graveyard – Mary Bastard Rider. Died January 26th 1878. Age 76.'

Younger than me, I thought, and a bastard to boot. What on Earth did I have to complain about?

On another scrap of paper and copied out in Julian's best hand: 'From Padstow Point to Lundy Light / a watery grave from day to night.'

In the privacy of his head could Julian have been as downbeat as me? Had he given in to despair?

On a small shelf further along were his workbooks. The bookshelves downstairs had the biographies and fiction titles of a well-read pair, plus bird and fish guides, their varied spines not a background pose for face-to-face calls. Up here were different size dictionaries, books and brochures on antiques, a guide to patent law, a rack of OS maps, and a couple of well-worn notebooks.

One notebook had passwords old and new listed, many crossed through. Had me feeling that I was invading his privacy. I told my over-sensitive state to not be so stupid: how many times in my career had I peeked into the private lives of people? And that had been for a not-worth-printing news story. Here I was trying to find Julian. By whatever means.

The other notebook was a collection of quotes. 'Einstein vis-a-vis Newton,' Julian had written. 'My own understanding came about conversely regards Mercator projections and Great Circle navigation. If the world (worlds) curve then so too must space. The natural shape is not Pythagorean crystallised and angular, but pebble-rounded like a planet. Is the universe entire then principally feminine, all curves, rather than spaceship sharp and jutting angles?'

The note wasn't dated. I guessed post Glynis. Post very nicely rounded Glynis.

There were no quotes from any of my books.

Here again the Padstow Point / Lundy Light quote leaping out at me. Why was that significant? Was it?

I reminded myself that Julian had been, having been brought up here, a keen schoolboy sailor. Moved on.

As my wandering approached that end of the lab my eye kept glancing to the cage, its open mesh door. I heard a clunk downstairs as the dishwasher began its cycle.

I reached the fully recharged laptop, took one last long look at the open door of the cage.

If I were to go in the cage, take Julian's last route, would my being in the cage then make it impossible for Julian to return? Or at any moment now would an invisible hand reach out of the cage and pull the door closed?

Experience told me not. Within the cage, within our sheds and spare bedrooms – Rhean watched by Bart, Julian here on video – we had at all times been visible, if only to ourselves, no matter where we had been in space or time.

Supposing that Julian had gone missing from the cage, what could have been his reason? Or had he fallen out? Had the cage come undone. No: aside from the door being open it looked to be otherwise intact. Or had Julian simply got carried away adding numbers to the data block's time section, have taken himself beyond dates, beyond years? Was he light years into the future?

Only one way to find out, go after him.

This may seem atypical of my unadventurous nature; but to have made an informed decision would have taken me hours of studying the data block. Even then mine would have been largely guesswork. Much simpler to repeat his journey. To wherever it was.

Add to that my then largely negative state of mind: what did it matter what became of me? There was also, I confess, an element of wanting to impress Glynis.

Putting aside my concerns about Julian's cage being irradiated, closing the laptop, reconnecting it to the gaming switch, the lead attached, I sat on the cage's low stool and pulled the mesh door closed, fixed the four hooks.

I noticed that the extension lead buckled out the lower corner of the mesh door. Would that affect the integrity of the cage? Had that been why Julian had taken the laptop unconnected?

This cage was much smaller than my shed. The slope of the ceiling was pressing my head forward and I had to lift my heels to keep the laptop level on my knees. But I managed to squeeze the laptop open, watched it light up, and saw the familiar program layout on the screen. The data block was out of sight, way down.

With a deep breath and a long sigh, I pressed Return.

I was on moorland. Strong twilight, the light grey that comes not long after sunset. My one effort at small talk over dinner with Glynis had been to mention the sunset. She, distracted, had said only Yes. Was I close to Ilfracombe?

The cage and I were sitting atop massed ribbon-like white grasses with a kind of plateau ahead of me. Over to my right a valley, tops of some trees visible, a few fresh green leaves. Why had Julian come here?

At some distance straight ahead – I had initially thought it low woodland, scrub possibly – but it was coming to have the look of some sort of barrier, dead black branches in among the little green. A long barrier.

Where was I? When was I? No sky trails. I turned best I could on the low stool with the laptop on my knees. Was that the sea beyond the far slope of the moor?

I heard a bird call. A large bird, not an Ilfracombe seagull. A crow, possibly a raven.

Of course, in time travel we could hear where we were. Could we be heard? I cursed my depressed slow thinking.

"Julian!" I shout-whispered. "Julian!"

I asked myself why I was being so quiet. Pulling in air for a full-throated bellow I yelled, "Julian! Julian! I am here! In your cage! Julian! Can you hear me?!"

I looked around the moor for possible sight of him, realised that being out of time he could well be as invisible to me as I to him.

Thinking that maybe I heard a response – my name? – I called out again, "Julian! Julian! I'm here in your cage! Julian! Can you hear me?!"

The evening was still, the flat blades of the winter grasses lying white and dead. Close by I could see the first green spikes poking through. No sign of anyone invisible walking over them. Some of the white grasses appeared almost woven together.

Another call. My name? From over there in the valley?

Should I wait for him to make his way up? What would be the point? For me to tell him that I couldn't take him with me now?

"Julian!" I shouted. "Be here tomorrow! I'm here in your cage now. Me, Ben. This cage is too small for the both of us. Julian! I'll go back to Somerset and come here tomorrow in my cage. Can you hear me?!"

I thought I heard a distant, Yes Yes.

"I'll be here soon as I can." My throat was getting sore. "Tomorrow Julian! Here! OK?!"

Thinking that I heard 'OK' repeated. Not an echo? No, there

124

it was again same strength.

My elbows tucked in I awkwardly pressed Control D and looked from the laptop to Glynis standing wide-eyed by the workbench.

"You were shouting," she explained her being there. "You find him?"

"Not exactly." I began unhitching the cage door: "But I think he may be on Exmoor." I disconnected the laptop from the gaming switch.

"Not Ireland? He did keep coming down talking all Oirish?"

"Could be, was heathland. No, was too high and near here. Pretty sure I heard him. I'm going to get hold of Steve."

I emerged crouching from the cage, clutching the laptop to my chest. "I need to copy this data block onto my work laptop," I told Glynis. "Get it sent to Steve. But really, I need to get back to Somerset. Julian and I won't both fit into this cage."

"Oh," she said, and appeared to look for alternatives. Decided: "OK, but no way I'm driving back now. Way too tired. Not slept much the last few nights. We'll go first thing."

Previously I'd had in mind that Glynis, unlike some of my suspicious partners, hadn't seemed the least bothered by Julian spending nights away. Then though she would have known, been told, where he was.

She did an exaggerated slump: "Must sleep." She turned and began trudging towards the stairs.

"OK if I work up here?" I asked her. "I'll fetch up my stuff."

Glynis waved a weary hand in acknowledgement.

"Can we leave about six?" I called after her. "Sooner we get to him the better."

"I'll set the alarm for five." She stopped part way down the stairs. "Give me time for a shower." Of course she was of the generation that daily showered. I wondered how Julian had managed the last couple of mornings on the moor. If he was indeed on the moor.

In following Glynis down to collect my office laptop and phone from the living room I realised that that was the quickest I had moved in days. The rapidity continued, once back up the stairs, with my pulling up Julian's stool-chair to the work bench, the opening of my laptop and copying over the the huge data block, and finally sending a copy of the file to Steve.

I called him on my mobile: "Think I've found where Julian might be. I've sent you the data block." I told Steve of the heathland where I thought I had heard Julian, and my intention to go collect him, which would require my going in my larger Somerset cage.

"Can you help?" I asked.

"Got the block in front of me. Jeez, looks like he's gone two thousand years ahead. Thought we were all risking it by going a few hundred. No idea why that should have scared me more than popping up to Saturn."

I had just unknowingly been two thousand years into the future.

"Sky was clear of jet trails," I told Steve. "Thought we were maybe in another global pandemic. Or further into the future. But two thousand years!"

"This wasn't Ireland," Steve said.

"I thought it was Exmoor. We passed by some of it on the way here. Sounds odd, but the sky felt the same."

"You're right. He used Lundy lighthouse as his first stepping stone, then went more or less back on himself but on a higher elevation. You should be able to work out the OS co-ordinates, use them from your base."

"Will I end up same place, same time?"

"A day later, yes. Our time travel, so far as I can make out, doesn't take into account light years. Probably because all of our time travelling has been done here on Earth."

There was a long pause.

"Hope you're right," I said to keep him talking.

"Leave the time section as is," he told me. "Only adopt the physical directions from your Somerset base. Why did he leave the cage? Never occurred to me to even attempt it." I could almost hear Steve shake his head in disbelief. Then briskly, "To the here and now what you need to do..."

What I needed to do took me the rest of the evening – searching through Julian's maps, finding a calculator, and looking for simple things like a ruler in centimetres not inches, which in my own office I could have put my hand to without a thought. Finally, though I had the data adapted to my Somerset shed, base zero, the Barrow Mump first step, then Willets Tower, Dunkery Beacon again, and on across – two thousand years – to where Julian had unwisely left his cage. His invisible cage.

Satisfied that I'd got all the co-ordinates right I took myself quietly to the dark downstairs, crept through to the bedroom where I had slept the last time here. This time an orange and red quilt graced the bed, a green towel folded on the corner.

I could hear Glynis behind their door lightly snoring. I had seen shades of blue in the quilt on their bed, recalled whiffs of pheromone musk in the car on the way over. Still adrenalin awake I wondered if she'd want my company this night. Tired as she was I doubted it, and I told myself to stop looking at her sexual potential, called myself a dirty old man.

The bathroom had a well-lit mirror, showed me my wreck of a face, its lumps, scars and creases, open pores, bristles and baggy eyes. What woman would want to wake to this? Not compact Glynis that was for sure.

'Men always have to spell things out to themselves.' Brian Aldiss

I reminded myself that I had never made advances, had never

once propositioned a woman. The women it has been who have approached me. I told my ancient self to stop indulging in adolescent porn fantasies and to grow up.

Sex is the one subject everybody lies about.' Robert A Heinlein

In the bedroom I shucked off my trousers and jumper, and my head full of numbers I slid under the quilt.

Next thing I knew Glynis in damp bathrobe was shouting Morning! She had put a mug of tea on the bedside cabinet. A rosewood antique, Julian had told me last visit.

"Five thirty," Glynis said as she left, big-breasted and still no wobble to her. "Leave at six."

Twenty Eight: Exmoor

One delay after another that morning, my brain a fug from over-thinking number sequences and from re-rehearsing plans for the day, so that while I remembered to bring my office laptop down to the car, I left my mobile on charge up in the laboratory. When I swore, told Glynis that I'd forgotten my mobile and went to start getting myself back out of the car, she said, "For fuck sake." Then apologised as she went bounding across the car park and through the door into the flats.

I had just about recovered my breath from coming down the stairs when Glynis came running back, dropped the mobile into my lap and slid her solid self into the driving seat. 'You're old,' I re-informed myself. 'So very old.'

Glynis took us zooming up out of Ilfracombe. Only to get stuck behind a tractor on a twisting stretch of the 'back road.'

"Knew I should've gone Barnstaple way." Glynis kept looking out around the red agricultural equipment at the back of the big green tractor. "Hadn't expected there to be anything this early."

"No help to Julian," I gripped my seat, "if we crash now."

"Where's he going?" she complained. "Must have passed two farms already."

"Agri-contractor," I gave her the benefit of my Somerset reporter knowledge.

Glynis made a pressed-lip noise close to exasperation – exasperated with modern farming practices and Julian and I, I assumed – and then we were safely past the tractor and speeding up hills, around bends and along beside moorland. I looked out over it, nodded an affirmation to myself.

The scare over I again rehearsed my rescue plans. But fell to wondering if Julian had intended to abandon the present. When I had first been told that he was missing I had gone to future Ilfracombe. The harbour and low-lying buildings had all been underwater, the kiln-shaped theatre's top awash. His small tower of flats was still there; but had Julian meant to leave that prospect, stay away?

In the car I had told Glynis that I had stuff to prepare before I could go to the shed and collect Julian. Even so she followed me into the caravan, put the kettle on while I set to checking through my last night's adaptations of Julian's data. I got out my own maps, confirmed angles and elevation from my own base zero to the beacons to get me up to Exmoor – Barrow Mump to Willets Tower to Dunkery Beacon and on to where Steve and I had calculated Julian to be.

When I was transferring the data block to the cage laptop Glynis put a cup of coffee into a space on the office desk. She asked if there was anything she could be doing.

"Food," I said. "He'll probably be hungry."

"OK. I'll get some ready. Won't start cooking though until he's here."

"Chest freezer," I told her, "is under the bike and trailer lean-to around the back. I've got to retrieve my left-over copper mesh from the Turdis."

She didn't ask me about the Turdis: I was one of Julian's funny SF friends, got their own lingo.

"Prep won't take me long." She still stood beside and over me. "You got the plans for your house handy? Be something for me to look at while you're busy."

I turned and pointed the length of the caravan to the long cabinet above the caravan's wide end window: "House plans are up there. Help yourself."

The plans for the changes I had to make to the shed cage were nowhere but in my head. These plans involved removing the swivel chair from the shed and then making a cage within the cage. All were based on the hope that half the cage would be wide enough for plump Julian. And if, for whatever reason, Julian couldn't make it, then I could – safely within my half of

130

the cage – return to this time, this place.

My shed might have been bigger than Julian's cage, divided in half though it meant my having to stand; and once within my half I would have no way – other than by breaking my cage seal – of opening the door for Julian. I didn't want to risk that. The shed door was therefore to remain open on my journey there.

Once Julian was safely in I had a piece of string looped through the inner mesh and tied to the top of the shed door. That way I could pull the door closed without breaking the mesh seal on my inner cage.

Preparation almost complete I undid enough of the inner cage to squeeze out, went into the caravan to tell Glynis not to respond to my shouting. "I'll be shouting for Julian. If I want you I'll shout your name. Otherwise stay in here." She had some of my house plans laid out on the coffee table and around the soft seating. Years since I had looked at them.

"I'll remain here," she assured me. "Good luck."

"Fingers crossed it works."

Glynis held up both hands, surprisingly small, fingers crossed.

At the shed I manoeuvred myself behind the mesh partition, and one-handed – my other hand holding the laptop – I took care re-fixing the partition. To open the laptop I had to balance it against the shed wall.

I made one last check. Shed door open, string attached, inner mesh unbroken.

I awkwardly pressed Return.

I was back on Exmoor. Not quite in the same place as yesterday evening, this time just off a green path that led through some bilberries to what, in today's full morning light, was so obviously a thorn barricade.

I could see all of the shed's copper mesh save for that attached to the door. That made sense; and this was definitely

131

the same Exmoor that I had seen from Glynis's car an hour or so before.

Geographically Julian hadn't gone that far from home.

A trodden path meant people. I could see no-one.

Yesterday Julian's voice, if it had indeed been his, had seemed to come from the valley. I was further away from the white grass and the valley's tree tops this day. I pointed my face in that direction, took a deep breath and bellowed, "Julian!" Another, "Julian!"

"Shush," he said from somewhere nearby. "They'll hear."

"Where are you?"

"Here." From in front of me. "I'm as invisible as you. Keep talking. So I can work out where you are."

"Who'll hear us?"

"People in the settlement. They'll think we're ghosts. Moor spirits." He stopped: "Where are you?"

"Sorry." I hadn't considered directing him by voice, had my laser pen and a torch in my pocket. "I've divided the shed cage in half," I told him, saw a bilberry bush squash down on my right. "You're the wrong side of the shed. Go past my voice to the east."

The sun had not that long risen: he would know where east was.

Another bilberry bush went down. "That's right. Keep going. Now turn."

"Don't shout."

"I'm not," I stage-whispered. "Two more steps. Now turn to your left. Feel for the door. It's forty-five degrees ajar." I felt the shed move slightly. "Work your way around the door. Got the edge?"

"Got it."

"There's very little room in here. No forceful movements or we're both fucked."

132

The base of the cage shifted.

"Think I'm in," Julian said. The inside mesh was being pressed towards me and I could hear him breathing. I pulled the string. Pulled again.

"Something's stopping the door closing," I told him.

"Not my foot. Ah no, a bush. Hold on, I'll press it down. That's it. I've got the mesh."

The shed's iron latch dropped into place, and I was looking through the inner mesh at the dishevelled back of Julian's head. Leaves and twigs were stuck in his hair; and there was a nose-curling smell, something akin to a dead and gut-bloated sheep I'd once come across.

I was about to ask what he'd stepped in when Julian partially turned, said, "Hi Ben." The side of his face had two deep scratches, smears of dried blood. "Can we please go home?" He tried to smile.

"Of course. Reason I'm here." I manoeuvred the laptop so that I could press Control D and we two were enclosed within the shed's wooden walls.

Julian lifted the latch and went stumbling down the small slope, bumped into the swivel chair and to stop himself crashing into the back of the caravan brought both his hands up, came to a stop with a slap.

He stayed like that, his hands splayed on the side of the caravan. I wondered if Glynis had felt the bump, if Julian had hurt himself. I had been about to ask when he turned slowly with both his arms held out before him. The left leg of his jogging bottoms had a big tear.

"You have no idea," he told me while rotating his hands, "what a relief it is to be able to see bits of my own self again. Dirty as they are. I had to climb a tree, get away from some boars. Thought they were boars. You try climbing a tree when you can't see what your hands are doing. Anyway, I fell out the tree. Hence this," he gestured to his scratched face and the long tear in his trouser leg.

133

"Glynis has been really worried," I said from within the inner cage with the smell, the kind of stink that clings to the insides of your nostrils. "She's in the caravan, cooking," I told him. "You must be hungry."

I left Julian and Glynis alone for their reunion, took my time getting out of the inner partition, wafted the shed door to and fro to disperse the remains of the smell. Then I undid the inner mesh, rolled it up and returned it to the portaloo. The swivel chair I wheeled back up the slope and into the now ventilated shed. I hooked the cage laptop back up to the extension lead. There hadn't been room for the extension with the two of us in the shed. Another risk taken, survived.

I smiled to see that Glynis had opened several of the caravan windows; and I could hear the shower going.

"I've helped myself to one of your refuse sacks," she said. "Christ knows what he fell in."

She was frying bacon and eggs, had slices from a frozen loaf leaning up against and in the toaster. "I'm doing a brunch for you and I as well," this self-contained woman told me. She wasn't even flushed from the stove. "Has the recently invisible man been compulsively touching you as well?"

"I kept well clear," I signified the open windows. "I'll look him out some fresh clothes."

"I took photos of your house plans and specs," she said as I went to my wardrobe room. "Interesting ideas. Hope you don't mind?"

"Fine by me."

"Your coffee went cold."

We both turned to look at the bathroom door as Julian farted long and loud, then chuckled to himself.

"I'll make you another cup," self-composed Glynis said.

Twenty Nine: survival?

Julian's belly and bottom filled out my blue sweatshirt and black jogging bottoms. Not that Julian or I ever jogged.

Glynis, the cooking finished, pushed him – still damp from the shower – past her and into the window end of the caravan. Soon as he and I were seated she placed plates of sausage, egg, bacon and beans on the low table before us. She herself ate standing in the kitchen corridor.

I cut off a corner of the toast and started into my eggs and bacon. I thought Julian would be as famished, but he was sitting beside me looking at the knife and fork in his hands.

"Being invisible to myself was such a weird thing," he told the pair of us. "Knowing where your limbs are but not being able to see them. Weirder than being blind, 'cos I could see everything else. But not me."

He turned to me: "It's not so bad when you're in the cage, knowing you're invisible to others. None of this makes easy sense though." He raised the knife as if lecturing: "Invisible within our own time we take our domestic sounds with us. Then, when we go beyond our own time, we're still invisible, but now we can hear and be heard."

"Why did you leave your cage? "I asked.

"Wasn't my first visit. Previous visits I kept within the cage and kept trying to get closer. To get into the settlement. But the best I achieved was to be right above it. Different heights, but always above it. Blinded by cooking smoke. Adjustments to elevation didn't get me anywhere. Too low and it would have got me going into ground. So, I decided to go back to my original setting and I ended up round about where you were, just outside the settlement. I got out and walked in. When I came back, I couldn't find the cage."

"Eat." Glynis's one sharp word was an order. While Julian

135

had been talking, I had almost cleared my plate.

"So where," I asked once I had judged him to have started into his eating, "did you stay? When you couldn't find the cage?"

"Didn't want to risk the settlement. Accidental discovery. So I went over to the valley. Masses of catkins on the valley's upper slopes. Lovely looking down through them. Well-tended, deliberately kept. For hazel nuts I assumed. Towards the bottom are oaks. For acorns? Acorn bread? Octavia Butler?"

I nodded.

"Is an oak tree," Glynis asked, "what you fell out of?" She didn't wait for an answer: "Those scratches need antiseptic."

I told Glynis where the first aid box could be found, asked Julian, "Did you fall because you were invisible?"

"No. The climbing up was hard because of invisibility. No, I fell," Julian talked between and through mouthfuls, "because some animal scared me silly. And my falling scared the animal. Whatever it was. Big I think. Heard it go crashing away. I'd thought I'd be safer up the tree. Slept there. Probably would've been OK if I hadn't woken in a panic."

He lifted his face up so that Glynis, leaning over the table, could apply Germolene to his scratches. I finished eating, lifted my plate to Glynis's waiting hand.

"Wasn't just me," Julian returned to his eating, "settlement people are really scared of animals. That's why the barricades. Behind what you could see, back of those dead thorns, are fences of tightly woven hurdles. And they're very keen to keep those hurdles closed at night. Being invisible I sneaked in during the day, wandered around. It's quite some size. Several hectares. If anyone goes out during the day they're very quick to close the gate hurdles behind them. Their fear of animals is very real. Which is probably what got me so on edge."

He finished up his plate by wiping a piece of folded toast around it.

"Was so weird being invisible." He really wanted us both to

136

know that, looked from Glynis to me, continued with his tale, "I had to wait until no-one was looking in my direction before I moved the gate hurdles, slipped in. Imagine one massive allotment, different beds for different veg. They even have a sort of house for plants. No glass. Sets of hurdles they move to let sunlight in. Houses are of different construction. Working sheds are mostly mud and wattle. But the live-in houses got thick walls, some sort of straw blocks so far as I could make out. No glass again, but shutters with some sort of dowel hinge. I frightened the life out of one woman. I saw what I thought was everyone leaving the house, assumed a nuclear family. So I carefully lifted the latch – wooden latch – to take a look inside. Which really confused this old dear. I had to stand right beside her when she came out to look around, see who had opened her door. Took an age – my belly pulled in, hardly daring to breathe – before she checked the latch and went back indoors."

"You really were a ghost?" Glynis said, back at her self-appointed station by the sink.

"I really was. Can't wait to tell Bart. Will have him trying to work out if his Welsh ghosts were time travellers from the past. Medieval probably. But the weirdest thing of all was having a poo. Inside me it was invisible. Once out though, there it was, a perfect stool."

"You actually looked?" Glynis laughed. "Expecting not to see it?" She chuckled, went to continue with the washing up, checked herself. With a wet hand raised she said, "You could have died up there Julian Featherstone. A dead ghost. Now that would have been scary."

She gave Julian a hard look before going back to scrubbing my frying pan. I don't usually wash frying pans.

"Wonder what the settlement people made of my shouting?" I looked from Glynis to Julian: "A moor spirit or some lost travellers stumbling upon them?"

"No idea," Julian gave me a small smile. "But I'll tell you

what the settlement reminded me of, rural Japan."

We four futurists have idealised Japanese culture, that sense of communal service. Not madcap-city-Japan, its technology shouting out of our screens.

"Everything in the settlement looks to be thought through," Julian said. "Nothing wasted. Every action precise. They have those long cart handles with ropes they hitch over their shoulders. Long shafts, and a high underside to the cart. So their heels don't catch on the cart." He paused. "Maybe more like the Amish. Minus the horses. Not one beast of burden. Throughout the settlement not one animal. None. Not even that signal of domesticity, a scratching hen. No doves, no cats, no dogs. All that we assume domestic. Not a one. No songbirds in a cage. No fish in their pond. They have a pond, but it is a covered reservoir. Covered, I assumed, so that it doesn't attract birds.

Glynis, leaning back against the sink, was drying her hands and looking fondly, critically on Julian. I couldn't help but note the contrast between compact Glynis and Julian right beside me, his belly stretching the seams of my sweatshirt. So different, so devoted.

"All animals they're frightened of?" she asked him. "Disease?"

"'spect so," he nodded. "From my other visits forward I'd say that the UK population then to be a tiny percentage of what it is now. Don't know about you Ben, but I've seen no war-ravaged landscapes."

I said nothing, keeping to myself that I had made few trips into this unappealing future.

"More likely crossover diseases the cause," Julian continued. "Covid, bird flu, swine flu, SARS, Ebola. BSE, et cetera. And the people must have become a-feared of every animal."

An outcome that vegetarian Steve would find pleasing.

"No glass? No iron?" Glynis asked.

"None. Ingenious contraptions though. A wooden turbine powering, I think, the well pump." His excitement for these artefacts, I guessed, came from his days of antique dealing and seeing old things made anew and again being in use.

"Pots were all earthenware from what I saw. But given that I was only there a few days..."

Glynis stood erect: "Have you thanked Ben for coming to your rescue?"

"I did. I think I did." Julian gripped my knee: "And I will do so again. Thank you Ben."

"Not me to thank. It was Glynis set it in motion," I said. "I was just, this one time, the technician."

"Can't help wondering why they've ended up on Exmoor of all places," Julian started to sink back into reflective mode.

"Wonder in the car." Glynis reached across the table to pull him up by his sleeve. "You can call Ben later. I've got work to do. Thank you Ben."

"Humanity has survived," Julian said, using my shoulder to heave himself up out of the soft seating. Once stood he patted my shoulder. I got up just as soon as he'd got around the table. Glynis waited until Julian had gone past her before she gave me a long hug, her body against mine as ungiving and solid as Julian's was wobbly and soft.

Thirty: more settlements

With Julian finally chivvied into the car, a sharp reverse and turn; and they were gone. I was left looking beyond the grey of the concrete platform and out over stands of silver birch, their new-leaf mauve haze. Julian had declared that humanity had survived. Hardly a success though, I thought, their hiding away up on Exmoor.

Sitting on the front steps, excitement of the rescue and pleasure in their company dispersing, I felt myself sink with one long sigh back into what I can only describe as the apathy of hopelessness. Birdsong muffled, the bright world an unfocused blur, I saw myself an amorphous lump, an adjunct to the world on the edge of a concrete rectangle. Even the cats didn't come curling around corners to keep my misery company.

Having had enough of telling myself how miserable I was, how squashed I felt, I was about to rouse myself when my phone buzzed. Steve. He said that Julian had called him from the car, had told him of the settlement. "'Millennial' he kept calling it."

"Numerically should be double millennial."

"Yea," pause as he adjusted to my mood. "Clever, your partition within the cage. His misadventure though will have me double check the door contacts on mine. No way I want to get accidentally abandoned, invisibly, in the future. Have my daughter break into the lav and not find me there. Something else though that settlement. I've already got the OS co-ordinates from you..."

And he chattered on.

Next to call was Bart. Another rehashing of the rescue, concerns about his wonky cage leaving him or Rhean isolated in the future. He too wondering about the Exmoor settlement.

All had somebody worried for them, or about them.

'They who had never wanted family are now lonely old men.'
Haruki Murakami

Glynis had extended her worry to me. Or so I thought then.

She must have called soon after they arrived home. She began by thanking me once again – for my 'forbearance.' "But poor you," she said, "cooped up in that caravan, staring at a square of concrete."

I was about to say that it was a rectangle when she asked, again, if I'd mind her showing the plans to a builder she sometimes used.

"Be my guest," I said to her. Thinking, would that I had a guest, especially a bouncy female one.

That was the one phone call out of what was to become my ordinary over the next few days, the sole topic being the Exmoor 'millennial' settlement.

'That high plateau where philosophy lives with despair.'
Norman Mailer

Bart was the first to come across, cage-travelling, to study the Exmoor barricades.

"Thought at first, like Julian, the thick hedges had to be a defence against other groups. Julian though has done a section by section search of the moor, can find no other nearby settlements. As he says the hedges have to be to bar animals. And it's truly weird not to see any hens, dogs or cats in there. I saw some of the older children posted to scare birds away from freshly sown seeds. To scare all birds. Fear of zoonotic contagion has to be our best guess."

"No iron," Steve told me when he again called. He had plotted an Exmoor visit over both Cumbrian and Cambrian

141

mountains: I'd been given a long list of bounced-off beacons. "Couldn't see one metal implement. Salvage from our time has to be long expired. Although I couldn't get a close look, I assume that, for things like the hand-pulled plough, the blade has to be hardwood. Hornbeam probably. For kitchen implements, and Rhean thought this might be the case as well, sharp ceramics for the cutting and chopping. My daughter has some. For the rest it'll be wooden spoons and spatulas, and earthenware."

Like Julian Steve was taken by their design of handcarts; and, being a keen gardener, how they managed their extensive vegetable plots, their fruit bushes and canes. He hadn't been able to see any vines.

It was Bart and Julian though who seemed to make the most trips to future Exmoor.

"They seem content," Julian told me when I had suggested that theirs had to be a miserable existence. "Not exactly happy. Not chirpy cheerful. Not Amish serene. But definitely engaged. Tanks and reservoirs in evidence, someone in charge of pumps."

My quiet hopelessness was on their periphery again. I simply could not share in their enthusiasm for a survivor's pre-industrial way of life. And while they were pleased to have found future human beings battling on, I was not so sure.

"This is what's left of our civilisation?" I said to Steve.

"Depends what you call civilisation. This is planet Earth still in the process of curing itself. Of us. This new humanity looks to have learnt not to exploit. As with Amazonian tribes of yore these new humans look to be living within their environment. Not seeking to dominate but living with. Which will probably prove easier for groups in the warmer south than for those few up on Exmoor."

When Julian one day was in raptures over their mechanical adaptations up on Exmoor, marvelling at 'the ingenuity of superseded scientific theories,' I dared say, "And what of our technology? What of all our digitised stores of knowledge, of know-how?"

"If," Julian took a careful moment before responding, "the whole of humanity was of a sudden, next week say, to be taken back to evolutionary/scientific zero, and given today's general public's working knowledge of, ignorance of technology, how many centuries do you reckon before even video would get re-invented?"

I had no come-back, nothing worthwhile to add. Knew only that the future had been everything to me. All kinds of futures. Little chance though of those Exmoor new-villagers going into space. Best they could hope for was that space would come to them. And that would suit Julian: he was also a wannabe believer in Van Danniken's theories regards extra-terrestrials. If only, when play-battling Steve, to throw doubt on their likelihood.

I felt so beaten down, so apart from everyone, so alone. Like a conspirator or a scholar, I started to look for messages behind messages.

Because their enthusiasm for this distant future didn't stop with Exmoor. Exmoor they left to Julian.

"Crop rotation," he began one of his new regular calls to me. "That's how they achieve sustainability. Crop rotation. Probably courtesy another folk memory become superstition. Against pesticides?"

"Could be," I half-heartedly responded.

"I've come across little salvage from our time. Has anyone else?"

Didn't know why he was asking me. I suggested he try Bart.

Bart and Rhean had begun a systematic millennial search inland from the Welsh Valleys. Two millennia ahead within the Valleys there were apparently still single terrace houses in use, their gardens extending up the hillsides. All kinds of fencing being used to keep animals out.

In some places people had – in reverse order of valley

bottom habitation – moved up the valley sides, away from floods and landslips. Some had dug into the softer hillsides, not for minerals but – so far as Bart and Rhean could make out – for easily defended living quarters. The new troglodytes. All these valley dwellings appeared to be for isolated multi-generation families.

Bart and Rhean had to go further inland to find an Exmoor-type settlement.

The one they came across was also on an upland plateau, a once-forested plateau, with similar thorn and paling barricades to keep out animals.

"Must have been plague after plague," Rhean said from their zoom corner. She and Bart were sitting side by side. "All of them crossover viruses. Has to be this that's given them their superstitious dread of all animal life."

"Not all animal life," Bart said to her. To us, "There is one surviving human-animal relationship – with the honeybee. Forget hens, a cluster of hives is now the signal of domesticity."

"Shall we call this," Steve smiled, "the New Apiacene?"

"I actually approve their keeping their distance from animals," Bart said with a this-is-no-laughing-matter face. "Must never forget mankind's capacity for cruelty. We can so easily regress."

Rhean's part blue face shared his seriousness. She and Bart had a regular booking to play at the annual anti-hunt ball.

"Not that long ago," Bart continued, "we had badger, bull and bear baiting. Dogs were bred specifically to attack those chained-up bulls and bears. They even dressed the spectacle up as culture, wore fancy clothes to go hunt a fox. Wore sequins to stick swords into bulls."

On that same zoom, to change the subject, vegetarian Steve told us and meat-eating Rhean and Bart, that millennial Workington, along with most of the coastal plain within tidal reach, had long been abandoned.

"In all the thousands of years between us and them," he said, "seawater and animals have come to represent danger." Human survivors, he said, seemed to have migrated deep inland. Searching inland he had expected to find Exmoor-type settlements near the larger lakes. Found none.

"Strange to see the mountainsides minus sheep. More trees. The very few sheep left seem confined to the rocky uplands."

"Got the same here," Bart put in. "Just a few sheep together. Wouldn't call them flocks. Ten to twenty at most. Ragged looking creatures, quick to disappear. Wild cattle too. Spiked barricades built to keep them out."

"Wasn't until I was some way inland," Steve continued, "that I found a settlement on a long, south-facing hillside. The long hill had been terraced; and, again, barricaded against beasts."

He laughed: "I know that while there I'm invisible, but I felt so out of place. Can't explain it. 'Cept there was nowhere I could be along those terraces where I wasn't looking straight at somebody or other. Came by another sensation too. Compared to the one on Exmoor this one felt too ordered."

Not enamoured of that settlement Steve looked elsewhere, found what he first thought were the remains of a settlement, "...on the heathland behind Blencathra. At one end could have been the remnants of fruit cages. Or could have been even older sheep or cattle pens. Had me ask," he directed this to Bart and Rhean, "did we exploiters poison and starve ourselves into near extinction?"

Although contributing little to such zooms the 'oft repeated future fear of animals had me feeling justified in not having let the two cats into the caravan.

"Their language on Exmoor, best I can tell," Julian said, "is based on English. I recognised one or two words. Although could well be a dialect that has evolved locally."

"We've called the dialect we picked up here," Bart said, "Cwnlish."

145

This prompted Steve to come up with, "As the late and greatly lamented Octavia E Butler said in *Eathseed*, 'Our new worlds will remake us as we remake them.'"

"Except this was our world," I blurted out. "Was our new world to be. And we human beings, having fucked up this world, we won't now ever get to the stars."

"Best then if another planetary species comes here," Steve said, "before our sun expires and while Earth is still a viable organism. Then they will find an intelligent species living as part of its environment, and not seeking to control it and in controlling bringing about its destruction."

"Could these new people," Julian piped up, "be the reconciliation to Butler's 'Human Contradiction'? That our intelligence is at the service of hierarchical behaviours? I've encountered no sense of any one individual dominant in the settlement, just tasks arising and jobs needing to be done."

"What did you expect of this future?" Steve asked me. "Some face-fanged, mind-melding cross-breed, courtesy Brian Aldiss?"

"Not at all. But is this the very best that future humanity can do? This the future we have left them? No longer Earth's apex species?"

That latter aspect pleased Steve, Bart and Rhean.

Steve told of shifting his area of search across the Solway to Galloway, where he found a settlement less rectangular, its lower end being the upper end of a loch. Again, it was fenced and barricaded. "Not in straight lines like Exmoor. More organic. Follows the lay of the land. That terraced inland hillside was all square corners, felt fascistic."

It pleased Steve to find that future human beings were existing in small pockets, their being unlikely to ever dominate the planet again. Steve held that domination of itself was not healthy, co-existence preferable.

*

146

On these check-in zooms the three of them, plus Rhean, seemed to talk of the future as if of the past. What had been happening in the Exmoor settlement, how Bart's green latitudes seemed to have struggled, how parts of the Galloway forest had mysteriously died... in the far distant future.

Each took turns telling of the many innovations being made, of their latest find/theory. They could just as easily have been talking of how clever our bronze age ancestors were, their deft use of materials.

I could not share in their interest or their enthusiasm. They had become archaeologists of the future rather than, as I saw our life's work, to be celebrants of the future.

"Hark at you," I said on a call to Steve, "talking about them as if an ancient civilisation. Next, you'll be saying how very clever were the Neanderthals."

"They were."

"No!"

Disagreements among us four were nothing new, heated arguments on conference calls a few times. Bart famously once switched himself off in a huff, claimed afterwards that it had been a technical hitch.

I wondered later if their enthusiasm for these millennial futures did have an edge of desperation. We had none of us leapt into time travel as we had into space. Julian aside we had all of us stepped carefully. Not wanting to know? The future unknown had been our dream world, possibilities endless in the many many realities of SF.

But there we millennially were, Earthbound survivalists, prosaically dull.

To be fair Bart did share many of my doubts and disappointments, took himself more often over to Africa's green latitudes and searched there for millennial settlements. He found a couple where, again, there was the fear of animals, no domestic pets of fowls, no beasts of burden. And Africa's

147

animals being larger their thorn barricades were that much higher and thicker.

"Why so few people?" I asked to bring him back to our reality. "Did they all die of Ebola? Or drown when the coastal cities went under?"

Bart sensed my mood and soon after cut the call.

Thirty One: manic

Seems I wasn't alone in being mentally affected by our future travels: at one point Bart and Rhean became decidedly manic.

How it began.

Bart had reported back that his green latitudes settlement had wheeled handcarts with the same long shafts. He furthermore discovered that another settlement, on the northern edge of Africa's green latitudes, had sand sledges, also with the same long shafts.

Steve, Julian and Bart decided that there had to be – if only because of the universal cart design – communication between settlements. And it was from Bart's green latitude settlement that a group, laden with produce, were first to be spotted leaving their thorn enclosure. They of course had no domestic animals with them. Not even a goat to milk.

To follow them entailed Bart letting them pass, going back home and resetting the data block to get him somewhere ahead of the troupe.

The troupe had in their carts, as well as produce, parasols and what Rhean called a gazebo, Bart said was an open-sided tent. Being hot they, men and women, were dressed in what Rhean said were long cotton robes. They also had with them – Bart believed for the purpose of scaring animals away – long sticks, twice the height of their tallest man, and wooden horns and drums.

"Certainly weren't used for any musical purpose," Bart said. Rhean disagreed, said, "Maybe not in terms of Western music, but when drums and horns were employed for their own amusement then there was a definite musical call and response."

They had taken sides on that before the zoom and in their zoom corner they continued to cheerfully argue.

Music though was not the cause of their mania.

In their tracking ahead of the troupe Bart had set himself off to the side of what was obviously a well-trodden track. He had had to get himself to ground level to be sure it was the track: tree cover meant that only parts could be seen from above.

Congratulating himself at having managed to 'land' himself in the shade, he was watching a large black millipede climbing a nearby trunk when a boy about ten years old came walking straight towards him. The boy's head was down as if looking for something on the ground. He was about to walk into Bart, invisible in his invisible cage. Bart instinctively shouted "Whoa!"

The boy stopped.

Had he been able to see him the boy would have been looking directly at Bart, who – as he would in a crowd elsewhere – said, "Sorry." At which the boy started shuffling backwards, almost tripped, turned and ran.

When he came back it was with a man Bart took to be his father.

Bart had been smiling to himself at the comedy of the boy's fright and flight. Now, seeing the father's impatience and irritation with the chattering boy who, pointing at the tree behind Bart seemed to be telling his father that it was the tree that had spoken, Bart decided to vindicate the boy.

"Pleased to meet you," he said.

This had man and boy looking to left and right, even up into the trees. Which set Bart to chuckling out loud.

Man and boy left, both looking warily around as if about to come under attack.

Bart lost track of the troupe soon after that, never did discover where they went. It was that one incident however that set the pattern for Bart and Rhean's behaviour – seeing where, who and how many they could 'ghost.' Such was the name they gave their game.

At first, they played, not so much planned pranks, but related to one another those moments when they had inadvertently given their future hosts a scare. While Steve – in a call to me – shook his head at their giggling together over their escapades, I saw in the pair of them an unacknowledged despair, one that had them manically nihilistic.

Rhean even managed to video one of her japes in their Welsh plateau settlement.

A woman alone was dismantling old bean stakes and laying them in a bundle. She then turned to pulling up and putting what was left of the bean vines into a handcart. She was in no hurry.

Rhean, hanging above her, said that she approved of her slow pace and decided to sing her a Welsh lullaby. The woman's puzzlement was funny, her going ever higher on tiptoe to try to see who, with no-one nearby, might be singing.

Rhean's sending the video to us all got Julian to set up a 'What are we doing with this?' conference call.

Thirty Two: only connect

Pranks discouraged, Bart and Rhean, Steve and Julian now gave serious consideration and time to how the settlements might be connected, if they were connected.

This was no easy task.

As already mentioned, to find where a track might go meant a constant back and forth, placing co-ordinates further along the presumed track, then home again to work out a new set of co-ordinates.

Bart, contrite, decided that the Welsh settlement presented an easier study than the one in the densely covered green latitudes. Even though some of the plateau – the foothills of the Brecons – still had the remains of pine plantations. In the interceding centuries although fallen trees had not been replaced there had been some natural regeneration. Overall however, the predation of sheep, deer and wild cattle meant that much of the land had returned to heath and scrub, potential tracks more readily spotted.

These back and forth trips into the millennial future took place throughout our summer's end and on into autumn.

At one point Bart, still contrite, excitedly suggested to Julian – as reported by Julian to Steve and Steve to me – their building a bigger cage and, as a money-making venture, offering trips into the future. "For people who want to disappear? Literally disappear?"

"And just who would want to become a ghost?" Julian had dismissed the idea.

For my part I didn't understand Bart's lackadaisical attitude to invisibility. Almost as if he had given up caring. And maybe he had, and these were just him attempting to keep friends with Julian.

I could see why he might have given up: the absolute

pointlessness of our existence. Even if his despair wasn't as mine. Would there be history, any of our history, these future millennia? For Bart the future would have been empty enough when there was continuation of a kind; but how now to relate son Lou's death to a largely non-future?

Rhean – also contrite – was making more trips than Bart. And it was Rhean who puzzled over the separate enclosure reached from within the Welsh settlement. It had the same barriers around it, but didn't seem to have a purpose, grass and weeds growing there.

Intrigued by this lack of apparent purpose she had a look every visit. One day a grave was being dug.

Steve and Julian then looked for, and found, similar graveyards within their settlements. The one in Galloway was a completely separate enclosure a few hundred metres away, but as highly protected as the settlement itself. While the one on Exmoor proved to be within the settlement and was not, as Julian had previously assumed, a field let go fallow.

Moorland tracks through bracken and those through willow scrub proved hardest to second guess, especially when a track descended one side of a valley and didn't rise directly up the opposite side. Steve in the Cumbrian hinterland decided that the long hillside settlement didn't have any regular connection with any other settlement, called the tracks that went seemingly nowhere 'foraging routes.'

By this time Steve had given up lamenting the desolation of his 'cradle of civilisation,' Mesopotamia. "Land of the ancients... To see it now and in the future did hold an awful fascination." A fascination I'd have thought, in my characterisation of the three of them, historian Bart would have been more prey to than techie Steve. But what do I know of people?

Rhean and Julian went on to find more foraging tracks. Ironically it was lackadaisical Bart who discovered the first active meeting site. A hilltop of course, open but easy to defend against animals.

The day that Bart chanced upon it, to the long west of his Welsh settlement, there were groups present from just two settlements. They had laid out their produce in an arc alongside one another. From the marks on the ground Bart supposed that when other settlements met there they would do so in a circle.

Encouraged by Bart finding that meeting place Steve went on to find, deep into Galloway, another circle, an old stone circle, and by old he said prehistoric. Looked like, he said, going by the tracks off, that each of the settlements had their own stone.

One of Julian's tracks eventually led him – visit by visit – across Exmoor to Dartmoor, and he too was excited to find a stone circle being used.

Most stone circles in the British Isles were built somewhere between 3,800BCE and 1,300BCE; some as old as 5,000BCE; and I was, going by my fellow futurists' excitement, supposed to regard their re-use as an advance?

Julian, with his interest in artefacts, had been intrigued to find metal being traded at the Dartmoor stone circle: "Didn't look that old. Someone somewhere in this future is smelting."

"But how is any of this an advance?" I asked Julian. "No evidence of electricity, and Rhean going all Wow they're using beeswax candles. Now you're the same, excited to discover they've re-invented metal."

"You're choosing to misunderstand what these millennial settlements represent. The Earth has restored itself to a slower evolution, to something approaching ecological equilibrium. Our homo-not-so-sapient having pretty much almost got itself wiped out. The outcome is these few settlements, and with humanity now too few to have a malignant effect. And with folk memory instructing them to be wary of waterways and animals."

"I repeat," I said, "how is a return to a solely pastoral existence to be considered an advance?"

Answer came there none.

Bart had his own recurring disappointment in this future: "Whistles and flutes is all they got. No catgut I suppose."

I had been moaning to him about our prehistoric futures, specifically about Julian saying that re-use of the stone circles should be taken more as a celebration of human continuity.

"They do have some sort of drum," Bart conceded. "Pumps out a beat."

"There is also," Rhean said from somewhere in the background, "some neat vocalisation." And she went off wordlessly singing.

Having further mulled over Julian's assertions I later challenged him, "Just how is this continuity to be celebrated?"

"We've gone," Julian said, "from a coal and iron economy to an oil and petrol economy to a plastic and all-electric economy; and they..."

"They have regressed to barter."

"The good news Ben, and it is good news, is that the human species has managed not to become extinct."

"All very well for these hilltop few, what happened to the rest of the people?" I asked that of each of them. "We now live in a world that is over-populated. Where did they all go?"

Going only by Bridgwater's flood I knew that most cities and coastal townships had been abandoned, the seas radioactive. Exeter cathedral, Julian said, was inexplicably in ruins. Carlisle, according to Steve, had gone, completely gone. No-one was living anywhere near water. The settlements all depended on wells. Save for the long hillside one, which had a series of small reed-filtered reservoirs.

"I suppose we could," Steve said, "if we're that concerned for our future selves, do a search ahead every hundred years or so. What though would that realistically accomplish? Pandemics, plagues can start anywhere in the world. Climate change? How to halt that? Us four? Five with Rhean."

In our time, the present present, Steve had become fascinated by the birdlife come to the flooded open-cast mines at Broughton. He had used them as an example of nature reasserting itself. Season upon season goosanders and mergansers, teal and mandarin ducks populated the ponds; all highly photogenic, especially before the mountainous backdrop.

Steve cage-went to see how the ponds had fared in the millennial future. Reported back that the birds still occupied the ponds. That visit he also spotted wild dogs, feral cats, and again passed comment on mountainsides with no sheep.

"Consider this," Julian said. "Of necessity the survivors have banded together. From what I've seen on Exmoor they look to be a pretty homogeneous bunch. By no measure white Caucasians. My guess is that there will have been a mongrelisation of the human race. Which will have led to a more robust populace, lessening genetic illnesses such as sickle cell anaemia. And if their folklore knows this, could be why contact between settlements is seen as important. For intermarriage if not barter."

Came to be accepted between us that somewhere "twixt our present and that distant future there had to have been, not only a massive geological event, but a series of plagues, crop failures, droughts, with each one further diminishing the human population. Nor was that our only speculation, my negative to their positive, arising out of this inland future.

"What if all the legends of drowned cities," Bart said, "weren't of the past but of the future. That Atlantis and Gondwanaland, Mu in the Pacific, were predictions and not a myth memory? What if someone in our own distant past had, like us four, accidentally found a way of travelling into the future? And what if they too had come across our drowned cities? What if the hieroglyphs they had left us were warnings, much as we try with various symbols to warn our successors of nuclear waste? And these warnings have been misinterpreted as history by our ancestors and us?"

Thirty Three: The New Neroche

The name as much as the arch surprised me. 'The New Neroche' was carved into the trunk balanced aloft two hefty supports, much like a torii before a Zen temple. The settlement lay beyond.

I had gone there fed up with feeling sorry for myself. Could still feel the lead weight of depression pulling at me; but I had come to realise that my emotional state was more of a justifiable misery. This was not the debilitating apathy as of yore. This time I had good reason to be unhappy: the future was fucked and there was nothing I could do about it.

That finally was the realisation that lifted me out of what might have become clinical depression.

I once was a reporter. In some respects still am, my hunger to know, to understand akin to the everlasting starvation of the harpy. To satisfy my need to know – in practical doable terms – I thought to wholly break out of my depression by looking for a millennial settlement local to me to study.

At first I had thought to make a search around Clayhidden. By repute remote Clayhidden had been the last place in Somerset that the Christian missionaries had converted. Latter-day Clayhidden inhabitants still boast of having been pagan long before the ever-trendy Glastonbury druids.

Having made one cursory visit – millennial Clayhidden was far too wooded – I made a study of local maps and decided that the most likely place, going by what the others had so far found, would be a flattish part somewhere on top of the Blackdown hills.

During the Second World War one flat part had briefly been an airfield for Spitfires and Hurricanes. After the airfield it had become part of Cheltenham's listening network, massive aerials with cables strung between like giant spider webs. It was/is called Trickey Warren. Which is why I was surprised to see it now – future now – called The New Neroche.

I was sitting above the road that used to run past the listening post. The road was still not totally overgrown, so I was satisfied that my calculations for getting there had been right and I was indeed a few feet above Trickey Warren. The actual Neroche forest I knew was over towards Staple Fitzpaine, the forest being named after the Saxon fortress once built on the promontory there. All that remains of the fortress in our own time is the earthworks, the wooden fortress having long ago rotted away.

The archway on which 'The New Neroche' was written was by any measure substantial. Made of three large trunks the letters had been carved, possibly burnt, into the flattened side of the crosspiece. None of the other settlements, not even the ordered one that Steve called fascistic, had an arch as imposing as this. Although the hedges, dead thorn trees piled one atop the other, were as those I had seen on Julian's Exmoor settlement and were as Bart and Steve had described.

At odds with the archway's enormous construction the gate itself was one tightly woven hurdle, waist high, and which looked to be scraped open and shut on a rope hinge.

Looking again I saw that the nearby hedges followed the old Trickey Warren fence line. The spider-work of aerials had of course long gone. But visible here and there in the thorn-heaped hedges were the concrete posts, their tops still angled at 45°. These would have been strung with barbed wire.

I had first come to know this place through the Greenham Common protests about the US Cruise missiles. Not that there had been any plan that I know of to also base US Cruise missiles in Trickey Warren. But as part of all the scary publicity and counter publicity, surrounding the missiles coming to Greenham, a map of the British Isles, purporting to have come from the Russians, was made publicly known, I think, on BBC's Panorama.

On the map had been the prime targets for Soviet nuclear warheads, each place marked with a red hammer and sickle. London and Greenham were each of course a target, along with all of Britain's other major cities; and in rural Somerset Yeovilton air base, the Royal Marine headquarters in Norton Fitzwarren, and Trickey Warren. I did a follow up piece on the map's disclosure, asked local residents how they had felt being targeted by Soviet Russia. None, I had to report, had seemed unduly alarmed.

Looking beyond the hedges of The New Neroche I could see similar squared-off divisions for vegetables that the others had described within their settlements, a countryside not so much farmed as gardened. There were small terraces, mixed kitchen plots, rows of leeks, brassicas, beans on poles, what looked like massed spinach, and lines of fruit bushes – I assumed blackcurrants and the like – acting as partitions. Further in there were what looked like lines of supported raspberry canes.

One vast allotment, Steve had called the hillside one; and here too were sheds dotted about seemingly at random. I could also see – this on my second, deeper-in visit – that old concrete buildings had been either adapted – grass grown over their roofs – or incorporated into wooden structures.

The arch aside what made The New Neroche markedly different from the other settlements were the extensive orchards. Some of the apple trees even had mistletoes balled among their branches. Which initially surprised me, that they should allow parasitical growth on what was there to provide food. Julian had laid great store on the Exmoor settlement's utilitarian approach.

There have however always been Druidic tendencies in Somerset. I got to report annually on wassailing, the dirge-like songs and the firing of a shotgun up into apple trees. These millennia on were they still wassailing? Mistletoe formed part of other Druidic ceremonies...

I watched the people moving about within The New

159

Neroche. Of all ages they went quietly about their business. A mother called out a warning once to her bare-legged toddler who had, possibly, been about to go onto freshly dug ground. Other people, pulling the long-handled carts that the others had all commended, stopped by to chat with those working on plots.

Subsequent visits – I really felt that I should persist – had me remark on the many collections of bee hives dotted about. No living creatures other than bees tolerated, but mead and cider always on the menu. And that was it, Somerset's millennial future.

Thirty Four: a proposition

When my phone buzzed, seeing that it was Glynis calling, my aged heart gave an adrenalin jump. What now?

Sliding the phone carefully off my desk I carried it still buzzing through to the caravan's front steps. If I accepted calls within the caravan they often cut out, which necessitated my having to call whoever was calling back, which could lead to several minutes of them trying to call me again as I was trying to call them, until finally one or other of us managed to get through.

The state I was in, hands all a-tremble, I didn't want to risk that. Arriving at the steps I took a steadying breath, said, "Hello?"

"Hi Ben. Got a proposition for you."

Another adrenalin heart-leap.

Unlikely as this may seem given my downbeat personality it has always been women who have propositioned me. Every one of the women I ended up living with, they first approached me.

Doesn't help that I have never satisfactorily worked out precisely what it was that all those very different women saw in me. Whatever it had been it hadn't taken them long to discover that the rest of me wasn't worth it. And now hyper-fit Glynis?

My never having been able to turn down an offer, my overriding concern at that moment was what would I say to Julian?

"What kind of proposition?" I asked.

"One that will be of benefit to both you and I."

I wanted to be safe, to not – if I could help it – betray a friend: "How does Julian figure in this?" Would let me know the state of their relationship.

"Told me to go ahead and ask."

That made no immediate sense: "Ask what?"

"If you and I could do a deal whereby I build your house, according to your specs, and you live in it rent free. But you make the house over to me in your will."

That was the nub of the deal.

Glynis went on to explain that she had been 'quietly' buying up higher properties in and around Ilfracombe. Since arty types had moved in however house prices had rocketed. She still though wanted to add to her property portfolio. She had come by this policy, she said, before Julian's descriptions of post-flood Ireland. Since then, and Julian telling her of most low-lying "...parts of 'combe gone. Capstone at best an occasional island. Harbour all gone. I've got my higher up houses on buy-to-let mortgages. Building yours will be cheaper than buying."

And it was so sad, she said, my looking out onto that square of concrete.

I had been on the verge of correcting her to say that it was a rectangle, when she changed her voice to a soft confiding tone, said that she and Julian wanted to start a family and to leave their progeny more than a dodgy cliff-top block of flats.

"Which I think I understand," I said. "What I don't understand is why now? I might be a miserable old git, but I have no intention of dying any time soon. Could be at least a decade, possibly more, before you take possession. So why?"

"That's all down to Julian and Exmoor. Now that he has established that humanity has a future of sorts."

'A man is a sperm's way of producing another sperm.' Phillip K Dick

Julian, his innate optimism carrying him ever forward, is more used to businesses begun and failing than I. A logic to that life philosophy; and made sense that he and Glynis, now in their thirties, should see this as their last chance to start a family. I was, even so, astonished by their bravery.

No-one had ever considered starting a family with me. So Glynis and Julian's partnership had to go beyond sex and domesticity, was love-based?

I looked back over the time spent with my women and accepted that I had never been loved. A pretence at partnership, a shared domesticity, nothing more. Love? Had I ever known it? At best my parents had tolerated me, had more often resented me. Faulty goods, I had not been what they had ordered.

A wry inner look should have had me laughing at all the sexual thoughts of Glynis that had passed through this sex-starved brain of mine, while all that Glynis had wanted of me had been my house plans.

"My specs?" I said. "Built to my exact specifications?" After all this time I didn't see the point of building something I didn't want.

"When I showed the plans to my builder, he got really excited about them."

"You're serious then?"

"I've drawn up a contract. Will send it over."

The contract was in my email folder by the time I got up off the steps and back into my office. The contract had none of the usual ifs and buts, was absolute in that I would incur no expense whatsoever for the materials and the erection of the house, that it would follow my construction specifications to the letter; and on its completion I would be able to reside in the house for as long as I wished, but that on my demise the freehold entire would become the property of Glynis Featherstone.

'So sad your looking out onto that square of concrete.' A re-hearing said that she had actually said, 'wet square'; and I wondered if Glynis had inadvertently diagnosed another cause of my depression.

That last thought had me burst out laughing. In that moment I had seen Glynis no longer as a threatening sexual possibility, with all the social entanglements that would involve, but simply as a friend; a friend who, having seen first-hand how I lived, had become concerned for my welfare.

Laughter settled, smiling to myself, I responded to her email with a thank you, and I agreed to the contract. My phone buzzed no sooner had I clicked on *Send*. I again wandered through to the caravan's front steps.

"You sure?" Glynis said. "Don't want time to think it over? Show it to your solicitor?"

"I'd like to see the house built."

"So would Mike. He's done more than a few renovations and repairs for me. Your plans though really excite him. You'll like him. He's as full of ideas. Can we come over tomorrow?"

They came, arrived before lunch. Glynis was as before, solid athletic meat; but who I now saw as comrade, as friend. While Mike was big with a gingerish look and smiling blue eyes.

"This is magnificent," he said as he paced out the rectangle of concrete. "Mains all in. Dirty work all done. Only half a job to do. And what a magnificent view."

I was to hear 'magnificent' many times over the next few weeks.

Thirty Five: an erection

Mike went away with the original plans and within the fortnight the materials arrived. Along with Mike's two-man crew.

Watching them unload the lorry that had followed them up the hill I wondered if they had got the idea – materials and men arriving together – from Julian's future Ireland visits. Which also got me to wondering how much Glynis might have told Mike of Julian's space/time travels (mishap). Had Steve and I been the only ones to keep our cages secret? Had Steve? I doubted that he had managed not to tell his live-in daughter something. I was the only one with no-one to tell.

Mike and his crew's daily industry surprised me: I had become used to the usual gripes about lazy workmen. But lorry gone, these three set to sorting through the piles and heaps, then stretched a membrane over the concrete, carried and placed timbers, got an extension plugged in... All done seemingly without direction from Mike, each occupied with their own task. A doubt raised by one would be responded to by another stepping away from their own moment's work, an agreement reached as to the best way to proceed; and within two days the first walls were up.

This meant that my only view from the caravan was now of a wooden frame filled with grey insulation blocks. Ladders were then leant against the new walls and the first joists were laid across.

I had to make one compromise on my plans.

"Hope you don't mind my saying," Mike's blue-green eyes smiled kindly on me, "but your oriel seems out of character with the utilitarian rest of the house."

His cautious approach had me smile in return. I have known near identical caution from editors who have wanted the removal of some interloping 'little darlings.' The oriel too had been pure self-indulgence: I had imagined myself sitting within the overhang, views all around, book in hand.

On having been told that Mike suggested keeping the window size but deepening the walls on either side, which would allow him to create a window seat.

"Aesthetically it'd be more pleasing."

"And less trouble? This is not the thin of the wedge? More changes to follow?"

"Not a single other." His big hand patted my thin arm. "Though if you're really set on the oriel? You've waited long enough."

"And it wouldn't be happening now without you and Glynis. I quite like the idea of a window seat. Make it long enough so I can stretch out."

"It shall be done."

Plans amended, first floor boarded out, roof trees installed; all done so far as I could make out on a diet of pizzas, burgers and all-day breakfasts. Monday to Thursday they stayed in the Travelodge at Chelston, Friday afternoons left for their North Devon homes. I made them their lunch time mugs of tea. On the first day I had been told by all three that they didn't stop for tea breaks: "Slows the job down."

All three men were softly spoken. Only if a thumb was banged or wood unexpectedly spilt were there curses. Their not pausing to chat I never managed to pin down their precise employment status, suspected that the one who did the plumbing might have been registered unemployed in that he had to 'shoot back' on the same day midweek.

Glynis only came over when the roof of integrated solar panels had been installed, floor bricks been laid, and the building inspector had nodding been. Doors and windows were in, wiring and plumbing complete. The external wood cladding was to arrive later that day.

"What do you think?" Glynis asked as she, Mike and I went

166

from room to room.

The south-facing window and heat-retaining floor of bricks were both smaller and bigger than I had imagined. But it was the speed at which the house had been put up that was hardest for my old brain to accept. Had I been able to afford the materials I had foreseen my wizened self-adding piece to piece over the years. Yet here it was near complete, walls plastered, bathroom ceramics plumbed in, gaps left for cooker and washing machine, window seat awaiting paint and new cushions.

Where Mike had deepened the window seat, he had built bookshelves on the 'backs' of the walls as well as under the window seat itself.

"What will you do with the caravan?" Glynis asked when we three came into the caravan for Mike to place his witness signature on the paper contract.

"Might let it out," I told her. "Provide a little extra income."

Two days later, with the wood cladding attached, I prepared to say goodbye to Mike as he and the crew loaded up the SUV for their final trip home.

"Thanks for everything," I said to Mike. "I know Glynis said she'd pay, but do I owe you anything?"

"All taken care of," he assured me. Then adopted a dealer's grin: "One thing though. Do you want to hang on to that portaloo? Could come in very handy for us."

They had been using the caravan lavatory when I had told them that I only used the portaloo to store tools. The house had an upstairs bathroom and a downstairs lavatory.

"Take it," I told Mike. "Leave the tools on the ground. I'll find somewhere for them later."

I was glad he hadn't mentioned the shed. On his asking for the portaloo I had briefly considered using the shed for the tools and at the same time had seen such a use as a betrayal of Glynis and Julian.

"You sure?" Mike said. I nodded. Mike told his crew to make space in the back of the SUV; and the three of them discussed how best to lift it in, whether to have it lying or standing. Method agreed, teamwork saw it lifted in and secured.

Contrast that with the fiasco of retrieving my house furniture from storage.

I cycled down to Wellington, locked up my bike behind the supermarket, caught the bus to Taunton, walked the mile or more out to the storage place and, as arranged over the phone, met the van there at the time agreed. The fat driver instructed two, could have been school lads, in the carrying out of my sofa, Ikea wardrobe, bed pieces, double mattress, kitchen chairs and table, and cardboard boxes. With everything packed into the van, shutter pulled down, I said that I'd ride back with them.

"Can't do that," the fat driver said. His every utterance up to that point had seemed to emanate from exasperation. The set of his mouth and the sideways look he gave me I sensed that I was about to become yet another of his life's exasperations.

"No space in front," he said.

"We'll ride in the back," one schoolboy nudged the other.

"Can't do that. Insurance."

"If I'm not in the house," I told the driver, "you'll be unable to deliver it."

"We'll leave it outside."

"Rain's forecast."

"Not my problem."

"OK," I said to the two schoolboys. "Open it up. Put it back in storage."

Long and short, Mr Exasperated with bad grace – silent save for long sighs – drove me and my worldly goods up to the house and had the lads take it all into my new indoors. Indoors I took care to quietly give the two boys a tenner each.

That day's second small act of defiance pleased me. And with my furniture out of store I now had one less monthly payment to be made. Things were definitely looking rosier. The forecast rain never came so I took a pleasant evening stroll down into Wellington and collected my bike.

Thirty Six: in residence

Even with my old furniture installed, kitchen table rebuilt, chairs arranged around it, still took me a while to move out of the caravan. Despite its many frustrations the caravan had been my home for so long, knew me as I knew it. My habits belonged there. And at my age I don't have that much physical energy, so took my time going over to the house to paint walls and skirting boards.

Once the new cooker and washing machine had been delivered however, I could no longer put off the day. The cats had already moved.

When I had agreed to Glynis building the house I had been sitting on the caravan's front steps. "You've had it," I had told the curling, purring tabby. When the walls had gone up both cats had moved deeper under the caravan. Come the clangour of the building work they had disappeared. I put out food for a couple of weeks after, but they haven't returned.

With all my office bits and pieces carried across I still had jobs around the house needing to be done; last walls to be painted, shelves to be put up, old pictures to be unpacked, placed, and hooks found. And yet... with rugs on the floors, rooms personalised, within a house built to my specifications, still it didn't feel like mine.

The house was my dream made manifest, and yet... Probably because of how it had come about, it didn't somehow feel as if I had earned it.

My depression, I knew, was lingering, waiting to reclaim me.

I had been prepared to be disappointed about the missing oriel, had to concede however that the deep window seat packed with cushions was far more comfortable than would have been my old sofa pushed into the oriel. And sleeping in

170

the house – my old bed frame finally reassembled – I soon came to relish waking in a quiet bedroom.

With no acorns clanging on the roof I could start my days not having to first quell my jangled nerves. Instead there I lay in my new bedroom, insulated and insular, not one workaday sound from outside breaching, shattering the drift of my slumber-filled thoughts.

And it was within those lie-abed thoughts that I tried to analyse my underlying disgruntlement, and so dispose of it. The disgruntlement was, I decided, because I felt – irrationally – that the house had been stolen from me. While having to concede that Mike and his team had made a far better job of it than could have single I. My dream though had seen my hands holding hammer and saw.

Mine and not mine, the house now belonged to Glynis. Or would on my demise.

Oddly what reconciled me to the house, how I found favour with it, came about outside the house.

I had picked up some more bookshelves and a small bamboo table – for a pot plant – from Taunton's fortnightly auction. Meant I could unpack more of my books; and look for a lemon-scented geranium and a maidenhair fern. I'd had the pair in my every house. It was those two plants that got me to thinking about other plants, but outside, make a garden again.

My reconciliation came about as part of that, the day I was making a path to my new front door. I had already dug a shallow trench for the laying of sand. Once, on a weekend break in Amsterdam, Lilith sofa-stuck recovering from a hangover, I had paused in my morning ramble to watch some workmen replacing cobbles. My intention was to do something similar with the path, but using end-on bricks.

While spreading the sand I wondered what Mike would make of my plan. From thinking of Mike my thoughts moved to Glynis; and it was in that exact moment that I accepted all that she had done for me.

Glynis hadn't needed to build this house. Yes, ultimately, she and her yet-to-be-born child would benefit. But for her it was a very long shot. One she hadn't needed to make. No, she had seen my unhappiness and she had wanted, as a friend, to make me less unhappy. Ambitious and resourceful as Glynis was, even she wouldn't have believed herself capable of making me actually happy.

Resting on my rake in front of this house built to my precise specifications I found myself smiling at the thought that I had a friend. More than the one: mustn't forget my three *Futuricity* friends. A house and friends... had to be enough for any man.

I watched a magpie, unaware of my still presence, come bouncing down the hill through a gap in the trees. Magpies please me, their black and white long-tailed elegance, their crow antics. Yes, I thought that day, the future can take care of itself, this now is much more than enough.

Thirty Seven: Galloway

As autumn dribbled into winter, I became used to the house's habits, creaking down the stairs to make my first cup of tea, cracking open a window to check the new day's sounds, match my day's planned activities to the weather.

Still wanting to be a part of Julian's experiment – an enduring reluctance to let go of knowing – I occasionally, and dutifully, went around to the back of the caravan and up into the shed, where I made a half-hearted visit to The New Neroche, contributed my observations to my friends' research. I told of the threshing of grain, the big vat of plum jam, the collaborative picking of apples, the self-imposed disciplines of seasonal cultivation.

All of the settlements under observation seemed determined to keep their self-policing communities small and independent. On that level I could understand their rationale: in such small communities' stupidity, especially the stupidities that cause harm, vandalism for instance, have to become readily obvious and can soon be quelled.

"Neroche are definitely making cider," I reported my Somerset amusement in this to Steve.

"The upper Galloway lot," he told me, "the one with the stream alongside?" A millennial oddity that, most of the other settlements relied on wells. "I'm pretty sure they're making paper."

"Paper?"

"I couldn't figure out why they were gathering up all this dry material. And keeping it dry. Straw, grasses, bracken even. But anything fibrous, near woody. Reeds and sedges. Then I came across a couple of men pulping a mix of it in an old stone trough. In the shed, the barn, call it what you will, they must be flattening out the pulp and laying it on drying racks."

"Sure it's paper?"

"I can't get inside the building, but what else? They threw some edges, trimmings, back onto the dry pile. Looked far too brittle for cloth. Besides they're using flax for cloth, all those blue acres. No, the raw material would be what you'd use for paper."

I had to leave the call with Steve, could hardly contain my excitement. Paper meant writing. Writing meant communication.

We had wondered about communication, how they knew where to set up their bartering circles. No coinage of the realm, straightforward exchange of goods, possibly of ideas. But if ideas then only person to person, group to group. Paper could see ideas move beyond the face-to-face personal.

There already had to be a supra-settlement organisation at work: most bartering sites, by stones or on heathland, were roughly equidistant from their nearest settlements, which were approximately equidistant from other meeting places. They couldn't all be arrived at organically. Could they?

We had all lamented the millennial loss of electricity, of electronic communication; and there seemed no appetite in any of the settlements to reinvent. As there wasn't also any vestigial hankering after animals. Although Bart and Rhean had seen some of the Welsh settlements starting to experiment forging small amounts of metals.

Bart and Julian had done some hundred-year dipping-in research to try to discover how the millennials had arrived at these settlements. But it was where exactly to dip, when to dip, for it to have any meaning. Could miss things by a day, a country, a mile. What they did find was that what had been predicted in our own time had happened. The moon colonies had failed.

"Lasted one generation only," Julian said. "I came upon a vox pop interview with a colonist about to leave. 'Won't staying there affect your bone mass?' the interviewer asked him. 'I won't be returning, the colonist said, 'so loss of bone mass won't be of any consequence. I have to go. We need more than machines on the moon, if only to carry on the human race.'"

The colonies failed. And on Earth the climate tipping points all got passed. The dustbowls came, then the mutated viruses, forest fires, tectonic events, then floods... Almost all as we had expected.

What I hadn't anticipated was that some of humanity would survive and create the settlements. What I hadn't taken into account was the lasting effect of those who had battled the oil companies, the coal corporations; their optimistic planting of trees, their protecting of forests; how psychologically that must have carried into the future.

So have the settlements become civilisation of a primitive kind. And now with paper..? I could feel the hope, like sunshine inside, being reborn.

Futuricity had been about exploring all kinds of futures, of toying with concepts, the one question, Would this be possible? Remotely possible?

As importantly *Futuricity* had been all about books, those reservoirs of ideas, of thought. *Futuricity* had relied on books, had recommended books, had promoted books.

Books need paper; and in upper Galloway the millennials had started to make paper.

I was, I am, a futurist. The likes of cider-making Neroche wasn't the future of my many times imagining. No electricity, no books, no intergalactic civilisation.

With Galloway making paper however books might, just might be on the way back. Books that will carry those complex notions that can't be easily expressed in person-to-person speech. Books the bricks with which we build understandings.

Earlier on, before I had moved into the house, Steve had forcibly – for him – told me, "It has only been a couple thousand years to the settlements. Civilisations get to be measured in the tens of thousands of years. You have to ask yourself, is what we are seeing but yet another cycle of homo sapien's creation/destruction? 40,000 year old temples and megaliths are all that remain of some previous cycles. This time, having almost destroyed the planet itself, will this next cycle finally be the one that gets it right? Theirs is truly a new beginning Ben, and nowhere near as futile as you would have us believe."

Steve had been right: I had been thinking short term. Even for the millennials it will be a million years or more until the natural demise of planet Earth. Time aplenty to succeed or fail in their own way.

My three friends had taken their hope for the future from that long term continuity. Continuity alone hadn't been enough for me. Paper on the other hand...

In paper there was hope of a future still. And what a future.

Maybe from this time, from this starting point, human beings won't turn out to be so cruel, so wantonly destructive. Just look at The New Neroche. Where once Neroche was the name of a wooden fortress now it had behind it a wooden community hall.

No beasts of burden in any of these new settlements. Not one animal under their control. These new humans won't learn enslavement, will be masters of none. Will no longer see themselves as superior, the apex species, will no longer feel the need to dominate.

This last notion had me feeling strangely safe. From the settlements onwards this new humanity could well become civilised without wiping out neighbouring species.

And there being no cuts of meat in these new books there will be none of the brutalising analogies so beloved by politicians.

Paper made of grasses; this is the future straw that I am grasping at. I have faith though: through paper is how information, how ideas get passed from one generation to the next.

When I was unpacking my books from storage, I had worn a smile as I had placed each on the long shelf. Old friends. Asimov's *Foundation Earth* at one end, all of my Harry Harrison's somewhere in the middle. It had been such a pleasure to just hold the books again, reacquaint my memory with their contents, arrange the spines to the bend of my neck, tilt of my head.

So very many of them. And before our sun's end there will still be time enough to create, to recreate another empire of books.

I have, as will have become evident in this tale, no high opinion of myself or of my efforts within the grand scheme of things. If scheme there is. But now there is, there will be paper; and possibly, just possibly, this tale of ours will be carried into the future. Unlikely as that is, but just say this book survives two millennia, it might explain their ghosts to them.

Throughout all this telling what has to be borne in mind is that I was only despairing of the future because I was able to travel there. So by what Earthly right did I, Benjamin Barraclough, have to become depressed when I, one of only four, five with Rhean, had so very recently been in space, had so very recently been forward in time. Where we found reasons for hope other than the re-invention of paper.

Bart for instance had been right when he said that we have encountered no future genetic mutations. Nor, with the settlements' segregation from other species, are there likely to be. My despair over one lot of flooding had been misplaced. All changes.

Dear old Fred Hoyle had been right: '...the Universe did not have a beginning and it will not have an end. Every cluster of galaxies, every star, every atom had a beginning, but not the Universe itself. The Universe is something more than its parts...'

This book had been intended as a record of our voyages into

space and into the future. It appears to have become something else.

All very well, I can hear a *Futuricity* critic carp, your smugly knowing of the distant future, but what do we do now? What do we do here, now?

I can only quote a character in Octavia E Butler's *Parable of the Sower* when she was also asked about a predicted future. 'We can get ready,' her heroine says. 'That's what we've got to do now. Get ready for what's going to happen, get ready to survive it, get ready to make a life afterward.'

Part Two: Out of Time

Testimony

Explanation [if I may?]

The form that you presented me with, the questions asked, and even though I was encouraged to answer fully, even though I was told that there could be no wrong or right answers, I looked at the first questions and I didn't know where to start.

Or rather there were way too many starting points. Each one of which would have taken me in a different direction, each new direction requiring an explanation, with that explanation requiring its own explanation, and so on.

And I'm not used to documents. Documents of any kind. Not used to writing things down generally. In Care I didn't take, let alone pass, any proper exams. And though your speech-text converter works OK, when I started to read it back it didn't look right. Didn't sound right, if that makes sense. So I did it all again. And then I did write some of it down.

Then when I scrolled further on down the form, I saw that some of my already explanations would have been answers, part answers, to further down questions. Although they weren't in the order I'd have used if I'd been answering the first question as I'd seen fit.

And that was when I called you and told you of the difficulties I was having getting started.

"Some candidates need the questions," you told me, "find them useful prompts. But you do it your own way. Answer best you can Question One, and if the answer you start with requires further explanation, then explain. And if you think that explanation needs more, then add more. But take your time. Time here is what we have plenty of. Come back to the form when you have reached a stopping point. That's what previous candidates have done. No rush. You're here. And you will find that, once you get going, that telling all will acquire its own volition."

And it sort of has. Not to begin with though. Even after your pep talk there were many impulsive deletions, crossings out, rewrites.

Reading this you will find that, regardless of the question on your form, I might begin by wanting to explain something more about what I had mentioned before. Add a detail important to me, and maybe to your understanding of me.

Where I have remembered to I have called some of these add-ons *Supplementaries*. They are there for the same reason – my needing to say more. Or my having been prompted to say more by your, my mentor's, intervention.

Only in the first *Supplementary* do I mention my mentor entering the room, your getting me to tell more. Other of your promptings took place in chance meetings in corridors, in the grounds, in one or two of the canteens, or elsewhere.

*

One thing's for certain if it hadn't been for Old Ben I wouldn't be here now in this place, [Is it a place? A real place?] sitting at this table, in this room and trying to come up with answers to these many questions.

So how did I come to meet Old Ben?

Answer to that will need me to tell of my occupation at that time.

What was my occupation? Could it be classed as an occupation?

[Am I now to come up with my own questions? Was that the idea all along? That I am to interview, to interrogate myself? Can see that it might get me over this cold start, these many wiped-out starts.]

My occupation? Well now... How to explain? I had become

a specialist, a technician in the field of illicit cannabis production. Not that I any longer tended the cannabis sativa plants. Or only occasionally. No, my main contribution to the business was in the building of internal rooms wherein the cannabis sativa could get grown.

Other drugs, MDMs for instance, don't need rooms within rooms. Any kitchen laboratory would do for their production. And cocaine can be cut and packaged on any table anywhere. Not cannabis. Although small scale, own use, can be done indoors, to make saleable amounts large scale production is necessary. Therein my specialisation.

A place would be found, say a disused factory, a house for rent, farmer's outbuilding, and I would be the first to go in, build rooms within rooms. By the time I met Old Ben I had come to rely on click-build.

I want to call the separate pieces angle irons, but they were actually made of reinforced plastic, and very versatile. Clicking them together I could make corners, reinforce ceiling spans; and once I'd got them up I'd cover the lot in thick black plastic sheets. The bright grow lights would still glow through the black plastic but become a weird kind of amber.

If it was a house, I'd also put up net curtains. Net curtains are never pulled. Then I'd hang behind the nets, or behind whatever curtains were already there, black-out material.

If anyone should try to peer in through the nets, even if the house was on its twentieth or thirtieth crop, day or night they'd not be able to see a thing.

If it was a rough old building, like a barn, as well as the black plastic over the clip-build frame I'd pin blackout material to the insides of the wooden walls. Or tape it to tin walls if that was what was there.

As for the smell... My innovation, part of my earlier experience working in such spaces, was to not have the air filters aimed up into the lofts. No filters are a hundred percent perfect, and some lofts can be loosely linked – in a terrace say

182

– to the other houses. The smell readily permeates; and there are always days, even if the reek is sent out through the chimney, when atmospheric pressure can bring the air sinking down. Bringing the skunk reek with it.

Where others, to keep the business out of sight in a house preferred to adapt the second floor upwards, if possible I always built my rooms within rooms on the ground floor and aimed the filters down through the floorboards. Sometimes I had to cut a hole. My theory was that the dry soil, or building debris, what-have-you under the floorboards, would absorb and/or filter away more of the reek.

Working on the ground floor also suited the live-in horticulturalists. If a house they could sleep more or less comfortably upstairs.

Only once did I voluntarily – I was between houses – live where I had built. My fellow gardener that time though turned out to be way too fond of the product. Made him stupid. We called him Orange. He was ginger, had very white skin and these large almost orange freckles. We were in full production and he actually opened a window to blow his smoke out.

With houses, if not the smell, it was usually the comings and goings that got neighbours curious, and talking. Which is why out of the way places were preferred. My masterpiece for instance was on an industrial estate.

I had built a whole shed within a shed, filters bubbling into tanks. Vans could come in during the broadest of daylight, collect product and leave. Nothing suspicious. Except that Hodges went and brought in some illegals. I'd had the locals on shifts there, regular workers coming and going. Nothing to say our shed was any different to anywhere else on the estate. The illegals though had to sleep there, and facilities were minimum to say the least.

Even if slaves don't actively look for ways to make themselves free they still make small acts of rebellion. Or they just don't care what they do. Which gets them noticed, and which got that site shut down.

It had been my masterpiece and I was angry with Hodges, told him that's what came from being a cheapskate. My verdict, 'Penny-wise pound-fucking-foolish,' though I didn't have nerve enough to use those actual words to him.

To be fair to Hodges he was as disappointed with the outcome as I. Hodges is a businessman, sees himself first and foremost as such. Albeit one without scruples. As I saw myself first and foremost as a technician. In my case as one who couldn't afford scruples.

Our main concern, for both of us, was not to get caught. Although we both had reputations, we both tried to avoid notoriety. That said among us workers our product was affectionately known as 'Hodges Home Grown, from farm to client, Quality Assured.'

I could speak some of my mind to Hodges because I was good at my job. I could get a site set up within a day and, as importantly, get it taken down even quicker – as if never having been, except maybe for some holes in the ground floor.

The County-Liners came to know of my specialism, asked Hodges' permission to use me. That did not please me. The reverse. Involvement in any illicit activity, unless you are particularly deluded, means that you have to expect to get caught. I worked with fools like Orange, depended on the foolish: I myself would have been a fool not to have expected to get caught.

Supplementary [recorded/transcribed]

Mentor has come back into the room. One hand resting on my shoulder she reads what I have written.

Mentor: Is this what is called 'organised crime'?

O/V: It's only a crime if caught and convicted. That is when, by definition, you become a criminal. Before then, doing what we did, I suppose we'd be called 'felons.' As to organised... I wish.

184

Mentor frowns as if not understanding.

O/V: we certainly tried to be organised. Organising fundamentally unreliable people though, often desperate people, is difficult. What 'organised crime' does depend on is trust. I made sure that I could be trusted. As for trusting others... You have to ask yourself, How can characters who are innately untrustworthy be organised? Can do it with fear. And/or with dependency. But either can only work for so long, until a way out can be found. Loyalty works. Give your crew a uniform, a badge, a special tattoo. But again, that only works up to a point. Should a better offer come along...

Mentor is still standing behind and above me, as if waiting, wanting more. I part turn in my chair, talk across her belly-flat front.

O/V: What you have to realise is that most people in 'organised crime' have no bigger picture. They often see nothing beyond the moment, beyond the self. Some are so selfish, wilfully cruel, destructive, act out of silly spite, and ultimately against their own self-interest. They don't see that their every quick theft hurts themselves, makes them untrustworthy. And most are people with no consideration of a secondary effect. Orange with his use of weed. He didn't see, or want to see, how it might be viewed by others. He wanted to smoke some weed on the sly so he craftily – in inverted commas – opened a window to blow the smoke out.

I paused. Mentor waits still.

O/V: Organised assumes a steady hierarchy. Maybe even a Mr Big. And there probably are a couple who see themselves that way. Hodges didn't. He may have had a broader view than the ground troops, but he still had to deal with fundamentally untrustworthy people. Look at his use of slaves. Someone Hodges had had dealings with, a gangmaster or a trafficker my guess, had a couple of slaves going spare and offered them to Hodges as a favour. Or maybe Hodges took them on as a favour. A sort of win-win that turned into a lose-lose for the tight-fisted twat. Businessman Hodges lost more in income than the wages he'd have had to pay to my locals. Maybe though, given the people he'd had to deal with, it hadn't been a favour he could decline.

Mentor: I was about to mention that. Within organised crime there has to be violence, coercion. Were you violent?

O/V: Didn't need to be. Apparently I have this look, this stare which unnerves people. A couple of foster parents called me Psycho Child because, usually when I didn't want to do something I'd been told to do, I'd just sit and stare at them. Wouldn't say anything, just sit and stare. For as long as it took. Did the same in care homes. When anyone tried to bully me – always someone wanting to be top dog – I'd just stare at them. Wouldn't say a word, would try not to even if their crew was knocking me about. Afterwards I'd say, 'Sleep well.' Just that. No locks on doors in care homes. 'Sleep well,' I'd say. Didn't have to do anything. Just stare at them. Each one. And me the victim would be the one to get moved. A disruptive influence.

Mentor is studying my reflection in the screen.

O/V: I need to tell you about Old Ben though. Before I get to Hodges.

*

I still haven't told you how I came to meet Old Ben.

First there was...

I've put his actual name out of mind. Let's call him David. David liked to present himself as normal, as ordinary, as respectable. Looked a bit like a salesman if not a businessman. Always well turned out – clean shirt, no tie, cuffs rolled back, trousers not jeans, shoes not trainers.

Given the precarious nature of our work we were often in need of new premises. David it was who hunted them out. A few times via online rental sites. More often just by driving around and spotting a likely building. Or on being told that up around so-and-so was an unused farm building. Surprising how many of those agricultural buildings are miles from any farm. Small industrial estates were another favourite.

It was in tracking down this one word-of-mouth farm building that had David stop beside Old Ben. Ben was in his garden out front of the house.

I was never sure just how deaf Ben was. Or whether he sometimes laid it on. Or if he was just not paying attention, had been thinking of other things. Which with him was often the case. Or if he had been that day truly deaf, had genuinely not understood what had been said and needed you to repeat.

Anyway, this day David swished up in his usual shiny model, lowered his window and called out to Ben. Ben must have done his usual hand-to-ear mime and come wandering over to the car.

David's spiel was that he was looking for workshop premises to rent and did Ben know of this supposedly vacant farm building? I don't know if Ben deliberately misunderstood, but he told David that he had space to rent and he stepped away from the car as if to show him.

David, thinking that Ben might have some outbuilding hidden in the trees behind the house – wouldn't have been the first time that someone had rented us an outbuilding, be it double garage or part-glass greenhouse – he got out of the car and followed Ben. Only to come to an old caravan behind the house.

Between house and caravan was a rough earth path, with the house back door not quite opposite the caravan's wooden steps.

"Been meaning to let it for ages," Ben told David. "I sort of tried. But the agency wanted to know about insurance for this, insurance for that..."

I'm guessing Ben said that last bit. He had a thing about insurance companies.

"Not actually what I'm looking for," David told Ben. "More

workshop premises I'm after. But I've got a friend desperate for somewhere to rent. Can I give him your number?"

"Tell him to just come up. An odd day when I'm not here."

Ben, like me, would take some persuading before he'd share his phone number.

I was at that time, had been for some time, living in a shared house on a Taunton housing estate. On the flat Taunton has this huge housing estate made of many smaller housing estates, one estate linking into another and that seem to go on forever. Take one wrong turning and it can take an age to find one's way out.

The houses, all of similar brick, are more or less anonymous, which suited me, kept me clear of officialdom. Inside the house though my fellow sharers were sub-clever been-to-uni types. They had jobs they claimed not to like, spent most of their off-time online gaming; and if going out coming back to boast to one another, a constant kitchen sneer of petty one-upmanship. I was the youngest, kept to myself, told them my irregular hours were down to agency jobs. They had all had mac-jobs, done deliveroos, sympathised and so didn't closely question me. But I was on edge living there and had told David so. Without bank statements and references though places for such as I were hard to come by.

For you to make sense of why I have done what I have done I'd best mention, make clear here, that I was brought up in Care.

My official designation was orphan. Orphan however requires both parents to be deceased. On a few forms I have been more accurately described as a foundling, parents unknown.

As a babe-in-arms I was adopted. Within a couple of years though those adopting parents split up. My guess is that they had been about to split up prior to my adoption and I was to have been the last-ditch cement to hold the marriage together. I didn't.

188

With neither of them wanting to keep me I was passed onto foster care, care homes, back to foster, more care homes, more foster... Decisions were made on my behalf and delivered to me as if their official scheming – the covering of backs to keep their jobs – had all been solely for my infant benefit.

From the false-hugging, emotionally-manipulating social workers to the of-course-I-have-room-for-another-needy-child money-making fosterers, I learnt early on not to trust officialdom.

In that Taunton house-share they had known me only by my first names, the name that I had given them. Colin I think it was.

When I got up to Ben, I told him that my name was Ollie, short for Oliver. Ben gave that passing attention, had been more interested in the electric bike that I had brought up the brick path to the front door.

"Can you go up hills on it? Without pedalling?"

"Sailed up here."

He had taken hold of the bike, was giving the wheels, its battery, a sceptical scrutiny.

"Give it a go," I said. "While I have a look through the caravan. If I may?"

"Round the back. Door's open. You sure?" he said as he began wheeling the bike back along the path to the road.

Hidden behind the house the caravan was gloomy inside due to the trees growing out above and the two storey house directly in front. Smelled fusty too from being closed up. I wouldn't be able to do much about the gloom, but a thorough clean and providing old Ben didn't want too much...

I needn't have worried about the last. Ben came back excited about the bike, "So easy," and wanting to know how the battery was removed, charged. I asked how much rent he wanted for the caravan. He didn't know, asked how much I thought. Thinking that he'd go higher I added half again to what I was paying for a single room in a shared house.

"Sounds fair," Ben said. He was wheeling my bike back and forwards along the path, testing the front brakes, the back.

"Cash OK?" I asked. "Month in advance?" I counted the twenties into his hand not holding the bike.

"This'll take care of my shopping," he laughed. And Ben's laugh, I have to tell you, was a strange thing. It was a kind of hissing laugh, one I came to know well. His thin body would kind of rock with the laugh and dribble would come out through a two-tooth gap in the side of his mouth. So while he was laughing he'd have to wipe away the dribble with the back of his wrist.

"Come on," Ben said. "I'll show you where I keep my bike. Not electric."

Ben leant my bike against the house wall and led me up around the back of the caravan to a wooden lean-to. In the lean-to was a road bike and a narrow two-wheeled trailer. The trailer could be attached to any bike by a compression clip on the saddle stem.

"You do your shopping with this?" I hadn't seen a car.

"Bit of a struggle with a full load. Tins'n stuff. Have to push it up the hills."

"Borrow my electric."

"Really?"

"Sure."

And that is how I came to live in the caravan behind old Ben's house. He gave me a key, I arranged a meet-up with David, and a couple of days later we collected my few belongings from the house-share, more from the lock-up.

I had found for the moment, always for the moment, my ideal home.

Supplementary [recorded/transcribed]

Mentor: Is this Care you talk of an oxymoron?

O/V: Dunno. What's an oxymoron?

Mentor: The dictionary defines oxymoron as a word or expression that means the opposite of what it purports to say.

O/V: Maybe. Yes and no. The system was set up, is meant to care for children. And we children were fed and housed. Not left to beg on the streets like in poor countries. But the care system, as it works, groups together children who have been, one way or another, denied parental love. And in care homes especially, if damaged themselves they can pass that damage onto other children. And they become easy targets for paedophiles and pimps. Fed, housed, clothed, yes. For the rest...

*

By the time I came to rent the caravan Hodges and I, along with David and a couple of others, had established a steady working relationship. As steady as any relationship can be in that cash economy.

We all of us preferred to be paid in cash and to pay in cash.

Say the police got a whisper of something going on some place, a house say. First thing they do is go online, see who the property belongs to, check the owners' bank account, their social media postings, company listings, criminal record, CCtv. If rent was paid in cash under an assumed name though, any police investigation stumbles to a halt right there.

I'd got to know Hodges over the years. And while to us he may have been Somerset's Mr Big – that end of Somerset anyway – he saw himself primarily as a businessman, not as a criminal. That self-perception was important to me. And Hodges did have legitimate businesses – a used furniture emporium, property portfolios and genuine investments. He paid tax [some] and contributed to local charities.

Crime as a career can become attractive to kids in care. Being in care children are unlikely to receive any formal qualifications. Recognisable qualifications that is. Because of the interrupted education – moved from a failed foster placement to a temporary hostel to another foster placement to a children's home – any education keeps going back to square one. Then the later, the final care establishment, will try to con them – adding to/deducting from their self-worth – with easy-to-pass grades from an unrecognisable exam board.

Most of those exam board exams were multiple choice and a piece of piss. Took less than half an hour. My thickest compadre took the whole two hours. And he'd been given covert help. We both ended up with the same 'qualification.'

Such a qualification wouldn't gain me entry to any well-paid profession. And without proper qualifications all I had was my street smarts. I didn't want to go on Benefit, have social workers looking out for me again. I needed to be shot of all that. What I wanted was to be able to look after myself. And with no career other than mac-jobs open to me crime looked to be the best option.

You have to understand that as soon as children in care reach puberty, not so much in foster homes but definitely in the larger care homes, then they get to be targeted by pimps and pushers.

And kids in care, often self-defensively, and way before they have committed any sort of crime, act as if they are criminals, or as what the screens have told them criminals act like. They do have actual role models, the pimps and pushers who hang about care homes. In one of my homes, they hung about in a nearby lay-by. In another they kept house in a local house.

Any of that type – tattooed, coarse, bullying – I walked away from. Some had cars that were made to look like gangster cars. Painted black they had flame stickers or extra coloured lights. Their clothes, their facial tattoos, all said loud and clear that they were criminals, that they wanted to be seen as criminals. Country boy gangsters with no real gang, more bling and tattoos than brain cells. The type who only knew how to steal and break stuff.

And they thought to impress and recruit such as we? They even boasted of jail time. I wanted to be out of care, not repeat it as jail time.

Some of those pretend crims, criminals, had massive dogs with spiked collars. To show how hard they were? And that they, the owners, were hardened criminals?

Any such who self-advertised in the city I was even more careful of. They could be recruiting for actual gangs. Where I, knowing no different, could be knifed by another gang just for being in the wrong place. Possibly even not actual gang members, as likely fulfilling some fantasy of their own. Either way best avoided.

If someone who didn't look like a crim though happened to say, "Like to earn a little something? No problems, cash in hand. Careful lad like you..."

"Doing what?" I'd say, but knew what, knew I'd be county lines carrying. Children's homes are county line recruiting agencies.

This is how recruitment went for me. Each time. Usually, it was with a co-worker around the place – handyman, cook, cleaner. Or friend, come to collect.

"Help out a friend of mine?"

"Doing what?"

"Not asking questions."

"Cash upfront?"

"Some."

A meeting place would be arranged, I'd be given a backpack and a package, told which bus or coach or train to catch, where to go from the station or coach stop. Where someone called Peter or Paul or Pat would relieve me of backpack and package, hand me my return fare.

I got into the habit – the first time a long wait for my return coach – of having a look around the town or city. Once or twice the local countryside. And I never once got caught, even stopped and questioned. Not being local anywhere I had no-one to proclaim my criminal status to.

I came to be trusted. By the intermediaries if not yet by Hodges. Not that I was by any measure complacent. In that world, unless you are particularly deluded, you expect to get caught. I'd already worked too often with fools, had had to depend on the sometimes foolish. I myself would have been a fool not to expect to get caught.

Understand that I had no family to fall back on, and I had learned early not to trust officialdom. I had to use what talents, what knowledge I had to survive.

At that time I got called Buzz. Not because I was always busy, I was, but due to my having hair like a guardsman's busby. As time went on I decided that the hair made me too identifiable; and once I'd got the bike that much hair was a squash under the helmet. Now that I'm here, no bike, no helmet, I'm thinking of letting it grow again.

Mind you I was pretty much at ease back there in the cash economy. Had its problems of course. Given the nature of my work I couldn't have an easily traceable, trackable iPhone. Or any vehicle with a registration plate. The reason for the e-bikes.

If somewhere was under surveillance police cameras might spot me on my bike, but with no numberplate and with my helmet on I was not so readily identifiable. Of course, I knew that if the police were really determined then their technology, their bureaucracy could find me. Eventually. The cash economy just made it harder.

Using the Oliver name David did later on get me an online bank account, and that meant that I could get an iPhone. Also later. Plus a debit card. But both are so easily traced that my first choice, especially when getting paid, was always cash.

David, I remember now, called himself a company director. He even posted annual accounts, paid tax. He saw himself as Hodges' progeny. They both, with a smile, referred to themselves as businessmen. David's recurrent complaint about Hodges was that he did so enjoy the riskier ends of making money. He used to shake his head over Hodges getting bored with a job/enterprise, inventing a risk and querying the game.

For David and I it was all about, and only about, the money.

When I had first met Ben and moved into the caravan, I hadn't reached the stage where I had built up funds enough to be able to masquerade as a businessman. But one of the first things I did when I moved into the hidden caravan was to ask Ben if I could log in to his router. I offered to pay extra on my rent so I didn't have the bother of setting up my own router.

"See if it works first," Ben had said. He had doubts about receptivity within the caravan. The router did work, intermittently but enough, putting me in contact under any name I wished in the big wide world.

I had a basic mobile, gave its number to only those who needed it. And I had what I called my lock-up. Which wasn't actually mine. Became mine, sort of, when one of my old foster mums had split up with her mechanic partner.

Theirs had been a strange, a strained relationship. Both were women, but the mechanic, the one who left, hadn't seemed to do much at home other than snarl at us children and bark at our foster mum. In the lock-up she had done mostly bodywork repairs, smelled of acetone.

I took over the lock-up, paid rent to my ex-foster mum – cash, with a tidy extra for her trouble – and she paid the council. It meant that if my comings and goings to the lock-up were being watched and they checked back with the council to see who I was my name wouldn't be found. I had kept my two bikes there on charge, and later on stacks of my clip-build. I had the only key.

Back then I did everything I could to be untraceable. Not so easy these days when online forms require an address, a post code verification. Although it's mostly a covering-of-backs bureaucratic formality, doesn't mean anything. What I do is give a genuine but old address. Like the Taunton shared house. Any ex-roomy mail they get there they bin.

I'm assuming intermediaries reported back my quiet reliability to Hodges, and I was gradually given more work. So far I had only physically met Hodges a couple of times. And that hadn't been in his office. Although I had checked his offices out. We met in car parks. Once I had to wait for him at a bus stop.

Aside from those in-car meetings, communication was all done by text or voice mail. 'Your expertise reqd. Call.'

Supplementary [recorded/transcribed]

Mentor: What are county lines?

O/V: The division between one county and another, Somerset and Devon, Somerset and Dorset. Each county has its own police force. We children were paid, some coerced, to take goods from one police force area to another. Communication between police forces was not that good. Say one police force started cracking down on one brand of our goods, then we'd shift promotion of the goods to another supply chain, another county, another force.

Mentor: These so-called criminals who target children? You make them sound grotesque.

O/V: They were. They are. What breed of moron wants to show off to children? As you are aware I have known real criminals, killers even, enforcers. Those who hang around care homes and show off to children are no more than malicious clowns. If not themselves paedophiles pretending, a double pretence, to be criminals.

*

My sex life?

Not much to tell. Not really.

Way before I'd moved to Ben's caravan I'd had a steady girlfriend. We'd both been in care, had briefly been together in one placement.

That foster home had had a donkey. I think we children had been supposed to bond with it. And that was what Jane and I laughed about when we met later. At a mutual friend's barbecue.

We recognised one another, talked of that one very sad donkey. And how weird it was that we abandoned children had been expected to identify with a beaten-down donkey covered in flies. It was Jane reminded me of its long lashes blinking away the flies.

I say steady girlfriend, but it was a bit more than our going on dates. Jane and I lived together for a while. Which sounds like we set up house. We didn't. Jane had a one bedroom flat in a social housing block, all red brick and concrete steps in Taunton's Priorswood. The flat was in her name, and I sort of moved in with her.

We got on well together. Didn't have to explain ourselves to one another.

Didn't last though.

Jane wanted an ordinary, a normal existence. Steady job, steady man.

She was working in an old people's home, had a bank account, a driving licence, a flat in her own name. And there was me in the cash economy not knowing from one week to the next where I'd be working or how much I'd be getting paid.

Jane and I effectively ended when I had a close call over a delivery I was supposed to have made. The man I was supposed to meet didn't turn up, left me holding. I'd been standing around the bus station so long, people coming and going, that I got to feel I was being watched. So I dumped the package in a locker there and came home. Back to Jane's flat that is.

There were lots of frantic phone calls. Some threatening, about where the goods had got to. And this despite their knowing that their own guy had crashed his car on the way to the meet. Nature of our uninsurable trade though was to suspect a set-up.

All ended with me asking for another meet, somewhere near, where I could hand over the locker key. Which I did while outwardly browsing in an antique shop down East Street. No-one compromised.

Had been a sweaty couple of days though; and it had been the many phone calls and texts coming at me that decided Jane that I was not a fit candidate for long term domesticity.

After Jane?

Took a while to get established, but up to and including the caravan I had a couple of occasional girlfriends. One in Exeter and one in Bridgwater. When I felt the sexual need, my body telling me it was time, I'd call one or other, fix a date and catch the train.

I'd tell Ben that I'd be away for a couple of days. Which I often had to be for work. Maybe though I took more care over my appearance for my sex trips. Because when I got back from them Ben nearly always smiled and said that I looked '...refreshed from my break.'

Supplementary [recorded/transcribed]

Mentor: You earlier said that you and Ben became close. Was yours a homosexual relationship?

O/V: Not at all. I wasn't, I'm not a homosexual. And from what Ben told me I'm pretty sure he wasn't either. As you will have gathered from *Futuricity* Ben had difficult, unfulfilling relationships with women. I think though it's safe to say that Ben was neither misogynistic nor homosexual. I became close to old Ben because I liked him as a person. And he me I think. There was a large age difference. And definitely no sexual attraction. Either way.

*

So many beginnings. The most important I guess was Ben breaking his legs.

He'd put a ladder up against the front of the house to fix some wires. The idea was to train some honeysuckle and jasmine around the doorway. My guess is that Ben, having tied off the last wire, got overconfident, came down the ladder too quickly, missed his footing on one of the rungs along with his grip on the ladder sides, one leg went through the ladder and...

I have seen violent incidents, bodies having the breath kicked out of them, those awful grunts. But I have never heard anyone howl in pain as Ben did.

I was out the back of the house, inside the caravan. Luckily, I had the windows open and no radio on. At first, I thought it was an animal, or a long tyre screech. But it went on and on. Then I made out a Help in amongst the howl and realised that it must be, could only be Ben.

Hurrying around the side of the house I found Ben dangling upside down from the ladder. His head and shoulders were on the ground, squashing a big peony. Ben was particularly proud of that red peony.

Actually, there wasn't a day when Ben wasn't doing something in his garden. Both sides of the path were a deliberate mix of flowers and vegetables. Hard to tell what was what sometimes. The beans climbing up their poles were obviously vegetables. But he had purple cabbages next to orange marigolds, big yellow flowers on courgettes...

I stepped carefully though the flowers to him. His legs were an unnatural tangle and his face was a sort of bloated beetroot with pumped up blue veins. His eyes were squeezed shut.

199

"I'll call an ambulance Ben," I told him as I dialled. "Don't want to make matters worse by moving you."

"Fucking move me!" Ben screamed. "Move me!"

Tucking the phone between my shoulder and ear I told the voice that I needed an ambulance.

"Please move me!" Ben screeched. "Move me!"

I put an arm under his legs this side of the ladder and, with him still screaming, I lifted his legs clear of the ladder. Then I skewed his shoulders around so that I could drag him over to the brick path and lay him flat.

The fearsome upside-down purple that his face had been now went a chalky grey. He had stopped howling though, panted more than breathed.

My phone had slipped to the ground, had been live while I had been moving him. Emergency control now said that they'd got my GPS and could I confirm the address? An ambulance would be with me very soon.

And it was. The two paramedics gave Ben morphine before trying to move him. Ben told me where his house keys were and to lock up.

I wasn't too happy with the emergency services, officialdom, having my phone's GPS. Had been about time though that I switched phones again. Can never, unlike Ben on a ladder, be too careful.

I took a change of underclothes into hospital, a towel dressing gown and his house keys. He'd managed to break both his legs and to crack his pelvis.

"Couldn't find any pyjamas," I told him. His scrawny chest and a few white hairs poked out above the bed covers.

"Never wear any," he sort of leered at me. Said, "I'm on a load of painkillers," and he drifted off.

Long and short was I visited Ben most days while he was in hospital. He trusted me with his house keys, asked me to fetch him this and that, change of clothes, phone charger, books, laptop. At home Ben had spent wet days typing. "Used to be a reporter," he'd told me. "My hunger to know matched only by my need to tell." He hadn't told me what he'd been typing.

One day, when he'd been a couple weeks in hospital, he asked me to hang on until his consultant came. Ben told me afterwards that he was Iranian, the kind who always look unshaven. The consultant asked me if I would look after Ben on his discharge. Ben had described me as his next door neighbour.

I agreed, but it was still a couple more weeks before Ben got discharged. He had to be able to get about on crutches.

By the time he was delivered back to the house I had rescued what I could of the peony, and I had taken apart his double bed and had reassembled it in his living room. It was a squeeze with the sofa being there but, having the downstairs lavatory, Ben declared himself able to manage.

For the rest of that summer, he lived downstairs. I did his shopping for him, fetched books from the shelves upstairs, some clothes; and on fine days I let him instruct me in the art of weeding.

Long and short of it was that summer our relationship became more than tenant and landlord. Although friendly enough any conversations we'd had up to that point had been about the weather or the bikes, maybe me asking to borrow the trailer. Or if he had come upon me sitting on the caravan steps he had asked – again! – "Cats come back?"

"Not seen them," I'd say.

"Must've found someone else daft enough to feed them," would be his standard response and off he would have doddered.

Other than that, the many things Ben had previously said in my hearing I had often felt that he hadn't actually been talking to me, that he'd had someone else in mind, a response from me hadn't been required.

For the rest of that summer, if I had a job that took me

away, I made sure that his phone was fully charged and his fridge and freezer were packed. That period it was that forged our friendship, built trust.

When he and his physiotherapist decided that Ben could manage the stairs I reassembled his bed upstairs. Much to Ben's relief. The living room, with its floor of bricks designed to keep its warmth, had proved an uncomfortable sleeping venue.

Indoors and out Ben thereafter had to rely on at least one stick, even to get out and along the garden path. That was when he asked me to help him to bring his shed indoors.

*

One look told me that the shed wouldn't fit through the front or through the back door of the house. I said as much to Ben as we stood together by the bike lean-to looking up at the shed.

"You sure?" Ben said, leaning sideways on his stick.

"No need to measure it. Can see from here it's too wide, too deep to go through."

Ben wasn't a quick thinker. I waited for him to decide. He didn't. When I suggested moving the shed instead to the blind side of the house, thinking that all he wanted was easier access to it, he shook his head.

"Why do you want the shed indoors?" I asked him.

He moved awkwardly, not wanting to tell me. This was autumn, the oak leafs a curling brown, one or two slowly falling near us.

"What do you keep in there?"

There was no padlock on the door. I realised that I had never seen him go to the shed.

"You not looked?" he asked me.

"No. Got my bike here. Your trailer too. Why would I?"

"Curiosity?"

"I'm no nosy-parker newsman." I gave him my no-offence-meant smile.

Ben had told me, often, what he used to do for a living. This day though Ben didn't want to play at even pretend good-natured banter. He remained silent.

"What I assumed," I said, "was that the shed was for more of your gardening tools." The tools that he regularly used, or had me fetch, were in a plastic chest on the blind side of the house.

He was moving awkwardly again.

"You OK?" I didn't want him falling over there, back of the caravan, with my then having to drag him all the way around to the house.

"Nothing in the shed," he blurted out. "Well, nothing's kept there. It's a Faraday Cage."

Which had me ask, my education not having amounted to much, what a Faraday Cage was.

Ben explained, all the while shifting about on his walking stick.

Since his falling off the ladder, so much of our time spent together, Ben liked to tell me of things, of books mostly, and of those books mostly science fiction. When I had read the last one he had pressed on me, he would ask me what I had thought of it and, depending on my answer, press on me another.

Up until the caravan I hadn't read many books. I'd had a few foster parents, mothers mostly, who had pressed books on me. But with them there had always seemed a college snobbery attached: "You must read this." And even if there was nothing superior said I had just known, childhood intuition, that among their own kind, as there had been with my house-share lot, sooner or later it'd be all Nah Nah Nah, didn't know that didcha?

Ben wasn't like any of them. When he handed me a book

he'd say, "Loved this. You might." And I didn't have to. Some I didn't. And I'd tell Ben I didn't. "Not for everyone I suppose," he'd say. "Pity. Try this..." If I liked a book he might quiz me on it, find out what it was that I had liked about it. Might've been a character, or a neat idea which had appealed. That would send Ben off to find another like it.

I told him that I really liked a Brian Aldiss book. In it Aldiss had said, '...prisons were filled by the products of poverty, unemployment, underprivilege and depression. The politicians were locking up the victims of sociopolitical crimes.' Aldiss had been telling there of so many people I had known, if only of their parents, hopeless cases.

As to other earnest authors: I have always known how small we each are, hadn't needed a book to tell me.

I read Ben's own books, both the crime series and some of his SF. They were all OK, but I came by the feeling that they had all been trying to be by somebody else.

"Why do you need a Faraday Cage?" I asked. The caravan could serve as one. He knew that my phone reception within the caravan was poor to non-existent, was why he had told me that the steps were the best place to take and make calls. And maybe the steps had been before the house got built slap bang in front of them. Dry days, calls I had to make, so I didn't get overheard I usually took a stroll up the road.

I caught Ben, in his discomfort, keep glancing at me.

"If all you want is a Faraday Cage indoors," I said, "I can knock you one up in a couple of hours. Internal construction being one of my employable skills."

"Truth is," Ben said, "I don't see why I shouldn't tell you. You did save my life. And they've all told someone else. Wives, partners. You're the closest I've got to a partner."

"Steady." I smiled.

"Yea, well." Now he was embarrassed. "Nothing like that. But no-one else near me. So why shouldn't I tell you?"

"Tell me what?"

"Go up and have a look."

I took the three steps up to the shed, pulled open the door and looked at the copper mesh on the inside of the door, the floor, ceiling and the sides.

"Could you take all that mesh off," Ben asked, "and attach it to your 'internal construction'?"

"Might rip it a bit taking it off. But yea, readily done."

"OK," Ben said. "My leg's aching. Let's go back to the house. You can make us a coffee and I'll tell all."

Ben's 'tell all' included cage travels into space and into the future. I didn't know what to believe. But so far as I was aware Ben had always told me the truth. My scepticism however must have shown and Ben got all old-man-shirty, said he'd show me.

Hobbling over to his laptop he sent me a PDF of his 'memoir.' The 'memoir' was what he had told me he had been working on when I had sometimes come across him typing. Thus my introduction to *Futuricity.*

I had already met Glynis and Julian when they and their toddler had visited. Back then Ben had introduced them as his 'old friends,' had told me afterwards of the 'arrangement' he had with Glynis; how she had built the house, he lived rent free, and how on his death it would belong to Glynis.

That had explained Ben's odd attitude to the house, his proudly showing me aspects of its design followed by a mouth-twist grimace of dissatisfaction. And when I had later on chatted to Ben about the deal with Glynis whereby the house had come to get built, his relationship with Glynis and Julian, and I said to be careful they don't bump you off, Ben had said, "That says more about you than either of them." And Ben had a way of saying such things, things that he thought might be taken as insulting, with a soft look and a sideways smile.

On the day of that first visit – while Ben and tubby Julian had been indoors talking – Glynis and her toddler had come wandering around the back of the house. Seeing me at the caravan's kitchen sink she had given me a wave, had signalled me to come to the door.

Glynis is a sharp woman, one of those who you almost instinctively do as told. Though on that day she was not telling me to do anything. To stop her toddler climbing up the steps and into the caravan she hoisted him onto her hip.

"Just wanted to thank you for all that you've done for Ben. It's so reassuring knowing that you're here to keep an eye on him."

"No problem. I like Ben."

"Looks to be mutual," she said. And that was it, aside from handing me one of her business cards: "In case anything else unfortunate befalls Ben."

"OK."

A simple exchange of words between two people, each trying to be smiling pleasant. Back then though, when she'd given me her card, I'd had no idea that this pleasant woman and her tubby hubby had been Ben's fellow space and time travellers.

Did I disbelieve Ben? Disbelieve is a big word. Bigger than believe. Disbelieving can cause offence. I had accepted what Ben had told me. Why would I choose to disbelieve him, make him out to be a liar?

In my life up to that point I had met many people, children even, with the strangest of stories. One boy had been kept in a cupboard, had had his food put in through a cat flap. He hadn't called it a cat flap, had said it was a little door in the door. He liked to sleep under my bed. During the day he would be an all-normal-runaround boy to our foster parents. Same too for bathtimes, a bedtime story, got tucked in and all that. Soon as the grown-ups were settled downstairs he'd come sneaking into my room and slide under my bed.

It was the foster mother first told me about the cupboard.

A foster sister, another place, told me of her father and

206

uncle who used to paint her. Literally paint her, head to toes, before getting her to do things to them. Some of the paint used to get in her eyes and sting. They filmed her, and it was that film being traced that got her put into care. She said that she missed her dad and uncle. Other than the painting she said that they had been kind to her, had let her have anything she wanted.

When I had first told Ben that I had been brought up in Care – this was before his fall – he had tried to say that my being in Care must have been pretty much the same as his having suffered private education.

"In *loco parentis*. Duty of care. Was all I'd hear from the house parent," Ben said. "Stop me doing what I wanted. Not that different."

"Very different." I was certain. "You had a home to go back to." Which had Ben stand erect and still. And after giving due consideration to my response he said, "You're probably right." Which sort of sums up how and why Ben and I got on so well together.

Wasn't a matter of whether I actually believed Ben had been in space or not. You could say I suppose that I indulged him. Whatever, I set to work making him a new cage.

In order to build the cage in his spare bedroom I first had to dismantle the single bed there and take the pieces across to the caravan's spare bedroom. Didn't then take much clip-build to knock up something slightly longer than his shed, a door at either end, partition down the middle. I did that at Ben's suggestion, so that he could take me into space. He referred me to his 'memoir', to the part where he had rescued Julian from Exmoor.

"What do you use these for?" Ben was watching me work. "In your job?"

"Various requirements." I'd had no other ready answer. I concentrated on the next section.

"Let me guess," Ben said. I knew from his voice that he was

smiling. "You make rooms within rooms. Don't forget I was a reporter, got taken along to more than a few indoor horticultural enterprises."

I said nothing, continued pressing clip into clip. Although I didn't look up I knew that Ben was giving me one of his long looks.

"Fair enough," he said after my determined silence. "Just so you know you can trust me. I can keep secrets. Never told anyone this," he said, about to tell me a secret, "but I had a pen with me when I went to Venus. I dropped it. We take our gravity with us. To see what would happen I deliberately poked it down through a gap in the mesh. Under the shed door. Because of the clouds I couldn't see where the pen fell. Truth is I was a bit ashamed of having done it, still am. A silly impulse. It was a sort of vandalism: I'd corrupted, polluted Venus. Which is why I've never told the others."

I still didn't comment, concentrated on the build.

Ben had laid out his requirements for this new cage. I was to include on his side a shelf for the laptop and the gaming switch. My design contribution was to build a seat that went through both sides of the partition. The new cage being slightly larger than the shed we had had to order extra copper mesh.

"Looks the business," Ben said when I had cable-tied the last of the copper mesh in place. "I'll fetch the gubbins."

He went wobbling off: he didn't use his stick indoors, helped himself along with a hand against the wall. He came back awkwardly carrying laptop, gaming switch and carbon fibre. As I helped him place them in the cage he swore me again to secrecy. As you are aware that is an oath that I have here of necessity broken.

"This is better," he sat on the bench seat that I had running through both compartments. "Bites into my old bones though. Can you fetch a cushion?" He pointed to his window seat. "Get one for yourself!"

At that point it had all felt like a game. One of those pretend games you play as children. Where you place chairs together and make believe you're on a train. Or you sit one behind the other in a cardboard box and make believe you're in a canoe going down a river. So I got us the cushions, took mine around to my side of the cage, settled myself and watched Ben get his cushion satisfactorily under his near fleshless backside.

"Ready?" he said, fingers on the keyboard, and before I could say Yay or Nay, I was looking beyond the dark curve of planet Earth to the big white disc of the moon and the sun shining bright on the copper mesh, on the back of Ben's bald head.

With starlight all above me, sun warm on my back, I don't think I spoke for several minutes. Ben had been muttering to himself, partly to me, that this wasn't where he had meant us to be. He was scrolling though his laptop and apologising again: "Sorry Ollie. I'd meant to get us much closer."

"This is just fine Ben," I managed to say. "And we can go into the future too?"

"I'll take more care of that. I'm a little out of practice."

Supplementary [recorded/transcribed]

Mentor: I am confused. Your relationship with Ben? I take it from what you have said that Ben must have, from early on in your relationship, have suspected your involvement in criminal activities. Yet he remained your friend?

O/V: Why wouldn't he?

Mentor: He wasn't a criminal. Was he?

O/V: He wasn't. I don't know what you know of Britain now, but for years and years, from the Right Royals downwards the wealthy and the powerful have been ripping everyone else off. And they've been doing it for years. And not only have their many scams gone unpunished, they and their mates get made into Lords and Ladies. Ben knew that whatever I'd been doing – me, the bicycle-riding tenant in his caravan – I'd been doing just enough to get by.

*

Even though we made a couple more trips into space, Ben saying he was trying to get me closer to the moon, I think Ben regretted ever taking me up there. I got the feeling that he was trying to backtrack. When I suggested another trip he decided that it was all too dangerous, what with gamma radiation and suchlike, me being a young bloke, how it might affect my gametes. Whatever they were, are.

"OK then," I said. "How about a mini-trip into the future?"

"Much more complicated," Ben told me, but shifting away. "Have to get it right. Can't have us lost somewhere. Who'll know to come and get us?" From which I gathered that he hadn't told any of his friends about the cage I'd built him.

He gave in to my persuasion and we did the one-time trip together, like his own first trip, over to Barrow Mump.

When I'd lived in Huish Episcopi, bike and I had made a couple of dry rides out around the Mump. Sitting with Ben in the cage, up above the bridge and pub, grey stone ruin on top its little green hill, all looked the same to me. Big basket works up the road. Ben was adamant though that we were ten years ahead.

I watched a cyclist coming from Othery. He was in no great hurry; and I guessed, by his only occasional touch on the pedals, that his too was an electric bike. Taking his time, he was having a good look round. He didn't see us though twenty metres up above the bridge. Whether Ben had taken us to the future or not we had to be invisible.

I said to Ben, "Let's go a couple hundred years ahead. Or up to your New Neroche."

Ben said, "Truth is Ollie I'm so old and shaky. I'm terrified of leaving you somewhere."

Ben's chin was all a'quiver, and his hands on the laptop

210

were trembling; so I said, "Fair enough." Though I acted a little disappointed, but still as if I accepted his decision.

I didn't. Despite my seeming to be unconvinced by time travel that was the day that I decided to get together the stuff I'd need to build my own cage. One of my life rules has been to never pass up an opportunity; and always to have a back-up, a way out. And whatever the cage's potential it was definitely not an opportunity to be missed.

At that very moment I didn't know the cage's precise potential, inklings maybe; I just knew that the cage had to be worth something to someone.

Took me a while to get all the bits together. I already had clip-build to spare; and the copper mesh and the carbon fibre were easy enough to come by. I got them delivered to my PO Box.

Any time of the day I pretty much knew where Ben was in the house. If in the kitchen he'd have the radio on. Not always. When he switched it off he'd shout, "Enough of this shit!" But I'd still be able to hear the noises he made as he put dishes away, closed cabinet doors.

When I'd made sure that day that Ben was out front in the garden I crept in through the back door, up the stairs, and I copied down all the numbers and letters I could find on the gaming switch. The physical set-up in the cage was laptop↔gaming switch↔carbon fibre↔copper mesh. That was how I wrote it down, my tech skills being updated daily.

I found and ordered the gaming switch online. The grey laptop, being an old out-of-date model, turned out not to be so easy to get hold of.

I don't have real techie skills. So what I did was search out on e-Bay a laptop identical in make, model and colour to the one in Ben's cage. Once found, complete with charger, I had that also delivered to my PO Box. Which is not a box but a shop where they hold stuff. What with people being on short term rental contracts, not knowing where they're going to be living next, there are a lot of places running PO Boxes now. You're given a card and you bring it with you when you want to collect your stuff. No other ID was required in the shop I used.

Another day when Ben was otherwise engaged – garden again: some sunny days he took one of his kitchen chairs out and just sat there – I made sure that the new laptop had the same Biro scratches that Ben's had, and I swapped them over. So far as I was aware, and from what he had told me, Ben no longer used the cage much. I left my new laptop to occupy the cage shelf.

I took Ben's laptop to one of Hodge's techies. He had cleaned a couple of phones for me early days.

He was a tall crouching man called... Let's say Tim. I told Tim to copy everything off Ben's laptop, to keep the copy and I'd bring another laptop to put it all on.

"OK," he said. "You gonna wait now?" I had thought the copying would take an age. I had nowhere else I needed to be, so I waited.

Tim had a small workshop in a row of workshops. One of the other workshops was a florist delivery service, buckets of flowers outside; another a bike repair shop. Tim crouched over his counter facing out. I sank into the sofa that backed onto the window.

"Busy?" Tim asked me.

"Yes and no," I said."

"Same here," Tim said.

For a man who craved company Tim was no conversationalist. But while the laptop's software was being copied I helped Tim out by asking if I brought in another laptop could he strip out the *Windows* and copy into that what he had just taken off, making sure the clock was still working?

"In the new one?"

"Yea."

"Might take longer." Tim screwed up his face, "A day no more."

Once back home, while Ben was busy in his kitchen, I called out to him that I wanted a book to read, "...that one about the Triffids," which I knew was on the shelf under his window seat; and I sneaked his laptop upstairs and took back my new one. Swap made I shouted a Thank You as I left the house and went over to the caravan.

Tim actually took two days cleaning out *Windows* from my laptop before loading up the stuff he'd taken from Ben's. And while Tim had been doing that I had built my own single person cage in the lock-up. With the laptop collected all that I had to do to make it operational was work out what went where in the data block according to the few instructions in Ben's *Futuricity*, and from what Ben had left on his laptop now copied onto mine.

I like to think that I was born careful. And I figured that so long as I stayed secure within the cage, even if I got the calculations wrong, so long as I was still in the cage I'd return to the lock-up.

I made a study of the data block that had taken Ben and I, allegedly, ten years forward in time to Barrow Mump. Then I went back and skipped through the copy of *Futuricity* that Ben had given me.

I identified, with hints provided by *Futuricity,* what had to be the ten-year time section in the block. Also easy to confirm were the co-ordinates for the destination. Took a while longer to figure out elevation's place in the block; and because we had gone straight across to Barrow Mump from upstairs in the house I had no idea how the Futurists had done the jumping from beacon to beacon.

For my own peace of mind/confidence my aim was to take the cage two millennia ahead to the New Neroche. If it really was there, had to be no arguing with future travel. Especially when, to make sure that it was in the future, I intended cycling up into the Blackdowns and seeing if the New Neroche had/will have replaced the Trickey Warren listening post.

Not being wholly sure what was elevation in the block, when I did by hit-and-miss finally manage to get two millennia up and over the Blackdowns I was miles too high. I could make out something in the green-cushioned woodland way below that could have been New Neroche. But not really, a possible rectangle within that dense tree cover, and within that possible rectangle some possibly squared-off sections.

I don't know why old Ben would have wanted to fool me, but my suspicion was that something like New Neroche might already exist, a hippy or a traveller camp say, and that like Barrow Mump I might not have been travelling forward in time at all.

Wind rattling the lock-up's tin door I sat at my work bench going top to bottom over the dense block of numbers and symbols – an asterisk, a backward slash, a colon, a forwards arrow... Such a jumble. I looked to a gust banging the door and when I looked back to the block saw the group of numbers that had taken me up above the Blackdowns but which were not the ones that I thought I had used. If they were the numbers though then from them I would be able, divided by a slash, to go from beacon to beacon.

"Just lay the trail," I excitedly told myself. "Lay the trail. Give it a try."

From my lock-up each stage would have to take me higher and higher so that I would be at approximately the same height as Trickey Warren. My guessing co-ordinates and elevations was no good.

Recalling Ben's stack of OS maps this need for accuracy had me bike into town, where I bought the OS map for Taunton and surrounds along with the two maps to the north and to the south. I also picked up a maths set in a tin which included a short plastic ruler, protractor, set square, compass and divider.

Maths was the one school lesson I had enjoyed. No arguing with it. Except that with my every foster move the lesson each time had gone back to basic numeracy.

"Know all that," I'd tell the new teacher. "Test me."

A lot of those teachers had been supply teachers, part-time tutors, semi-retired, on maternity leave. Some had known less maths than me. One though, a strange woman, never once smiled nor tried to ingratiate herself. She just said 'Good' a lot. I think she may have had illnesses, was on disability benefit and was tutoring on the side for a bit extra. Her greying hair tied back she hadn't been at all feminine or motherly. What she did though was take me way past trigonometry.

Back in my lock-up, map spread out over the bench, new protractor in hand, I smiled recalling her lessons. She hadn't been at all strict. She'd just present me with something, "Think you can do this?"

I'd do it.

"Good. Try this." And she'd show me how if I got stuck or went wrong.

With her remembered help I managed to work out how to get, forward-millennial-wise, from low down Taunton up to Willet's Tower and back across the Deane to just above the New Neroche.

Those millennia ahead the New Neroche was as described by Ben – name on the cross trunk, thorn hedges; and inside people walking between or at work on some of the vegetable beds.

Inbuilt uncertainties in my upbringing had taught me to consider, as a matter of course, all eventualities. So, using the same map, folded wrong, I then took the fully charged bike up the hills and along to the wire fences, tall gantries, hanging cables and bare grass of Trickey Warren. All was as Ben had said: no psycho-trickery involved. Not that my caution had truly expected any. I could for instance have more easily checked by going in my cage and repeating the visit using present day settings. But I had wanted to be objectively, absolutely certain, beyond the cage's influence.

With the bike and I back in the lock-up, helmet off, cheeks tingling from the mad flight down the hills, I had one more cage-testing trip to make, out to Taunton racecourse.

Mid-afternoon I hung out, unseen, alongside the main yellow building. No races that day. The car park though had quite a few more cars than would be needed just for staff. The long second storey room of the main building looked to have a bar at the back. Although, going by the way heads were pointed, this afternoon had to be some sort of meeting. Then I noticed the screen at the far end, someone standing before what could have been a power point presentation.

Turning away from the building I looked out over the white rails and the rough grass track. That afternoon I was so very fond of Old Ben.

Supplementary [recorded/transcribed]

Mentor: A common reaction to space travel has been for individuals to have brought home to them their insignificance. You barely mentioned it.

O/V: Had no need of a trip into space, or way into the future, to tell me I'm insignificant. I was raised in Care. Decisions were made about me without me. I was consulted of course, that box had to be ticked, but only after the decisions had been made. They then asked me how I felt about them. Didn't matter how I felt: I was told what would be happening to me, where I'd be going next. I was nothing of significance already, a parcel to be packed off somewhere else for someone else to make decisions on my behalf.

Mentor: Did Ben publish *Futuricity*? We can't find record of it anywhere.

O/V: Don't think Ben ever got it into actual book form. He wasn't sure his friends would want him to publish. Ben thought – so he told me – that if he presented *Futuricity* as a bestselling

216

fait accompli his friends might be reconciled to it. So he tried to get himself a new agent. Apparently he needed an agent in order to get a publisher. Ben said he then spent a year cursing agents because, he said, all they looked at was his age. They, the agents, wanted someone young, someone they could develop. After that year of trying, so far as I was aware, Ben gave up.

*

When I opened the caravan door that morning I didn't know that Ben had died. I did though come by the feeling that something was wrong.

As usual first thing I had pushed the caravan door open wide – to encourage some air through. Being between the back of the house and under the trees the caravan rarely got a decent ventilating blast. Interior could feel over-breathed.

Almost without being aware that I was doing it I listened for activity in the house. Wasn't so much that I kept an eye out for Ben as on him. We knew too much of one another. His welfare was my own.

That time of day Ben was usually in the kitchen, the radio on. Or not. But even if Ben had, as was his wont, shouted at the radio, "Enough of this shit!" and switched it off, I'd still have been able to hear him moving between sink and chair. Through the glass of the back door his movements too would have subtly changed the reflected light. Or there would have been the clatter of a dish, bang of a cupboard door being closed.

And if Ben had hobbled back upstairs, was sitting on the lavatory even, I'd still be able to hear a cough or a grunt. Or Ben would have been as usual muttering to himself, swearing at his 'aches and crakes.' "Fuck's sake," accompanying many a twist and turn.

The stillness in the house had me leave the caravan door

ajar and pick up Ben's house keys. My one hope that moment was that Ben hadn't left the keys in the locks on his side.

We'd had scares before where Ben had locked up at night and had left the keys in the locks on his side. That quiet time, my key having failed to turn the locks front and back, I'd had to go around the outside of the house, hand to glass, looking in. Through the big south window, I had seen him collapsed half-on half-off the sofa. I had to bang on the glass to wake him up. He had that time, "Sat down for a mo," and had simply nodded off in an awkward position.

This time, no inside key left in the door, I unlocked the back door and called out his name. Listened.

Ben wouldn't have been out, not without my knowing. He rarely went out. When he did he made big preparations, taxis booked to take him down to Wellington or to hospital in Taunton. Even if this time he had kept it secret from me, I had been there all the day before, and would have heard a taxi.

Ben was nowhere downstairs.

Still calling his name I went slowly up the stairs, found him face down on the floor part way out of the bedroom. A skinny old man, flat and still, grey, naked and dead.

From his position it looked like he had got up in the night for a pee. There was a dark damp patch on the rucked-up red rug either side of his hips. During the day his bad leg often gave way. That night he must have lost balance, stumbled and fallen.

Most evenings Ben went to bed early. If I'd been out and about, coming home I'd see the glow of his bedside lamp. The night before though I'd already been home, had heard nothing. My caravan bedroom window opened to the woods.

I stood looking down on the buttock hairs and rumpled skin for a few minutes. Then I pulled the duvet off the bed and covered him. Using his phone – it had been on charge on the bedside table – I called the emergency services, explained that I was Ben's carer and that I had found him dead.

Going downstairs I used the doormat to wedge open the front door. I had put up little hooks beside both doors for the keys to be hung on when Ben locked up at night. Had me sort of ruefully smiling to see that, with the doors locked, Ben had dutifully hung up both keys.

Going back through to the caravan I made myself some toast and orange juice. From the soft seating end of the caravan I could see around the side of the house to enough of the pulling-in bay to get sight of the yellow and white ambulance when it arrived. Waiting there I told myself that my time in the caravan was over. Almost over.

When the ambulance finally came, I went through the house and showed the green-uniformed man and woman up to the body, stood by and watched while they checked – thoroughly, machines and wires – for Ben's vital signs. That grey body though was no longer Ben, was definitely not Ben. Me telling myself that was when I had to consciously stop myself crying.

Next to arrive was a police car. Blocked the road. Out of the police car emerged an 'evidence gathering' Community Support Officer. She was tubby, wore plastic-rimmed glasses, and had as much grey hair as Ben. She kept saying, separately, to each of the ambulance crew and to me, that she was only there evidence gathering.

The ambulance crew told her that the death 'had the look of natural causes.' The Community Support Officer wrote that down, then stepped around the body taking photos on her phone. I had to give her my name. I told her Oliver Whatever, the one I had used with Ben. Seemed only right. The ambulance crew – given the go-ahead after she had phoned her Sergeant – wrapped the body in a blue blanket and strapped it to a red stretcher, carried the stretcher down the stairs, out the front door and wheeled it along the brick path.

The ambulance-woman came back to ask the CSO, still taking photos, to move her car. Fussing and apologising she left.

Standing in the front doorway I watched the police car reverse down the hill, the white and yellow ambulance make a difficult turn, and leave. When satisfied that the police car wasn't coming back I closed the front door and nipped through to the caravan to collect my tools, clattered back up the house stairs to the spare bedroom – I'd shut the door earlier: the photo-taking CSO hadn't gone in there – and fast as I could I set about dismantling what I had come to think of as my half of Ben's cage.

Ben had impressed on me that I wasn't to let any of his *Futuricity* colleagues know that he had taken me into space. Nor did I want any of them to now even suspect that I had copied the cage. They had to already know though that Ben had kept his cage. At that point I didn't think I had time enough to return all the bits to the shed, removing all speculation from myself. Taking a chance, I left it in this new half-form.

Taking the now spare clip-build bits and the spare copper mesh over to the caravan, I collected up Ben's dismantled single bed that I'd stored there, plus mattress. It took a couple more trips to return all of that up to the spare bedroom.

Having checked that all was complete, nothing obvious to connect me to the cage, using Ben's phone I called Julian.

He didn't respond. Ben had said that he rarely answered.

That last year Ben had often appeared petulant and peeved. He hadn't been able to find a publisher for *Futuricity* and had told me that he felt that his friends had somehow let him down. "Fuck 'em," he said; and he had looked sort of puzzled, as if he hadn't known why he felt that way.

I called owner-of-his-house Glynis.

"Ollie here," I said, "Ben's tenant. Afraid I've got some sad news..."

Supplementary [recorded/transcribed]

Mentor: I'm not clear about your name, your names. You said that you were known as Colin to your house-mates. Ollie to

Ben. Did you have an official name? On your birth certificate? The one your parents gave you?

O/V: I was a foundling.

Mentor: Even so you must have been named. A legal requirement.

O/V: I was. Not at first though. The local paper called me 'The Back Door Baby.' I'd been left in one of the hospital's service doorways. One without cameras. I couldn't though be officially named Back Door Baby. The cleaner who found me was called Vincent. I was looked after on Roberts Ward. So I was officially named Vincent Roberts, parents unknown.

Mentor: Did you ever try to trace your parents? Through DNA?

O/V: They hadn't wanted me. I was nothing to them. They were nothing to me.

Mentor: Now as a woman I naturally feel some concern for your mother. What might have become of her.

O/V: When I was thirteen, and I was an uncooperative pushing-back teenager, the head of that institution – felt to me that the Home was being run as a racket – but the Head told a member of staff to look into my pre-birth background. For their publicity I think, something they could maybe use as a distraction. And to keep me quiet.

Mentor: What did they find?

O/V: DNA didn't find anything. I said at the time I didn't see how it could as they had no-one in particular's DNA to measure it against. All it said was that I was a genetic mix of some Viking, European Caucasian and some West African.

Mentor: That it?

O/V: No. The member of staff got his teeth into it. I've got a faint memory of him having researched his own ancestry. Why he was so keen on it. What he went on to do with mine was research later issues of the local paper who'd called me The Back Door Baby. Reading between the lines of other news reports he thought that I might have been an accidental pregnancy within a religious cult. He also came across the results of the Name the Baby competition. The winner, which luckily for me came too late – hospital had already named me – was down to my having been born in August. The winner wanted to call me Augustus. I'd have become Gus. And, given those I lived among, Gusset more than likely.

Mentor: A religious cult?

O/V: The way it looked to him, from both the before and after local papers, was that my unmarried mother had been part of a strict religious community. She had an affair with an outsider, got raped maybe, but whatever the circs got made pregnant. The others in the community took the child from her and sneaked me into that hospital doorway.

Mentor: But why a religious cult? Why not just a young girl unable to look after you?

O/V: He found two young female suicides in the months after my birth. Both women had come from a cult. One was a Jehovah's Witness, the other a Plymouth Brethren.

Mentor: You never followed it up? Found out their names?

O/V: What would've been the point? Both were dead. Here I am. Call me whatever you like.

Mentor: Vincent? Vince? I don't think Ollie. That belongs to another time, another place.

O/V: OK.

*

No unseemly hurry, Glynis had assured me; but I knew that I had to move.

First though was Ben's funeral.

Glynis did most of the arranging from Ilfracombe, who to notify, what words to have on the stone. My being local I was asked to organise the flowers.

222

Bart and Rhean drove over from Wales, got introduced to me at the crem [crematorium]. Which was odd, my having known, from Ben's book, their imagined younger versions. What was even odder - given the construction of the cage in Ben's spare bedroom and with all four of them having to know how close Ben and I had become and that there had to be a chance I knew of their space and time travels – no mention was made of the cage.

There was only the five of us at the crem. Not anyone from the local paper even. Poor Ben.

By that time though I was no longer poor.

In my lock-up cage I had time-travelled ahead to the next Taunton meet, had hung there above the line of bookies' stands, checking the odds. That afternoon most of the favourites either won or came second. Only one outsider, 'Sod's Law,' came in first at twenty-to-one.

The next time, real time, that I'd been in Taunton town I had popped into the bookies and put a hundred quid, cash, on 'Sod's Law,' and another hundred on one of the also-rans in an earlier race. I hadn't wanted my win to look too obvious.

'Sod's Law' turned out for me to be aptly named. When I went to collect my winnings, just under a grand once tax had been deducted, I discovered that the bookies' maximum payout in cash was two hundred and fifty pounds, the remainder of my winnings to be collected in a banker's draft in a couple more days.

As I've said before I didn't then have a proper back account, only an online one. I took the banker's draft along to David.

Like Hodges, Company Director David liked to keep up a respectable front. He even had a couple of Limited Companies registered, kept accounts, paid some tax. I had told the betting shop not to put a name on the draft, asked David if he would cash it for me.

When he readily agreed I told him that there could be more.

"All banker's drafts?"

"Yea. They won't pay out cash above two fifty."

David knew where the cash had come from: "Insider knowledge?"

I shook my head: "Clairvoyance."

"Spread your bets," he said. "Dangerous territory this. And I'll only be able to cash a few. Banks're on the lookout for money laundering these days. You're going to have to come out of the shadows, get a High Street bank account for yourself."

That I didn't want. Survival up to that point had meant my, wherever possible, steering clear of officialdom. Cash was anonymous, was more or less untraceable. Nor did I want to have to follow, and get the wrong side of, officialdom's many petty rules.

I felt myself being pushed into the public gaze. Because it was also during this time that I was looking for somewhere new to live. Somewhere with reliable Wi-Fi. While I'd stayed on in the caravan, I'd okayed it with Glynis to keep the house electrics on to power up Ben's router.

Newbury was my next meeting. I'd bought a load more maps, was on the way to getting as big a stack as Ben's. In the lock-up I used the maps to go ahead a few days, found another outsider. And this time, in my own time, I placed a two hundred to win bet at a Bridgie bookies, part of a different betting shop company to the one I'd used in Taunton.

The day after the race I caught the train over to collect my winnings. In the bookies, before being given my two hundred and fifty pounds, I was told where to stand so that their cameras could get a good shot of me.

A week later David agreed to cash the banker's draft but was uneasy. As was I: being made to be videoed had me feeling all kinds of vulnerable.

And that was when, due to these betting shop visits, I remembered WeiShi.

WeiShi and I had been fostered together in a village outside Honiton. He had absconded twice from there, once back to

Plymouth, another time he'd been found in an Exeter betting shop, another in a Torquay amusement arcade.

On his being returned to the Honiton foster home I had asked why he gambled. Didn't he know that the machines were programmed to win? Betting shops too? The odds would always be against him and for the bookies.

WeiShi – he was taller than me, which was why he could, almost always, get away with the betting shop visits – said he knew all that, was basic maths. He reckoned that his gambling was only partly to do with hopes of a big win, said that it was more cultural. In the arcades, he said, you'll often see Chinese men and woman lined up on the one-arm bandits. They go there not expecting to win, he said, be happy if they come out in pocket. Mostly though, he said, for them it's a form of relaxation, meditation even.

I started trying to trace him – through others from Care who might have known him, WhatsApp groups, Social Media... It was the Honiton foster mother, retired, though who found an old address, which led me to his sister who gave me his number. A text and a call later had us arrange to meet up in Plymouth railway station.

WeiShi and I sat side by side on a curved metal bench in that charcoal-grey station. We didn't talk of the past. No point. I explained to him what I wanted.

I had come prepared, had gone to a future meet in Newton Abbot and had found an eighteen-to-one winner for later that week.

"Will cost you nothing." I gave WeiShi a hundred and fifty pounds, told him to put it all on 'Belly Boyo,' and I'd split the winnings fifty-fifty, but he had to pay me my half in cash.

'Belly Boyo' won by a head; and a week or so later I collected from my PO Box my half a grand, or thereabouts, in twenties and fifties folded in foil to fool the Royal Mail scanners and any felonious postmen or women. Us criminals guarding against crimes against us.

225

With that incentive I became a time traveller par excellence. I went ahead and around the nation's race tracks, from Redcar to Ascot, Epsom to Aintree; impressed myself with my growing time/navigation skills.

Looking back there was so much happening, being planned at around the same time that it's difficult now to bring a before-and-after order to the muddle. The plan, for instance, that WeiShi and I had agreed was that that I would text him the odds-against winners and he would pass that good news on to one or other of his Chinese relatives and/or other contacts scattered around the country. Not too many at once for a single horse: if they all started betting on that one horse it'd lower the odds.

The winnings being spread around, absorbed into shops and restaurants, we hoped to also avoid money-laundering suspicions. WeiShi's contacts took half the winnings, WeiShi and I a quarter each, my quarters arriving foil-wrapped in my PO Box.

Home at that point, at least after the funeral, had still been the caravan.

Texts from Glynis had told me not to worry about moving. A couple of times she'd asked me to show prospective tenants around the house, even though no-one had yet come to clear out all of Ben's furniture and belongings. Glynis had told me to take anything I wanted from the house.

I had pointed out to both lots of prospective tenants that if they took the house the caravan would most likely be removed. My telling them that had told me that it was me who had to move.

Straight after the crematorium though, pretending that I had business to attend to, I had gone to my lock-up. By the time bike and I got back to the caravan the four of them had gone. So too had Ben's clip-built cage. I wondered if it had been Bart and Rhean had bag-sied it. Although, according to Ben's *Futuricity*, my sturdy clip-built version would have been an improvement on either Bart's or Julian's cage.

Turned out that it wasn't the caravan put both pairs of prospective tenants off but the house having only two bedrooms and limited parking space. People who could afford the rent I supposed would be having guests to stay and big cars to park.

Like Ben I had only my bike, which could have made me the ideal tenant. Even though I now had more money than ever before I doubted that it would be enough, month on month, for me to rent the house. And did I really want to live in dead Ben's house? I did make myself seriously consider the possibility, went from room to room and in each tried to think what my life would be like there. And decided that my being there would be placing myself open to casual speculation.

With my newfound income I did think of moving permanently into a no-questions-asked hotel that I had used once or twice before. Living in the caravan though had got me used to the luxury of having more than one room, space enough to store stuff.

I got hold of David, told him that I needed to rent a proper house, but behind someone else's name.

"Cash I take it?" David gave me his salesman's smile. "Bit flush are we?"

"I just need somewhere not too obvious."

"See Hodges," David gave me the wink, "he's come by a block of flats in Bridgie."

*

I don't think I have ever felt so vulnerable as I did in Bridgwater. Could have been the contrast after all my years tucked away in the caravan, back of the house handing my monthly rent to Ben. The money had always seem to come as a surprise to him.

I still paid cash for the rent of my Bridgwater flat, but to do it I had to go into Taunton and up to Hodges' upfront office.

"Oh you again," the bustling about woman said every month. "One who pays cash." And she'd go off looking for the paperwork, not find it, search through her computer's folders, finally say, "Got it." And kind of tut at me for paying in slippery notes, which she now had to count, usually twice. My guess was that all the other tenants in my Bridgwater block paid by direct debit.

I felt exposed, noticed, up there in that office. I kept getting noticed too in the block of flats.

Although my flat was on the floor above a suite of offices, there were three more floors above mine and we shared the stairs. I had assumed that those living above would use the lift rather than the stairs. Except Bridgwater is flat, lends itself to getting about by e-bike and scooter. So the rather fit and well-off young people living up there, rather than wait for the slow lift, they came skipping down the stairs to the caged bike shack. In the bike shack each flat had its own dedicated charging point. Same for cars in the garage.

"State of art. For contemporary living," salesman David had assured me.

I had known, with all the money coming into my PO Box from the betting, that I had to somehow emerge from the shadow economy. What I was beginning to learn was that I hadn't yet got that right. I also made the mistake of turning up for my occasional Bridgwater date on my bike.

"Didn't know you were so local," she said. I usually stopped over at her place.

"Am now," I told her, not having had a credible lie prepared.

"Where are you?"

After the caravan's perpetual gloom, I had relished the flat's big windows and even larger rooms. And with Hodges not having stinted on the décor and furnishings, I made the mistake of taking her back to the flat to show it off.

Previously, after our restaurant meal, we had wandered back to her room in a shared house, where we'd had to be quiet. In the flat though she gave full rein to a night of enthusiastic sex. She even went twirling off naked to the bathroom, on her return struck a model pose, one arm straight up in the air, wrist bent. I'd never known her so unreservedly happy. Come the morning she enthused over the shower.

Didn't take a psychologist to see how attractive living there with me would be to her. I didn't call her again. Although she did come to the flats a couple of times. Door camera showed me it was her. I didn't answer, didn't let her in.

I was becoming less and less confident about all my recent choices, especially with my ability to remain out of officialdom's sight. Some shops, not having change, had difficulty taking notes. Buses and trains preferred apps to cash. Apps required a bank account. I felt that my now having money but not technology was driving me into a way of life that I didn't want.

At one despairing point I even considered moving back to my uncomplicated life in the caravan, rued the day that I had texted Glynis to let her know that I was leaving. According to Ben's memoir Glynis had lots of properties in and around Ilfracombe. I found myself wondering if, on the strength of my friendship with Ben, she would also be happy taking cash for rent. Sensibly though that thought I didn't pursue: Ilfracombe was too far away from everything I knew.

My Taunton lock-up was the only place where I did feel safe. It was from there that the cage and I went ahead to racecourses all over the country – Sandown, Chester, Wolverhampton, Aintree, Wincanton, Ascot, Goodwood, Chepstow, Cheltenham... I favoured races with jumps, reasoned that outsiders winning there, what with horses falling, would be less likely to attract suspicion.

I soon came to recognise each racecourse's bookies'

electronic boards. Those racecourse bookies always had two names, Billy This, David That, Archie Other, as if such first name familiarity created ready-built trust. The same false bonhomie as social workers with their Call-me-Mary, Call-me-Sal...

By this time, I had perfected my placement tweaking.

On my initial arrival at a new racecourse – was very handy most racecourses giving directions on how to get to them, some even including SatNav co-ordinates – I'd see whereabouts I needed to be to get a better view of the bookies' boards. If at first in the wrong place I'd send myself back to the lock-up, make the necessary adjustments to the data, and be back at the course within minutes.

The races over, the odds-against winners I sent off to WeiShi and he informed his countrywide team.

Secure as my lock-up excursions were, I welcomed a return to my normal, an indoor construction. Quite a large one, in some old chicken sheds near Steart, opposite the grey bulk of Hinkley Point power station. Wasn't pleasant working with the residual ammonia stink of chickenshit but was at the same time sort of reassuring that the chicken stink would go some way helping to mask the other notorious odour that we normally went to great lengths to quell.

Wasn't long after that job that Hodges asked to see me. Or rather he sent David. I was to meet up with Hodges on the Taunton-to-Minehead charity-run train. David gave me the printed ticket. I was to join at Bishops Lydeard.

"Hodges has booked a compartment to himself."

"Any idea what it's about?"

"None. Only that it's urgent. Can you get there OK?"

"Be easier for me to get on at Norton Fitzwarren."

"Has to be Bishops Lydeard."

I took a chance and, having made sure that the bike was fully charged, early in the morning I coasted up through

Enmore, pedalled up over the Quantocks, glimpsed a thin-legged deer and, holding tight to the handlebars, I flew down through Cothelstone and whirred along to Bishops Lydeard.

Invigorated, pleased with myself, paper ticket checked, I waited on the low down platform with a family of four. Before the wheezing train came to a halt I spotted Hodges. He wasn't in his normal attire. Looked to be a thin jacket and a blue t-shirt.

Not knowing what this meeting was in aid of, but curious why he should be dressed so different – usually it was a suit or, his jacket off, a white shirt – I found his compartment. When I'd got the sliding door closed he said, "Bookies have found your WeiShi. You're done. Permanently if you don't let them know how you did it. So tell me. And none of that clairvoyance shit."

*

As the train puffed and rattled along I told Hodges – in his day off disguise of cheap blue sports shirt, binoculars and backpack, red baseball cap on backwards – that I had found out how to go forward in time and that I had been to racecourses all over the country. When I am nervous and asked questions, I become very precise: "No-one could see me."

"You're hidden away?"

"No, invisible."

"You're invisible?" I nodded. "So why go all that way? To all those places? Why not the local bookies?"

I explained that the device I used couldn't go inside buildings or underground.

"So what is it?" Hodges asked.

No point lying to the likes of Hodges: practised in deception men like him have a nose for falsity.

"Know the clip-build? I made some into what's known as a

Faraday Cage. Once closed inside it I have gizmos that take me into the future."

"Invisibly?"

"Yes."

He had grasped its two most important elements. Didn't ask for further proof, the bookies' upset I supposed being proof enough. Hodges quizzed me some more on how I had come by the cage. I told him of the caravan, of old Ben and his three friends, their trips into space and to the distant future. By which time the train had chuff-chuffed and whistled into Minehead.

He and I joined the other trippers wandering out from the station. Most seemed to be making their way to the oriental canopies, rides and entertainments of Butlins holiday camp. Hodges and I found a little walk-through park with a lichen-crusted bench. Once settled on the bench, checking that we couldn't be overheard, Hodges continued his paternal questioning.

I don't mean to go on about what he was wearing but whenever I'd met him before or had seen him around his office, he had been either in a suit, or he'd taken his suit jacket off, had been easygoing in a smart white shirt. His hair going silver had always been carefully swept back. And here he was that overcast day, his cap crammed on backwards, sitting on a grotty park bench which, going by the cans thrown behind, was a hangout of daytime drinkers.

Hodges wanted to be certain that Ben's three friends didn't know that I had a cage.

"I left Ben's back there in the house. I'd copied all the gizmos way before he'd died. They have no idea I made him a double cage."

"A double?"

"Ben wanted to take me into space, show me the New Neroche place."

"Long term future's fucked you say?"

232

I nodded but knew that wasn't what interested him. I could see him considering other uses for the cage.

He went back over what I had told him: "You can't go inside buildings?" I shook my head.

"Pity. I'd been thinking of taking a step up from your bookies, and going for stocks and shares. Pretty penny to be made there."

He grimaced that notion away.

"When it's double," he said, "the other person is invisible as well?"

"Both of you." I told him of Ben having to rescue Julian from future Exmoor, invisible for all the days he had been stuck up there outside his cage.

Hodges looked at his successful businessman's Rolex, very much at odds with the blue sports shirt. A plastic Casio would have been more in keeping with his day's apparel. We are all though prone to oversights.

"Let's get back to the station." He stood.

We didn't talk again until seated in the carriage, a table between us and away from the other travellers, steam train enthusiasts. The return compartment had been taken over by a group of cheerfully loud pensioners.

"No more racecourses," Hodges quietly told me. "We can earn more with this than putting a few bookies' noses out of joint. First of all though what I'd like you to do is go forward, just a few weeks, and check out that Creech building."

I had put up internal rooms in a large corrugated shed that had once been part of a Creech smallholding. Or some such. The clip-built rooms inside had been in full production for several years. I had filled in on a few shifts. The shed was nicely tucked away among trees and houses off a narrow lane. A single concrete track led up to the shed, no-one to see who was coming or going.

Until lately, Hodges told me, when a new owner in one of

the houses next to the track, or the existing owner, had removed a tree and some of one hedge. A few times a man in the garden had appeared to be watching workers arriving or leaving. A police car had also been spotted going slowly along the lane, with no obvious purpose there.

"Could well be paranoia," Hodges said, "but can you go forward a few weeks, check out the place is still intact?" Better still, go forward week by week. If they do raid they'll leave crime scene tapes over the doors. And let me know. We can get everything moved out beforehand."

We didn't talk much after that. I watched wisps of steam going past the windows and listened to the trainspotters up the other end of the carriage telling one another what they'd seen where.

I had once asked old Ben, "If, as you say, your friend Julian is an inventor, why doesn't he go forward in time and snaffle some new tech, come back and invent it?"

"Most of that new tech," Ben had said, and this is after he'd taken me to Barrow Mump, "will be solid state, needs team input when being put together. Single man stuff is altogether different, add-on gadgets and gizmos, maybe some neat software. What Julian likes is the inventing itself. I also very much doubt, Julian being a man of principle, that he won't have even considered stealing someone else's patent."

That had been me told. Sitting now opposite a man prepared to consider everything.

"I'll have you check out other sites too," Hodges told me. "Forewarned as they say." And he smiled. Had me feel slightly peculiar, was the first time I'd seen serious businessman Hodges smile. And what else was there to do but try to smile back?

Although I had been amused by his disguise, I can't emphasise enough that I approved. I have only ever worked with crooks who haven't wanted to be seen as crooks. Operating outside of the law characters such as Hodges and I had no wish to be identified as lawless.

Before I got off at Bishops Lydeard he told me that he'd make up my losses from the bookies, not to come into the Taunton office anymore, my rent would be taken care of and that someone would be around to my flat with the other addresses that he wanted checked out. He also had in mind a big money earner for me. "This has so much potential. Don't know as yet for what exactly. Or who'll pay. But pay big they will."

Relief that the bookies weren't going to be sending their heavies after me was my overriding emotion as I got back onto my bike. Worries lifted I actually enjoyed my ride along to and up over the Quantocks. I wasn't aware then that I was about to enter the world of real villainy.

*

My having to go forward week by week to the same place turned out as expected to be tedious work. The only thing that changed about the shed under observation was the weather, the vegetation, and which vehicles were parked outside.

There would be the shed, the concrete drive, nosey-parker neighbour or not, worker's car, van or motorbike. I would go back to the lock-up, type in the numbers for a week ahead; and there was the shed door closed, motorbike covered in a polythene sheet, brick on the seat, neighbour nowhere to be seen.

Versions of that carried on right up to week eighteen. When a blue and white tape was looped across the drive, with more of the tape in a large X across the shed door. No car, no van, no motorbike.

I made a note of the date, texted it to the number Hodges had given me.

David appeared on my door screen that evening.

"Don't like this one bit," he said as soon as he was in the flat. "Told me it was all OK but," he took a sheet of folded paper out of his trouser pocket, "this feels very unsafe. Very unsafe."

I unfolded the paper, warm from having been in his pocket. I recognised some street addresses of houses used, names of other places. All of them probably first found by a hereby incriminated David.

"He said to point out on the map where the others are. And not to bother week by week. Do a month by month. For a year. Whatever that might mean. Got local maps?" he asked.

"Not here." Mine were in the lock-up.

"Have to use mine. They're in the car." David hesitated twice on his way to the flat door. He was far from his usual easygoing self, the very embodiment of in-charge confidence. "Why do I feel I'm being set up?" He actually looked around, as if for the benefit of hidden cameras.

"You're not being set up," I told him. "This is just so new. And probably best you don't know why."

He was no more at ease when he came back up with the maps. So determined to be careful was he that, once I had taken a photo of each of his pencil marks on the maps, before he would let me move on to the next location, he took a minute rubbing them off. For each place I made a brief note – map 1, map 2 – on the piece of paper with the addresses, which I mock-solemnly promised David that when finished I would eat and shit out the pieces.

David left unhappy. I remained unhappy. I was going to have to spend day after day shut in the Taunton lock-up. And I did, checking all the houses first, month by month. Any difference was where cars in the street might be parked. Just one of the houses got busted, month seven.

For the places – outlier farm buildings, small and not so small industrial estates, a walled up cave best I could make out – I saw through every season. All bar one of the big sites was still in operation after a year.

*

With the forward searches finished I heard nothing from Hodges for nearly two months. Until a strange looking lad turned up on my door screen.

"Message for you," was all that he said into the screen. Which in my circle was identification enough.

His whole get-up was odd, a goth's white make-up, heavy black eye-liner, but no black garb or heavy boots. Once in the flat – blue jacket embroidered with flowers, green trousers and red shoes – unimpressed by the flat's décor he said in a soft effeminate voice, "I'm a helper. Very cloak and dagger this, but I'm to tell you that you have to be in Lidl's car park at eleven ten tomorrow. Message delivered."

His staying made me uneasy. I could see that the voice, make-up and clothes were part of an act. I couldn't though see through to the intent. He wasn't being camp, nor was he in any sexual way trying to impress me. The act looked to have become part of who he was.

"OK," I said. "Anything else?"

"Sum total." And he clicked his red heels, turned smartly about and left.

Next day it was raining, one of those thin windblown rains. I didn't want to shelter in Lidl's doorway, have to keep getting out of the way of wet people and their trolleys. I took myself around the side of the building. All that I had to avoid there were the drips.

When Hodges' long grey car came cruising through the car park I shuffled along to stand on the corner. He brought the car up to me. I made to step around the front of the car. He opened his window, said through the top of it, "In the back." Today he was bulky in his business suit.

As Hodges drove out of the car park, I took my time buckling the seat belt around my wet anorak, trying to see if I knew the man in the passenger seat beside Hodges. Middle-aged, white-ish; I think he was what is called swarthy, had dark groomed hair and bristles down the side of his jaw. I didn't know him.

Windscreen wipers on intermittent, Hodges waited patiently at lights and junctions, eventually took us out of Bridgwater on the road towards Brent Knoll, the hill that sticks up on its own beside the M5.

"My friend here," Hodges said to me in the rear-view mirror, "wants you to take someone into the future. Can you do that?"

"Theoretically yes." I thought of the double cage that I'd built for old Ben in his spare bedroom. "I'll need somewhere bigger to get set up though." I didn't want strangers coming to my lock-up. Enough were already coming to my flat. "It's OK where I'm set up now for what I do now," I told the pair in front, "Not space enough though for a double. And can't be in my flat."

Soggy fields going slowly by Hodges took his time responding, finally said, "I got an empty shop. Concrete floor, concrete ceiling." Consequently of no use to our usual enterprise. "That do?"

"How big?"

"Twenty by thirty?"

"Can anybody see in?"

"It's in a small arcade awaiting redevelopment. Big boards up, back of the windows. So it don't look derelict."

Hodges had to negotiate a roundabout going into a recent housing estate, followed by another roundabout, then another.

"Can you do it?"

"Won't know for certain until I get set up in the shop. Iron rods in the concrete might interfere."

"And if you can get it to work?"

"Where do I have to take them?"

The passenger, who had had his head turned away as if looking at the new-build out the side windows and had so far just listened, now glanced across to Hodges and said, "We'll let you know once you're set up."

"OK. But I will need to know beforehand precisely where you want to go. Do a test run, see if it can be done."

"No test run," the passenger said. His accent wasn't West Country. Midlands possibly.

"I won't be seen," I told the back of his headrest. "I literally won't be seen."

"What I told you," Hodges said to his passenger. "How this will work. You'll need to get your man down on the ground. Mine will need to do a test run. You'll have to let him know."

The man looked down at his trousered knee, realigned a crease. Hodges took the turning that would take us to the motorway and back to Bridgwater. The wipers were switched to regular.

The passenger reached a decision: "Job's in Bristol. You'll wait outside. Be eight in the morning. I'll let you know precisely where on the day."

"OK," I said to Hodges. "I'll let you know when I'm set up and running in your shop."

And with that I knew that I had entered the realm of real villainy, that my life was now not to be my own.

As I think I've said before most crime these days is corporated. I was sitting in a too comfortable car uncomfortably silent behind two corporate executives. Me in the back was a technician to be managed. The two executives wouldn't talk to each other about anything important while I was present. Whenever they do so talk, and on other occasions I have overheard them, their terminology mocks business usage. Street dealers hold a local franchise, franchises grouped

239

together become a syndicate; and being corporations there will of course be hierarchies, the further up the more remote. That remoteness reinforced that day by their not talking together in front of me. Me the technician, owner of a unique skill-set, an asset to be passed around as a favour. I had become no more than an indentured retainer, to be bought and my services sold on. I could expect to be protected, but only for so long as I remained an asset. And how long was that likely to be? How long before I became a knowing-too-much liability?

*

The Bridgwater shop of Hodges was in a pedestrian cul-de-sac. Filling the shop's one window was a large blue and green picture of lambs in a field. Two of the neighbouring shops in the cul-de-sac had similar full colour country scene boards. The only shop in actual use, directly opposite Hodges', housed a cobbler-cum-key cutter. Being on the edge of the precinct I guessed the cul-de-sac would get little footfall.

The shop key had been brought to me last evening by the same mock-goth, but this time wearing a huge diamanté belt around baggy red trousers, the ensemble topped off with a silky blouse.

"I'm told that I may be working with you."

"OK," I said.

The lengthy eye contact that followed – mascara and eye shadow again – told me that I was being assessed. He made a show of nodding before finally leaving.

The inside of the shop was a huge empty space with just enough lights left for me to see what I was doing. Wires hung from the false ceiling where there had been other lights. Grit and dust formed scuff patterns on the grey floor, intercut by right-angled old silver tapes with curling edges.

I had brought the clip-build in my big backpack, began to assemble the cage in the middle of the shop. This time, as I had

240

initially for Ben, I was going to make the cage a double.

I had taken my bike into the shop. Wheeling it out I glanced over to see if the cobbler was looking my way. He was towards the back of his narrow shop, bent over something dark that I assumed to be his lathe.

I cycled over to my Taunton lock-up, collected a few more clips, the copper mesh, laptop, gaming switch and the carbon fibre. I didn't want to keep going in and out of the Bridgwater shop, so stopped off to buy another set of maps that would take me in forward time over to Bristol. The bookshop didn't have all the maps I needed. Those two I ordered to my PO Box, paid extra for next day delivery.

Back in the shop – bike leaning against the wall, double cage incongruously in the centre – I added the extra clips, a shelf my side for the laptop, and the copper mesh, between passenger and myself as well.

I was still not sure that this was what I should be doing with the cage, but for the moment I had no alternative. And whatever was to happen with the cage I wanted it to look slick, professional. So for this version the bare minimum, no soft cushions; and the carbon fibre this time was no longer just stuffed into the mesh: I spread it out so that it interlaced with the mesh.

Satisfied I laid the opened maps over the shop's concrete floor. I had more space there than in the lock-up, and I began looking for high points as of old to take me from low-down Bridgwater over to Bristol. I must have spent an hour, squatting or kneeling, jotting down trajectories and co-ordinates, had in my mind's eye the data block getting bigger and bigger. But I wanted to be thorough, the consummate technician, however the more beacons the greater chance of error.

Why didn't I, I asked my sensible self, do as I had so casually done for the races and site checks, and go really high the once, then across to Bristol? Two directions. Maybe three,

241

and then fine tune to get to the ground in Bristol once I had the actual address.

That I did, entered the co-ordinates into the data block, pressed Return; and there I was above Bristol docks, River Avon disappearing down the gorge under the Clifton suspension bridge.

Iron reinforcement in the shop ceiling hadn't stopped the cage working. All that I needed now was the precise address.

I sent a text to Hodges: 'All set for another day out. Need corroborate venue details.'

Next evening the tall thin one delivered the address on a pink post-it.

This time he was very much the non-Goth. No white face paint, instead two roundels of rouge below his still heavily mascara-ed eyes. The same willowy height and soft speech, and this time topping off the red trouser ensemble – slightly grubby – an embroidered waistcoat.

"What it doesn't say," fingertips held the pink post-it out to me, "is that you will need to be at that address before eight, day after tomorrow."

"OK."

Again he gave me a lengthy study as he left, then said, "Think I'm going to call you OK Man."

I did a trial run the next day, got briefly down to the pedestrian precinct in Bristol's Broadmead. I was ahead of, two shops away from, a jewellers, which had to be the target. I would have to pull back my final distance to place the cage outside the jewellers. A man on an electric scooter started coming straight towards me. I hit Control D.

Back in the shop I stayed in the cage trembling.

My worry about the following day, aside from the purpose of the visit, was that, although there weren't likely to be hordes of shoppers in Broadmead that early, there could easily be workers hurrying through and any one of them could come walking slap-bang into the cage.

A night of not much sleep saw me up early. By seven I was in the shop. I had been told to leave the door on the latch.

At half-seven a slim man, my height, came in and locked the door behind him. He had on a maroon baseball cap, peak pulled down over his face.

"Gotta get changed," he took off the cap, lifted off his crossover shoulder bag. He looked around the floor: "Where's the least dusty corner?"

I shrugged. He went to the back of the shop, took off his bomber jacket, tee-shirt and trousers, folding each into a neat pile. Despite the pattern of dark body hairs, he looked gym-toned. His shoes he put upside-down on top of the clothes pile. From his shoulder bag he shook out a white cover-all with hood, blue scrub slippers and plastic gloves. The last thing out of the bag was a hammer. Some white material looked to be wrapped around the black rubber and metal handle

"In two weeks time," he said, "they should open at eight for the cleaner. Two weeks ahead. We clear on that? Two weeks."

I nodded.

"Coming up to eight now," he said. "Let's go."

I directed him to his side of the cage and, as I went around to mine, told him that he would become invisible as soon as he left the cage, that the cage would also be invisible, for him to find local markers so that he could get back into the cage.

I adjusted the time ahead, double-checked the entry, and closed the cage door my side: "Ready?"

He glanced around the shop, nodded, said, "Whoa!" as we arrived in Bristol.

Broadmead had the damp deserted feel of early morning. The metal shutter on the jewellers was being slowly rolled up.

My passenger was frowning down at the floor of the cage. Directly under his blue scrub shoes was one discoloured paving stone.

"Alarm will go off," he told me. "Don't panic."

I realised that my nervousness had to be in some way showing. His coverall rustled as he opened the cage door his side and became invisible.

He must have sprinted across to the jewellers. I saw the shine on the glass door move as it was opened almost immediately. I heard a bang and the shop alarm start. It was a bit like a car alarm, not a continuous ringing. A red light on a box above the shop was also flashing. The cage door was grabbed, closed. My all-in-white passenger was holding a white fabric bag and the black hammer.

"We can go now," he told me.

And we were back in the Bridgwater shop, empty aside from my bike, his neat pile of clothes and the slew of maps. He looked all around, then at me, smiled and said, "Wow." The hammer was still in his hand. He hefted the white fabric bag, said, "Job done," and he began to get out of the cage. "They tell you to bring a rubbish bag?"

I shook my head.

"You'll need one." He started to squirm out of the white coverall. "Glass fragments in this. Hammer's got to go too. When you've got a rubbish bag use somebody's skip."

I was still sitting in the cage when he left the shop, fully clothed, cap peak pulled down over his face, and with whatever he had stolen in his crossover shoulder bag.

Left alone I set about composing myself. The violence, although so far as I knew not to anyone, had nonetheless got my heart racing. After a couple of slow walk-around circuits of the cage, and a few deep breaths, I locked the shop door and took my time wandering around to the supermarket, where I bought a roll of black bin bags and two fresh doughnuts.

When I got back to the cul-de-sac a slow old man was about to go into the cobblers. The cobbler hadn't been open when I had left.

I waited around the corner, bendy roll of bags tucked under

244

my arm and I ate my two jam doughnuts. When the old man had shuffled off deeper into the precinct, and by my reckoning the cobbler would be back at his lathe, I went to the shop.

Alone again I spent a good while just looking at the cage, licking the last of the sugar and jam from my fingers, and wondering what the cage now meant for my life.

The main decision reached that morning was that I didn't want anyone other than myself using the cage for whatever purpose. Unplugging the laptop, I slid it into my backpack. And with that decision restoring a small sense of control I set about completing the job. Stuffing the white coverall, gloves, scrub slippers and hammer into one of the black bags. I carried it out with me, dropped it into the first unlocked bin I came to in a line of commercial bins.

*

I was not at all at ease with this new set up, with where it might take me. Or who might take over my cage. I felt it to be at risk. So I got another laptop and Tim to make another copy of it, and I bought myself another gaming switch.

My lock-up was known. My flat was known. I stored the new laptop and gaming switch in another self-storage unit, along with some clip-build. If needed I could, as and when, easily get more copper mesh and carbon fibre.

Should there come a time when I was no longer flavour of the month with Hodges, or there happened to be no other work, I could make a new cage and bet on the occasional odds-against horse to keep myself in money.

Getting all that sorted kept me busy for just over a week. Then the willowy and winsome one paid me another visit.

"I am to be your next travelling companion," he informed me. "Meet me at the shop, seven tomorrow morning." He leaned forward into eye contact, "Say OK"

"OK."

Another one been told where the shop was. My life was feeling increasingly crowded and insecure.

My bike and I were in the shop, lights on, way before seven. At seven precisely the willowy one slid in through the door. He too had a shoulder bag strapped across him. Door locked behind him – an instruction both had been given? Or learnt caution? – he stood looking around the shop, empty apart from the double cage and the bike.

"I was told to expect the unexpected." He walked across the shop, touched fingertips to the cage, lingered a glance over the open laptop and the gaming switch. "This is to be our vehicle?"

I nodded: "Where is it we have to go?"

"Oh, so you can talk. Have to say I'm not sure that I actually want to go anywhere. But this is where I have been told to go." He showed me the address on his phone, had a Gloucester postcode. "And I need to be there two weeks from today. Leaving now. If that makes any kind of sense to you?"

No rouge on his cheeks today. Skin was a pitted white and there was an acrid smell about him. Something unclean? His clothes?

"Have to check my maps." I indicated the stack beside my feet, the stack topped by scribble pad, protractor and ruler. "Will take me a minute or so to work out. If you want, you can go find yourself somewhere for coffee."

"I'm sticking with you like gum to a shoe. So, while you do your working out, whatever it is you have to work out, I'll pop myself down here, quiet as a mouse." He took himself to the furtherest corner and, folding his legs under him, appeared to sink into stasis.

Brushing away grit I knelt before maps and measured trajectories, scribbled beacon points. I wanted to be accurate, so took me almost half an hour. Going into the cage I entered all into the data block.

"I'll do a recce first," I told my day's companion, closed my cage gate. "Want to come?"

"Yes I do." He rose. "My gum to your shoe. First though I have to change."

No surprise that he pulled a white coverall from his bag, shook it open and began climbing into it. Once dressed, bag re-strapped across his chest, I told him where the latch was for the gate his side, and to make himself comfortable: "I'm taking us to above the address." I pressed Return.

A tree-lined crescent was below us, the shining roofs of a few cars visible below the trees. The only sign that my companion had registered our arrival had been a sudden gripping of his seat edges.

We were a few metres short of the address, visible ahead on our left, a large modern house, beige walls, big glass, and a gravel drive behind remote-controlled gates. Typical villain attempt at upmarket respectability, leastwise according to TV's Mr Bigs.

The tree cover side to side of the road, with cars below, had me tell my companion, "Have a job getting you down onto the ground here. If ground is what you want?"

"I need to get inside the house. Is that correct, we can't be seen?"

"While here we're invisible. In and out of the cage."

"In that case can you get me onto that big lawn. There, behind the house."

"I'll have to take us back to the shop. Make adjustments there."

Our arrival in the shop startled him as much as had our arrival over the trees. His languid confidence was a show; he was as nervous as I, kept touching whatever was inside the shoulder bag.

Adjustments took only a minute or so. My racecourse trip had made me adept, and as with the racecourses I used my last

247

position as a beacon and, with a guessed-at elevation, dropped us down onto the lawn, sideways to the house.

"That was quicker than expected," he almost smiled.

"I thought it'd take at least another go." I returned the almost smile.

He didn't respond to my friendly tone, was looking past me to the sky-reflecting windows this side of the house.

"To be absolutely certain," he said, "we are now two weeks ahead, and invisible?"

"Two weeks yes, and the cage is invisible to anyone up there looking out. Once out of the cage you will become invisible even to yourself. As I will be invisible to you."

"I have to get inside the house." He was again looking beyond me, eyes searching windows up and down. "Shouldn't be more than half'n hour." He turned to the latch.

"Find something distinctive on the ground," I quickly told him. The hammer robber had picked a discoloured paving stone. "So you'll know where the cage door is. Don't come to my side."

He nodded, opened the cage door and, the mesh seal being broken, became invisible. A moment later, time enough to adapt to his invisibility, a mud line got heel-scraped through the close-mown lawn grass. Then I knew that he had gone.

I waited, watched the house. The patio doors this side remained closed.

Nothing seemed to be happening. I wondered if my passenger was having trouble getting inside. But no sooner thought than I felt the cage shift, the latch clicked and he was sitting beside me, panting, and with red blood splashes on his white sleeve and shoulder.

"You get in the house?" I asked, thinking at first that he may have climbed and fallen, tried to see where he may have injured himself. Imagined getting him to A&E, decided that I'd call Hodges first.

"Rang the front doorbell," he said as he squared himself on the seat. Then impatiently, "Can we go?"

I did a Control D and we were back in the shop.

He took a steadying deep breath, made no attempt to leave the cage.

"I made a mistake," he told me. "Shouldn't have taken the bag. It's my own." The crossover bag. "I was told you'd dispose of the paper suit, and this." He lifted a long-bladed knife out of the bag. "Can the bag go in a separate rubbish bag, different bin?"

"OK."

He glanced to my face, smiled briefly at my OK.

We both got out of the cage. I picked up my roll of rubbish bags, ripped off two. I was watching to see what he would do with the knife. I had been sole witness to whatever he had done two weeks from this day and I was therefore a danger to him. But the knife got dropped handle first into the same rubbish bag as the white coverall. Crossover shoulder bag went into the other black bag.

"Apparently," back in only his own clothes he had recovered his drawl and and his willowy composure, "as with a previous passenger of yours," a fingertip wave to what was passed, "I too, passport in hand, am off to the antipodes for a gap month. Perfect alibi. Or so I have been promised." With another soft wave he slipped out the shop door.

Given the blood spatter my guess was that I had become accomplice to a slash warning if not a murder.

Supplementary [recorded, transcribed]

Mentor: I have to ask, were you the assassin?

O/V: No

Mentor: Did you kill Ben?

O/V: Ben? Course I didn't. Why would I? Once Ben was dead everything started going wrong for me. Granted at the time I thought I was being clever, but I got caught up in all this other stuff.

Mentor: With Ben dead though you were able to do the horse betting, make yourself lots of money.

O/V: Then I got warned off. And recruited into a bigger mess. I lost the caravan, the most secure I'd felt for years. And Ben was old, had been ill on and off for years. Why would I have even thought to kill him?

Mentor: We have to be sure.

*

How did I feel?

Vulnerable. I felt vulnerable.

I'd taken risks before. I've stolen things, been afraid of getting caught, being found out. Those one-off fears though were nothing like this day-in-day-out feeling of being vulnerable.

All the defences I'd built up over the years had gone. I had no hiding place. David of necessity had known of my lock-up for years. And he'd probably told Hodges. But now? Now far too many of Hodges' errand boys knew of my Bridgwater flat. And who knew how many of Hodges' 'associates' he'd told of the cage?

People I didn't know now knew of me. On top of that I was getting letters from the bank and credit card company.

I'd even been invited up to Hodges' North Curry house. Twice. Never met his wife. Both times she was 'off somewhere.'

His house?

Cedars, wooden controlled gates... The thing with big players is that they try to appear, and I think want to be, respectable. So they buy these big houses like in the posh adverts. Floor to ceiling windows and polished pebbles in bowls. And they like me because I'm quiet and polite, and I go along with their life as in an advert.

"Hear you can make people disappear?" One of Hodges' contacts said straight off.

He was a big man, a heaviness about him, sitting square and filling the armchair. Not fat. Frightening. Big car parked out front, driver inside watching me get off my bike. I'd taken a detour across the Levels.

"Not exactly," I said. I didn't know how much Hodges had told him.

"Exactly how then?"

"While we're travelling, we're invisible. And invisible while we're there. Back here we're not."

I could see him working out how that might be of use to him. By the look of him I hoped I was going to be of no use.

Hodges had his own big men who he used as frighteners, but reluctantly. Hodges was more for everyone playing fair and getting their cut. This armchair-filling man though had the look of someone who'd take pleasure in hurting anyone who, for whatever reason, failed to deliver. Where someone like Hodges would probably have just stopped using them.

I was back with the kind of criminals, criminals who if they didn't want to be seen as criminals nevertheless acted as criminals, that I'd done my best to avoid when starting out from Care.

You know about the other future robberies I did? Like the jewellers? The one on the ATM refiller?

For that first ATM [a cash machine] I landed the cage beside the security van, outside the shop. The security guard, helmet on, took the refill into the shop, put it on the floor. My passenger, muscular but sharp and quick with it, had invisibly followed the guard through the slowly closing shop door. Said afterwards that he waited while the guard opened up the back of the ATM and began to take out the long metal box of money. The guard's hands being occupied my passenger picked

251

up the full refill and walked out with it. By the time the guard had processed what was happening, my passenger was out the door and we were gone.

Before that job Hodges had had me take another of his heavy and be-suited 'business associates' forward to case out the ATM.

"Going to be interesting this," he told me on our return to the shop. "All new currency in the refill. We can flood the market with it before the notes have even been issued, and way before they're reported stolen. Endless possibilities this."

So had said one of the men who knew me, knew of the cage, knew of our Bridgwater shop.

I lay awake nights trying to figure a way out. I had the funds now. Where though could I go? Bear in mind that I had no passport. I could probably have bought a false one. But I was so known now, and any good forger would be known to my circle. Where could I go where I wasn't known?

I did consider teaching someone else to navigate the cage. That would have made me less uniquely valuable to them. Except that I already knew too much about them. Would they let me go my own way that easily?

I'd taken 'business people' from Belfast and Aberdeen for future trips back to Belfast and Aberdeen. I'd become known all over the country, had nowhere obvious to go where I'd be safe.

Bridgwater evenings an errand boy or girl would turn up with a note, 'Shop tomorrow 11.' That time would mean a sightseeing trip. An even more perfunctory text, 'six,' meant for a job; and if I hadn't already been asked to case it I'd have no idea where or what was intended.

'Five thirty,' was the text that brought me to you.

Another sleepless night, alarm set, I was up at four thirty, bike lights on to take me to the shop.

Five thirty inside the shop was another man changing into a white coverall while I worked out a route to a month-ahead

252

Gloucester pedestrian street.

Another cloth shoulder bag was strapped across another white coverall.

No boss-man this trip out for a time-travelling jolly. This was a technician, a worker. Another fit-looking one, like the robber at the Bristol jewellers. Could have been ex-military.

We made our first trip over by six, clouds breaking grey, street lights still on, cobbles below damp and gleaming. We were rooftop high, the pedestrian street sloping down from a bollarded T-junction.

"Get me down there," he pointed to an alley's dark entrance.

Back to the shop we went. I adjusted the elevation; and next time we were at ground level among the tall buildings and side on to the alley.

The man, technician to technician, nodded his approval to me. Before opening the cage door, he took a black pistol with silencer from the shoulder bag, turned off the safety catch.

My previous passenger's knife could have been a slash warning only. That was what I had been telling myself. This pistol though, unless a kneecapping was planned, and a kneecapping could be either punishment or warning, but a warning to who in the future?

Man and gun disappeared as soon as he opened the cage door.

I thought I saw movement in the alley. A lit-up bus passed along the road at the end. I turned back to the alley and you were walking towards me with a smile.

I actually looked around to see if you were smiling at someone the other side of me and the cage. On you came. I braced myself for you to bump into the invisible cage. Instead, still smiling friendly-like at me – you were so confident – you caught hold of the invisible cage door and stepped in, sat down and closed the door. The whole cage was now visible to me and you were inside it.

Not knowing what else to do – a boy's voice from the past yelling at me to run – I reached forward to do a Control D.

"Don't bother," you said. "Won't work. You're coming with me."

"What about him?" I pointed to the alley.

"Already back in your shop. A very puzzled man. Wasn't him we wanted. It was you."

And here I am.

Part Three: The Enquiry

Session One: Part One

Present are Senior One, Inquisitor and Moderator 28.

Senior One: We are here to inquire into the disappearance of the recruit variously known as Vince/Vincent and/or Ollie/Oliver. Our task is to discover both why and how he has disappeared; and, if possible, where he might have gone. We have before us his testimony, which we will take as our starting point.

Over to you.

Inquisitor: In his testimony, telling of how the 'Supplementaries' came about, he says that some were casual encounters 'in the corridors, canteens, and elsewhere.' Am I to take it that 'and elsewhere' was your bedroom?

Senior One: Can we stop there? Moderator 28 is not on trial here. A less accusatory tone please.

Inquisitor: Apologies. I had the page open before me. I sought only clarity.

Moderator 28: For clarity's sake I am happy to confirm that some of the 'Supplementaries' did take place in the bedroom. In other rooms too.

Inquisitor: You became lovers?

Moderator 28: As his mentor I had to win his confidence. Lovers, if that is what we were, came later. At the case meeting where we decided on the intervention, not knowing just how dangerous a criminal he might be, it was agreed that I should make the intervention. My appearance – that of a young woman – was considered the least challenging. This is the form I have long adapted for store visits. One of us as a man he might have been viewed as a threat and have had him respond aggressively.

Inquisitor: Did he? Respond aggressively?

Moderator 28: Not in the least. If anything, he seemed to shrink into himself. From his testimony we know that it was under duress that he brought the assassin out of the present. When I entered his cage that morning he did try to escape back to his present. But at the same time was uncertain that he should be doing that as I had already been sitting in his cage contraption. What would he have done with me back in his present?

He really had been in a funk, fingers dithering over his laptop. I told him not to worry, that he was perfectly safe; and I brought him here. Early afternoon, I think. And once here, human dress no longer necessary, I reverted to our loose robe.

Inquisitor: Could he have escaped in the cage?

Moderator 28: Not that day. I had him under my control.

Inquisitor: I meant his recent disappearance. Could he have used the cage to make good his escape?

Moderator 28: Escape? By the time of his disappearance he was a recruit, not a prisoner.

Inquisitor: Could he?

Moderator 28: The cage is still here. Archived.

Inquisitor: What was it made you decide to become his lover?

Moderator 28: Those first weeks he was very guarded. But I noticed, during our early interactions, that he had been showing an interest in my physical form. When I go to the store I am, as intentioned, inconspicuous. A nondescript young woman doing her weekly shop. Here though, just him and I, I noticed his eyes coming to rest on my bust. Or looking me over as I walked away. I was being sexually assessed. So I began enhancing those attractive aspects, breast and buttocks, as well as altering my genitalia to that of an adult human woman. Should it prove necessary. And in light of gossip can I say that I was assured, mentor to mentor, that in order to win his confidence seduction was considered an acceptable ploy.

Inquisitor: Why did sex with him become necessary?

Moderator 28: The more that I had to do with him the more I realised his potential as an Adjuster. We knew from his testimony that from a young age he had been versed in duplicity, had early learnt to espy falsity and fraud. Which is why we became so keen to recruit him. We often have difficulty not knowing what lies behind the actions of some human beings. We believed that he could be, indeed he became, if briefly, an asset.

Senior One: This is interesting, but I can't see that it is telling us why he chose to disappear. If choose he did.

Inquisitor: I suspect that the key to his disappearance might lie in the close relationship that he had with his mentor, Moderator 28. Her motives I believe might prove as important as his.

Senior One: Continue.

Inquisitor: You say that you changed your genitalia. Were you not concerned that doing so might affect your psychosomatic reasoning?

Moderator 28: At that juncture I had incorporated only a limited amount of human DNA. I embarked on further adaptation – vagina, ovaries and uterus – only in order to seal the compact when and if the need arose. And the need didn't arise for some time. Because, despite those changes, he continued to be less than confidential, secretive even. So I boosted my pheromone output. And that did have him become increasingly attentive, seeking me outside of our mentoring sessions. I invited him to dinner. He had been asking to see my quarters. This was, comparatively, early on. When he was interested in all of us, how we'd come to be, what he then called, The Time Police.

Inquisitor: I have no record of him entering our quarters.

Moderator 28: I used one of the temporary quarters, got it set up as if for a human woman. I prepared a meal according to a recipe book; and that is when we became lovers.

I have to say that the pleasure this body took from the sexual act came as quite a surprise. I had already experimented with masturbation, to see if the new parts were in working order. And I'd felt my lips, breasts and labia becoming increasingly sensitive. When it was him who touched my clitoris however the sensation was of an entirely different order. Not knowing what he was about to do next had my whole body in a state of high excitation.

That first time proved quite a revelation, gave me fresh insight into the importance humans attach to the sexual act. Especially regards the infidelities of otherwise subservient females. Once I had experienced orgasm, and the desire for another, the dangerous urgency of those subservient women became clear.

Inquisitor: The sex act succeeded in gaining his confidence?

Moderator 28: Not immediately. He was still suspicious of me. The sexual act was just a step along the way. You have to understand that he had already had several sexual partners, and that he hadn't wholly trusted any of them. I believe that it was more through our domestic familiarity, resulting from the sexual act, that he came to trust me.

Inquisitor: Yet he didn't tell you that he was about to disappear?

Senior One: If I may?

When did you tell him that you weren't human?

Moderator 28: Prior to his recruitment. He had to know or he couldn't have worked with us.

Inquisitor: His knowing that you continued as lovers?

Moderator 28: Yes. Right up to the time he failed to return.

Senior One: Can we establish that it wasn't shock at learning that you weren't human that had him leave?

Moderator 28: He was fascinated by my non-human state, wanting to know how I had changed, what I'd had to do. If anything his knowing of my non-human state revitalised his interest in me, in my body. Sexual activity certainly saw an

259

increase. And, if only by comparison, he confided in me more about himself.

Senior One: Enough for now. Let's take a break.

And can we, Inquisitor, when we resume keep to a sequence of events? I feel that we have been jumping back and forth a bit here. And one more thing, if I may: how did he address you? I can't imagine that he, in intimate moments, called you Mentor or Moderator 28?

Moderator 28: On our arrival here, as I led him to the interview room, I introduced myself as Myra. An arbitrary invention.

Inquisitor: What did you call him?

Moderator 28: O/V.

Senior One: Before we resume can I check that we all have copies of *Futuricity*?

Inquisitor: We do. Benjamin Barraclough stored a copy in the Cloud.

Session One: Part Two

Present are Senior One, Inquisitor and Moderator 28 [Myra].

Senior One: I have been looking back over the initial transcript. Taken along with the Supplementaries during his testimony it makes for confused reading. In the Supplementaries you are listed as Mentor, here as Moderator 28.

For the purpose of future transcripts I shall remain as transcribed. And that being his/her function here the Inquisitor too. Regardless of who that session's Inquisitor might be.

Moderator 28 though is a mental mouthful. It is also a title from outside this Enquiry, not a function here. We will henceforth therefore use the identifier you have given yourself, Myra. Research tells me that it means 'consent is given.' Is that so?

Then we are agreed.

Myra: Regards nomenclature can we in future also call our disappeared colleague O/V? Rather than any, or all, of the four versions that he has given us?

Senior One: Agreed. From first contact if we may?

Myra: First contact was when I stepped into the cage and he realised that his device wasn't doing as it should. He went into a state of controlled panic, kept glancing from his laptop to me sitting calmly beside him. What he was looking for, he told me later, was to see if I had a weapon. Seeing none he resigned himself to capture.

Once satisfied that he was in my control, assuring him that he was safe, we came here.

House and grounds were a surprise to him. He had expected, or so he told me later, some sort of police station.

At that point though all that I was doing was assuring him that no harm was intended towards him.

We left the cage out front and I brought him through to our group room.

Inquisitor: Did he see others of us here?

Myra: No. The taking of him had been meticulously planned. With any other transgressor we would simply have removed their time-travel capabilities and popped them back into their present. We didn't though know what back-up O/V had. That if we had only taken the cage from him, we didn't know how soon back in his present he could have built another.

No, our aim had been to cause him the least harm, let him see as little as possible of what was here, who was here. So, as you must be aware, we cleared the grounds that day of all personnel prior to our collecting him. Soon as we left the cage I led him up the steps and straight to the group room.

Senior One: That is the interview on record?

Myra: Yes. Although it is missing one minor point. The recording wasn't triggered until we were both sitting on the settees opposite one another.

As we had been coming up the steps into the house, I had told him that we were going to the interview room. Which he had acknowledged with a nod. When he saw the room though, the furnishings, having anticipated a grim police room, he actually gave a little laugh, and said, "So where's the soft toy I'm supposed to hold this time?" Referring back, I believe, to his time in Care. "Or do I make do with a cushion?"

Inquisitor: Can we take the interview as read?

Senior One: Agreed.

Myra: If I may?

What the transcript doesn't wholly convey is his curiosity about us. Even back then. That curiosity I believe can tell us much about his disappearance. Yes, he readily told us, was eager to tell us – once he was convinced that we were nothing to do with the police – that it was only under duress that he had brought the assassins into the future. He was equally interested however in how we had come to know of him, in just who we were.

Inquisitor: At that point, according to the transcript, you gave him only basic reassurances – that he would have his own quarters, would be required only to give 'a full and accurate' testimony. Did you offer further reassurances when you showed him to his quarters?

Myra: Of course. With each and every introduction to domestic life here I kept the conversation easy and expectations of him at a minimum. He was by that time, I believe, relieved to be here and free of his criminal associates. He seemed satisfied with his quarters, was particularly pleased that he had his own kitchenette and bathroom. He did though comment on there being no screen.

When later he saw others in their robes he asked if I too usually wore a robe. That was the first time I caught him looking me over. I told him that while he was here he too could wear a robe. He said that day that he'd give it a try. He came to prefer it.

Inquisitor: I take it that he had seen the canteen?

Myra: Not that first day. But certainly within the first few days.

Once I had shown him his quarters I lifted the embargo on the ground. He would have seen others of us wandering about out there.

Before I left him to himself that day, I again told him that he would be expected only to give a full testimony. He asked if he could leave. I told him not. He asked what was stopping him. I told him that there was nowhere to go.

He hadn't at that point seen our offices. Everywhere I'd taken him had been front of the house. He had asked if we were the Time Police.

Inquisitor: How did you respond?

Myra: Non-committal at first. But he kept on. Am I in Time Prison? Are you the Time Police? Time Bureau?

I'd like to emphasise here that when I say, 'This is what I told him,' it does not mean that is what I believed. I told him that he had been causing Time Upsets and that, to make life easier for ourselves, we had brought him here. I told him that what we needed was every detail of how he had become capable of travelling into the future.

Inquisitor: If you can, what precisely did you tell him that we are?

Myra: Temporal Adjustment Bureau. Time Correction Officers. Varieties thereof.

Inquisitor: If this wasn't a prison, he must have wondered why there was nowhere to go?

Myra: Back then I think that I told him that we were out of time. But you're all visible, he said. I told him that house and grounds existed within a pocket of time all its own. That he was free to go where he wanted within the pocket of time, house and grounds; but that we were the only people, the only place within the pocket.

So far as 'the pocket' was concerned I let him presume that the rest of the globe was unpopulated wilderness. To begin with, I confess, I encouraged that presumption.

It wasn't until he was a few days into his testimony, and he had become used to the place, and his being curious about what we all did, that I showed him the office building. Not inside it, just the building. More Time Adjustors than police, I told him. That we had no interest in crime *per se*.

Senior One: I think we have covered enough this initial session. Thank you both.

Session Two

Present are Senior One, Inquisitor and Moderator 28 [Myra].

Senior One: To discover where O/V might have gone I think we need to know what was his understanding of Time.

Myra: If I may?

Inquisitor: Go ahead.

Myra: From the very first O/V was curious about what he called Time Travel. Specifically, my Time Travel. How I, without a 'vehicle' of any kind, had transported him here; and how, just by one touch, I had sent the assassin back to his own time.

Inquisitor: You told him that?

Myra: He was not only curious how I had managed that, but concerned that the assassin, at the behest of someone else, could be coming after him.

"So you just touched him?" he said several times. "Just touched him. How does that work?"

I told him that the assassin and I had been two entities out of time. I told O/V that I had said, "Good morning," to the out-of-time assassin, as if welcoming him to a meeting, a convention say, and with a fingertip touch to his sleeve I had sent him back to the shop.

Inquisitor: O/V was content with that explanation?

Myra: Not in the least. Even when the initial interviews/debrief were over, and he was satisfied that we weren't in any way seeking to 'punish' him. Other than not allowing him to return. Which he emphatically didn't want.

"What if you touch me now?" he asked out of nowhere. "Will I go back?"

I assured him not. Told him that here in this place we were in sync, both of us out of time, but in our own present.

Inquisitor: And that was enough?

Myra: No. He was a young man, eager to learn, needed to know where he was, how we Time Police – he insisted on calling us that – worked.

Senior One: I have to say that I have always preferred the characterisation Time Philosophers. His being young though I can see that he needed to attach a purpose to our being. One we ourselves have yet to convincingly decide.

Myra: Our purpose, I told him, was to interfere, and then only very occasionally, with human ventures into forward time.

Inquisitor: It was your decision to recruit him?

Myra: Not mine alone. Although I didn't see what else we could do with him. Was he, for the rest of his natural span, to just wander the grounds here? Accost others for conversation? He had an active mind, a cerebrum that needed to be exercised. So, together, we talked of time.

Inquisitor: Of time travel?

Myra: Naturally. Was how he came to be here. His own experiences had already shown him that going back in time wasn't possible. Of course I...

Inquisitor: Where did these conversations occur?

Myra: Some began way back in the interview room. Some in the canteen. We also used the counsel/council chamber outdoors. Those two benches set in a corner? By the large white oak?

[Myra's hand is held up to indicate a pause.]

I don't know if you have ever tried to describe time concepts to someone with a limited scientific understanding, but it requires repetition, and different approaches. The concept of time not being a constant, for instance, he found difficult to grasp. He knew nothing of time dilation. I had to explain to him how time had slowed after the Big Bang. Time and again – sorry – I had to tell him that space and time travel, as he had

266

experienced them, were entirely conceptual. That he had seen and heard only what he had, reinforced by groupthink, expected to see. Known in science and law, I told him, as confirmation bias.

He took some convincing.

"Those trips of mine ahead," he said, "the odds-against winners I found. They all came home in real time, paid off. If I'd just imagined them, how were they so accurate?"

I told him that he'd have to ask an actuary, that people not numbers was my forte.

Senior One: Do we have an actuary?

Myra: Not as such, but the statistician I sent him to came some way to convincing him that statistically some odds-against winners had to every so often occur.

O/V still found it hard to believe that forward-future doesn't actually exist, except via the groupthink of the present. Visitors to that groupthink future, I told him, shamans and seers and suchlike, are generally of no concern to us. You however became, I told him, an active participant in that future. And that was a concern.

Inquisitor: With none of these conversations recorded can you tell us just how you got him to understand 'time travel.'

Myra: I tried telling him about Schroedinger's cat. How we could believe the cat was in the box but we couldn't know without opening the box. You can believe the cat is in there but you can't know it's in there. Your belief is real, cat and box less so.

Don't think he got it, Or I didn't explain it well. So I reiterated that neither the future nor the past truly exist. As say a place. One was, one will be. The past has left remnants, the future is a mental projection. We can imagine life in both. The past though is fixed. There are objects, buildings, machines from the past among us now. We ourselves are a consequence of the past. We can see back through light years to the birth of the universe; but beyond how that affects our knowledge of the past, we can have no actual effect on the past.

I felt that I had to emphasise the inviolability of the past. The past is, I told him. We can argue over interpretations of ancient artefacts and hieroglyphs; but they are what they are, fixed. I quoted Margaret Atwood: 'You don't look back along time but down through it like water.' Time physics says that we cannot alter the past. If only for the simple reason that it would be the undoing of ourselves.

Futures on the other hand, I told him, can be surmised, invented, speculated and disagreed on. Bearing in mind always that time itself is an invention. One that keeps getting reinvented. And once reinvented becomes a logic that has to be followed through. Time confused with speed of light say and used as a formulaic constant, which took its adherents back to the Big Bang and beyond. Until it was decided otherwise.

In considerations of Time every fact is a theory. Concepts of future time always get challenged, become superseded. New maths will do it every time.

I quoted Cixin Liu's, 'Time is the one thing that can't be stopped. Like a sharp blade, it silently cuts through, hard and soft, constantly changing.'

I tried to explain effect/non-effect to O/V by calling on the Brunnant Morphail theory. But as I've never truly understood its temporal contradictions myself it was of no help to either of us. I further muddled us both with my attempts at explaining Heisenberg's uncertainty principle.

Senior One: You have my heartfelt sympathies.

Myra: So I came back to emphasising that the future is at best a projection, is imaginary and is therefore malleable. And that is what O/V found most difficult to grasp, that any future is a mental construct.

"But I've been there," he said. "I've placed bets, won money. Wasn't just me imagining. I found odds-against winners."

I agreed: the future he visited wasn't reliant on only his own imagination. I told him of Jung's 'collective unconscious,' of

Huxley's 'doors of perception,' of time's inconstancy, of time dilation again, that although time may be used as a mathematical constant it isn't. That any future is dependent on the present, on the culture, on the Zeitgeist.

To begin with he hadn't known what the Zeitgeist was. I had to tell him that he had all this knowledge that he probably wasn't aware of. Something glimpsed on a screen say that he hadn't been consciously looking at. A newspaper headline long forgotten. The future is, I told him, what you as a people believe it to be. Except that most of humanity give no thought to how little time they have alive, how small their life. Always comes as a shock to them how close death is, non-existence. Yet they too will have absorbed the Zeitgeist view of the future.

To convince him I took him back to what he did know, to old Ben and Ben's three friends. I told him that they went into their future and met despair. Futurists themselves what they had most feared had happened. Nothing they could do to change it. So they lost faith in their probable future. Ben gave up even going, concentrated on his house, book and garden. Glynis and Julian gave themselves over to child-rearing, to looking after what they already had. Steve too, up in Cumbria, let his family and photography take over his life. Bart and Rhean filled their present with music, formed a folk ensemble with three others. Their distant future, if not forgotten, became an irrelevance.

The future is what you as a people believe it to be, I told him again.

"But I won real money betting on horses that I'd seen win in the future," he came back to that. "I was there. At the races."

Were you? I asked him. Were you? Did you ever arrive at a racecourse when it was raining? Did you and your cage ever get wet? No he hadn't. Because, I told him, on your wet return that future projection would have been difficult to sustain. Imagine Ben's friend Steve getting caught in a future rainstorm, the inside walls of his lavatory covered in wet? Did you ever check, I asked him, come the actual day of the race the weather at the course? He hadn't.

Forward time, the future – I tried a different tack – began with oracles, seers and suchlike attempting to foretell the future. Ally that with prehistoric attempts at divining the heavens and discovering stellar repetitions, reappearances of comets... all used by seers to forecast human doings. This happened then, might well happen again.

Inquisitor: Did that help? Did he accept that?

Myra: Sort of. He has/had a quick mind. When I had first broached that aspect he said, "So future and space have always been linked together?"

Not always, and not directly, I said; but yes, the future was born along with knowledge of the stars. When the sky-watchers had worked out repetitions, had got the lunar months measured. Recurrence of orbits.

Human beings construct futures that have meanings in their present, I told him. Take a look at old European paintings, their gross depictions of hell. The religious had their own futures, which they thought of as an after-life. When religions lose their influence their after-worlds/ after-lives more or less cease to exist.

I told O/V that we know that your sun will die. That is when our future stops.

Inquisitor: When did he accept that futures aren't absolute?

Myra: I don't think he ever did. He was stuck with the evidence of his own eyes. I had to tell him, again and again, that of course some of those near futures will exist in the material sense. You can go there and view them. You can even exploit them as you did with your horse races. But they all remain a conceptual realisation; and to mess with those futures is to de-conceptualise, to de-construct them. As with an incomprehensible crime – that jewellery robbery – and even more so with his enabling those future killings. That we had to stop.

Inquisitor: Please tell me he accepted that.

Myra: Reluctantly yes. Even so I had to retell him that human beings have been here on Earth, in one form or another, for hundreds of thousands of years. Most of those peoples wanted human life to continue after they had died, and to continue more or less as, or better than, they had known life. Throughout those hundreds of thousands of years the futures had been very different to the futures we have now, each of their futures having been a projection.

"But I went two millennia ahead to Ben's New Neroche," he objected. "And Ben went two millennia ahead to Julian's Exmoor settlement. I was nowhere near as well read as either of them, so how could I, how could we all see the same things?"

I could only tell him again of the collective unconscious, doors of perception.

"OK, so what is it that you know of the future?" he asked me. "Were Ben and Julian right when they saw the ecological troubles to come?"

Probably, I told him, or something close to it.

"So, what is it you do know of the future?" he asked again.

I know, I said, that this star of yours will die in about ten million years. And I can imagine, given global trends, a reduced version of humanity a few thousand years hence. But no imaginable future for human beings close to those ten million years. Your species will be long gone before your sun starts to die.

Senior One: A short break here please. If we may?

Senior One: Welcome back. Inquisitor?

Inquisitor: From what you have told us so far it would seem that he took some convincing regards the nature of time. I thought you said that he was quick to grasp concepts?

Myra: His was more an emotional reluctance.

Inquisitor: So what was it that overcame that 'emotional reluctance?

Myra: As I said, to his every doubt I repeated 'collective unconscious.' One day I added 'auto-suggestion.' It was the 'auto-suggestion' that sent him off to the library. And it was from the library that he usually sought me out day and night with questions that began, "So what about...?" or "I thought you said..."

Inquisitor: You were completely open with him?

Myra: By this time, he was accosting others. You yourself I believe? [Inquisitor nods.] And we were considering his suitability as a Moderator. To be a Moderator though he had to wholly accept the nature of forward time.

Inquisitor: At last.

Myra: What finally convinced O/V was my telling him of previous travels. Of how, even in prehistory, people found themselves in a 'future.' Although they didn't then see it as the future. Their triggering concept, their preoccupations were with the afterlife. Their collective unconscious focussed on that. And this afterlife, these other worlds of angels and devils, was where trance states, mushroom concoctions and suchlike took them. In his own Northern Europe, I told him, ergot was what was used to induce the trance states necessary to travel beyond. Orpheus to his underworld for one.

That mention of Orpheus sent him back to the library. From where he emerged to say, "So you're saying that...."

Inquisitor: He still doubted you?

Myra: It was more that he sought corroboration. Or a construct credible to him. It pleased him, I think, to be told that when atheism, rationalism, came to be near universally acknowledged – that is scientific rationalism being accepted, if grudgingly, by even the religiously-minded – that the afterlife ceased to be where the collective unconscious went.

Senior One: A good student?

Myra: An eager student. He asked if all forward travellers were travellers beyond death, Orpheus coming back from his other/underworld. Not all, I told him.

So we talked of how shamans had pursued their daemons into the 'spirit world,' whether by hallucinogenic substances or by – as in sweat lodges – enforced trance states. Howsoever the trance might be managed, they go out of their bodies and into another place. Which nine hundred and ninety times out of a thousand has no consequence other than for the individual. Unless, as in prehistory, the travellers found themselves in the land of the dead and required our help to return.

He leapt on that. Which has to be of interest here.

"So you return them to their present?" It was almost an accusation.

Inquisitor: You think he wanted to return to his present? Might that be where he has gone?

Myra: We don't think so. We're pretty certain that he hasn't.

I believe it was him simply trying to catch me out. For instance, he wanted to know if his absence back in his own time would create an imbalance. Unlikely, I told him, millions on Earth die and/or disappear every hour of every day. You will not be missed.

That indisputable fact seemed a visceral offence to his ego. Consequence being that he played with the idea that we had created a 'shadow self' of him. That shadow self, according to him, had arrived back in the shop minus the cage and had somehow continued his life there. Or – and this shows how sharp he had become – "What if me here is my shadow self?"

Senior One: Did he really believe that?

Myra: Was a passing fancy, part of his trying to find the limits of what we do. What he found most difficult to grasp was the little that we do do. I had to tell him that most who travel into the future cause no damage, no upsets. That there are moreover so many futures existing simultaneously that it can be hard to say which will eventually happen. That there's the possibility, still unproven, that they all do. Although statisticians assure us that most futures will align.

O/V referred back to my having told him that, generally, in the warp and weft of time all future interferences balance out. Even the one future death, the stabbing that he'd helped to bring about, had balanced out. In which case, he asked me, why had he been brought here?

Inquisitor: You told him?

Myra: Yes of course. Told him that we couldn't be certain that he wasn't able to recreate the cage back there and ferry more assassins into the future.

Inquisitor: Apart from O/V himself accosting others here, you made no attempt to pass his education onto anyone else?

Myra: It was me he came back to with his every new quibble. And it was strange what he could and what he had difficulty accepting. He readily accepted all of the flukes that had enabled him to travel through time. And he readily came to accept auto-suggestion: "Seen that practised by social workers."

His own experience was his base-line verification. "I was told where I'd be going," he said of his trips into space, "so I got to see what I expected to see." When I agreed, said that their being unprotected outside of Earth's atmosphere, but while still being able to breathe, the four futurists had practised auto-suggestion upon themselves, had found a radiation rationale that allowed them to give space travel up.

"So here we have to be," he said, "within Earth's atmosphere?" Told you he was quick.

Inquisitor: Meaning here?

Myra: Yes. And it wasn't so much that he was trying to catch me out as his leaping on aspects, clues to what puzzled him about the entire notion of the future, and of us.

He accepted that futures had differed throughout time. Accepted that last century the imagined futures had been mostly of a post-nuclear holocaust; while in this century they have been of climatic despoliation. He also conceded that his taking more assassins into the future would really have messed with time and had had to be stopped. By a fingertip touch. The quietness of that really appealed to him.

Inquisitor: You knew him best. I think it best therefore that we move on to your sexual relationship with him. How and why you brought that about?

Senior One: We have covered a lot of ground today. Can we save this for the next session? Agreed?

Session Three

Present are Senior One, Inquisitor and Moderator 28 [Myra].

Senior One: I have been told by the Inquisitors that we won't get to the bottom of O/V's disappearance unless we also get to the bottom of your relationship with O/V.

I can understand, Myra, that you needed to win his confidence: was it necessary though to go to such lengths?

Myra: Such lengths?

Senior One: I'm given to understand that you amended your pathology in order to have sex with him?

Myra: Yes.

Senior One: Why? That seems so extreme. For a Moderator?

Myra: I was chosen for the initial contact in the hope that my appearance as a young woman would be less likely to cause him alarm. In Earth years we look approximately the same age. And beforehand I had deliberately softened my look to appear less threatening. In that I succeeded.

As to gaining his trust once here...

As a child O/V successfully navigated himself through the British care system, and then as successfully through the lower echelons of organised crime. This, ironically, has served to give him a clear eye: he takes nothing for granted, assesses every new circumstance.

Unfortunately growing up in Care, compounded by his subsequent criminal activities, has also left him with an innate distrust of authority. Here I was authority's representative. So yes, he was friendly enough, but as an authority figure I was being allowed to only know so much.

In our subsequent meetings as his mentor, I began to notice his glances lingering over my faux feminine shape.

Long before O/V's arrival I had added small breasts to fill out the human clothing. Determined to win O/V's confidence, should it turn out to be necessary, I set about altering the intricacies of my groin. The urethra was easily shortened, inconvenient as that was. Then I self-engineered a vagina, labia and clitoris. I subsequently made further studies of human physiology to ensure that I had everything in place, including – almost an oversight – pubic hair. And finally, I added a pheromone musk to what I had come to think of as my armoury.

The effect of the last was quite remarkable. We talked as usual; but I was aware of him all the time edging towards me, almost as if he himself wasn't conscious of it.

Inquisitor: You had sex?

Myra: Yes, but not immediately.

He couldn't think that I was trapping him into a relationship. The initiation had to be his. And he did seek me out. Not ostensibly for sex. Not then. From the beginning he had wanted to know as much about us as we wanted to know about him. So we talked. Went for long confiding walks in the grounds.

You have to understand that O/V isn't in the least an aggressive human being. He is careful in all his approaches to others. As he was to me. So physical intimacy came about gradually. A guiding touch on my arm as we changed paths, a bump against me as we squeezed through a doorway, a joke-sharing pat on my shoulders. Pheromone closer all the while.

Inquisitor: I have grasped the tactics. They worked?

Myra: Yes. We were walking and talking in the grounds, in the woodland, when I happened to turn against him. He kissed me.

"Oh dear," I told him, "this could compromise our relationship."

"Don't see how," he said. "We're both adults."

"True," I said, "but let's not continue this here."

I had to appear both concerned for my professional reputation as well as appealing to the side of him that delighted in underhand activity. I went that evening to his apartment for one of his-turn my-turn meals. That was when we had sex for the first time.

And it was a true revelation.

I had read of female orgasms: to experience one was something else entirely. The strength of my first was due possibly to my endogenous increase of pheromones. The muscular force of it however really took me by surprise. Him too I think.

I knew that human pairs couple more than once, that coupling is not solely for procreation. What I hadn't realised was the degree of physical pleasure sex gives. Not only in the pursuit and relief of orgasm, but in the preceding sensory delights. Although they came later.

Inquisitor: You became more intimate? Continued the affair?

Myra: Certainly. Spent hours at a time in his bed or mine.

Senior One: Did he at this time talk of time? What did he make of our part in it?

Myra: In the beginning there was nothing much in depth. Enough to reassure him that he was safe here.

Inquisitor: To be clear, you began your sexual relationship during his testimony?

Myra: Towards the end. After the death of Ben and when he began telling of the criminals taking over his time excursions. In his telling of how life had been slipping beyond his control. He was in remembered distress. I offered him comfort.

Inquisitor: In giving him comfort you learnt more?

Myra: He opened up about all sorts. He was still putting together his testimony. We kept on with our sex through his recruitment, right up to his disappearance.

Inquisitor: The 'elsewhere' mentioned in his Explanation/Introduction, that was in both your bedrooms?

Myra: And the kitchens, living rooms. Shower room once. But indoors mostly.

Inquisitor: You have kept all your female human attributes?

Myra: All. I still take my turn, with Oen and Tere, going into town. Store trips. And O/V's disappearance can still have been accidental. Temporal displacement. He might yet find his way back. In which case I will welcome his return, go back to having sex.

Inquisitor: It is that important to you? That gratifying?

Myra: As I said, to know about human sex is one thing, to experience it quite another.

From his explorations of my body, his previous experience of sex, he asked why my nipples didn't become erect. I hadn't realised that they should. Texts I'd consulted hadn't specified how they reacted. Nor how many other body parts are reactive. Lips especially, clusters of nerve ends there. Before they would respond as he expected I had to make several adjustments to my autonomous nervous system. Once I'd got it fully functional, I found that I could orgasm solely through kissing. Not every time. Occasionally

What you have to realise is that these were discoveries for the both of us. New sensibilities, new responses, which seemed to strengthen with use. My body, with no conscious effort on my part, continued to finesse what I had begun. These two nipples, vestigial for those of us who have them, came alive. I was never sure what was going to happen next. During one orgasm I felt my vagina wall muscles clutching onto his penis in peristaltic waves. Unsure of what was happening I looked to his face to measure his response. All that he did was smile at me and say quietly, "Wow."

Inquisitor: Now that he is not here you retain those human 'sensitivities'?

Myra: Yes. Though they have dulled since his disappearance. I have come to believe that they are a part of the human pairing process. His presence is probably required to stimulate that acute sensitivity.

Inquisitor: You mentioned recruitment: he must by then have become aware that we, that you, aren't human. How did he respond?

Myra: With his usual curiosity.

Inquisitor: He wasn't deterred by your bodily adaptations?

Myra: Quite the opposite. He wanted to explore every nook and cranny of this body. As I his. Human sex is a collaborative venture.

Inquisitor: Doesn't the human male have only one orgasm? When they ejaculate their semen?

Myra: Ejaculation can be delayed, deferred. And while his orgasm is being deferred, during his sensory approaches, using fingers or tongue, or part penetration even, the female can have several orgasms. The male in that instance takes pleasure from the pleasure he gives. It is an emotional, psychological, physical collaboration.

You have to understand that with my full adaptation to the female human my entire skin became over-sensitised, became one vast erogenous zone. Initially I thought that I may have miscalculated my autonomous adjustments. But it seems, from the literature, that such increased sensitivity accompanies heightened sexual activity. As it was for the both of us.

I took pleasure from teasing his penis erect. Gave me insight into the origins of their phallic worship. While what his tongue did, to what he called my yoni, went some way to explaining those impractical ceramics. Because he explored my made self with as much interest as he did the general environment here.

Within the arc of our sexual intimacy, he also felt able to explore aspects of himself, of his making past. The downside of that was that he would keep going back to what might have happened to his 'shadow self.' To the extent that I regretted my part in its invention.

Inquisitor: Could the 'shadow self' have some bearing on his disappearance?

Myra: Don't know. Only that it bothered him.

"How do I know I'm not my shadow self?" he would say out of nowhere.

Senior One: If I may?

Can we put the shadow self aside for another session? I would like to know what he made of us. As a species?

Myra: When naked together our talk tended to focus on the personal. But elsewhere, and as I said, he was naturally curious about all of us. Wanted to know our history, where we came from.

I gave him a potted version, that we know only our post-cataclysmic role here. That we have no real knowledge of our pre-cataclysmic history. What time, what place we might have originated from: all that has been lost. That we know only that our supposed life purpose is to analyse the sun's activities and to protect the forward flow of time.

I had of course to tell him that we are all clones, that I am the forty fifth. He wanted to know if our knowledge was cloned along with our bodies. I told him that each new clone had to be re-educated. That we are all generally raised as any child in any grouping. Never though by the one that we have been cloned from. We had learned that lesson early

All of this he related to his own upbringing, to his own orphan self. He wanted to know, at first mention of his recruitment, if he too would be cloned. Depends, I told him.

"On what?" he asked.

"How useful you turn out to be."

Inquisitor: Have we kept cells?

Myra: Not so far as I'm aware.

Senior One: He was that accepting of us?

Myra: Not initially. Acceptance was difficult. He kept trying to make of us another human race. I had to tell him several times that he misunderstood, that we are not of the human genus.

"But you look like us." It was said almost as a complaint, almost an accusation. I apologised, told him that was how we had let humans perceive us.

"So what do you look like?" he asked.

"Like this," I had to tell him. "Since the cataclysm this is what we have made of ourselves, accommodating this form to this role."

Nor did I have to tell him that only the once. Time and again I had to explain that, whatever we are we are not human. That I nor anyone else here knows precisely what we are. That pre-cataclysm we would seem to have been adapted for different purposes many times. A carbon-based life form was the best I could come up with, that making us so readily adaptable.

If anything, he was cross with himself for having assumed that we were all human: "Always tell myself, never assume. And here I made the biggest assumption ever, that you were human."

Earlier on, when he had assumed us to be all human, he had asked me if being here, out of time, he would live forever?

"Entropy is entropy," I told him. "Time is both meaningful and meaningless here." I assured him that he would inevitably die. At some time. Whenever. And talk of his individual death brought him, of course, back to his shadow self.

Senior One: Much to consider. We'll call a halt here.

Session Four

Present are Senior One, Inquisitor and Moderator 28 [Myra].

Senior One: Who was it made the decision to recruit O/V?

Myra: Wasn't one person's decision. Followed from discussions of his Testimony. Being his mentor, I of course contributed. But I don't think anyone set out to recruit O/V. It arose more from our wondering what we should do with him.

Inquisitor: You didn't lead the discussion?

Myra: Not in the least. Although decisions were based on some of what came out of mentor-on-mentor evaluation. And my noting O/V's restlessness. How it might cause problems here.

Inquisitor: How did this 'restlessness' manifest?

Myra: At first in his wanting to know why he couldn't return to his present. Why he couldn't leave the grounds. For instance he wanted to accompany me to town. Just a day out, he said. I told him that he couldn't, that his being English would attract attention.

"Your being an alien species doesn't?" he said.

I had to tell him that the shopkeepers had got used to us, that they had accepted us in the human forms that we had adapted. But that he was new, novel, and would therefore be of interest.

"So what am I supposed to do here?" he asked.

Inquisitor: Your sexual relationship wasn't sufficient?

Myra: The sex was important to him, but only as a part of his life here. He complained that he wanted more than to 'shack up' with me and to 'forever' wander the grounds.

Inquisitor: It was you then who brought his restlessness to the discussion.

Senior One: I think we have established why O/V was

283

recruited, to occupy his time here. Tell me please Myra how the recruitment came about?

Myra: This is an uncomfortable memory.

I had employed his own make-believe 'shadow self' to explain why he couldn't return to his present. One of the reasons, but the one I feel shame for. I led him to believe was that a chance meeting with his 'shadow self' could cause a 'temporal dysfunction.'

"Your shadow self will continue back there," I had told him, "on the course that you have set for him. Your shadow self will probably go to prison at least two or three times."

That rang true to him, and the fiction was so readily accepted that, as I think I have said before, he used to wonder what his shadow self was up to, where his shadow self might be. If he asked if I knew what the shadow self was up to all that I had to do was shrug. He was happy with his own version.

Inquisitor: How could he be recruited while believing such nonsense?

Myra: Exactly. When it was finally decided to recruit him it was left to me, his mentor, to disabuse him of the fiction. The loss of his shadow self had him almost enter a state of grieving.

Inquisitor: Had the decision to recruit him not been made would you still have disabused of the shadow self fiction?

Myra: Yes. Contingent on him not being found suitable for training.

He couldn't stay here indefinitely, so would have had to be returned to his present. In which case what we had in mind was to tell him, if not that it was a fiction, then that his shadow self had fallen off his bicycle on the wrong side of a lorry, and the mangled body had been difficult to identify. With him safely back his real present, him having been unaccountably missing, his life could trundle on. No radical ramifications. No great surprises.

Inquisitor: So you had in mind to recruit him before he was

284

brought here?

Myra: When we discussed the intervention, we posited several possible outcomes for O/V. Training was one. Giving him a start elsewhere another. We doubted that he could go back to his own present. We didn't know what tech he might have stashed there.

Inquisitor: I've been told that he was an eager recruit?

Myra: Oh he was. From his arrival on he has been full of questions. What happened to his assassin passenger? What...

Inquisitor: What did you tell him?

Myra: The shadow self has been our only out-and-out deceit. For the rest I told him the truth as we know it; and that his passenger, at my physical contact, my touch on his arm had immediately found himself back whence he came, in the Bridgwater shop. When O/V asked what his colleagues would make of his own failing to return – after we'd dismissed the shadow self fiction – I said that they'd probably think he'd been the victim of a temporal mishap.

[Long pause.]

Inquisitor: Why have you stopped?

Myra: I was wondering what to tell of next. Because O/V has been curious about all things here. With time travel. He wanted to know, for instance, if Ben hadn't rescued Julian from Exmoor, what would have become of him.

I told him that Julian would probably have lived out his life there.

"Invisibly?" he asked me. I told him yes. "And you wouldn't have rescued him?"

I told O/V that we might have monitored Julian's stay there, but – and as with the majority of human time travels – his stay would have created no great change.

I have told you how O/V was fascinated with our not being human, how that had increased his sexual interest in me. At mention of recruitment, he wanted to know where were the other humans we had recruited. I told him that only one other had been recruited, Náay, from Mexico.

I told him how Náay, a shepherd, had cooked himself a stew of berries, fungi and leaves, that had sent him into an out-of-body trance. Náay had, in that future trance, gone down into the village and bitten out the throat of one of the villagers. And Náay had done it again and again, with the villagers and the nearby townsfolk becoming more and more troubled by this invisible 'night beast.' Even in that sparsely populated part of Mexico the social disruption had been immense.

Having already seen or heard Náay's name mentioned, O/V wanted to meet him. I had to tell him that the original Náay had died almost three centuries ago, that this Náay was his fifth or sixth clone.

He thought on that, then asked if we weren't worried that Náay might eat us. I told him not, that it had been the original Náay's spirit guide who had led him to eat his victims. That it had been the accidental ingredients making up the hallucinogenic compound that had induced in him an appetite for human flesh. I assured him that we had thoroughly checked the original Náay and had found no subconscious cannibalistic desires.

Reassured he went off to meet Náay clone 6. Before he did he asked why Náay should have been the only other human to have joined the Time Police.

Inquisitor: Time Police?

Myra: That's what he first called us and what I initially went along with. It is approximately what we do. Even then I did tell him that we weren't interested in planetary crime as such. And that most Time crimes, if that is what they are, have been self-remedying. As with his betting on horse races. That what might be a crime in one part of the world can elsewhere be looked upon as acceptable behaviours.

"Can they be crimes when committed within a criminal society?" I asked him. "Usury for instance. And certain sexual practices." Given his background, his having mingled mostly with those who had little alternative to crime, O/V rather enjoyed that notion.

It wasn't that we condoned his criminal background, rather that we appreciated his open outlook. He took nothing for granted. He assessed. He questioned. And as I have tried to get across O/V was not well educated. I'd had, for instance, to explain what usury was.

"So my crimes," he said, "don't count here?"

Only when you began messing with the temporal flow, I told him. When you went into the future and placed your bets in the present, we saw that and let you be, knew that it was self-correcting. It was only when you took that robber into the future that we became alarmed. We would probably not have intervened even then, had that been all that you had facilitated.

The video of the robbery caused some confusion – a cabinet seeming to explode, jewels disappearing, hammer and bag invisible. The local police put that down to some clever clothing blanking the camera, with the cleaning woman's near incoherent testimony discounted as shock.

That was just about tolerable, I told O/V. Even when you transported the knife-wielder into the future. That stabbing, of another criminal, also recorded. The police that time believed that someone had somehow interfered with the door-cam and the hall recordings. But it was then that we knew that we had to stop you.

Inquisitor: How does this relate to Náay? So far as I am aware original Náay had no recall of his trips into forward time.

Myra: Relates to Náay only in their shared humanity. Although I did use Náay's story as part of my explaining, best I could, the nature of time. Used it to tell him that he was not alone in his forward travels, how human beings have been taking trips into the future for millennia.

Much of what I told him he went to our library to validate. I told him that cages like the one he had acquired were but the latest device used for trips into the supposed future. [Myra sighs.] So I had to tell him again of the nature of human futures.

[Myra sighs again.]

I will tell you all that I told him. Then you can judge for yourselves where what he knows might have taken him.

I told him that the future anyone visits is a projection. That any future is the collective unconscious married to the Zeitgeist. For him, given his present's concern for the globe, there are probably only a standard two or three futures. No more. O/V's cage inventors therefore almost inevitably beheld the ravages of climate change.

"But," O/V said again, "I saw actual odds-against winners. How could my Zeitgeist have predicted them?"

I had to explain that any pre-existing future is both as anticipated and follows a real-time statistical curve. That curve will have included a possible change of jockeys, trainers, a new saddle even. Those same statistics were what showed the bookies that you shouldn't haven't been able to pick that many odds-against winners.

The future that we go to, I told him, is and isn't a shared perception. For us to go to it there has to be a future, and it has to be mutually imagined. Which isn't to say that the imagined future is what will happen.

Time travel has rarely been intended, I told him. Most travels there have been a fluke, like your Julian's. Quite often future travellers have been unaware that's where they've been. The Lydians for instance. Nor were they the first to have come bumbling into the future. Shamans from prehistory have come in awe. And ignorance.

Most of those early travellers believed that they had come beyond death, had taken Circe's potions and suchlike. Beyond death being as equally improbable as time travel. And yet there they were, those few Orpheans coming back from beyond death, from our/their over/otherworld. Time's multidimensional fabric.

O/V, having checked with the library what I had told him, came back with more questions. I had to explain how others might have seen 'beyond,' often through trance states. I drew on the example of Náay again, how Náay's ingestion of an hallucinogenic compound had sent him into the mid-American spirit world. In itself no problem. Unfortunately, the mix of berries and leaves that Náay had taken had also turned him into a cannibal. He went into his future and ate people. Ate men, women and children. Raw.

That original Náay hadn't known that his eating of people was what had been keeping him healthy and well-fed. While his neighbours all around had been starving, as well as being in terror of the spirit killing and eating them.

Although Náay's forward killings were random, as random as disease contagion can often be, the cannibalistic mutations of the bodies led to suspicions, led to retributions, to other killings... Which was why we'd had to bring Náay to us, away from his hallucinogenic compounds.

That scenario O/V readily accepted. What he found difficult to accept was that, as his sixth or seventh clone, Náay had no knowledge of the first Náay other than what he had been told.

Inquisitor: We have interviewed Náay regards his association with O/V. O/V's questions to him, conversations with him, match your own recollection.

Myra: What did take O/V a while to grasp was how futures change according to expectation, how not all hallucinogenic voyages beyond the present arrive in a future. I told him of the bronze age Ring of Gyges that rendered the wearer invisible. "Sound familiar?" I asked him. And that was in old Anatolia, I told him. Then there were the Enochians, necromancers, all of whom claimed to have 'gone beyond.' Their beyond being post-death, that being their preoccupation; and seeing in their beyond what their religion had told them to expect. If hell, then dragon-tailed imps and sprites. If a heaven, white light and fields of ambrosia.

Inquisitor: How did he respond to training?

Myra: He thought, prior to going into the offices, that they'd be full of tech. Was surprised to find individuals sitting in rooms on their own and seeming to be doing very little. While in other rooms, as here, people gathered together to discuss, learn, be interrogated.

Senior One: This is not as interrogation.

Myra: Apologies. It has though at times felt like one.

Inquisitor: He resisted the training?

Myra: As with any clone new to the training he took a while to subsume himself. Remember from his Testimony that his being raised in Care had created within him an innate scepticism, It therefore took time for him to re-order his experiences, his expectations. Bear in mind also that O/V had little formal education. But which could also be seen as beneficial so far as training went, it having left him open to the new.

In fact he was almost the perfect candidate, had so few expectations, didn't believe that he deserved anything, good or bad. Even so he continued to question everything. As he himself said, "I learned early to doubt, to question. Most children in normal households come late to the realisation that those who have charge of their upbringing, that those who are bigger, who know more, can also be quite stupid. Because the adults around me changed so often I learned to assess them, and so realised early on that many had less a grasp of my reality than I."

Like us here O/V does not know his own ancestry. Even so it has been a lot to ask of a human.

Then again has to be emphasised that what made O/V such an attractive recruit was his looking clearly at whatever new circumstance he found himself in. He initially held our enhancer to be the equivalent of a human acid trip. Our wafer on the tongue he likened to acid-treated blotting paper. Acid, I had to tell him, creates a sensation of temporal simultaneity, of everything happening at once. Our wafer does the opposite, creates an awareness of temporal divisions.

Inquisitor: He completed his training?

Myra: Insofar as any of us ever complete our training. But yes, he was well on his way when he disappeared.

Senior One: Enough for this session. A deeper look into his training and disappearance next time. If we may?

Session Five

Present are Senior One, Inquisitor and Moderator 28 [Myra].

Senior One: I think we need to establish how conversant the training made O/V with our activities here. You said that even by human standards he wasn't well-educated. Was he difficult to train?

Myra: He did have difficulty grasping certain concepts. As do we when we are new clones. Although we do have the advantage of familiarity, growing up here with time concepts figuring in everyday speech.

Inquisitor: How did he respond to your proposal? For him to become a Moderator?

Myra: "Me? A Time Constable?" was his initial reaction. Followed by a period of my trying to disabuse him of all police comparisons. Still at times though, and out of nowhere, he was apt to laugh and say, "This Jack-about-all-crimes now an officer in the Time Police."

"You're not," I'd tell him.

"So what will I actually be doing?" he asked me when recruitment was first mentioned.

"You won't be doing a lot," I told him. "Watching. Monitoring."

"That it?"

"Ingenious as your laptop and cage were," I told him, "they were limiting in how far ahead you could go, how much you could see. We will metaphorically plug you into our mainframe." And I had to tell him that our trance states were not originated by us, that as far we could surmise, they had been gifted to us by our ancestors.

What this Enquiry has to bear in mind is that, not only was

292

O/V's lack of a general education a barrier to his comprehension, I also had to rid him of his time's fictions. "There are no alternative universes, no separate timelines. The very worst damage any ignorant time traveller can do is to create a bump in an otherwise straight line. Most of those bumps however will be self-rectifying. The bookies for instance rectified you. Even the fatal stabbing of that one gangster caused only a minor blip. A generation on the social circumstances that had created and sustained that gang will be no more. With or without their leader that gang will have ceased to exist."

I told him too of the chronically jealous clinician who went forward to substitute his own sperm for that of his ex-wife's new partner. The pair were undergoing IVF. We monitored it. DNA was never checked, the child accepted.

Inquisitor: This sounds very much like incomplete training.

Myra: Granted we had a slow start, nor was it straightforward. Any Moderator will tell you that our training is rarely complete, rebegins with every novel incident.

Where we'd got to before O/V disappeared was to posit scenarios whereby our intervention might be required. Although he was by no measure ready to intervene.

"Our task is to engineer outcomes," I told him. "We have to make the consequences of blind time travel, as with the assassins you assisted, as if executed in real linear time."

"But you stopped the shooter that I took to Gloucester," he objected, "before he did anything."

"Exactly. We had you under close observation. If we had allowed that future killing to go ahead the ramifications were so large – no-one able to say who had done it, so many possible culprits, outcomes – that we had to stop him. The putative victim is still alive."

Inquisitor: How many interventions did O/V make?

Myra: None. He was nowhere near ready. Still sometimes called himself a Time Cop. He used to put on this strange, back-of-the-throat voice to say, "Where the Endless Past meets the Endless Future. I. Now. Somewhen."

He would annoyingly keep returning to the concept of Time Police. I had to, again and again, impress on him that the powers we have at our disposal are of a different order; that while we may work within the space/time continuum we are there mostly to observe.

I also had to again and again press him to leave behind all considerations of predestination.

Inquisitor: Did he?

Myra: Not by my estimation. But I knew him better than the others. The direct flow of time, its asymmetry, seemed beyond him.

"Rarely is there any need for our intervention," I told him. "Most odd circumstances, coincidences, pretty much cancel themselves out. Which is not to say that coincidences can't have lasting effects. If David hadn't stopped his car beside old Ben you would not have got to live in Ben's caravan and in all likelihood you would not have ended up here."

[Myra sighs.]

That again had O/V bringing up alternative universes, secondary timelines. I tried telling him that even when there is a temporary parallel track, given the probability quotient – if something is likely to happen it probably will – then the two tracks will merge at some point.

"So there could be," he leapt on that, "alternative futures."

"But only briefly." And I had to again explain that someone like his pistol-carrying assassin might actually kill in the real future and may appear to get away with it. Probability though says that while he goes to hide in the antipodes his wife will leave him. As she will have left him had he been imprisoned for the killing. So their own timeline will continue regardless. A massive explosion however, many dead, that will indeed create a new future.

"Old Ben's village folk in the New Neroche then won't be the only future?"

Once O/V came by a notion he wouldn't let it go. I tried to convince him that what happens in the future all depends when the break is made between now and then. That so far as New Neroche was concerned there had been, before this current coal and oil disaster, many breakaway societies. All defunct. I had to tell him again that all future trips can only go so far ahead as the present is capable of imagining. But that in any actual future there will be quantum leaps, changes of state which the present is incapable of predicting. Which is why any shared mind-state of distant futures is fundamentally flawed. That as a thinking species we all have to await the unknown.

Inquisitor: I take it by this time he must have been told of forward travels in pre-history?

Myra: His training didn't happen sequentially. I will remind you again that O/V had very little basic education. Often I'd have to digress with explanations that, even by this stage of training, will have been taken for granted by us.

Inquisitor: Such as?

Myra: Duality. Double thought. When it comes to the future being both perception and probability. I had to refer back to Schroedinger's cat being there and not being there. And time dilation... I had to explain Heisenberg's uncertainty principle. Which, bless him, he questioned.

"What I don't get," he kept saying, "is you say that the futures we go to are what we expect to see. You say that once Julian had decided that his Faraday cage had taken him into space then all his friends were primed to believe that they too were able to go to space. Having been told what to expect space travel became credible. Got reinforced by them. Time travel too. No surprise therefore that Ben's sci-fi lot saw the effects of climate change. All of that being what you say is statistically probable. But I went ahead and I saw odds-against winners, winners that were statistically improbable."

"No you didn't," I again had to tell him. "Going by their

previous form their winning was improbable. Going by the bookies' overall reckoning however occasional odds-against winners are highly likely. It was your consistent betting that went against bookie probability."

That though wasn't the only concept that O/V had difficulty with. He argued...

No, argue is too strong a word. What O/V did was to query my assertion that forward time is solely expectation. He said that he had a job getting his head around the fact − fact for us a doubtful assertion in itself − getting his head around the fact that the future could exist as seen and yet not happen.

"Not everything adds up here," he said, almost an accusation. "Ben for instance pushing his pen through the floor of his cage when he was on Venus. How come? His shed floor was solid wood. How did the pen go through? Nor does everything add up here. If as you say the house and grounds are a nano-second ahead making us invisible to the locals, how come there's only wilderness out there. Doesn't add up."

I hadn't at that point retracted the wilderness fiction. Nor had he then been aware that we are in North America. So I could only join him in doubting what Ben had said he had done. One explanation, I suggested, could be that Ben had pushed the pen under the shed door and then down as he thought onto Venus. More likely though was that the pen had rolled down from the shed and had disappeared under the caravan.

"All of future time is a construct," I had to once tell O/V. "With some of those constructs more complex than others. All sufficiently imagined however to convince more than one's own self. Your blundering in," I told him, "upset some of those constructions."

"So they're not real?" he challenged me. Again.

"Define real," I came back at him, asked, "How do you authenticate anything? All reality is but shared illusion."

"Evidence. Hard, independent, objective evidence."

"In which we choose to believe. We can only go as far ahead

as is presently imaginable. Only as far ahead as you humans are capable of imagining."

"Explain then, if I was only seeing what I expected to see, how come the robber had me get rid of – in the present – his hammer and the glass bits stuck to his cover-all?"

"Yes." I said. "You became a participant. Not an observer. That and the killings upset the time flow and was why we brought you here." That could have been when, I think, that I sent him off to the library to study statistical probabilities.

Inquisitor: I have never had to train anyone. I'd have thought though that to render the concept more readily palatable you would have had to tell him of pre-history time travels?

Myra: Of course.

Senior One: Last session's transcript?

Inquisitor: Apologies.

Myra: In all of this you have to understand that O/V hadn't even known what the Zeitgeist was, let alone how it can create futures. So yes, I did refer him back to early Christendom with their seers and shamans. I told him how when they went out of their bodies they saw, as their belief systems had told them to expect, either the white light of the hereafter with its ethereal beings; or, as with Ben's friends seeing ecological disaster, the medieval trancers found themselves – as expected – in hell, among leering imps and fork-tailed beasts.

On several occasions I referred O/V to pre-history, when the concept of future time had not yet been embedded in the human psyche; and as I said I told him how in most early human civilisations the shamans and seers took themselves to places beyond death. And this insight into the past, as you have surmised, did help O/V to an understanding of how we travel forward, and moreover that mechanical contrivances such as his were not necessary.

Inquisitor: Did we analyse the cage?

Myra: As a matter of course. The laptop's wasn't a set code. It was the four elements – program, data block, gaming switch and cage – working together, feedback feeding back and creating its own codes that tricked the human mind into credulity.

I didn't though discuss that in any depth with O/V. By this stage he was more taken with the notion that travel beyond the self can be achieved through prolonged fasting, as well as by the ingestion of various psychotropic berries and plants. Or a measure of both. Native Americans' sweat lodges intrigued, how they managed to follow their 'spirit guides' to somewhere other.

All that O/V readily accepted, said that it made sense to him. What he doubted was future times being 'solely expectation.'

"Not solely," I had to keep telling him. "Both. With communication being global now most futures are alike. They weren't always."

Inquisitor: He didn't question your use of 'always'? I have to ask, did he come to understand time?

Myra: I don't think he did. Not fully. He couldn't grasp, despite our being here, that none of us are wholly out of time. That we are all within time, briefly within the billions of aeons that this universe will be here. That we are all here, clones and originals alike, within each our own birth-to-death clock. All part of the double-think that I tried to get across.

Senior One: You must though have been confident of his understanding to allow him to continue his training? What was it that led to his gaining that understanding?

Myra: The clincher – to use his terminology – had been my asking him why it had been that nowhere that he, or any of Ben's friends, had visited had it been raining?

Inquisitor: Can we go back to Náay?

[pause]

Myra: OK. They became friends. Even so it took O/V a while to realise... No, not realise; to accept that this Náay hadn't come here recently, that he was the last of a line of clones. Though once he had accepted that I noticed that he sought

298

Náay's company less. Náay as a clone not having had any human experience. So less common ground. Little common ground with any of us, once he had accepted that we here are all clones.

Inquisitor: Was he reluctant to train? Did you have to persuade him?

Myra: Not at all. He struggled to master concepts outside of his direct experience. That experience being his lens. Generally though he was quick to learn.

Náay's cannibalism for instance he readily accepted, said that he was '...used to transgressors.' Which had us go over again why he and Náay had been brought here. What had motivated original Náay's trance-killing, Náay already not liking the people he had grown up among. Was why he had become a shepherd in the first place. And we went over again why O/V himself had been brought here, his transporting of the robbers and assassins.

Inquisitor: Can we move on from Náay? To O/V's training? An able recruit?

Myra: Able? Yes and no. He was impressed that by the power of thought alone he was able to move himself into the future.

Inquisitor: Could he?

Myra: Took him a while. That leap of trust, the subsuming of the self in order to enter a trance state. I'm not certain however that he ever became fully functional. Even when he had fully mastered trance, he often came excitedly to me, eager to tell of his latest excursion. He said of one that it had been like looking into different mirrors in different houses.

"Saw something different of myself, another self, and I became that other self. Saw different aspects of that self."

Another time he had to tell me that it had been as if he had been on the very edge of a weather system, the rain falling on the other side of the street.

Inquisitor: Can we assume that, once trained, he reached a level of competency?

Myra: Was yet to be tested. What had also been difficult to get across to him was that we can go centuries with no call for direct intervention. Then a sudden rush. Something gets concocted in home chemistry. Or something mechanical, like his, a fluke of engineering. Or someone finds some berries, squashes them with some leaves, lets the juices ferment, takes a sip and... As with Náay we have a time blip.

As to actually spotting anomalies in time's flow... Yes, he got that. He knew that he had to regard the spherical whole, note the effect, search out the cause, any side effect, judge the consequence, consequences of the consequence...

"Like looking for fossils on a beach," he told me. "At first you find them difficult to spot among the other stones and pebbles. Once your mind has the pattern though then the fossils leap to the forefront."

Senior One: Looking for, searching... That has to bring us to his disappearance. Next Session?

Session Six

Present are Senior One, Inquisitor and Moderator 28 [Myra].

Senior One: Did you suspect that O/V might remove himself?

Myra: With hindsight, yes. My suspicions unacknowledged. With hindsight there were many clues. As you will be aware from his testimony, he always felt safer when he had a 'back-up plan,' a way out.

With hindsight I can see that he became increasingly distant. At the time I had put it down to the arc of our relationship, as related in the literature on human monogamy.

Inquisitor: The arc...?

Myra: The tentative approach by both prior to pairing, then the absolute involvement with one another, followed by a cooling down period, then a slow return to the insularity of the self, while remaining within the partnership. O/V said that he wanted to study uninterrupted, began to spend the odd night back at his own apartment. Even then we still took time cooking for one another, and I still oiled and braided his hair. We gave every appearance of caring for one another. Our training though had made him aware of how little he knew, and he had become so very keen on educating himself. Self-education having become his new passion.

Inquisitor: And you encouraged this passion?

Myra: Yes. I was pleased. Saw it only as a gain for us. For all of us here.

Inquisitor: From conversations he had with Náay he had apparently wanted you to have a baby?

Myra: Which was another reason for the increasing distance between us. In his estimate the arc of our relationship should have meant increased domesticity and parenthood. I pointed out that we here are all hybrids and are therefore incapable of natural reproduction. He said that if I could change my genitalia then I should be just as capable of changing my ovaries. He just wouldn't accept that as the clone of a hybrid I was doubly incapable.

I also had to remind him that human females are born with all the eggs that they will ever need. And that on reaching maturity every month one of those eggs will make its way to the uterus and, if unfertilised by a sperm, will result in that month's menstruation.

My telling him this, while he may already have known some of it, had not before been delivered in such forceful detail. With hindsight I now believe he came to resent my educating him.

Inquisitor: If you could have made yourself fertile, would you?

Myra: Given our strained relationship there was little incentive. I told him that even if I could effect the changes the chances of my conceiving were extremely slim. Say, for instance, his space ventures had indeed damaged his gametes.

"Whatever they are," he said. And he wouldn't be told.

I did briefly think that his disappearance could have been his punishing me. For not getting pregnant. And for having lied to him about his shadow self.

I said to him time and again that we had been together from his testimony onwards, and throughout his training, why couldn't we just go on as we were?

But no, for him there had to be more.

Inquisitor: Is he dead? Did you kill him?

Myra: Really? You think that I, fearful of losing him, became like some jealous human and illogically terminated him?

No, I didn't kill him. Although his being dead could explain our having been unable to trace him.

Inquisitor: His having mastered trance, could he have returned to England?

Myra: First place we looked. No trace of him there.

Inquisitor: Where else do you think he might have gone?

Myra: The present, worldwide, was where we first looked. Despite our best efforts we found not a trace. My suspicion is that he may have created his very own time pocket somewhere.

From the very outset he became very interested in how we remain hidden here. Even though he hadn't been at that point aware that we are in North America. That had what looked like wilderness was just the blurry effect of our being a nano-second ahead. (Another lie I had to apologise for.)

When he had finally been told he was really impressed by our being able to see out, sort of, but with no sound entering. Likewise no sound escaping. He wanted to know how we had come to create 'so effective a barrier.' I had to tell him that, as with many things, we didn't know the precise cause, we simply exploited it.

He had assumed, prior to recruitment, that we were somewhere on moorland in the north of England. Then, once he'd found out about our taking turns to go into town, he'd assumed – from the unfamiliar goods brought back – that we used a specialist store. He'd had to be told, quite early on, that when we needed people from the present to come here, to make specialist repairs, then all of us had to individually make ourselves nano-second ahead invisible.

That said it is hard for us to know what O/V did and didn't know. I do know that when the training became too much for him, he used to slip out beyond the barrier and into the present to fill his head, he said, with birdsong and bee buzz.

Senior One: I sense O/V's confusion. His confusion confusing us. Best we can, I think, is we nonetheless determine what he does know of us. That being as important as what we know of him.

Inquisitor: He was definitely told how we are established here? Undetected?

Myra: Yes. Our nano-second into the future, undetectable even

303

to any like ourselves. Early days I think it was his love of criminal deceit that had him excited how we went back into the present, driving our truck into town for supplies. How the house, office and grounds can be visible to the present, yet we wandering the grounds, our nano-second ahead, are not.

Inquisitor: Could his slipping into the present, for his birdsong and bee buzz, often undetected by any here, have been him practising for his disappearance?

Myra: Very likely. The barrier, largely unquestioned by us, grateful of it as we are with our fears of bird flu and other wing-borne diseases. It denied him, he said, his pleasure of birdsong. He was however always but a blink away.

But yes, if to practise his escape was his intention. Yes, possibly.

Yes, he understood the too brief a future for any of us to get a fix on.

"Nanosecond there and gone," he smiled saying it. Didn't though like our combined nanosecond invisibility stopping us from seeing out. Except for the grey wilderness. He said it was such a relief to pop himself into the present, to look out over the cornfields, let his mind take the track leading to the highway...

Inquisitor: Would his training have enabled him to singularly replicate our base?

Myra: The training? Doubtful. Certainly not at the stage I think he was at. He hadn't even made a practice intercession. With hindsight though...

With hindsight we should take into account that avaricious self-education of his. Because his was a mind that, whatever the subject, needed to know more.

More. All the time, more. Same with our relationship, his wanting a child, his personality having to have an objective. So, possibly, my being unable to have his child he shifted his objective to finding a place to disappear to. Most of his adult life he has spent trying, as he put it, to fly under the radar.

If I may remind you? In his testimony he said that he always sought a back-up, a way out. So if no accident, no misadventure, can we assume that he did find a way out?

Inquisitor: Do you think now that he lied in his testimony?

Myra: Definitely not in the beginning. No point. He was relieved to be here and not in prison. Relieved too that he had been removed from his criminal associates. And he was then telling of his early past. Later maybe he shaded the truth in trying to be kind to me. You know how human beings misread one another. Misread us too when we are pretending to be human. Yes, there had to be times in his testimony when, if not being kind to me, he had been trying not to be unkind.

Senior One: So... All that we look to be left with is a cautionary tale. How not to... abduct a criminal human being? How not to... recruit a criminal human being?

Inquisitor: Did O/V never talk of staying? Did cloning hold no attraction for him?

Myra: Náay had let slip that not all who come here get to be cloned. Only if they prove to be of use. O/V assumed that he would not be of use. Although at that stage we hadn't even considered if he'd be acceptable for cloning.

Yes, I have to say that for him cloning held no appeal. That clone would grow up here, he said, and it might well look like him, but it would be one of us.

Inquisitor: Which seems odd as he wanted to part-replicate himself in a child. There is no rational to human beings. Nor you apparently. From what I can see you have retained your human form. Why? When there is no longer any need?

Myra: The possibility of his return? And I still take my turn going to the store.

Inquisitor: If he does return your relationship would most likely be discouraged. Especially after his disappearance. I have been told that you have kept more than your outward human appearance, so why?

Myra: I retain a fondness for O/V. And yes, I would like for us to be reunited.

Senior One: We appear to have completed a circle. Which leaves me to ask if, in the long term, his having been here, and his disappearance from here, matters? We know that, as in all organic life, that our own and human beings go on, one after the other. In those terms what can this one human life matter?

This enquiry closed subject to further information.

Part Four: Confession

i) I am here with O/V and I am pregnant.

Here is not where we will be when I allow you to read this. We have made space and time meaningless.

Here now is our time pocket. As where you are, but here in Bulgaria. This is where O/V has been hiding throughout the Enquiry.

I don't really know why I'm telling you this. Feel that I should one moment, the next tell myself that you're not worth the bother, that you simply won't get it, that you will read this all wrong, misinterpret it all.

I feel though that I must. If only to stop myself having more imaginary debates with one or other of you. Debates where I forcefully justify my every deed, those done and those about to be done.

On a lesser level I feel the need to explain myself. And it is only you, one of you who might understand. Disapprove, but understand.

I am not proud of us. By which I mean you.

What you won't admit to, but it's true, is that day in day out, year in year out, we have been taking for granted where we are, what we do. It came as a real shock to O/V that our house and grounds were in North America; and that we could switch so easily into the present to go into town for supplies.

I told you that O/V has a clear way of looking at things, that it was his lack of preconceptions that made him valuable to us. Except that the more I told him about us the more contemptible to me did we seem.

"And you've been here for over a century?" he said. "How did that work out when it was the Wild West?"

"Not that wild," I had to tell him; and of our French château before their revolution, right back to our Roman villa. How we have kept ourselves time-remote, distant from the local population. How in every generation we have acquired expertise enough to render ourselves self-sustaining. Aside from food. Which has required our predecessors to adapt to local trading systems. Making ourselves of benefit to the locals, but never a part of the local community.

"Our aim always," I told O/V, "has been to be remote. But still of benefit to the locals."

"Complicit," O/V had laughed. "Got it. Make it worth their while."

This was how O/V applied what was commonplace to us to himself. A mirror I didn't want to look too closely into.

This was when he first started looking for somewhere that he and I could live out our lives together.

"Have you seen a film called *The Accountant*?" he asked me. "Where the criminal accountant keeps a Silver Stream caravan in his lock-up? Has his whole life in that caravan. Money, guns, paintings even. Could say I kept a time-travelling cage in my Taunton lock-up. 'Cept I never got to use it. But that's what you and I have to do here." This was back at the house. "We have to create a couple of mental lock-ups. Our means of escape."

This is where, I confess, O/V's criminal mindset came fully into play.

Late at night he and I slipped undetected into the near future and distant Bulgaria. We reckoned that at that time of night a sleepy on-duty trance in house or office would be unlikely to pick up our in-and-out-of-time activity the day side of the planet. They didn't.

In Bulgarian daylight, and under assumed names, O/V and I switched to the present and opened bank accounts. He and I, much as our duplicitous selves have done over the centuries, made ourselves local gentry, lords of the manor. Except that for O/V and I it was nothing quite so grand.

Employing the fabricated intelligence of the internet it didn't take O/V and I long to fill our new bank accounts and purchase this old farmhouse. Big houses like this in Bulgaria have been going relatively cheap, Europeans buying them up for holiday lets and second homes. Our occasional presence/absence was therefore nothing out of the locals' ordinary.

Before O/V 'disappeared' he and I, during our nights at the house, slipped into the present here, got local builders to renovate the house. So many English had bought cheap in Bulgaria no-one questioned our gesturing and struggling to explain what we wanted – to the builders or in the shops.

We bought a car for the garage and I taught O/V to drive, at first up and down the farm track. And when we were confident that he could take care of himself, that this was where he could safely hide, only then did he 'disappear.'

I can tell you all this now with no fear of our being found. We are together and way beyond your capabilities. At O/V's insistence we have discovered how to live with birdsong; and you will have no idea how we managed to undetectably achieve that.

As I told the Enquiry O/V's main complaint of house, office and grounds was no birdsong. "Flora is fine," he used to say. "But being out of time all we got is grass and trees. And, OK, bushes. But no animals. Not even a bee. Never thought how much I'd miss 'em."

O/V believes that it was he taught me to live with guilt. Do I really feel guilty though? Or have I imbued O/V's life outlook along with his child?

Like you I was trained to think objectively, no emotional, no egotistical justification. Is this then ratiocination-al retrospect, and not guilt-ridden hindsight? Or is this yet another hormonal reaction like my emotional highs and lows, manic laughter followed by copious tears?

O/V told me to use near-truth to confuse the Enquiry. Ask yourselves, so sure of yourselves are you, is that what I am doing now?

As to the Enquiry... I smile now at my descriptions of

sexual pleasure proving such a useful distraction. And that was my very own initiative, happy to know that I was feeding the gossip that I'd heard whispered in house and office.

An unearned guilt though still seems to lie behind my every other word, my every other thought. I did lie to you. But I loved O/V; and O/V wanted us to live together, just him and I. And maybe our children. Not beholden to you. To any of you. Not whether or not, spoken or unspoken, you could bring yourselves to tolerate our relationship, indulge us.

And I... I wanted a new life, not a repeat.

We are all aware of, philosophically acknowledge, the nothingness at the core of ourselves. We clones always needing to go beyond what we thought we were before, give meaning to this our latest incarnation. And in so doing doing largely as our clones have done before. Even to joining the same sub-groups.

Have I been driven here solely by love? Or was it that I was driven to love, and am acting now as if in love, wanting to please my beloved? Or is this wanting to please but a symptom of love?

At this Bulgarian remove I think it is more likely that I have long craved change, and in O/V's sexual interest in me I saw an opportunity for change.

We have lived so long with repetition, repetition upon repetition, us self-appointed guardians of time's asymmetry.

Or is it that we, our ancient past lost to us, we are self-made victims of time? Just where have we been letting time take us? To what end? To the rarely-voiced, and then say it quietly, hope of a reconnection with other survivors from the far side of the cataclysm?

I wanted more. I wanted new. Not continuation for continuation's sake. Not repetition.

What I have growing inside me now is new, is indisputably new.

I am a clone of a clone. And all of us clones, whisper it,

have had suicides. Mine was number 12. Which has been why, every number thereafter, mentors have encouraged my clones towards sub-group time studies.

There would have been clones of me to come. May yet: you have the material and the means. And all of them will initially look like me. But not be me. What's the betting though that they won't be encouraged to either philosophy or time sub-groups?

O/V has offered me more than repetition. He and I are about to create something unique. We two beings without ancestry are about to go out of time. And knowing that is what we are to do has made misleading you that much each easier.

I do however owe some loyalty to you and I consequently feel the need to put your minds at rest. That said, you won't find us, not where we're going. I have let you know though how we both managed to initially disappear.

Throughout the Enquiry I kept as close to the truth as I dared, made myself believe that I didn't know where O/V might have gone. I allowed you to believe that I was reluctantly allowing uterus and vagina to become reabsorbed, that I was becoming almost as I had been. I know that I looked as if my body was preoccupied. That though had been from exhaustion – lack of sleep from all those nights getting set up in Bulgaria, worrying how O/V was managing... And while I was telling you things about O/V that you hadn't known, I was surreptitiously making further changes to my body, which is now as near human as it is possible to be.

Time for my daily rest.

ii) O/V wanted more. More than our birdless grounds, more of life, more of me. More of our relationship. The sex wasn't enough. I said in the Enquiry that O/V has to have a purpose. That became fixated on my getting pregnant.

The pressure began in our bedroom.

But what will you know of that? Apart from a knowing sneer? We have been clones for so long, what can any of you know of love? The desire to please, and the physical sensation of warmth that comes from a loved one's smile? Your own hurt when they appear sad?

In love your whole being is wrapped in theirs. If O/V and I were a fruit, an orange say, we would be the many segments inside the same peel, enveloped, as one.

"You will go on," O/V said. "There will be more clones of you. Of me? Not even a proper name."

I had to tell him that the 28 in my titles didn't mean that I'm the 28th clone. That no-one has kept an exact count since the cataclysm. Apparently took a while for the survivors to work out what they, what we had to do. But I'm way more, I told O/V, than the 28th version of me. And the next clone will be another lookalike version of me but will know nothing of secret me. Ours is not everlasting life. For me, I told him, death still represents the unknown.

It was long ago, I told O/V, that we concluded that we are all hybrids, which is why we clone. We can't reproduce any other way.

"But I am not a clone," O/V said. "I'm not a hybrid. What if we two can?"

I tried again and again to explain to him that as an ersatz woman I very much doubted that I'd be able to conceive.

Yes, he put pressure on me, but that pressure came from the evolution of our relationship. We were no longer two separate entities, our identity now came from our unity. And O/V wanted us to be free of the constraints that we back there had placed on him.

To be just us two, free to decide our futures. The I that was a part of just us two helped to plan his escape.

O/V wanted us to have children. And that want came from, not just the growth of our relationship, but from his never having known his parents. He wanted a child that would at the very least know its mother and father.

And love wanted to please.

Even so I was full of doubts. I am false, a fabrication. I am treacherous, knew that I was about to betray you. Betray you, you clones of hybrids, made beings who have needed to exalt philosophy to the level of an unquestioned creed because we haven't known who we are.

That not knowing we have come to tell ourselves we take a pride in. Rarely though do we acknowledge our true not knowing. Our ancestral species suffered a cataclysm that has left us historyless and with only a few clues to what we should be doing. We have interpreted those few clues into a not-to-be-questioned historical mission. That has become our this-is-what-we-do-here existence. And if any questions proper have been asked then they have been left philosophically unanswered.

O/V asked many questions, sought practical outcomes. Here he and I are making our very own history.

I was, I am nevertheless still full of doubts. How could O/V love this self, this faux human body I have made?

There are many degrees of nakedness required of love. I had to reveal the truth of myself to him. And he... He told me of his desire to be free, free of the confinement that I was in part responsible for. And it was love that had him confide in me his want for a child.

Naked to me O/V became the hurt child that he had hidden from himself. And he wanted the two of us to make a child and give that child a better childhood that his own.

"You've changed your body this far, go further," he said.

314

And love needs to please. Or what was I? A double-betrayer? A self-miscalculation? A misdemeanour?

In love I was afraid of losing love. In love though things can be done as clumsily as in an unloved life.

"I don't menstruate," I told O/V. "No eggs unfertilised don't get rejected by my non-womb wall. Nevertheless, I will try."

That was neither the beginning nor the end of the matter.

"What if we do manage to have a child here?" he asked. "Here with the Time Police? Out of time? Will they take the child from us? Will they know how to look after a non-hybrid child?"

"You will age and die here," I told him. "While I will neither visibly age nor die within your life span. Our slow maturation is how – somehow – who knows how? – we became Time Watchers. Or we made that our purpose."

"Say I do manage to get pregnant," I said another time, "will it bother you that our child might have some of my avian DNA?"

"Does it bother you," he asked me, "that in my mother's womb, whoever she was, I will have briefly been a fish?"

He was nevertheless as full of doubt. "How small we two are," he held me one night. Had just said that he felt unworthy of me. "I know how small I am," he said, "Mister Nothing-Much and Never-Has-Been. And that's not only this one life. I mean small," his grip tightened on me, "tiny within aeons."

Love wanted to please. Was not so easy though to render this fake human body fertile.

Converting the cloaca to the semblance of human female genitalia had been readily achievable because, I think, this clone has since maturity presented as a young human female. A form that I was used to, the making of her vagina but the next step. A seeming physiological inevitability say. Then the vagina's active use seemed to provoke further glandular changes. Or could that have been psychosomatic? Nerve ends would tell a different tale.

315

To build in uterus, fallopian tubes and ovaries, equipment necessary for human breeding, became a mammoth task, the ersatz cervix proving the most difficult.

Why persist, you may ask. Simple, succeed or fail, love wanted me to be thorough.

The lymphatic system was, to my surprise, the easiest to replicate/adapt, almost textbook additions and insertions. I modified a few of my own. Although I had already come by the sense that our mammalian coupling had of its own accord stimulated some endocrine production. My breasts for instance had become increasingly sensitive. Begging the question that if I went on to self-create the rest of the equipment would it wholly change my autonomous nervous system?

We hybrids, and we know not why, have long been capable of corporeal mimicry. Would this though be beyond my capability? So many worries: would my unalterable pituitary match that of a human?

Having everything in place was one thing, getting them all to function together something else entirely

Time-watch colleagues saw my self-absorption as sadness following O/V's lengthy disappearance, and they left me to my changing self. During the Enquiry even I was still making some changes – uterus afloat within, fallopian tubes unconnected... The ovaries turned out to be not-as-human. Female humans are born with all the eggs they will ever need, on reaching maturity lose one a month. I had to employ my cloning knowledge to fabricate what might pass as a human egg.

The production and fertilisation of one of those 'eggs' didn't come about until I was reunited with my love. A whole world/time in two smiles and hands reaching out to touch and to grasp and to hold. And there was such urgency. An 'egg' to be released and fertilised. We also had to vacate our Bulgarian time pocket, cosy as it was.

iii) Pregnancy has been a time of wonder and of worry. Because we did it.

No sooner had I arrived in Bulgaria for the final time than O/V came crawling across the large bed we had there, saying in a strange accent, "C'mon darlin', release one of 'em platerpussy eggs. Let's get you up the duff."

Saying that amused him greatly, in those first weeks together was almost a preliminary to his foreplay.

I had told O/V that I had modified my 'platerpussian' egg-laying apparatus to mimic human ovaries and fallopian tubes. This successful modification, marriage of my research into human DNA along with our cloning know-how, was what succeeded in making our species-incompatibility compatible.

But for every positive a negative, such is the universe.

I had to tell O/V, when he was once again fantasising on our forthcoming life together, that as with most carbon life forms heartbeat rate predicts life spans. A hamster's heart rate beats much faster than that of a human being; but over the hamster's three year life span that hamster's heart will have beaten the same number of times as that of a human heart during his or her 70 plus years.

"Your heart averages out at 63 beats per minute," I told him with my palm to his chest, "mine at about 19."

Undaunted O/V came back with, "So that means that you'll live on long after me. Be there to look after our brood." He was determined that we have children. More children.

Being pregnant, the increased blood flow, has no doubt accelerated my maturity. O/V however has been unremittingly positive: "You'll still outlive me." Nor did death hold any fears for him: "Death serves a purpose. Unalive flesh becomes carrion. Vegetable matter becomes compost. We cannot go beyond death. Imagine if we could, Earth would become even more crowded."

His sperm met my ersatz egg, if not quite in the human way. And once safely lodged in the uterus wall the dividing cell began making its own alterations to my biochemistry.

These human breasts tightened and grew. I tell you I have never felt so alive, every nerve end inner and outer sensitive to every sensation of every second of every waking hour. The almost overwhelming worries as my abdomen swelled. A spasm: what did it mean? A heavy, hip-dragging feeling, as with the three previous failures: was this too to be a miscarriage? And, as if proof that human sex is not solely procreative, a disproportionate desire for sex, awkward sex, especially later on given the size of my belly.

My belly... O/V's delight at my expanse was in itself a joy to behold. Offset by worries – over the outcome of this thing growing within me, increasing my blood flow, my need to urinate. I felt the thing move uncomfortably within me. Middle of the night thoughts – O/V small, still and asleep beside me – what if he and I had created a monster?

Come daylight the worries dissipated, and pride in my magnificent size returned. I was all life, two lives, the centre of and the most important being in the universe.

Having done this, having altered my body in so many ways, has been an expanding education to me. Should have been to you too. Clones of clones, we are capable of so much more.

The false labour pains undid any smugness I might have been harbouring, were worrying for an hour or more. I had several days of those start-stop pains. Until finally, finally, I was so huge, clumsy in everything that I tried to do, and it was then that my waters broke. They came pouring and splashing from me, so much so that I thought that maybe I hadn't been pregnant at all. Then the real contractions gripped me, had O/V fussing around, excitedly checking all the info he had collected on midwifery.

What a mess it was, blood and shit, and more pain. Pain for hours and my not knowing what this pelvis of mine, of ours, would do. Would it spread out sufficiently to allow the baby egress? Or would O/V have to resort to his meticulously sterilised scalpels and clamps? Our ancestors laid eggs; I kept telling myself. It will work. Hurt yes. Be the biggest egg ever. But cloaca-like the pelvis will open...

And yes, finally, finally our child forced its way into the world, followed soon after by the womb-sac that had nourished it as an embryo.

That O/V and I had succeeded we were ecstatic; but believe me in this: eggs I am sure have to be an altogether neater method of natural reproduction.

I am not going to tell you of our child's gender. I want to make it doubly difficult for you to find this child born out of time, this child our very own sub-species of *homo erectus*. This child beyond perfect.

I have to tell you that we three are no longer in Bulgaria. We abandoned that time pocket, cosy as it was, for a safer and even more undetectable other. The three of us in our pursuit of love have now moved even further on. We three have gone way beyond how we kept ourselves hidden in Bulgaria, with O/V's nervous if discreet trips into the present for market groceries. Now? What a life O/V and I together have achieved. I am so proud of us. Us three.

Set against that happy pride is an occasional niggle of regret, of shame even, a feeling that I have betrayed you. Which, when it starts to take hold, I dismiss by telling myself that you, collective you, have betrayed us all by continuing down our/your dead-end path. A time path that we have been amending and which will be forever lost to time anyway.

A sub-species on repeat we philosophise the futility of the repetition away, accept its pointlessness with a wry turning aside, return to your/our oh-not-so important routines and divertissements.

O clones of clones I so pity you, that you will never know this, the pains and joys of motherhood,

My baby's mouth makes a narrow tube of itself, tongue poking through; and I know – without instruction – to cup the back of the small round head and press the mouth to my nipple. Then I feel the milk start. Sensations I devoutly wish were known to you.

Clones of clones we have reared one another; and those clone children, new to just our small portion of this planet, they have always been a joy to behold, their comic stumbles, the pleasure we have taken in their accelerated understanding. Pre-cataclysm I can imagine, had we not been infertile hybrids, that same concern for the young among us would have been as if for our own hatchlings.

That would still have been nothing like this hungry, alt-human gaze one has for one's singular offspring. Imagine if you can how much more is the joy and watchful worry when the child has been planned and striven for, has come from just... a pair of you.

While I have been feeding the baby O/V has been sitting opposite, watching with a wide contented grin the two of us. At long last he has a family all his very own. We three.

Feed over I lift the baby up to him, and he walks cradling the baby to his shoulder, his own body taking up the baby's morphic rhythm. Once the baby has burped to O/V's satisfaction – babies swallow air while sucking – O/V carefully sits, but still softly moving to the baby's metabolic rhythm, and continuing even when I lean over to embrace the pair, lay my cheek atop the cushion of O/V's hair. We three.

"Let's go populate the wilderness," he says later.

"Only ever been a conceptual wilderness," I tell him, "and it has no need of us three."

O clone of clones I was so innocent when with you, thought myself content. Thought I knew so much. Thought us, although never acknowledged, superior to all of humanity. But now that I've known O/V, now that I have matched his desires, see where it has brought me... I scoff at my then ignorance, my then superiority.

I so wish that you could experience all that I have.

Doesn't mean to say that we too now feel safe, secure. With children come worries.

"Even for you," O/V said in a quiet time, "one day will come an end. What then for our child? Where then for our child?"

Where then for you? Another you?

Signed: Moderator 28, Myra

Part Five: Analysis

Senior Two: Our time enthusiasts have been misled, have been so cleverly misled, and in so many ways.

So much of what I write here will, of necessity, be supposition.

First let me iterate what we do know and what we don't know.

We know that if O/V and Moderator 28 were ever in Bulgaria then we have been unable to find the actual site. I have to doubt therefore that they were ever in Bulgaria.

O/V is a man practised in deceit. My guess therefore is that the two of them are – at the time of writing – somewhere in a place within a place, a time within a time.

It is reasonable to assume that O/V learnt how to achieve that here with us. Not necessarily by tuition, simply by observing how we live, our nano-second ahead invisibility. Interesting for instance how he kept stepping out of nano-time to 'listen to the birds and bees.' How curious he was in how we day-to-day maintain ourselves here; our rota of trips into town; and how the house and grounds remain visible to the present while we, our nano-seconds ahead, don't.

Anger serves no purpose. But angry I am. Angry at the pair of them. Angry at us for being so easily duped.

O/V confided in Náay that he, O/V, had found his *Instantistan*. Náay didn't report O/V's boast because, wanting only to be left to himself, he resented the company forced on him by O/V. Náay did all that he could to politely discourage O/V's visits, even to on occasion hiding from him. Left to himself Náay therefore tried to put all thoughts of irritating O/V from his head; and if he thought at all of what O/V had said he assumed that O/V's *Instantistan* had been but his nano-steps beyond the barrier.

Náay now believes that O/V's *Instantistan* was more, a nano-second ahead within our nano-second ahead. All achieved when he had been supposedly been listening to the buzz of bees and the songs of birds.

We did manage to recreate his *Instantistan* here. For all the good it has done. O/V's devious thought processes I am sure having taken that concept beyond anything we have yet attempted. O/V has been steps ahead of us way before his disappearance; had also, I suspect, conceptualised a place within a place. And that, despite my urging, we haven't managed to achieve here.

It was only through Náay that we were led to *Instantistan*, would have been unlikely to have discovered it if left to ourselves. What I am left to wonder is why O/V, so practised in deceit, had let us know via Náay. His every motive has to be questioned.

Despite further searches, increased watchfulness, we still have no real idea where the pair of them may have gone. And, given our present capabilities, I doubt that we will ever find them.

Some colleagues have expressed the belief that, if the pair continue alive, their aura is bound to flare at some point. That, if on the surface and despite the noxious state Earth is presently enduring, their auras will have to become evident.

I believe that naïve in the extreme, hope winning over expectation; and in denial of our own nano-second ahead being undetectable to ourselves when beyond the barrier.

I have also noted a general reluctance among us to believe that the pair of them were working to a plan. A belief that Moderator 28's disappearance might be unrelated to his; and that belief sustained despite Moderator 28's own confession.

Yes, I am angry. May I remind everyone that no other among us has disappeared. Even those who have become disaffected have asked only, going by the equal disaffection of their predecessors, that they be the last of their clones. A wish generally acceded to.

This unhappy episode leaves me mostly angry at myself. Firstly for having been one of those who agreed to bring this dissolute here. But I ask you all, what sort of sentient being seeks to breed with another species? And brings pressure on that other to tinker with her own morphology? I also have to ask what brought our once-trusted colleague to comply with the demands of her paramour? Leaving us to reconcile our having been misled by one of our own, besotted by a man practised in deceit.

I believe now that Senior One's Enquiry allowed too much emphasis to be laid on the sexual act and too little on the pair-bonding, on the sharing of food, on the mutual preening. We looked at their self-absorption through a false human lens while forgetting our own avian pathology. We ignored not only the initial bonding, but the re-bonding following migration. Look at the pattern here: he went ahead, made a nest, and waited for her to arrive, and only then did they commence breeding.

O/V may be adept at deceit. What we have to uncomfortably look at though is our having been deliberately, and convincingly, misled by one of our own. That should be where our concern is now directed.

I believe, from what Moderator 28 has not said, that the two of them have created another *Instantistan*, a time pocket within a time pocket. I say this doubting that we will now pursue their *Instantistan* with any vigour. As a technician I have come across many time pockets. As I am sure many of you have. Undetectable by us there is usually nothing the least sinister about them. Accidental creations, nothing odd happening in them, they have tended to be disregarded.

Looking back over both their testimonies I can't help but nurse the suspicion that they may have been planning their elopement from almost the consummation of their relationship. That said, I nevertheless also believe that O/V had disappeared for Moderator 28 throughout Senior One's Enquiry.

Possibly that had been part of their plan, and O/V had given a promise to return. But a year had passed and still he hadn't come back, hadn't contacted her. Had that uncertainty been how she had been able to convince the Enquiry?

Loathe as I am I can imagine, in Moderator 28's defence, another scenario where he unexpectedly contacted her and she, self-seduced, followed her desires. Those selfish desires nonetheless outweighing our collective goal. Leaving us having to wait beyond her life expectancy before activating one of her clones. Which, with no consideration for us, will create an unnecessary gap in future staffing.

To conclude, we must hesitate before bringing another human among us. Their needs are not as ours and the more that we try to accommodate to them the more we will lose sight of ourselves, of what we are here to do. Which is, and not a one of us should need reminding, is to monitor and measure the sun's rate of decay. Boring as that may be.

What previously has been viewed as a harmless divertissement has with this episode taken precedence over our reason for being here, and may even have placed our mission in jeopardy. So enough of time-watching and other distractions, enough of those various and disputatious schools of philosophy, all of which should only ever have been indulged side issues.

Human time misuse is not why we are here. Nor is philosophy. Of course we will carry on tidying up errant time excursions and we will continue to ensure the maintenance of time order. And of course there will be those among us who will question the cosmos. We are here first and foremost though to measure this star's evolution.

To do that we have needed a base on this planet. The Earth however is becoming increasingly unstable, both geologically and psycho-socially. Preparations for evacuation from this place need to be prioritised, materials gathered and provisions readied for removal.

Over the aeons our kind has survived the end of many nation states, the ends of many so-called civilisations. Before us, our kind has survived the ends of worlds, as we have been assured that we will survive this world's end. All that we have to do, wheresoever our new base on this world may happen to be, is to keep on monitoring the sun. And with a total solar eclipse imminent we need to concentrate our efforts.

The monitoring of human time inconsistencies has not been, cannot be the sole reason for our being on this planet. If I may reiterate, as mind-consuming as this unfortunate episode has been, we must now return to our prime consideration.

From what we know of our pre-cataclysm history we preceded human beings by several thousand, if not millions of years. Legend has told us that we have to await contact from our pre-cataclysmic brethren. When that time comes, we will learn what our ultimate purpose is. Should we however still be here when the sun dies, or another cataclysm should overtake us, then we will be no more. This damaged world will certainly have no need of us.

Given our longevity and the ever-forwardness of time I believe that we will go on, that our kind, spread as they are throughout the universe, are here to witness what comes after the final black hole, the black hole that will have drawn in every other black hole.

What then? That I believe is the greater purpose of our brethren's survival.

The end?